Critical Dawn

By
Darren Wearmouth

This edition published in 2014
by Darren Wearmouth

Chapter One

Charlie Jackson felt like they were on the edge of a great discovery. Pippa had emailed him earlier to say that she'd "made the find of the century" in an archeological dig to uncover what happened to the missing colonists of Roanoke Island.

Typical Pippa, he thought. Keeping the huge news to herself and making him wait. It didn't help that she'd told him to start work on the report. It was the worst part of his job. He preferred to be out in the field being the one to make the finds.

He looked up at his screen and grudgingly continued to work on the report, all the while trying not to be distracted by her excited email.

4:00pm, April 2014, Manhattan

On August 18, 1590, a privateering expedition on its way back to England from the Caribbean stopped off at Roanoke Island. John White, the governor of the colony and passionate advocate of the new world, took his men ashore. They found the settlement completely deserted. Infrastructure had been dismantled, no trace existed of the hundred-and-eight residents, and they couldn't find any signs of struggle. The colonists were never found.

The only clue was the word 'CROATOAN' carved on a

fort post and 'CRO' carved on a tree. Events surrounding the disappearance remain a mystery to this day.

The aim of the Quaternary Productions dig is to try and establish the fate of the colonists with firm evidence. After geophysical surveys following the investigation of aerial photography in the Alligator River National Wildlife Refuge, the initial findings are as follows ...

Charlie pushed the keyboard away after those few hundred words, unable to concentrate. All he could think about was that email. What had they found? More than just bones, that's for sure. His mind raced with ancient artifacts, caches of treasure. Unable to stand it, he got up and decided to go chat with the temps.

He poked his head around the door leading to the next office and cafeteria and listened for chatter around the coffee machine.

"They're not in today," Mike Strauss, his colleague in their open plan office, said.

"Want me to get you a brew?" Charlie asked, welcoming the distraction.

"Sure."

Things had changed since Quaternary Productions agreed to a deal with National Geographic to make a documentary about finding the lost colony at Roanoke. The place had become louder and more congested with contractors, but not today. Mike and Charlie were pulling overtime. It seemed the others weren't so keen.

The small coffee room was deserted. Charlie got the pot boiling and prepared two mugs as he pondered the current project. His main job had been site identification for potential pitches to places like the History Channel and National

Geographic. His team traveled the country, surveying and digging. After winning the contract, the focus shifted to how quickly information could be cobbled together, rather than how thoroughly, because of the production targets. It was always that way when they landed these kinds of deals.

He wasn't about to get pretentious over projects that paid the bills. Charlie felt lucky to have a reasonably paid job to do what he loved. Most of his friends from college had to find work in other industries.

Finishing up the coffee duties, he headed back into the office.

"Here you go, Mike. Black, no sugar," Charlie said. "What's with the plain purple sweater? A little dull for your usual tastes."

"It's casual Friday. Thanks."

Mike had regularly freelanced with Quaternary Productions during the last six years. Charlie got to know him well since joining the company three years ago. He was renowned for his tasteless and bright woolly sweaters, usually stretched over his bulky torso, and his long, greying hair made it look like somebody had placed a mop on his head. A few of the production crew called him 'the mad scientist.' He liked the nickname.

"One more hour and I'm out of here," Charlie said.

"Hey, Pippa says she's got some really exciting news about the Roanoke dig. From the areas you identified."

Two weeks ago, Charlie had carried out a ground-penetrating radar survey in Alligator River National Wildlife Refuge. The uniform sandy soils made it an ideal method, and the results were encouraging.

Due to budget limitations, he'd returned to the office while a small team of archaeologists used his tomographic images to guide their excavations.

The team was restricted to certain areas because of the nature of the land and had sought special permission to dig. He was confident they'd find something with the results. Whether or not that had anything to do with the lost colony was another matter.

Charlie checked his watch. "She emailed me yesterday. Said it would blow my mind. Didn't reply when I asked for details."

Mike laughed. "A broken piece of pottery or the stem of a clay pipe blows her mind. I wouldn't get too excited."

Mike's skill was in the identification of finds. He loved the big-ticket items recovered from digs. A four-hundred-year-old Scottish pistol found in a well at Jamestown was the kind of thing that got his juices flowing.

Charlie could always see a look of disappointment on his face when he was presented with a clear plastic bag of buttons and buckles to sort though.

"She'd better hurry up," Charlie said, "otherwise, she'll have to wait a couple of days."

"You'll wait. I can tell by the way you look at her."

"Whatever. I'm not the one that calls her a younger version of Halle Berry."

Mike shrugged. "It's the hairstyle. You going climbing again this weekend?"

"Yeah. Heading to Keene Valley. Should be a blast."

"If you say so."

Charlie shook his head and continued with the interim report. The aim was to complete it by the end of the day, using the information provided by Pippa if she showed. He disliked leaving work unfinished.

Three sites were targeted with Ground Penetrating Radar

to identify anomalous signals that might correspond with subsurface archaeological features. The inland locations were selected in the hope of shedding new light on the fate of the colonists.

The Roanoke site two contained hyperbolic reflections indicating the presence of reflectors buried beneath the surface possibly associated with human burials. Priority was given to this location due to time and financial constraints.

Pippa Quinn breezed through the door. She placed her laptop bag on the desk between Charlie and Mike and ripped open the Velcro fastening. "Afternoon, guys. I hope you're sitting comfortably."

"Comfortable as any other Friday afternoon," Mike said.

She fired up her laptop, connected it to a docking station, and smiled at Charlie.

He loved working with Pippa. She exuded infectious energy and always had a healthy appetite for their projects. When he studied geology at Stanford, he found the subject dry. The lecturers seemed to beat the life out of it, and he doubted he'd ever find a satisfying job upon graduating.

Pippa helped change all that.

At twenty-eight, she was two years older than Charlie. He had vague memories of her from college when he turned up for his interview. The enthusiasm and sparkle she showed for the role made him desperate for the job, and he wasn't disappointed in the three years since.

"This could be potentially ground-breaking. I'm serious," Pippa said.

"Don't tell me. You've found animal bones with signs of butchery and a nineteenth century comb?" Mike said.

"Come on. You think I'd come all the way back here for

that?"

"Uh huh."

Typical Mike. He often helped provide some balance with his healthy skepticism, although he occasionally fell into cynicism. He amused Charlie, probably without realizing it.

"Seriously. Come see this," Pippa said.

Charlie wheeled his chair across and looked at the monitor. It displayed a high-resolution photograph of site two from the Wildlife Refuge. A deep, square trench had been cut into the ground, surrounded by a taped safety cordon and a selection of digging tools.

"You were right, Charlie. We found burials at the second site. A little deeper than expected," Pippa said.

"How many?"

She clicked to the next picture, saved as "Eight skeletons."

Three sets of bones were fully exposed on the right-hand side. The rest poked through the dirt like pieces of nut in a large chocolate brownie.

"These were all laid out next to each other, arms by their sides. We couldn't find any traces of coffin nails ..."

"Christian burials?" Charlie said.

"They aren't aligned east-west. But that doesn't mean they're not Christian."

"Is it some sort of mass grave?" Mike said. "If they were just placed like that?"

"Of those three," Pippa said, pointing her pen at the monitor, "we couldn't find any immediate signs of injury on the bones, or arrowheads or musket balls. They're going to be taken away for analysis."

"Are they sixteenth-century?" Charlie said.

"We found ceramic pieces and a decorative ring in the layer above, possibly from the sixteenth century. We're carbon dating skeleton number one and should know in a couple of days."

"Makes sense they're below the finds. Being buried," Mike said.

"Nothing with the bodies? No buckles? Leather …" Charlie said.

Pippa shook her head. "Nope. This is the part where it started to get weird."

She clicked on the next photo, showing a close-up of a scapula bone. Below it, a dirty blue bead rested on the dirt. "We found one of these around the shoulder area of each of the three fully excavated skeletons."

Mike frowned. "Grave goods? Do you think they're from the Chowanoke tribe?"

"We'll probably have a clearer picture after the tooth isotope analysis. Our hunch is that they're European. Carbon dating will be the key," Pippa said.

The next picture showed a cleaned blue bead, broken in two, sitting in a finds tray. It had a smooth, shiny quality.

"We x-rayed the bead to try and see the elemental composition in order to establish the production process and origin—"

"I thought you said you'd blow Charlie's mind?" Mike said.

"I'm just building the picture. Here's the first x-ray. Can you see the small rust marks running through the internal lattice toward that space in the middle?"

"That's pretty intricate," Mike said. "The local tribe didn't use any metals that rusted. Must be European."

"We couldn't identify the row or trace elements of the

glass to anything we've seen before."

"Seriously? Have you sent it away for further analysis?" Mike said.

"Not yet. Just wait a minute."

Pippa clicked to the next picture. "The next skeleton's bead was intact."

She sat back. Charlie and Mike leaned forward.

The intricate internal lattice had dark lines running through the channels like circuitry. In the center of the bead was what appeared to be a rectangular microchip.

Charlie scratched his head. "What the hell is that?"

"You've got to be kidding me," Mike said.

"Trust me, I'm not. These things were found in situ, below undisturbed earth."

"Oh Christ, we haven't stumbled on a modern murderer's—" Charlie said.

"Didn't you just hear me? The ground above was *undisturbed*, with finds from the sixteenth century above. If we carbon date the skeletons to that time …"

"This has to be a hoax," Mike said. "It's the only explanation."

"I've been racking my brains all the way here. I thought about one of the team planting it, but I was there when these things were uncovered."

Charlie sat back and puffed his cheeks. "Beats me. Where's the bead now?"

Pippa reached into the front pouch of her laptop case and pulled out a small plastic bag. She produced a bead and passed it to Mike. "Be careful with it."

He held it toward the strip light on the ceiling, rolling it between his fingers. "Holy … We need to get to work on this."

Mike passed the bead to Charlie and wheeled away to his laptop.

Charlie's first impression was the weight: a lot heavier than he expected. He switched on his desk lamp and held the bead underneath in the palm of his hand, ducking to get a side profile of the object.

Dark, formal lines with an angled shape in the middle. Unbelievable.

"Seen anything like this before?" Charlie said.

"I called a few of my contacts. Janet from England reckons she's seen something similar to our broken one," Pippa said.

"Really? Like this thing?" Mike said.

"Where did they find it?" Charlie asked.

"Cheddar Gorge. In two pieces. No body. They bagged it up as unidentified."

She flipped to her emails and opened one from a team member at the Roanoke dig site. Charlie sat back in his chair trying to think of a logical explanation. The problem was, one didn't exist based on the evidence. He looked over to Mike, who was furiously typing.

"Blue beads found near the shoulders of skeletons four and five," Pippa said.

She spun her seat toward Charlie. "I think we need to start thinking outside the box on this one. Preferably in the bar. You two coming for a couple of cold ones? It's been a long day, and I need something to take the edge off."

"I'm calling my techy guy, see if he's ever seen anything like it," Mike said from behind her. "This could change the whole way we view history. I'll stick around here for a few more hours, but you two go ahead."

"Surely, you're not suggesting this is …" Charlie said.

"You've seen the Vijayanagara Empire carvings in India, the Nazca lines in Peru, Puma Punka, and the strange ancient cave paintings all over the world," Pippa said. "This is potential compelling evidence, but we say nothing until we get all the evidence in place."

Charlie didn't want to believe it. Yet deep inside, he was left to wonder. Could this be extraterrestrial technology?

"So?" Pippa asked. "You wanna come buy your boss a drink and posit some theories?"

Ordinarily, he'd jump at the chance to spend some social time with her. Despite working closely together, and despite renting a room in her apartment, they rarely got to see much of each other with Pippa whisking off around the country doing deals with media execs and the like while Charlie kept Mike and the other crew company in the office.

And of course, there was the climbing weekend.

He'd been planning it for months with three of his old college pals. Every few months, they'd take off on some adventure, whether it was caving, scuba diving, mountain climbing, or his favorite activity: finding a big old forest to explore and surviving for a few days off the land.

Before he could even say it, Pippa gave him "the look." A special pout she had developed that would hit at Charlie's heart. "You've got other plans, G.I. Joe? What are you doing this weekend then? Paragliding with endangered falcons into the caldera of a live volcano?"

"Hah, not quite, Pip, but that does sound epic. Let's do that in the summer. I've got a climb planned with the guys. I'm designated driver, so I can't really let them down. I need to take off tonight."

"Well, your loss, G.I. But you know where to find me

if you change your mind." She gave him a quick smile and returned to her desk, packing up her files for an evening of analysis in their favorite haunt: a small, old-timey bar called The Rusted Shovel, the coincidence of which was never lost on Charlie.

If he didn't know any better, he would have guessed that Pippa had agreed to the lease on the office space purely because it was less than a block away from the bar.

He grabbed his bag and keys and headed for the door. "Don't you two work too hard. The mega discovery will still be here on Monday morning."

"And don't fall down a mountain," Pippa said over her shoulder. "I need you to develop a presentation for an extended features set on the Nat-Geo product line by Wednesday."

"Gee, thanks, boss."

"Anytime, action man. Now get out of my office and go get your adrenaline rush."

"Take it easy," Mike said, mumbling as he frantically searched the web for anything that could explain the bead.

Charlie exited the building and headed for the elevator, all the while thinking about that little blue sphere. It must be site contamination, he thought. Had to be. Couldn't be anything else.

Chapter Two

Generation Ship 5A

Ben Murray sat in the enclosed Operations Room wondering if he would be remembered by future generations. The lucky ones who would reach their destination—still nearly a hundred years away. His life would be spent rumbling through space.

All eight measurements of visual status display fluctuated green between the bottom three bars. Everything at a safe level. Then again, it always was. He must have had the most boring job on the ship although he couldn't show it today.

Sitting next to him at the console was a new replacement. Jimmy was retiring, and it was Ben's responsibility as the new senior team member to bring new operator Ethan Reeves up to speed.

Ethan was clean-shaven with neatly-combed, mousy hair and wore a crisp, dark blue uniform with red piping along the arms and legs. Ben had shaved that morning, his first in a month. There was nothing he could do about his frayed jumpsuit. Best to try and keep up appearances, at least initially.

"The four on the right are the critical measurements. You escalate immediately if one touches the red," Ben said.

"I do it by pressing here?" Ethan said, pointing to a

square on the console screen.

"Yep. One of the engineering team will fix it. The backup systems automatically kick in. If they don't, you have to switch to manual override. You do that here."

Ben patted a group of four safety-locked switches.

"How will I know if it's worked?" Ethan said.

"You'll be sitting in the dark with somebody from master control shouting at you through the speaker if it doesn't."

"Does it happen a lot?"

"Do you remember any service outages?"

Ethan looked to his left, frowned, and paused. "No. Anything else I need to know?"

"Our job is to monitor and control the ship's internal power source for stability. That's about as technical as it gets."

Ben figured they didn't fully automate the systems as it gave people on the vessel something to do. It also helped with compartmentalizing the crew.

"Can we go through it again?" Ethan said.

"One of us will sit with you for your first few shifts. You'll be okay."

Ethan sighed as he gazed around at the sparse, metal-paneled walls.

"Not what you were expecting?" Ben said.

"Have you ever seen outside? I mean, space?"

"Nope."

"My teacher told me that the fleet had been built in a hurry, functionality over comfort. I just thought … Once I was up here …"

Ben shrugged. "Listen kid, it's six hours a day in front of the display. The rest of the time, you can watch as many old movies and shows as you can handle. The food's no different up here. We're all in the same boat—"

Since a flu virus spread early into the two-hundred-year voyage, all sections of the ship were isolated. He'd been in Two. A child section containing five orphans, where he was fed and educated by a single adult who avoided any kind of relationship with the children. He'd only ever met orphans and often wondered if they were being singled out for the Operations Compartment.

"I get that. Survival of the species. We'll be honored as the forefathers ..." Ethan said.

"My advice is to make the most of your time here. Get a bit of mental stimulation, study the old books; it'll keep you sane. I've got two years left, and reading kept me going."

Six hundred and seventy days to be exact. It was close enough for Ben to start counting toward the promise of better things. He wasn't surprised about the retirement age of thirty. Anybody who suffered more than fifteen years of this kind of confinement would surely go mad. His rewards waited in the retirement village. A new life. A chance to see the stars.

Maria Flores appeared by the door. "Jimmy's leaving in five minutes. You better go. I'll take care of Ethan."

"Thanks, appreciated," Ben said. "Don't do anything stupid while I'm gone."

Maria smiled. "Get out of here."

She was his idea of a perfect colleague in the Operations Compartment. She'd been part of the team for five years, was always polite, punctual, and never complained. Jimmy was the opposite: loud, usually late, but he was still likeable.

"Don't forget, I'll be testing you later on pseudopodia.

Make sure you bring your A-game," Maria said.

"I will."

Ben enjoyed the gentle pushes she gave him. They studied microbiology together. It was the most interesting material they'd found on the hard-drive in the common room. When his motivation waned, Maria was always there. She made his life in the compartment feel like more than just watching the visual display and eating slop on his bunk. Before she came, he felt like a ghost.

He clanked along the dimly lit, grated corridor, squinting against a pink glow emanating from the airlock door timer. It had started its five minute countdown in bold, red digits.

A burst of loud laughter came from the common room. Ben passed the sleeping quarters and supply hatch before entering. Erika Kosma and Jimmy sat on two of the three chairs. Ben leaned against the kitchen unit. Having three in the room always made it feel cramped.

Today was different though. His colleague of over thirteen years was leaving.

"Thought you were never going to show, buddy," Jimmy said.

"The timer's running. You all set?" Ben said.

"I've never been more ready. Fifteen years in this place … I can't believe it's over."

"We've been talking about what he's going to do on the other side," Erika said.

"Damn, I missed it," Ben laughed. This was a regular and worn conversation, especially from Erika. It was all she talked about in the two years since arriving. "Are you still expecting a welcome party?"

"That's the million dollar question," Jimmy said.

His idea of money was probably as abstract as Ben's, but Jimmy loved to use lines he'd seen in movies from their MP4 collection. Every day for the last thirteen years, Ben would find him in the communal area watching something. It lost its sparkle for him years ago, after he'd been through his favorites for the fifth time. Would the crew on the other side think Jimmy sounded strange? Like an actor, he thought.

"You better wait by the airlock," Erika said. "Time's ticking. You don't want to miss it."

The group of three walked back along the corridor and stood facing the countdown timer.

Jimmy sighed as he looked up and down the short corridor. "You know, a small part of me will miss this place."

"A very small part, I'd imagine," Erika said.

"We know which part that is," Ben said.

Jimmy playfully punched his arm. "You know what I mean. We've been together for years. We're almost like family."

It was strange for Ben to hear Jimmy being poignant. He probably was the closest thing Ben had to family. He was also usually the life and soul of the place. He was going to be missed.

"Say hello to Billy and Tracey from me," Ben said.

"I'll let them know things haven't changed. Same food, same clothes, same movies, same old Ben."

"If you can send us a message through the supply hatch, let us know what it's like?" Erika said.

"You know I can't do that," Jimmy said. "I asked the same thing before seeing my first retirement. Why take a risk once you're out of here?"

"I wouldn't," Ben said.

Jimmy was the third retirement since Ben started in the Operations Compartment. He tried to push the jealous feelings to the back of his mind. They'd done their time, and he was next.

"Have you said goodbye to Maria?" Ben said.

"Five minutes ago. She didn't want to watch me leave. Thought she'd give you the pleasure," Jimmy said.

A faint, whooshing noise came from behind the airlock door. A white light winked above it.

"Thought this day would never come," Jimmy said.

"I haven't seen that door open for two years," Erika said. "Not from this side."

"Any final words, Jimmy?" Ben said.

"I'll see you soon. Don't work too hard."

The airlock door smoothly slid open with a hiss. Jimmy stepped into a bright, silver space and turned to face Ben and Erika.

A neutral female voice came from a speaker next to Jimmy. "Door closing."

"Good luck," Erika said.

"See you soon," Ben said.

Jimmy raised his hand and smiled. The door slid shut.

***

The corridor returned to its usually gloomy state after the airlock timer blinked off with a low click. Ben leaned against the chilly wall.

"That's it?" Erika said.

"Yep, that's it. I'm going back on shift."

"What do you think he'll—"

"Not now, Erika. Not now."

The whooshing started again. Jimmy was on his way. Watching the door close brought his departure firmly into reality. Ben had to keep his emotions in check. If not for himself, for the other three. They had ten years plus left in the compartment. As the senior member, he wanted to keep up morale.

"We've got to complete our weekly aptitude tests by tonight. You done it yet?" Ben said.

"I'll get it out of the way now," she said, and headed back toward the common room.

Ben returned to the Operations Room, finding Ethan and Maria hunched over the console in conversation.

"Going through the procedures again?" Ben said.

"Repetition, repetition, repetition. That's what you told me when I first arrived," Maria said.

"I'll be quickly up to speed," Ethan said.

Ben resisted the urge to crack a cynical, time-related joke. He sat next to them on the spare plastic swivel chair. After decades of shifts, cream foam was visible through the worn, blue threads of the cushioned seat.

"How'd it go? Any tears?" Maria said.

"It was all bit abrupt. I'd prepared myself, but …"

"I get what you mean. You've been together years. It's impossible to prepare for something like that."

"Where's Erika?" Ethan said.

"She's doing the weekly test," Ben said. "We all need to complete it today."

"Weekly test?"

"Forgot to tell you about that," Maria said. "We get a set of twenty multiple-choice questions on a weekly basis. Most are around the Ops compartment, pretty basic stuff. There's a couple about our mission statement that never change."

Ben stiffly saluted. "We gave today so they could have tomorrow."

"Where do we take it?"

"You take it on your own in the common room," Ben said. He glanced at the two small cameras in opposite corners of the Ops Room. They were positioned all around the compartment. Did other crew members really monitor their mundane lives? He hated the thought of it.

"What if I fail? Know anyone who has?"

"There's a rumor that one guy did thirty years ago. Apparently, a pair of huge men in protective clothing grabbed him—"

"Stop teasing him," Maria said.

"You'll be fine, trust me. A chimp could pass it."

"Is that rumor true? What if someone refuses to do their job or screws up?" Ethan said.

"You need to drop the paranoia. Seriously, give it a couple of weeks and you'll wonder what you were worrying about."

Ben had heard stories of people refusing to comply, going crazy in the isolated environment just as he'd heard the rumor about the test failure. It was always large men in protective clothing appearing out of the lift and dragging the crew member away.

The clear embellishment was the offenders being fired out of the waste disposal hatch into space. How could any of the shift know? Besides, it seemed these stories were passed down through the decades. He'd never met anyone who had physically witnessed it or knew a person who had.

"There's a comments section at the end of the test.

You're supposed to report any strange behavior from other crew members," Maria said.

Ethan frowned. "Like what?"

"We've got an agreement to leave it blank," Ben said. "It's sort of a tradition—"

A loud scream echoed along the corridor. Erika.

Chapter Three

Charlie stopped a few doors away from The Rusted Shovel and waited for Greg, whose voice was cutting in and out through Charlie's cell speaker, to stop moaning about the cancellation of the trip.

Eventually, his old friend from Charlie's time as a National Guardsman stopped for a breath.

"I know it's super last minute, but something's come up at work, and I've got to stay over the weekend."

"You know we're psyched about this one. We won't have another chance until next year. This was the last weekend they'd keep the place open to visitors," Greg said, the disappointment all too clear even over the crappy line. For the last few days, Charlie had noticed that it was becoming increasingly difficult to make a solid call. There was something on the news about increased electromagnetic interference in the atmosphere these days.

"I'll make it up to everyone," Charlie said. "Next trip is all on me. With this work we're doing at the moment, I should be in line for a big fucking bonus, and I'll share the wealth, bro."

"It's not the money, Chuck, it's the time. But fine, I get it. I know it must be important for you to grovel like a whiney bitch."

"Yup, that's me. Okay, I gotta run. The boss is giving me daggers. I'll be in touch next week when I know my schedule better, and we'll arrange something else. Say sorry to Manny and Bill for me."

"Will do. Laters." Greg hung up just before his words were cut off from a blast of static. Charlie pulled the cell away from his ear before dropping into the front pocket of his cargo pants.

The truth was, as eager as he was to make the climb and meet up with his buddies, the discovery just wouldn't leave his imagination. He'd only got two stations away when he knew he couldn't concentrate without digging further into it. And then there was of course the opportunity to share a beer with Pip, something he hadn't had a chance to do in months.

Since they took on the Nat-Geo contract, it had been fifteen-hour days for everyone. Not that he thought he really had a chance. She was his boss for one, out of his league for another. Her parents were some big shots in D.C. He doubted she'd be the model daughter if she showed up at their mansion with a bottom feeder in hand. Charlie didn't even own a suit: just cargos, chinos, and jeans.

He mentally shrugged away the issues and walked into the Shovel, savoring the sound and smell as he stepped inside. A home away from home, he felt more comfortable there than he did in the room he rented from Pip.

Being in her place was like borrowing someone else's life and being scared that his lackadaisical ways would break it indefinitely. Even her cat, Timbo, looked down at him as though he were nothing but a wild peasant, but then that was cats for you.

The barwoman, Patty, gave him a nod, a smile, and a saucy wave with her fingers. Nope. Not his type. Lovely girl, friendly, but the face tattoos weren't his thing, nor the biker gang she rode with. Two of their larger and hairier members were sitting at the bar, their back to the door, working on a pitcher of budget beer.

The two bikers turned round, froth caught in their beards. Together, like coordinated dummies, they said, "Evening, Charles," doing their best-worst posh accents. It was the same every time.

"Jace, Geoff," Charlie said back.

"She's over there, stud," Jace said, nodding his head toward the booths at the back.

He was the one with the slightly larger beard. That's the only way Charlie had learned to tell them apart.

Charlie gave him a "Keep your voice down, fool" face, which elicited a laugh from the pair and a disappointed scowl from Patty. Looks like he'd have to leave a bigger tip later to keep her sweet.

Charlie weaved in and out of the narrow path between booths and stools. An elbow came out from the left, nudging him in the ribs. A bottle of beer was in the elbower's hand: his favorite imported ale.

"What the … How did you know?"

Pippa grinned up at him from within the booth. "Like you could go climbing with a discovery like this rattling around in that empty head of yours. I thought you'd at least reach the apartment before you changed your mind."

The bottle was cold in his hand.

He took a deep swig and slid opposite his boss, putting the half-drained bottle on the table, avoiding the carpet of paper and files she had spread out on its surface. She reminded him of one of those off-duty detectives who couldn't leave a case alone and took it with them everywhere, looking for that crucial loose end, that missed but vital piece of information.

"It's in here somewhere," he said, using his best Columbo accent, realizing he was both terrible at it and completely out of time. All the cool kids were doing Horatio Caine one-liners these days apparently.

Pippa groaned. Shook her head. "Don't you watch anything newer than the early '80s?"

"Don't watch TV. Don't have time. Except for our productions, of course."

"Liar. Who did we get to present the Rogue Pharaohs of Egypt production?"

"Umm … it was that woman, you know, the one with the hair. She was in that thing with that other woman …"

"You mean Zahi Hawass, the superstar Egyptologist … A guy."

"Yeah, that's the one." Charlie flashed her a smile.

"Zahi is a megastar in the field. You really ought to brush up on this kind of stuff. You never know who might drop into the office." She took a sip from her beer and avoided eye contact.

That was her way of putting him in his place.

He'd come to recognize it over the years.

The "not looking at you while I'm being the boss" effect started out with her getting tired of him leaving ropes and carabiners laying around on her sofa or his various outdoors pursuits magazines piled up in the bathroom.

It crept in at the office too. There was no problem when she was giving someone else a piece of her mind.

Her forthrightness was one of the many things he liked about her. Her ability to communicate her thoughts and ideas helped get her to her current position in life.

With Charlie though, she was different. Tempered,

almost coy.

Charlie took the advice on-board and finished his beer. He felt a bit stupid now. Although he was technically excellent at his job, he had to admit that it wasn't his true love or focus in life.

That would be the outdoors. He'd much rather be climbing down into caves to look at the rocks, feel them with his own bare hands, than survey them from above with GPR. Even during his time in the National Guard, he would prefer the weekends away on training out in the wilds than back at the barracks doing endless drills.

Again, technically, he was excellent. He wondered if that wasn't actually part of his problem; things came too easy to him at times, and he lost focus.

Nature wasn't easy. Nature wasn't something you could conquer like stripping and cleaning a rifle or running acres of radar surveys. It required respect and a humility to know you're not top dog.

Being in the wild outdoors taught him that.

"I'm sorry," he said. "I know I sometimes don't focus on the everyday details as much as I should."

"No, it's fine. Forget about it," Pippa said. "Besides, this stuff with the bead is more important than any of that. Though I'd totally recommend watching Rogue Pharaohs. That was a great production. It's what nailed this job with the Geographic. One of the production workers over there knew a guy who knew a guy … Sorry, I'm rambling."

"Must be exciting," Charlie said, pointing to the files over the table, "to have stumbled across something like this. It could be huge if it checks out."

Pippa leaned forward and rested her elbows on the table, a single piece of paper in hand. "I'm still trying to work out if we're being scammed. I know the guys and gals on the dig. The site manager and I were present. The beads were definitely within the skeletal remains. If someone had put them there after the fact, they'd have had to have somehow dug beneath the old soil on top without disturbing it."

"And that there," Charlie said, lowering the paper, "is the crux of the issue. It's not possible. We're talking basic physics here. Unless David Blaine does have magic abilities and is for hire for archeological pranks, I think we have to realize that this bead, whatever it is, was with the bodies at the time."

Leaning back against the booth, Pippa sighed and let the piece of paper fall to the table. It was a printed photo of the dig site as the skeletons were first exposed. She had ringed a blue bead with a red pen.

"I don't know about you, but I need another beer." Pippa got up, waited for his answer. "Hey, dufus, the boss is offering to get you a beer. Yea or nay?"

"Nay, boss, I'm good. Just a Coke will be fine if you're buying though."

Charlie inwardly sighed with relief as Pippa approached the bar. Patty hadn't stopped giving him awkward looks since he arrived, and he didn't really want to address that issue.

While he waited, he rifled through Pippa's reports and printouts. One of them was the close-up shot of the bead, showing the intricate, almost circuit-like patterns. One thing that struck him was the uniformity.

If they were manmade and from the sixteenth century, then whoever had made them had developed technology way beyond anything previously discovered. The straight lines and complicated pattern weren't possible by hand.

There was a painter, Giotto di Bondone, who was famed for painting a perfect freehand circle, but even with that level of excellence, Charlie had a hard time imagining someone carving these circuits so accurately.

He sat back and looked up at the old TV hanging down from behind the bar on a wall mount that always looked entirely inadequate for holding up such an old, ancient device. The TV had those wood panels on the front and a thick, bulbous glass screen. Despite that, the speaker still worked, and as the bar hadn't yet filled up, Charlie could make out the sound.

CNN was covering an extreme weather report. From the pictures, he guessed it was somewhere in the Far East—China or the Philippines perhaps. The graphic showed a satellite image of a massive hurricane building its power over the … Wait, that's not the Indian Ocean, he thought.

Charlie got up and approached the bar to get a closer look. Pippa joined him, passing him a Coke. "What are you watching? I thought you didn't watch TV?"

"I don't, but it caught my eye. Listen."

The reporter squared in the corner of the screen brought a mic to her mouth. Her hair was blowing wildly, and she had to shout over the noise.

"As I was saying," the reporter said, "I'm on Ocean Beach, California, and already the wind is reaching in excess of eighty miles per hour. The satellite imagery is showing hurricane Mel gaining power. The reports from the National Weather Service are suggesting it's a Category 3 storm with potential to hit Category 4 by the time it reaches land." The reporter leaned into the wind. Behind her, trees were bending and snapping.

A branch flew past her, hitting against the camera.

"Back to the studio. I have to go. I can see it from here … I've never …"

The report cut off. The anchors took over. "Thank you, Hilary, that's looking terrible out there for Californians. Just to confirm, a state of emergency has been called as citizens find safe places to wait out the storm. In other news …"

"Holy shit," Pippa said. "A C4? What the hell's going on these days?"

"What do you mean? It's one storm."

"You must have missed the broadcast. India's been hit with a tsunami, and there's two more storms gathering in the Atlantic."

"Man, the Earth must be pissed at us for something."

"Yeah, hardly surprising though. It's cyclical. Mini ice ages, mega storms, all that jazz. Glad I don't live on the West Coast. You got any friends or family out there?"

"Nah, you?"

"All East-coasters."

Charlie and Pippa sat back in their booth.

"So what are we gonna do?" Charlie said. "About the bead. Publish our findings?"

Pippa took a long drag on her beer, placed the bottle to one side, and sighed. "You know. I've been doing this job for a while now, and never have I been so stumped. It's just beyond explanation. But we're scientists, we don't do non-explanations. We do rational logic. I have to admit, it's freaking me out a little. I mean, just look at this damn thing; it doesn't even look like it's made from a terrestrial material."

Pippa took the small baggy containing the bead from the inside pocket of her favorite biker's jacket, its elbows and collars worn with use. She opened the bag and let the bead drop onto the stack of papers before picking it up between thumb and forefinger.

They both leaned in to look closer at it.

"The light doesn't fall on it right either," Charlie said. "Unless I'm being stupid."

"No, you're right." Pippa held it up at an angle beneath a low hanging lamp. As she turned it, the light didn't seem to shine on all surfaces.

"That's fucking weird. It didn't do that earlier when I checked in the office."

"Maybe it's just an effect of the type of light in here," Pippa added, still twisting the curious blue bead in the light. "But look, on the sections where it's not glossy, you can kind of see a texture. Almost like a finger print, but much finer."

"I think we should wait until Mike's done his digging. You just never know what he might find. It could be the rational explanation we're—"

"Jesus fuck!" Pippa jerked back in her chair, shook her hands. A small spark burned her fingers. The bead fell from her hand and bounced off the tabletop.

Charlie launched forward to try and catch it, but he was too slow, and it hit the floor … and stayed there, in place, as though it were a magnet attracted to another magnet. It didn't shake or roll away. Nothing.

"Are you okay?" Charlie said as he bent down to reach for it.

Pippa grabbed his arm. "No," she said, showing her fingers. A burn blister had come up on her skin. "The damn thing electrocuted me. Here." She handed him the plastic bag.

Turning it inside out, Charlie covered the bead and lifted it off the ground. There wasn't any magnetic resistance as he was expecting. Patty and the bikers stared at him. He just smiled and leaned back into the booth.

"There's only one thing we can possibly do," Charlie said, sealing the bag and placing it on top of the files.

"What's that?"

"We go to the dig site and do some more research first hand. Just you and I." Charlie checked his watch. "If we set off now, we can get there in the morning. I'll drive."

"It's eight hours away," Pippa said.

"So? I was going to drive about that with the guys anyway. Don't worry, I won't play any cheesy '80s rock. Let's grab some supplies and head off. Think of it as an adventure."

"I'm thinking of my bed and the need to sleep," Pippa said.

Charlie gathered up the files and placed the bead in his wallet. "Come on, you can sleep in the truck. Where's your sense of adventure?"

"Fine, fine, but let's stop off at the apartment first. Let me feed the cat and get a change of clothes."

"Excellent!"

Charlie escorted Pippa out of the bar, his heart racing with the excitement of everything. With the electrocution and odd behavior, he knew humans couldn't have made the bead, and he was going to go to its source and find out what the hell was going on himself … with Pippa by his side. Things didn't get much better than that in Charlie's world.

Chapter Four

Ben leapt from his seat and raced out of the Operations Room. He was thrown against the corridor wall after the ship jolted. *Space turbulence or a meteor shower, he thought. This happened occasionally. Deep space wasn't quite the smooth cruise depicted on 21*st Century movies. It was an incessant rumble with the occasional bumps and rattles.

He skidded around the entrance of the common room. Erika sat hugging herself, shaking.

"Are you okay?"

"What was that, Ben?"

"There's all kinds of debris out there. Relax, it's nothing we haven't been through before."

She pointed to the internal wall. "Didn't you feel it? Before the bump, I heard a bang below. The wall vibrated."

"Probably the same thing. Don't worry about it."

"No. I was sitting with my back against—"

Ben was lifted off his feet and slammed against the wall. Erika screamed, grasping her chair. Plates and cups fell from the dish drainer and smashed on the floor. The whole place seemed to shudder.

An electronic alarm started to loudly pulse, drowning out Erika's cries. Ceiling lights flickered. The common room door started to steadily slide shut. It was probably an isolation procedure in case of a fire. Ben hadn't seen it before.

He didn't want to get trapped inside. Maria might need his help in the Operations Room.

Ben dove to the door and held it open with the sole of his boot, using the opposite side of the frame for support. He strained against the power, but was slowly losing the battle.

"Quick, jump under my legs," Ben said.

"What's happening? Where we going?"

The force increased as the door mechanism's pitch grew louder.

"Just do it, Erika. I can't hold on for much longer."

"Shouldn't we stay–"

"Do you want to get trapped in here?"

Ben's words seemed to propel her into action. She dropped to the floor and slid underneath his quivering right leg. He immediately jumped to the side and rolled away. The door sprang across and hammered closed with a thump.

He pulled Erika to her feet. "All hands on deck. Come on."

The Operations Room door was closed. Ben peered through the thick plastic window, which had frosted through age. He could just make out the blurred figures of Maria sitting at the console and Ethan standing over her. He thumped his fist against the plastic. The two inside both turned. Maria ran to the window and shouted something. He couldn't hear a word above the alarm blasts, shook his head, and gestured to his ear. She pointed to the console. He couldn't see clearly past a few feet.

"Is there a way to open it? An emergency switch or something?" Erika said.

"No, they're controlled externally. We might have a fire

on the ship. Wait here."

He opened a cupboard next to the supply hatch and rummaged through the tools. Ben grabbed a wrecking bar and returned to the door. Erika was trying to communicate something through the window.

"Stand back. Give me some room," Ben said.

He'd got used to the squashed confines, but now it felt like the walls were closing in. Ben faced his first real situation. The bellowing alarm and blinking lights had made the place come alive in a way he hadn't witnessed before. The prospect of having more excitement in his life suddenly became a lot less appealing.

After managing to jam the toe of the bar into a groove, he placed his foot against the wall for leverage and heaved. The door opened a couple inches then snapped elastically shut.

"Give me a hand. Grab the end of the bar," he said.

The door squeezed open a few more inches. Ben felt sweat running down his back. He was about to let go when a chair leg shot through the opened space. The door banged against it and settled, leaving a small gap.

Maria stood on the other side.

"We need you in here. There's a serious problem," she said.

"Get Ethan over here. It'll take the four of us to get this open," Ben said. He turned to Erika. "Find something solid to wedge in the gap."

"Like what?"

"Grab the toolbox. That should do it."

He gazed into the Operations Room. Three of the critical measurements were red. The fourth was green, stable. An electric crackle came from the console followed by a wisp of smoke.

Four hands appeared, gripping around the door.

Ben positioned the bar. Erika returned, leaned under him with the toolbox by her feet.

"After three," Ben shouted. He tried to count down between the rhythmic pulses of the alarm. "One … Two … Three."

They managed to create a two-foot gap. All seemed to be shouting through exertion in unison. Erika grunted next to his ear.

"Now. Do it," Ben said.

She ducked down. The door closed a few inches against their pull. Erika slid the box in place.

Ben couldn't hold any longer. He let go and bent over double, resting his hands on his knees, gulping for air. The door crunched against the toolbox, but it held firm and did its job.

He straightened and edged through the gap. A burning smell hit him as he approached the console. Not like the type when he over-cooked food, this odor had a bitter edge. The crew converged around him.

"We've escalated the problem. No response," Maria said.

Ben looked at the switches on the console. "You tried the manual override?"

"Same thing. What can we do?"

He was struggling to hear a thing. "Take the bar and stop that fucking noise."

Erika grabbed the tool from the floor. Ethan dragged a chair to the corner of the Operations Room. In each area of the compartment was a circular plastic speaker on the ceiling.

Ben flicked the override switches. Nothing. He pressed

the console screen to escalate. No response.

He pressed again several times. "Come on."

The fourth critical measurement shot from green to red.

Sparks fizzed from behind the console, spitting across the room. Maria jumped back.

Thumping came from behind him as Ethan and Erika attacked the speaker.

Ben depressed the call button. "Master Control. This is the Operations Room. Do you copy?" He waited for a response. "Master Control. Are you there?"

Maria shook his shoulder. "All eight are red. All eight are red."

He glanced at the status bars.

The alarm took on a high-pitched whistle. Ben turned to see that they'd broken off the protective plastic cover. Maria cupped her ears from the piercing sound. Ethan winced as he thrust the bar against a concave, black internal structure.

After what seemed to be minutes but was probably seconds, the shrill stopped. The jarring pulse continued in other areas of the compartment.

"You want us to do the rest?" Erika said.

"Okay. You two do that. We'll deal with the fallout later," Ben said.

Ethan and Erika left the room.

He tried the console screen again, pressing harder against the glass. Trying to get any kind of response from the icons.

He thumbed the call button again. "Master Control. Are you there? Master Control …"

"It's no use. I was trying before …" Maria said.

"Well, we keep trying—"

The light flickered off, leaving the Operations Room dimly illuminated by the red status bars and green console screen.

"Master Control. Can you hear me?" Ben said.

The speaker buzzed and crackled. "This is Control."

He bolted toward the speaker. "Thank God. Can you update us?"

"Activate stasis preservation in two minutes."

"Roger that. What's happening?"

Maria yelped after a loud, electric snap from below the console. Sparks shot across the floor. The screen faded to black, leaving only the red status bars to give off any kind of ambience.

"Control, are you there? … Control?" Ben said. He turned to Maria. "I think it's died."

"What did they mean?"

"Stay here, I'll tell you when I get back," Ben said.

"Ben, wait …"

"We've got an option. I'll be back in a minute."

Ben squeezed through the gap in the door. The toolbox was reinforced with a metal table from the sleeping quarters. The door mechanism unsuccessfully shunted against the obstacles.

At the end of the corridor, Ethan hacked away at another speaker, and Erika held the chair steady in support.

"Meet me in the Ops Room," Ben shouted. Neither acknowledged. They probably couldn't hear him from their position next to the alarm. He'd grab them on his way back.

Ben entered the sleeping quarters, a small room with two bunks on either side, four lockers at the end, and a door to the bathroom. The lights had cut, and the alarm boomed overhead. Ben opened his locker and swiped his spare clothing to one side. He fumbled in the dark, grabbed a metal card from the back shelf, and stuffed it in his pocket.

He flinched as a hand grasped his shoulder.

"What are you doing?" Erika said.

Ethan appeared in the gloom, holding the wrecking bar. "Just this one to go. We can't get in the common room."

"Come with me. Now. We're getting out of here," Ben said.

"Leaving?" Erika said.

"I'll explain when we're all together."

"Okay, lead the way."

He felt his way along a bunk and headed back toward the red glow of the Operations Room. Maria sat away from the console, which was starting to smoke.

"Come out here. It's not safe in there," Ben said.

She stepped over the toolbox and table. They stood in a huddle next to the supply hatch.

Ben pulled the metal card out of his pocket and held it up. Six numbers were stamped across the middle. The crew leaned toward him for a closer inspection.

"Listen up. A week before Jimmy left, he gave me this," Ben said.

"What is it?" Maria said.

"It's a code to use only in emergency situations. While you two were smashing the corridor alarm, we had an instruction to activate stasis preservation."

"You heard from Master Control?" Erika said.

"Briefly. We managed to get instructions."

"What's stasis preservation?" Ethan said.

"If we take a big hit, come under attack, lose power, or whatever, all operational resources are to concentrate on restoring or maintaining essential services, the main engines, and stasis units. We're earmarked for the stasis wing. There's a lot of important people down there."

"Why didn't we know about this?" Maria said.

"It falls to the senior member to take responsibility, which is me since Jimmy left. Priority-wise, we're a second tier service."

"Is it a code for the airlock?" Erika said.

"It's exactly that," Ben said. "We're going down to help the stasis team. My guess is that engineering will sort this place out later."

"Do you think they'll let us stay? Send others here?" Ethan said.

"It's not even worth thinking about—"

The compartment rattled after a loud, external boom. They skidded sideways. Ben grabbed the handle of the supply hatch to maintain balance. Erika screamed. Ethan grabbed Ben's shoulder. His face contorted with terror.

"Keep your cool. We'll get through this," Ben said.

The crew pressed themselves against the metallic wall for support.

Maria clutched Ben's wrist. "Two minutes, they said."

He nodded. "Let's get out of here."

Ben traversed the corridor to the airlock, held the card next to the silver keypad, and started punching in the numbers.

The three joined Ben, crouching around him in anticipation for another jolt.

A green LED to the side of the buttons lit up after he keyed in the last digit. A white light winked above the airlock, and the countdown timer started at fifty-nine seconds.

"Bet you didn't expect this on your first day?" Maria said.

"It's going to be okay, right?" Ethan said.

"We'll be fine. Trust me," Ben said.

The truth was, he didn't know what the hell was happening. For the past thirteen years, he'd robotically carried out his shifts, eaten, slept, and studied. This was as new to him as it was to the new arrival.

Whooshing from behind the airlock grew louder. The timer neared zero.

"Ready guys?" Ben said.

The airlock slid open with a reassuring hiss. Light filled the corridor.

Ben stepped into the bright silver space. The others joined him. He looked over to Maria, who returned his gaze.

A neutral female voice came from the internal speaker. "Door closing."

Chapter Five

Charlie yawned and reached over the dashboard of his truck to get his Wayfarer shades. The sun's glare reflected off his rearview mirror. The clock on the dashboard indicated it had just turned 8 a.m.

Some overly loud radio presenter was just finishing up the morning show. He mistook himself for Robin Williams in Good Morning Vietnam, only he didn't have the talent and this wasn't the '60s, but still, the next track on was James Brown's "I Feel Good."

Despite himself, Charlie sang along as he cruised across the deserted Virginia Dare Memorial bridge that connected Roanoke Island with the North Virginia mainland. They'd be at the dig site in the Alligator River National Wildlife Refuge in less than thirty minutes.

"Jesus," Pippa said, sitting up from her slouched position in the passenger chair, wiping at her eyes. "How can anyone be so damned perky at this time of morning? Especially after that journey."

"It's only been nine hours. We've made good time. Come on, Pip, sing with me. I feel nice! Sugar and spice."

Pippa turned the radio down. "I don't know what's worse: your singing or your chirpy mood. Have you taken something while I was asleep?"

Charlie grinned. He hadn't taken anything, but the thrill of the road trip and the discovery was enough to keep him buzzing all day. He loved these kinds of trips, driving across the state, watching dawn approach. It had a sense of change to it, the colors in the sky brightening, bringing with them a new sense of momentum, a promise of new adventures and truths waiting to be uncovered.

"Don't be a grouch, Pip. We could be making massive news by the end of the day. Think of the opportunities. You'll be more famous than Zavi Rammas."

"Zahi Hawass," Pip corrected.

"Yeah, that dude."

Charlie continued on, taking Highway 64 through Manns Harbor, leaving the glistening Croatoan Sound behind. A few gulls were busy fishing as he continued toward the mainland.

A few more cars appeared on the road, but being an early Saturday morning, the place still felt like it was deserted. Charlie always liked this part of the world. Lots of greenery. It felt natural. The Wildlife Refuge itself was one of the first places he had visited here once he was approached to survey the place.

"If we have time, you fancy hiring some kayaks for a trip down Mill Tail Creek? I hear it's a real nice trip heading up to Alligator River."

"I don't do boat trips," Pippa said. "I prefer a nice quiet bar and some food. I'm starving."

"There's still some donuts in the back."

"Want one?" Pippa asked.

"Nah, I'm good. I'll get some eggs in town after we've finished at the dig. So tell me, if we check it out and prove the beads were definitely there at the time, and by now we know for definite the freaky little bastards aren't human-made, at least from that period, what's your guess? Or let me rephrase: What do you want them to be?"

Pippa pulled the small brown bag into the front. The bottom was darkened by grease. She took out a chocolate-covered donut and bit into it, her cheeks puffing like a hamster as she talked. "Well. It's got to be aliens, right?" She swallowed the donut and washed it down with a bottle of water. "I mean, it needs to be something that was technologically advanced beyond anything we've seen before. Even now, they would be a technological marvel. So other than extraterrestrial origins, and that could either be aliens or perhaps they came down on a meteorite or something, the only other explanation would be time travel, and that's just as crazy."

Charlie slowed as a tractor pulled out on the road from a farm to his left. He waited for a clear space and throttled his Ram truck, speeding past the farmer. He held his hand up as he passed and got a wave back from the farmer.

"Friendly people," Charlie said. "I wonder how they'll react when this place becomes home to a million news reporters. You realize that if this is what it seems and it gets out, it'll be the biggest news story in human history."

"That's what scares me the most. It's so ... out there. What if we're discredited? You know what the media is like. We could have our careers ruined."

"Or it could make our careers. Why be pessimistic about it?"

"I don't know. I just don't trust the media. How many times have we seen a historical program butchered for accuracy to sensationalize something or to make it more entertaining? The media don't do truth. They'll have us as crazy scientists with a crackpot theory."

"Fuck them," Charlie said. "We'll do this right. We'll

figure it out based on evidence. No one will be able to accuse us of not doing our due diligence."

A police cruiser with its light flashing shot past Charlie's truck, its siren blaring. Behind, a fire truck followed.

In the distance, Charlie saw a dust cloud rise. "Is that … from the dig site?"

Pippa leaned forward and squinted. "I don't know for sure. It's in the same direction."

Charlie floored the accelerator and followed the fire truck and police cruiser. With each mile, the anxiety built inside. It seemed they were going the same way. As they approached a turning, he muttered to himself, "Please don't turn."

But they did.

"This doesn't seem good," Pippa said.

Charlie followed but hung back from the emergency vehicles. They took the exact route he had planned to get to the site. When he turned out of Cedar Drive, he saw the cruiser and the fire truck pulled up at the dig.

By the time Charlie had negotiated the rough dirt track and pulled up to the gate, police tape was already being dragged across and around a section of the clearing. Charlie leaned out of the window. "What's going on?"

An officer came to him. "Please turn around, sir. This area is closed to the public for now."

"I work here," Charlie said. "I'm with Quaternary Productions. This is our dig site."

"Not anymore, son."

The anxiety was turning to ice inside his guts as he turned off the ignition and approached the officer. "What exactly do you mean?" He showed him his ID to prove that he was who he said he was. Pippa got out of the passenger side and joined Charlie at the gate.

"What's happening?" she said.

The officer held the tape up, satisfied they were who they said they were. "It's probably best if you come and see for yourselves."

They followed him under the tape and into the clearing. Dust and dirt clung to the air, obscuring the trees. It felt like they were entering the eye of a twister. The fire truck's lights were flashing, giving the place a surreal feel. They reflected off the flapping, white fabric of their finds tent that they had set up. Its poles were snapped, and it covered the ground. The fire truck obscured the actual trench. The police officer led them through and then stood with his arm out. "Don't go any further," he said.

"Holy crap!" Pippa put her hand to her mouth as her eyes widened with surprise. Charlie followed her gaze, and his jaw dropped.

The trench was gone.

In its place was a thirty-foot-wide hole. A sinkhole.

Stephanie Marks, one of the senior archeologists, was standing at the perimeter, her face against the police officer's chest. She was crying and talking, the words coming out in a frantic jumble.

Charlie and Pippa rushed to her.

"Steph, what's wrong?" Pippa asked.

The brunette woman turned to face them. Her eyes were rimmed with red as tears streaked down her craggy face.

"Take your time," Charlie said.

Stephanie took a few deep breaths and wiped her face, getting control of herself. Behind her, the rest of the tent slipped into the hole, the wind pushing it over the edge.

"Oh my God. I came over early to double check the site as you suggested in your email. Luke was supposed to meet me here, but I can't find him anywhere. He's not answering his phone. I think he might have gone ..." she broke away as tears came again. She turned to look at the sinkhole.

A group of firemen were preparing a camera on a rope to send down the sinkhole. "Are you sure he was here?" Charlie asked. "Mine and Pip's phones haven't had a signal all night. The cell reception's all screwed up. He might not have fallen in. Have you tried his home number?"

Steph nodded. "No answer. It just keeps ringing."

That was odd, Charlie thought. He knew Luke, one of the local college kids helping out on the dig, had an answering machine. If he weren't there, surely the machine would pick up.

"You have to get someone down there," Steph said to the officer. "He could be down there now waiting to be rescued. What if he's badly hurt?"

The officer turned out to be Sherriff Mackelson. He'd come from the local town. "We're doing all we can, Ma'am; we're low on resources right now."

"Why?" Pippa asked. "Surely you could spare more than one fire crew and yourself. There might be a kid stuck down there."

"This isn't the only sinkhole," Mackelson said. "Another one opened up in Franklin's Farm a few hours ago. Lost a cattle shed and two farmhands. I don't know what the hell's going on, but in all my years, nothing like this has happened before. We're dealing with it all as best we can."

"Where are the finds, the skeleton?" Pippa asked, her voice sounding distracted.

"At the college's archeological department," Stephanie

said. "They were all transferred over last night. The kids and Professor Marsh are doing the cataloguing."

"Okay, good. At least that's one thing we don't have to worry about. What else has gone down there?"

Stephanie looked around for a moment as if taking an inventory of things that were no longer there. "Just the tent and some digging equipment and a few trays. Nothing valuable. But I'm worried about Luke. I said I'd meet him here … This is all my fault. I should have left well enough alone. He wasn't even supposed to be working with me this weekend."

"Nonsense," Pippa said, clutching the woman's shoulder. "It was me that asked you here. If anyone is to be blamed, it's me."

The officer excused himself and approached the lead fireman. They had hooked up the camera to a rope and a cable. A small laptop had been set up on a temporary table about twenty feet away from the hole. Ignoring the safety tape, Charlie marched forward and joined the firemen.

"Don't mind me," Charlie said. "I work here … or what used to be here."

"Sir, please, stand back. I can't guarantee your safety."

"It's fine, I'll sign a damned form if I have to, but I'm going nowhere. Now let's see what's down there. I don't know about you, but I kind of want this to get a move on if there's a kid down there. Do we even know how deep it's sunk?"

A grizzled, grey-haired man gave him a stern look and gave up trying to be authoritative. Charlie had the demeanor that he wouldn't be fucked with. "Well, on casual inspection, at least sixty feet. Possibly deeper. We'll find out shortly."

The image of the screen started to change as the camera slipped over the edge and was fed by one of the firemen down into the sinkhole. At first, the image was too blurred and dark to make out, but then the light came on, creating a glow around the center of the camera. The focus worked for a few seconds before sharpening the image. In the upper right corner of the screen, a digital readout of the depth increased in foot increments.

"Slower," the fire chief said.

Charlie leaned in to get a look at the rock. "Looks smooth," he said. "Is that normal for a sinkhole?"

The chief shrugged. "First one I've experienced."

During his college course, Charlie had briefly covered the massive sinkhole network in Florida. Most of those were caused by clay covering a limestone cave system. When the weight on the clay cap got too much, from building works or excessive rain, it'd crack, and the material above the clay layer would fall down into the weak limestone. He knew that wasn't the case here. The soil wasn't rich with clay, and there was no known network of limestone erosion beneath.

The camera reached just over one hundred feet when something glinted under the light of the camera. "What's that?" Pippa pointed out excitedly as she and Steph joined the others huddled around the screen.

"Zooming in," the chief said. "Shit, it … it looks like the glass screen of a smart phone."

Steph shrieked and clapped her hand to her mouth before mumbling, "Oh my God, it's Luke's. He must be down there. Oh my God." Pippa took her away from the scene.

The sheriff returned after finally finishing his call.

"What are we looking at?"

"A cell phone," the chief said. "And … Wait … I can see a jacket among the debris."

Steph's face when white as she looked at the screen. "That's Luke's."

Charlie rushed away to his truck. Pippa followed him. "What are you doing?"

He moved to the rear of the truck, opened the door, and pulled out a rucksack filled with ropes and climbing gear. "I'm going down there."

Chapter Six

Ben had vague memories of being in the elevator as a frightened teenager. More like déjà vu than a physical recollection.

The slight rock before perceiving motion. A strip of blue lights attached to a wall panel, changing tone as the cab moved between floors.

He felt a slight sense of weightlessness as they started to descend.

Ethan crouched in the corner, rubbing his palms on his forehead.

"Hey, you just might be the first member of the Ops Compartment to use this thing twice in a day," Ben said.

"Or maybe the first in a century," Maria said.

Ethan lowered his hands. "You've never been to stasis before?"

"First time for all of us. I doubt they're expecting technical experts," Ben said.

"Who's in there? I mean, who got lucky enough to sleep their way through this?" Erika said.

Ben had heard rumors of rich celebrities, politicians, and corporations buying or imposing their way in. It was always that way on the ship. He wasn't sure he believed it. What use would an aging rock star be when trying to build a new civilization from the ground up compared to a talented tradesman?

"Who cares?" he said. "It's just our job to make sure they get there alive, isn't it? We won't be around to see the results of their work. *This* is our work."

"Did Jimmy tell you anything else about this procedure?" Erika said.

"I've told you all I know. That's all he knew. To be honest, I wasn't expecting it to happen."

"What about the segregation? The flu …"

"All that's probably out of the window when the shit hits the—" Maria said.

The elevator juddered to a halt.

Maria took a sharp intake of breath as it jerked up. A cherry red, thimble-shaped light above the door flicked on and gave off a waspish, electric buzz. The door swished open.

Ben shuffled his way to the front of the group. "Follow me."

He stepped out of the cab into a dimly lit metallic corridor leading to another airlock with a glowing keypad next to it. Ben's breath froze in the air. Goose bumps formed on his limbs. He tried to remember Jimmy's directions.

Ethan hugged himself, put his hands under his arms. "I've never felt cold like this."

"I doubt any of us have," Erika said.

Ben shook his head. "Me neither, but it has to be this way."

He'd always been in a regulated temperature, although his recollections of childhood were limited to a few flashbacks, all of the same thing: controlled atmospheres, comfortable, unremarkable.

They could have at least given them proper suits to wear in these emergency situations. He doubted he could work for too long in the stasis segment when his fingers became too cold to even feel.

Another thought came to him as he remembered Jimmy's procedure for entering the airlock. As a disobedient child, he had been dragged away, kicking and screaming, never to return to his classroom.

The children were told by the teacher every day that any misbehavior would lead them to being fed to the ship's monster. Those kinds of myths are hard to remove.

Looking back, Ben hoped that one day he'd get chance to meet the teacher again and give him some lessons in attitude realignment.

He retrieved the stamped code from his pocket and started to punch in the numbers. It wasn't like the warm, loose mechanism in the Operations Compartment. Each button required extra force to snap inwards.

"I bet Jimmy's pissed. Imagine, on the day you retire, all this happens. All those years on the job, and nothing interesting happens," Erika said.

"Jimmy won't be the only one. Remember, I said this only happens in an emergency. Let's make sure we do a good job. Don't want them thinking we're a bunch of clowns."

The group collectively murmured approval.

After depressing the last button, the countdown timer started at five seconds.

The airlock door hissed open.

Ben stepped into a small room, facing another larger door.

"Door closing," a computerized female voice said.

"Come on, get moving," Ben said, urging the others inside.

Erika was the last through. She screamed and dropped to the ground as the door slammed against her trailing leg. It opened a few inches, crunched against her ankle.

Ben forced his shoulder into the gap and shoved the door with both hands. "Pull her through."

Ethan and Maria hooked their arms underneath her shoulders and dragged Erika back. Ben jumped to the side, and the door thudded shut.

"Goddamn, that's a bit vicious," Ben said, testing the door.

The room was twice the size of the cab and was lit by a single red light on the ceiling. Through the gloom, he could see Erika squeezing her eyes tight, gritting her teeth, breathing in sharply.

"Are you okay?" Maria said.

"Does it … does it … look like it?" Erika said.

"How bad is it?" Ben said. "Can you stand?"

"I don't know. Give me a minute."

He checked the larger door. Felt around its edges. No keypad. The other side was the same. No internal way to get out of the room.

"What the hell? This isn't like what Jimmy told me. Something's wrong here," Ben said.

"Maybe it's controlled from the other side," Ethan said. "They might get a notification or something that we're here?"

"Perhaps it's the wrong door?" Maria said. "Could it have been possible to have come into the wrong one? I mean, it's all our first time down here."

"No," Ben said. "I don't screw up like that. I remember his exact words. This is definitely the airlock to the stasis chamber."

Maria had her arm around Erika. She glanced up at Ben and shrugged.

"Looks like we don't have a choice," Ben said. "Hopefully, they'll be here soon."

"You know what?" Maria said. "The Ops Compartment seems comfortable compared to here. And I thought we pulled the short straw."

Erika groaned, rubbing her ankle. "Tell me about it."

Ben hoped the first person they encountered would be sympathetic and take Erika away for treatment. The last thing he wanted was for word to get around that their team wasn't capable of making it through a couple of airlocks.

Especially on his command. He'd worked hard throughout his time and didn't want any blemish on his record. Or worse: have to go visit the superiors. He remembered one guy, Brad, who screwed up. No one ever saw him again. Must have been transferred, but no one knew for certain.

Just another of the many mysteries of life on the ship.

However, this was a chance for the team to prove themselves outside their enclosed domain. Maybe they'd land better job roles. Go up the levels, remove some of the restrictions of working in Ops.

He also wanted to find out if they were really being watched. There were so many stories that they were always monitored.

He considered it might just be a case of a rumor to keep the workforce from slacking off, which he could understand. When you were relying on people to maintain a generation ship over the centuries, you didn't want a group of ill-disciplined people putting everything in jeopardy.

"Hey, what's this?" Ethan said.

He leaned down and picked up a thin piece of metal.

Ben instantly recognized it by its shape. It was in a letter 'J' cut from a foil tray that their food came served in. Jimmy's bookmark.

"That's Jimmy's. He's been here too," Maria said.

"Must have dropped it on his way out," Ben said.

"Don't blame him. He'll have a real bookmark," Erika said. "Can you help me up?"

Ben began to crouch but bolted up after a siren started to blast. It sounded similar to the ones he'd heard watching clips of twentieth-century car chases. It was different than the usual warnings alarms.

A cold shiver of dread crawled down his back. Something wasn't right here. He could just sense it.

The light on the ceiling began to spin, accompanying his previous thought.

Behind the large door, he heard a rattling sound, like somebody dropping a chain. The bottom edged shuddered and lifted up a couple of inches, sending bright light streaming into the small room.

"Hello?" Ben said, "We're from Ops. Come to run protocol checks on the stasis chamber as per the—"

The solid door jerked up a few inches at a time. No one responded. He could see shadows beneath the door. He held his arm toward Erika. "Come on. Let's get you on your feet."

He looked down and saw a pair of dark gray, smooth leather boots on the other side. They looked huge, much larger than usual. Just who was that on that on the other side? Ben took a step back as the door continued to rise.

Chapter Seven

Charlie ignored Pippa's protests and headed for the sinkhole.

The sheriff stood in front of him, his arm pressing against Charlie's chest.

"I'm sorry, son, I can't let you get any closer. It's not safe."

"I've done this kind of thing before. If that's one of our kids down there, I want to get down there ASAP. Your guys don't seem in much of a rush."

The fire chief joined the sheriff. "We have to use procedure to make sure no one else gets hurt. We're doing all we can. We'll be mounting a rescue shortly."

"How?" Charlie said. "You're busy watching the monitor. You should be having people down there with ropes and climbing gear. But you don't have any of that stuff, do you? Where are the resources for this kind of rescue?"

The sheriff looked sheepish. "We're stretched at the moment is all. We're managing with what we've got."

Pippa joined Charlie. "He's right, Charlie, let's not do anything drastic here."

"I'm sorry, but I'm not waiting. I know what I'm doing."

With that, Charlie turned away and tied the end of his two-hundred-foot rope to the grill bars on the fire truck. He followed his usual climbing prep procedure, fit his harness, checked his knots, put on his head-mounted flashlight, and headed for the hole.

The place smelled of fresh dirt. It reminded him of days spent in the summer working on farms picking strawberries.

The fire crew remonstrated with the sheriff but ultimately realized like Charlie that it was quicker if he went down there.

The chief came over to him. "Son, don't do anything stupid, okay? Take the camera with you. Pull it up and show us what you're seeing as you go. We'll be right here if anything happens. We've got resources on the way, but with the sinkhole on the farm and one opening up in the town, we're really pushed at the moment."

"Don't worry about me, Chief. I've done this a thousand times. Is there audio on the camera?"

"No, but take this radio. It's already tuned to our frequency." The chief handed him a small but rugged two-way, which Charlie clipped to his harness around his chest.

"Are you sure you want to do this?" Pippa said, reaching out for him. "I mean, it's dangerous. What if … I couldn't …" she broke her eye contact then, looked off into the distance.

Charlie gave her a hug and while close, whispered in her ear, "I'll be right up, you'll see. No worries, no stress." He gave her a reassuring smile, but she didn't look convinced and held onto him a few moments longer than would be considered usual for just friends.

He had a brief thought of holding on, staying on the surface, but seeing Steph's pale face as she stood by the fire truck gave him the motivation to carry on and break away. "I'll be back," he said with a wink.

The chief and another fire officer explained the controls

of the camera and discussed a few rote safety procedures, but Charlie had heard it all before. "Okay, I got it. I'm going in."

He had hooked a second climbing harness over his shoulders. If Luke was down there, the others would be able to lift him or use the winch on the truck.

A tug on the pair of ropes ensured the knots were solid.

Charlie stepped backwards until he found the edge of the sinkhole. He leaned his weight back until he reached nearly ninety degrees, dug his heels into the topsoil, and walked his way down into the darkness.

His light shined against the dirt. As he continued to abseil down, he noticed there was little clay, and the walls were smooth. He reached out and touched the edge, feeling it with his hands. He didn't recognize the sensation.

It was too smooth. Unnatural.

The further he descended, the more he recognized a degree of uniformity on the surface. There were striations, spiraled like the inside of a gun barrel. Even the various layers of rocks, halfway down, were smooth, almost to the point of polished. Charlie thought that perhaps it was more of a burnishing, done with great heat. And yet the smell was of cold, damp, earth.

He shivered slightly, thinking of the temperature.

The entrance hole was shrinking away, the angular morning light dissipating, unable to penetrate the gloom. His head-mounted flashlight cast a single, weak beam into the void.

The two-way radio crackled to life.

"Charlie, this is Pippa. Are you okay? Over."

He stopped his descent, ensured he was secure, bent his head to the radio, and responded, "I'm fine, Pip. Just over halfway by my reckoning. The surface of the hole is strange, smooth. It's like I'm going down a steel tube or something. Over."

"We're not getting the video, Charlie. Can you check the camera? Over."

"Shit, sorry, I forgot. I was distracted. Let me sort that out now, and I'll head lower. Talk soon. Over."

The camera was attached to his harness. Its umbilical cord twisted up to the surface alongside his own rope, the last two things to connect him to the real world.

His movements didn't echo.

Any sound was hungrily consumed by the hole, snatched from the air as soon as the sound waves birthed. Even his heartbeat that pulsed through his ears seemed muted as if shrouded and stolen by the darkness.

Filming with one hand, Charlie slowly panned the camera round and down, giving those on the surface a chance to see what he saw. His hand shook as vibrations ran up through the hole.

Fragments of dirt fell away from the sides as the noise of moving earth roared louder, gas and air and debris shot up, making him cough. He swung forward, hooking the camera to his harness but pointing down. He dug his feet in firmly and clung to a half-inch-wide groove.

The shuddering vibrated through his hands. It felt like an earthquake.

He'd experienced a number of them during his time in California, but there was something about this that just didn't sit right with him.

One particular time, he was half a mile underground, exploring a cave system when a quake struck. That was more violent than this one, but the roar of moving earth and air beneath made it seem like the hole was alive and devouring anything within its gullet.

He wondered then that if Luke were indeed down there, he'd likely have gone lower as the hole continued to sink.

"Charlie, what's happening down there? Are you okay? Over." Pippa said over the radio. He looked up to see her face poking over the edge.

Taking one hand away from the groove to depress the radio he replied, "I'm fine. The hole has sunk further I think. I'm going lower. And stand back. I don't want you falling in. It's hard to tell how safe the ground is around here. Over."

"The camera showed the basin of the hole fall away," Pippa added. "There's a shelf of some kind not far below. I think Luke's there. We can see a coat among the dirt. Over."

"I'm heading down right away. Over."

It took a few minutes of descending into the darkness until he found the shelf. The material was solid rock, jutting incongruously out of the sides of the hole. The edges were smooth, rounded, almost as if something had shaped them that way for some unknown purpose.

Letting the ropes dangle a further twenty feet below the shelf, Charlie crouched down and looked over the side, shining his flashlight into the gloom and pointing the camera down.

Something shined beneath the light.

A piece of fabric.

It moved.

"Luke? Is that you? Can you hear me?" Charlie shouted. He cupped his ear, waited for a response, but could only hear a low, subterranean rumble and his own pulse.

"I think I've found him. Over."

"Is he alive? Over," Pippa said.

"There was movement; I'm going closer. Hold on. Over."

Charlie turned his back to the hole and repeated the abseiling procedure and back off the ledge, letting the rope rest with a notch on the edge of the ledge. He zipped down the rope and stalled his progress a foot above the mound of dirt and debris.

The rumble continued from below.

He tried to ignore the idea that it sounded like some great beast, its maw open just waiting to swallow him whole. Tentatively, Charlie placed his feet on patch of soil and tested his weight.

It seemed solid enough.

Luke's blue windbreaker stuck out of the soil, his arm and hand held up, the fingers moving. Charlie reached down and grabbed his hand, traced his body until he found his head cocked to one side, half-buried in debris. Charlie cleared some of the soil and turf away from the kid's face. His eyes were open and glinted with recognition beneath the flashlight.

"I'm here, buddy," Charlie said. "We're gonna get you out. Can you move? Is anything broken?"

"I … don't know," Luke said, his voice barely a whisper, the weight of the soil on his chest making him breathe in shallow breaths. "I thought I was going to die …"

"It's okay, buddy, don't talk. Conserve your strength. I'm going to help get you out and put this harness on. You'll be lifted out of here. You're going to make it. Just squeeze my hand if I hurt you, okay?"

Luke nodded gently and squeezed his hand.

Before Charlie started excavating him from the debris, Charlie informed the others. He could feel the relief over the radio.

"Okay, I'll go slow," Charlie said as he lowered himself until he straddled the boy. With his free hand, he started to shift the clods of earth from around the boy's arms and legs. He made quick progress, but Luke hadn't moved a muscle.

Paralysis, Charlie thought. He could have broken his back.

For a brief moment, he wondered if it was such a good idea getting the harness on him, but with the rumbles getting louder beneath him, he didn't think he'd have enough time to get an EMT down there to assess him properly.

Charlie made a judgment call: he'd get the kid out and worry about the rest later. It was better he took him out alive and injured than leave him to die.

"I'm just going to let go of your hand for a moment, buddy. I need to get this harness on you. Just nod or make a noise if I'm hurting you."

Luke did just that, nodding and making a breathy, squeaking noise that sounded like, "Do it."

Each moment felt like a lifetime as Charlie worked on freeing the boy. He could feel the vibrations of the rumble below travel up his legs.

Five minutes later, or what felt like five years, Charlie had managed to clear enough debris from him that he could slip the harness over Luke's legs and waist. He attached the ropes and various safety gear and applied tension to test the connections. It was solid.

Luke didn't budge or make a noise.

"Can you grip the rope?" Charlie said, handing it to him.

The boy's grip was weak, but he'd only need it to stop himself from falling backwards as they hoisted him up.

"Good lad. This might hurt, but it'll only be for a short while, and you'll be back on the surface. Try and keep hold of the rope as they lift you up, okay?"

"Okay," Luke said. "Thank you."

Charlie stood back and reached for the two-way radio, readying to call up to the others. But the surface beneath him rocked and shook, making him drop the radio.

He lost his balance and fell backwards, cracking the back of his head against the rocky surface. He slumped forward as pain bloomed in his skull, making him see white flashes.

Before he knew it, the dirt below dropped away in a roar that made his ears pop. The pressure changed, and below him, watching in horror, the remaining debris fell away into a dark void.

The harness gripped around his legs and waist as he swung out, his weight making the rope twang with the sudden tension.

Luke yelped as he too tensioned against his rope. His grip failed him, and he fell backwards, his limbs flailing. The harness held him to the rope, but his eyes flashed wide with sudden terror.

"Oh shit," Charlie said, "Hold on, Luke. I'm coming."

With a twist of his body and pushing off against the hole, Charlie sent himself swinging out to the center of the hole, reaching out for Luke. He grabbed him by the arm and helped lift him upright.

"Grab the rope," Charlie said as he helped direct the kid's hands. "Are you hurt?"

"I can't feel my back or my legs," Luke said, his eyes

closing tight.

"Don't worry, we'll get you out of here."

Charlie looked up to the hole and was about to shout up when he heard another roar from beneath him.

This time, it was different. It wasn't the sound of earth falling but rather something mechanical. When he looked down, he saw a belch of smoke bubble up. It made him choke and cough. The white smoke continued to fill the hole, tightening his throat so he couldn't yell out.

And in the smoke, gaining on them, a large, metallic object the same diameter as the hole rose up.

An eerie, yellow light came from the front of it as it kept on climbing.

Luke screamed when he saw it.

Charlie's spine went cold when he saw electricity flicker on the shape's surface. He tried to lift his legs as the machine within the smoke came closer, but he wasn't quick enough, and a bolt of electricity shot out, striking against his leg.

His vision closed to tiny specks, consciousness dancing on the edge, the darkness consuming him, taking him away until he could no longer feel anything. His last image was the light at the top of the sinkhole, the small silhouette of Pippa looking down at him.

He wanted to scream a warning, but it was too late.

Chapter Eight

The door raised to waist height, revealing stocky legs covered in dark gray rubber trousers with a meshed appearance. Shiny, black-gloved fingers curled around the bottom edge and pulled upward.

Ben decided to help. He gripped the bottom left of the door and heaved. It quickly rumbled upwards and banged fully open.

Blinding light filled the room, surrounding the silhouette of a person outside.

Ben squinted away, eyes in pain. "We're from the Operations Compartment. We've been ordered down for stasis preservation duties."

A single pair of footsteps entered.

Erika's nails dug into Ben's arm. Her grip sprang free. She screamed, dropping to the ground, head slamming against the dirty metal floor.

Ben looked down. Two arms ripped the prone Erika out of the room by her legs.

He cupped his eyes, trying to get used to the light. Images started to become clearer.

Maria screamed next. "Oh my God. Ben."

Outside, a large platform came into focus. A vehicle stood on the right side. It looked like a futuristic motorcycle apart from the lack of wheels. In the middle was a large man in a gray suit adorned with various pieces of body armor around the chest, shoulders, upper arms, and thighs. He pulled Erika to her feet by her hair.

Ben could see blue sky, trees in the background on one side, the edge of a forest stretching as far as the eye could see.

Ethan shook his shoulder. "Have we crash landed? Ben, what's happening?"

Ben brushed off his hand and stepped toward the exit. "What the fuck are you doing?" he shouted.

The man on the platform ignored him and grabbed a handle protruding from a long, thin pocket on his thigh with his spare hand and slid out a glinting blade with a serrated edge on one side. Circular holes ran along the middle.

"Help me. For God's sake, help ..." Erika flailed her arms, thumping against his unmoving, sturdy frame.

Ben rushed out.

The man's head twisted around toward him. His reflective helmet visor shone with a blue sheen and glinted in the light. Ben froze a few yards short. Two tubes ran from his helmet to a square backpack. Metal spikes ran along the back of his boots.

He thrust Erika into the air by her ponytail as if lifting a trophy. She frantically kicked her legs to little effect.

"Get off her," Ben said as he stepped forward. "Now."

Erika's eyes widened, and she opened her mouth. The man plunged the blade into her chest three times in rapid succession before Ben could act.

"No," Ethan said.

"What do we do? What do we do?" Maria said from behind him.

The man threw Erika off the side of the platform without ceremony. He continued to face Ben, wiping the blade clean with his gloved hand.

"Holy shit," Ben said. For a moment, he seemed glued to the spot. "Quick. Round the side of that vehicle. To the edge of the platform."

"Where are we?" Ethan said.

"Save the questions," Ben said. "We need to find something, anything."

He darted behind the vehicle, skidding to a halt at the right ledge. The drop below appeared at least sixty feet. He frantically tried to process events.

Maria crouched next to him, quivering. Ethan panted behind. The man circled the blade above his head, stalking around them in a wide arc.

The area to the right looked like plowed farmland. Uniformed brown lines reached into the horizon. To his left, forest. Behind the ship, a deep gouge furrowed through the earth, running from the back of the ship into the far distance.

He wondered if they had crash-landed, but how could he breathe?

Black smoke belched from the ship into the clear, blue sky. He heard the noise of an engine straining and stopping, straining and stopping. The platform was around thirty feet long and twenty wide.

He scanned the platform for a makeshift weapon. The surface was clear apart from the bike, a pool of blood, and the man approaching with a raised blade. As the man closed in around one end of the bike, the three of them all scuttled to the other. They faced off, nine feet apart, separated by machinery.

"Why are you doing this? We're part of the crew," Maria

said.

Ben detected a low, clicking sound coming from the helmet. "Who are you?"

The man sprang up onto the seat, landing into a hunch, then rising to a towering position above them. He raised the blade over his head and then pointed it at them.

Ethan gasped. "We're gonna die."

Ben ducked to one side as the blade swung down. It whistled past his ear and clanked against the metal chassis. He staggered back, dropping to the platform to avoid momentum taking him over the side.

The man's focus seemed to zero in on Ben. He leaped off the seat and advanced toward him, sheathing the blade and reaching for a hip holster. He pulled a black, angular-looking weapon out and aimed with a straight arm, head tilting to one side.

Ben closed his eyes, thinking his time was up.

Two loud cracks, seconds apart, split the air.

Maria screamed.

"Ben," Ethan shouted.

Something hit the platform, two items clattering with a thud. Ben opened his eyes.

The man was on both knees, clutching his throat, weapon on the platform beside him. Another crack rang out.

The man sprawled back, his blue visor splintered with a small hole in the middle. He slumped against the vehicle, motionless.

Ben jumped to his feet and grabbed the pistol-like weapon. It was smooth and black with just a trigger and a button on the side. No insignia.

He held his finger on the trigger and trained it on the

armored man. Hopefully, the threat would be enough if the man was even still alive.

Ben had never seen a real weapon. The closest he got was a wooden toy in the orphan compartment. It felt heavy and solid in his hand. Deadly.

"Get behind me," Ben said. Maria cautiously approached the body. "Stay away. He might get up."

She ignored him and reached out. Fumbling with the handle on the thigh, sliding out the long blade, still smeared with blood. "If another comes along."

"Who the hell was that?" Ethan said. "Where are we?"

"I've no idea. We'll figure it out eventually; let's just get safe first," Ben said.

Ben glanced over the edge of the platform. Something moved in the trees below. A threat perhaps? More of these armored people?

"Down there, movement. Do you see it?" Ben said.

Three dark shapes cut through the trees alongside the ship.

Maria pointed. "Oh my God, Ben, look, someone's coming."

He followed Maria's direction to the gouge behind the ship. Erika lay directly below, face down in the mud. Thirty feet along, another man lay flat on his back, dressed in the same uniform.

Jimmy.

From what Ben could see, his former colleague had suffered a similar fate. Jimmy's twisted figure was deathly still, mouth open, face reddened with blood. His friend of over thirteen years butchered at the moment of retirement. He took a deep breath, trying to remain focused on immediate events.

Ethan sunk to his knees and started to sob. "It's over. We've failed."

"Pull yourself together. We need to find a way back into the ship. Get somewhere safe, warn the crew," Ben said.

He searched between the trees for signs of movement.

"How do we get back?" Maria said.

Two figures covered in foliage along with a dog broke from underneath the canopy cover. Two weapons aimed upwards toward them.

"Shit! Back to the airlock," Ben said.

He grabbed Ethan by the epaulette and dragged him back. Ethan stumbled to his feet and quickly overtook Ben. To the immediate right of the door was a circular, charred indent; the ship appeared to have taken a considerable blast from something.

They all crashed against the internal wall after staggering back in.

"Jesus, Ben. Erika, Jimmy …" Maria said.

"I know it's hard, but try to forget about them for a moment. We'll get some back-up soon. They won't just leave us here."

"Who was that?" Ethan said.

"No idea, but stay out of sight. They can't see here."

Ben checked around the room, now assisted by light. What he originally mistook for grime had a dark purple color, spattered and speckled across the walls. He shoved against the internal door with his shoulder to no effect. Ethan slammed the bottom of his foot against it, grunting with every blow. Maria felt around the room, patting the stained surfaces, running her fingers down the corners.

"What are you doing?" Ben said.

"I don't know. There might be a hidden button or something."

Ben crouched and peered over the back of the ship into the distance. Nothing looked familiar. A group of black specks circled in the air. The trees had a white tinge, and the outline of buildings jagged against the skyline, reminding him of the broken fence posts on the toy wooden farm in the orphan compartment.

"Did you hear that?" Ethan said.

"Hear what?" Ben said.

"Shouting. Listen."

The engines continued to strain and lull below. Ben heard a voice drifting up on the breeze between the mechanical screams.

"I'm going to check it out. Give me a minute," he said.

"Stay here. We'll be safer," Maria said.

"It might be the people that saved our ass. I'll crawl to the edge and have a look."

"*They* might not be people. How are you going to communicate?" Ethan said.

"He's right, Ben. You've seen the trench behind the ship. Doesn't take a genius to work out we've crashed."

Ben peered back at the fresh brown trail chewed out of the ground. "We need to do something. I'm not waiting here for another psycho to show up."

He slid onto his stomach. Maria grasped his ankle. "Don't do anything stupid. We need you."

Ben held up his thumb. He leopard-crawled across the platform, shooting glances at the body by the bike. A star shone brightly in the sky directly above him, warming his neck. The small dimples in the metal gave him a decent grip, and he quickly progressed.

He reached the edge, took a deep breath, and looked

over.

A single figure stood below, looking directly at him, the bearded face of a man. Ben thrust himself back with his elbows.

"Hello. Hello," a male voice called out. "Do you understand me?"

He spoke in English. Another member of the crew? It made sense. That's why they shot the attacker on the platform.

Ben leaned over the edge. "What the hell's happening? Where are we?"

"I'll explain when you come down. You've only got a few minutes."

"What happened to the ship? Did we detach?"

The man appeared to start laughing. His shoulders rocked as he looked down, shaking his head.

"I'm glad you find this funny," Ben said.

He gazed back up with a stern expression. "Far from it. If you and your buddies want to live, you'll do as I say."

"What do you mean?"

"I'm not going to stand here debating. You'll get us all killed. Come down in the next minute or I'll leave you to join your friend," the man said, pointing toward Jimmy.

"We can't get off this platform, can't see a way down," Ben said.

"Look around the edge. There's a ladder that runs up the side."

Ben edged around the corner and looked along the side of the ship. It was a few feet away, rigid, and running from top to bottom. Easy enough to navigate. The view enabled him to get a handle on the size of their craft. Roughly two hundred feet long and seventy high. Colored a dull black but with something painted on the side he couldn't quite see because of the angle.

"Get moving, boy," the man shouted, all humor gone from his voice.

Ben weighed his options. They couldn't get back into the ship and needed some form of protection. This man and whoever he was with provided it. They could have shot him, Maria, or Ethan on the platform. It seemed like the Ops team only had one choice.

He ran back to the internal space. "Did you hear all of that?"

"Not quite, but we did hear some English," Maria said. "What did he say?"

"We need to leave, now."

"Where are we going?" Maria said.

"Who is it?" Ethan said.

"Possibly a member of the crew. He says we need to leave or we'll die. Do you want to try and prove him wrong?"

"No. Where are we?" Ethan said.

"He's going to explain when we get down. We've got a minute. There's a ladder on the side. Ready?"

"Okay, let's do it," Maria said. "I don't like it but ..."

Ethan returned a vacant look. Ben shook his shoulder. "Are you ready?"

"Yeah ... Yes. I'm with you."

Ben jogged back to the edge of the platform. "We're coming down. There's three of us."

The man nodded and took a couple of steps back. He crouched on the dirt, surveying the area through the sights of his rifle.

"It's just around this edge. I'll go first," Ben said.

He reached out and gripped the cold, square ladder rail.

Composing himself, he took a deep breath and swung his left leg around onto a rung, grabbing the opposite rail with his left hand.

The sixty-foot drop had a dizzying effect. He hugged against the ladder, squeezing the rails hard.

"Don't look down," Ben said.

He descended the ladder, concentrating on his deliberate movements while glancing up at the other two. After Ben climbed down twenty feet, Ethan swayed out onto the ladder with a youthful fearlessness. Maria followed shortly after, and all three clanked toward the ground.

Ben flinched after the man shouted, "Denver, deal with that driver!"

He felt the man's presence as he neared the dirt. With only four feet to go, Ben jumped off the ladder, twisting as he landed.

The man stood only four feet away. He wore a camouflage jacket and trousers with pieces of greenery attached, giving his clothing a strange organic appearance. The jacket hood had three ferns attached. They twitched as the breeze caught the edges.

A pink scar running down the center of his forehead wrinkled as he smiled through a thick, dark blond beard. His striking blue eyes were rimmed with weather-beaten wrinkles, giving him a hard look. He looked at least ten years older than Ben.

He held out his hand and with a low, rough voice, said, "Charlie Jackson. Your only hope for survival."

Chapter Nine

Charlie waited for the uniformed man to take his hand, but he stood there, staring at Charlie with wide-eyed confusion. There was a degree of terror in there too. Charlie had seen that expression hundreds of times before. Usually when people realized their planet was no longer theirs, or in the final moments of their life.

"What's your name?" Charlie asked as the other eventually took his hand. The man's grip was weak, the shake clumsy. He'd obviously never shaken someone's hand before. Wasn't surprising.

The croatoans wouldn't have bothered to go to that level of education for their ruse. They only needed people within the harvesters to believe they were on a generational ship and give them some bullshit procedures to follow in order to keep the harvesters on track for their yield of root.

"I'm Ben," he said, releasing his grip. Two others joined him. Ben pointed to the younger male. "He's Ethan," and to the woman, "that's Maria. What the fuck's going on? Who are you? Where are we?"

"We crashed, didn't we?" Ethan said.

The three of them turned to look at their 'ship.' Charlie noticed Ben angling his head to take in the giant tracks—the same tracks that were now jammed and splintered apart by Charlie's land mines.

Ben looked back at Charlie, a sudden realization

making his face muscles tighten and his eyes narrow with fear. "It was all a lie," he said to the others. "None of it was real."

"Damn right it wasn't," Charlie said, pointing to the two bodies of their former colleagues and brainwashed lab rats. "The croatoans use you as tools, nothing more. Well, that's not strictly true. They use you … us … for lots of things."

Maria shook her head. "I don't get it, what's a croatoan? Where are we?"

"Let me spell it out real quick. We've got about five minutes before these bastards return. We need to get you lot into cover ASAP. That," he pointed to the great harvester, "is no goddamned ship. You're not engineers or pilots or any other bullshit role they've brainwashed you into believing. That's an alien harvester. You're on Earth, your home. You've never left the planet."

"So we're not going to Kepler B?" Ethan said. "Is it still 2451?"

"No," Charlie said. "2044. The shit hit the fan in 2014."

Ben stepped down the gouge in the earth and knelt. He pulled up a bright orange root, its tip sheared off from the harvester. All down the gouge, more roots with the same sheared tips lined the dirt like a carpet, and in amongst them were the bodies of his two colleagues.

Ben placed his hands on the dead male's back and bowed his head for a moment. After a few quiet seconds, he stood up and returned to the others, his eyes glossy with tears. "What do we do?"

"I don't believe this," Ethan said.

"Me neither," Maria added, both of them on the verge of hysteria, the cold truth making it hard for them to comprehend.

Denver's dog barked twice and ran up to Charlie, licking at his hand. The grey-haired gun dog was excited about its find. Denver followed close behind, dragging a small croatoan by the alien's scrawny, leathery neck. Denver's wiry, strong frame loped forward and deposited the four-foot-tall alien between Charlie and Ben's group.

It collapsed into a huddle. Its weak, spindly arms, sufficient only to press buttons and type commands, huddled around its naked body. It shivered, and its widely spaced eyes narrowed. At one time, Charlie had pity for them. They were at the bottom of the croatoan hierarchy, but the slit for its mouth sneered, betraying its feelings for humans.

"Good job, Den," Charlie said, patting his son on the shoulder. Denver stood nearly a foot taller than Charlie and bowed to the others. "Meet your captor," he said.

Ben and the others leaned in but remained cautious.

"Holy fuck," Ethan said as the croatoan let out a gurgled hissing noise and spat at the ground, choking up phlegm and blood, the earth's oxygen already at work poisoning its lungs without the breathing apparatus needed to enrich the oxygen with root compound.

Denver kicked it forward into the dirt. "Shut up, scum."

"Easy, son," Charlie said. Denver nodded and stepped back, running a nervous hand through his red beard. He looked up into the sky, anticipating a croatoan scout group to arrive any second. Charlie had to fight the urge to dive into the forest this very second, but this group needed to see for themselves before they'd go willingly.

The last thing he needed was for a reluctant group of lambs to slow him down.

Ben looked from the alien to Charlie. "Where did you get him … it, that, whatever it is."

"It's your *ship's* driver. Younger version of that fucker up there that killed your friends. It's what's taken over this planet. Well, I say take over; they were here long before we were, waiting deep inside the earth for when conditions were right."

"My God," Maria said, "It's all true."

"Evidence enough for you, Ethan?" Charlie said.

The younger man said nothing, his face pale.

"This is crazy," Ben said. "I can't get my head around it."

"No," Charlie added. "I suppose you won't. But we really have no more time. They'll know their harvester is damaged and send out a patrol. The one on the platform is one such member. The next patrol won't be long. They have quotas and some such shit when it comes to harvesting the root. That orange stuff you see there. Here's the thing, kids; that there is your enemy. Everything you knew was a lie. You're nothing but meat and resources to them. You can stay and deal with them yourself, or you come right this second and earn a chance at living a true life."

Charlie turned to his son. "Den, want the honors?"

Denver looked at Charlie with a grim expression before pulling his machete from the leather scabbard around his waist. He approached the mewling alien and cut him once across the throat, letting the creature bleed out into the dirt.

Its tan-colored leather skin hardened and crinkled to a grey, paper-like texture.

"Christ," Ben said as the others gasped.

Turning his back to them and lifting his rifle to his chest, Charlie headed to the forest. Denver and his dog followed. "We're leaving," Charlie shouted over his shoulder. "Your decision on whether you follow or stay."

***

Denver scouted twenty feet ahead of the group, hacking through the dense forest with the machete. His ever-faithful dog scurried along by his side, forever within a few feet of him. They were like siblings attached at the hip.

When Denver was just fifteen years old, he'd found the pup along with a dying mother in an old, crumbled apartment building. They couldn't save the bitch, but the pup had survived after close attention by Denver.

Charlie thought it was a dangerous waste of time and energy. They needed to be able to move quickly from one safe shelter to another if they were to remain alive, and looking after a yapping dog didn't aid general survivability.

But with Denver losing both of his parents when he was still a toddler back in the mini ice age times, Charlie saw a parallel there. He had taken Denver in, looked after him, made sure the croatoans didn't find him.

Denver did the same thing for the dog.

"What's he called?" Ben said, joining Charlie, helping to make their way through the thick foliage. Ethan and Maria had taken the flanks.

"Pip," Charlie said. "The dog's a she."

"Nice name."

"It has … sentimental value." Charlie thought back to his Pip. Pippa. Even after all that time, it still hurt as fresh as the day she passed. He unconsciously reached up and fondled the blue bead wrapped in croatoan graphene thread that hung from a leather thong around his neck.

The day in the bar still shone in his memory. The look of Pippa's beautiful face as she held up the bead in wonder and awe. How excited they both were at the discovery; how they didn't realize it was an omen.

Charlie continued to trek in silence for the next fifteen minutes, occasionally stopping to check through a break in the tree cover, expecting to see those hover-bikes flying above, searching for them. With the GPS chips buried within Ben, Ethan, and Maria, every minute out in the open was another minute the scouts had to zero in on their location.

If they were found, he'd make their deaths quick to spare them the scouts' torture. They seemed like good people.

Clueless and frightened, but good people.

Ben had adapted the quickest, focusing on tasks rather than worrying too much about the situation. Charlie recognized some of himself within Ben. Whether that was a good sign or not, he couldn't say, but at least it'd keep the kid alive for a while.

As for Maria and Ethan—he gave them a couple of days, tops.

Denver took a knee and held his hand up. Pip sat by his side, her tail still.

"Wait," Charlie said, pulling Ben to the ground. He looked to his side and indicated for Ethan and Maria to hit the deck. He pressed his finger against his lips to gesture to be quiet. He hoped they understood. It was difficult to tell what they had picked up or didn't within the harvester.

They at least managed to read his body language and sat still. Charlie crawled forward to Denver, whispered, "What is it, Den?"

"Two surveyors, thirty feet up ahead."

"Shit, that's near the shelter's entrance. Any others around?"

"None that I can see."

Charlie crawled a further few feet and pressed himself against the trunk of a giant redwood that wasn't there a decade ago. Since the mini ice age burned off, the growth of trees and plants had increased at an explosive rate, fuelled by the croatoans' introduced farming, which seemed to cultivate the atmosphere.

Looking through a thick bush, parting the leaves a few inches, Charlie saw them. Den was right; there were just two of them. They were small like the harvester's pilots, but these wore the helmets and backpacks that recycled oxygen, enriching it with their chemicals. He heard their clicking, percussive language as they took a series of soil samples. They were identifying new routes for harvesting.

The only problem was that they were right above one of Charlie and Den's shelters.

Within the trees and bushes, the remnants of a town showed through in places: old apartment buildings that had collapsed, sending concrete and steel to the ground, now reclaimed by nature.

His shelter was actually the basement of what used to be a three-story commercial building. From his position, he could just make out the southern wall. It collapsed years ago, leaving only a crumbled reminder of its previous use.

If one of the surveyors found his shelter, that traitor bastard Gregor would have the place carpet-bombed, especially now that Charlie had taken out another of his harvesters. His quotas would be way down, and he'd face increasing pressure from the administrators.

Charlie heard movement from behind. He spun round to find Ben crouching beside him. "What's happening?" Ben said.

"Get down, you fool," Charlie whispered between gritted teeth. He grabbed the idiot and pulled him away from the bush. Leaning close to his ear, Charlie added, "Give me the pistol you took. Do it quietly."

Ben handed Charlie the croatoan pistol with a shaking hand. Charlie handed it to Denver, who took it with saying a word. "Now be quiet and don't move," Charlie said.

To Denver: "Take the one on the right after three. Headshot preferable."

"Okay, Dad." Denver buried his foot into the dirt, pressed his shoulder against a tree for support, and aimed the pistol through a gap in the bush.

The surveyor on the left hand side used a small control panel that resembled a TV remote made from glass to raise a five-foot-tall metal tube used to analyze the soil. The tube extended out of the ground, held up by a tripod of thin croatoan metal.

Charlie grinned. That would make a fine weapon. With a little heat, their metal could be shaped and sharpened to a razor's edge like Den's machete. That used to be one of the alien scums' backpacks.

When the two surveyors faced each other to discuss their findings, Charlie extended his rifle through the foliage of the bush and brought the scope up to his eye. With his quarry in sight, Charlie whispered, "One … two … three …" Two shots fired simultaneously, his shot muffled by a suppressor, the alien pistol making an ear-popping, low hum.

Checking with his scope, Charlie saw both aliens lying on the ground, the shells of their helmets shattered.

Pip growled low.

"Shit, we've got company," Den said, pointing upwards.

Charlie looked up and saw the shadow of a hover-bike fly overhead. Damn it, they were quicker this time. They had to get to the shelter before the scouts landed; they wouldn't survive a full assault on their own. Perhaps if it were just Charlie and Den, but not with these lambs holding them back.

Leaping to his feet, Charlie turned to Ben and the others. He shouted, "Follow me, now, sprint!" He dashed through the bush and sprinted forward, leaving everyone but Den behind. He leapt over fallen trees and thick roots until he came to the surveyors. He and Den took one each, lifting them on their shoulders.

"Grab the gear and follow me," Charlie shouted to Ben and the others.

The whine of hover-bikes came from a hundred feet or so away. The GPS chips within the lambs would give their general position away, but below a hundred-foot-radius, Charlie's scramblers within the shelter would make it difficult for them to pin-point them.

At the very least, it'd buy them time to get set for a fight.

The crumbled wall lay just a few feet away. Charlie dashed forward and dumped the body at its base. Den followed. When the others caught up, Charlie pushed them along the wall until they came to an old tree. He rolled it away to reveal a hole in the ground. "Get down there," he said, pushing them in. Ethan and Maria had brought the tubes and tripods and handed them to Charlie and Den as they descended underground.

"In you go, son," Charlie said, waiting for Den and Pip to follow inside.

"They'll be more this time," Denver said before he went inside.

"I know. We'll figure something out."

Den nodded and smiled. "You always do." He scrambled inside the hole with the agility of a weasel.

Charlie laid the equipment at the base of the wall and, along with the bodies, covered them with foliage. He heard the guttural clicks and grunts of the croatoan scouts. Looking through a gap in the wall where a tree's branch had penetrated, he saw a squad of three armed with rifles scan the area. The lead grunt wore a gold-sheened-visor—one of Gregor's personal crew—and referred to a wrist-mounted locator.

They wouldn't be able to stay in the shelter long. They'd update their location, and others would arrive. They would soon be found. Charlie slowly backed away from the wall and made his way to the hole that led into the old building's basement.

Crawling into the darkness, he reached up and rolled the trunk back over just as the sound of yet more hover-bikes landed to the south of their position.

This was not going well.

Chapter Ten

Gregor Miralos threw a blanket to one side, splashed his face with stagnant water from the bedroom sink, and sprayed his armpits with a rusty can of deodorant—his typical morning routine. Dressed in only a towel, he fried a breakfast of fresh salmon left on his kitchen counter by one of his team. Despite a few hiccups, for the last two months, the North American operation was going well.

The salmon started to blacken. He scraped pieces onto a plate with a spatula and took the dish to his office, placing it on his desk.

He sat in a brown leather chair and caressed the mahogany arms, enjoying the squeaking friction against his back.

Scanning three croatoan-installed screens on his desk while tossing chunks of salmon into his mouth, Gregor checked the productivity statistics against operational harvesters in the field. The results were at least on par with other continents, if not slightly better.

He looked around the office, the main room in a sparse one-bedroom house on the edge of the croatoan camp. Whitewashed walls and furniture he'd looted from local derelict buildings. The aliens supplied power and water from their centralized source.

This place was better than the trailer at the last location, but he thought it was time for an upgrade. He wanted the top job of global director, currently taken by Mr. Augustus. Gregor knew that asshole lived in luxury.

The front door rattled against the jam three times.

"Enter," Gregor shouted.

Alex, his temporary second-in-command, opened the door and entered the room, stopping short of the desk. She fidgeted with a drawstring at the bottom of her yellow waterproof jacket and wiped a thin covering of sweat off her brow.

"Good morning, Gregor—"

"Cut the shit. What have you come to tell me?" Gregor half-closed his eyes, looking Alex up and down. Thirty years ago, Alex could light up a room with her rich dark brown, wavy hair and glamorous features. Today, she looked old, concerned, her graying hair in a tight ponytail. "Spit it out."

"Harvester five. It's down."

Gregor shifted in his chair. "Down? Down how?"

"We've lost contact with the driver and guard. It happened during a resource switch."

"Do the croatoans know?"

"They're on the way. I contacted a mobile unit to intercept."

Gregor slammed his fist on the desk. "Send out our croatoan team. If it's the little wasp, I want him dead. Even if they get a sniff of him, bomb the whole area. I don't care. The harvesters will just have to work longer and harder."

He hoped he'd seen the last of the little wasp, someone who had already taken out two of his harvesters in a similar manner: land mines coupled with a direct assault. This might be the third time in five months, denting Gregor's statistics, making him appear out of control.

The croatoans didn't seem bothered up to now. They

claimed it was mild resistance compared to other planets.

Their patience would only stretch so far before snapping.

"They might not like it. They only came in from patrol an hour ago," Alex said.

Gregor slammed his fist on the desk again, knocking the plate off. Alex winced as it smashed on the floor. "They're attached to this facility and will do what I say. Send them. Now."

"I'll get right to it," Alex said.

"Where's Layla?"

Out of all the humans attached to the operation, Layla had a level of competence that Gregor admired. If something was happening, he wanted her there.

"I think she's already gone out to investigate."

"I can always replace you with Layla, Alex. Send you back to the farm?"

Alex backed away from the desk, turned, and stumbled out of the door.

Gregor doubted Alex's abilities, but with the business with Marek, she'd taken over as Gregor's second-in-command two days ago. Marek had been Gregor's friend since childhood, growing up in Yerevan. They'd stolen together, fought together, and graduated into the same gang until they came to run it. Alex was just a junior member when the shit hit the fan in 2014.

Everything was fine, Gregor thought, until Marek went missing for twenty-four hours, then turned up on the edge of camp, semi-conscious, tied to a tree. A plank was hung around his body with 'Fifth Columnist' painted across it in bright red letters. Two of his fingers had been snapped backwards, and he'd taken a beating. The little wasp, that fuckstain Charlie Jackson who fancied himself as some kind of vigilante hero, had interrogated and beat Gregor's lifelong friend for information.

Gregor slipped into a pair of jeans, pulled on a brown, woolly sweater, and fastened his steel toe-capped boots. They were always useful when delivering kicks to the farm animals or his junior staff. He clipped on a hip holster and inserted his pistol.

The door rattled three times again.

"What?" Gregor shouted, not even trying to hide his annoyance.

Alex half-opened the door. "A shuttle's coming. Just thought I'd—"

Gregor could already hear the humming engines growing increasingly louder as a shuttle descended toward camp. The mother ship had turned up in 2025 near the end of the ice age.

It always held a faint white presence when the sky was clear, hanging up there like a specter or a spiritual portent, but then what did Gregor have with spirits? He knew there was no God the day the Earth was taken from them by the croatoans.

Fuck 'em, he thought. Just play the game, survive, climb the ladder. That's all there was left now. No point in fighting them; humanity had already lost too much.

Gregor retrieved a plastic tortoiseshell comb from his back pocket and smoothed his thick, black hair into a side parting. Shoving Alex out of the way, he stepped outside into the bright sunshine bathing the camp.

***

Six pink rings appeared over the camp. The humming took on a sharper edge as the shuttle plunged through the troposphere, its cobalt outline becoming visible against the sky's blue-orange surroundings.

Ever since the croatoans started harvesting the earth for their root, the orange dust floated up into the atmosphere, giving the sky a strange, permanent tan.

Gregor stood by the landing zone at the back of the farm surrounded by trees. Solar-powered markers ran around the edge of the two-hundred-yard square strip. It had already been turned into scorched earth from repeated take-offs and landings, a regular, twice-daily occurrence for the last three months, usually for the transportation of croatoans. But never this early in the morning.

Alex stood by his side. "What do you think they want?"

"It's obvious. They're going to complain about the harvester. We're going to need a sacrificial lamb."

"Do you want me to dress a human from the paddock?"

He drummed his fingers on his chin. "No, bring me Igor."

"Igor?"

"You heard me."

Igor, it had been reported to Gregor, thought he knew better on how the facility should be run. Additionally, Igor had been seen fraternizing with the camp's allocation of croatoan scouts and engineers.

They weren't supposed to mix. Gregor suspected the worm was up to something. Igor had been one of the few to survive the ice age along with Gregor and his fellow gang members. Used to run a small protection racket in Moscow, fancied himself as some crime lord.

Gregor had ways of dealing with competition. It was

dog-eat-dog these days, after all.

The shuttle steadied a hundred yards above. Its pink circles took on a darker glow for the final descent. The ground rumbled. Gregor pulled the woolly sweater over his nose and mouth and shielded his eyes.

Dust and burnt grass showered him as the shuttle gracefully dropped and bounced softly to a halt.

He was always struck with how bland these craft looked. Nothing as exciting as what he'd seen on TV but a lot more deadly. Two years ago, somebody fired on one from the ground. The response from the pulse cannon mounted on the roof was devastating.

Although violence was rarely the croatoan way.

That was more Gregor's domain. As the human resource officer on the ground, he had to maintain discipline with the local team and livestock.

A door on the side of the shuttle punched open and slid to one side with an electric groan followed by a graphite-colored ramp extending onto the ground. Through the darkness, a human male strode out in a long, purple robe flanked by two croatoans in their gray armored suits, carrying black rifles.

Mr. Augustus. The human-croatoan chief liaison. The only human to have visited the mother ship, and the only human to have visited and worked directly with the alien hierarchy.

Augustus thought he was some sort of king. Strutting around dressed like a fool, treating everyone with lofty derision. He wore a creepy mask to hide his facial features. Gregor thought it was an attempt to intimidate or for Augustus to make himself appear alien.

Gregor raised his hand and swallowed his hate. "Hello,

Mr. Augustus. Nice to see you again."

Augustus didn't acknowledge the welcome. He looked into the sky and then approached Gregor, stopping inches from his face. Gentle clicking came from the two croatoans behind him. Their shiny gold visors always had a way of making Gregor feel uneasy. Not that he could read their ugly faces anyway.

"It's been reported that another harvester has gone offline this morning," Augustus said. "Are you aware of this?"

"I've sent my force to deal with the situation," Gregor said. "I'm expecting a report back within the hour."

Augustus shook his head and sucked in his breath before stepping back and taking on a calmer composure.

When the sinkholes happened and the croatoans rose out of the earth in 2014, Gregor's gang thrived into a position of strength during the decade-long mini ice age, taking advantage of the confusion in the dwindling population. As the aliens approached Armenia, he spied on them and noticed them dealing with another human who wore a mask: Mr. Augustus. He brokered a deal with the pompous old man. They'd provide an interface for the operational arm. Help control things from the ground.

"This is the third in five months. We're not having these problems in South America or Africa," Augustus said.

"Come back to my office. I'll show you the results from the last two months. I think you'll find—"

Augustus waved his hand and sniffed. "I'm not going to your filthy den. Take me to the farm's command center."

Gregor closed his eyes and counted to five. If only he'd met Augustus before the aliens arrived. He'd be using his skull as an ashtray.

"Jump to it," Augustus said. "We haven't got all day."

"Yes, Mr. Augustus."

He led the way through a small group of trees into a wide expanse of open ground. Yet more orange tones blanketed the distant landscape as a sea of root crop grew from the soil. A healthy view—from an alien perspective at least.

Gregor headed right to the croatoan quarter—an area consisting of twelve metallic warehouse-shaped buildings with lightly-tinted windows thrown up in a matter of days. Three on each side completed a large square.

In the middle, forty hover-bikes were parked in a uniform row.

The three buildings on the right provided barrack accommodation for the aliens. They were pressurized to allow the aliens to remove their breathing apparatus, the barracks having their own internal atmosphere. Through the window of one, three croatoans lounged in front of a large screen.

The three warehouses on the left were workshops. Croatoan engineers constructed and repaired vehicles and equipment either brought by the shuttles or from the field after malfunction or damage.

The three nearest were for surveying, training, and breeding.

Gregor nicknamed the closest building *the chocolate factory*. Smaller aliens, that he thought looked like Oompa Loompas, used it to chart the land and test soil samples. He would assist them occasionally when selecting the next slice of land to farm as they worked their way up North America.

The command center took up one corner. One of Gregor's team always sat at the monitors, tracking the harvesters and areas covered.

The two warehouses next to it were a breeding lab and rarely used training rooms. The training rooms were used to school humans from the farm to bring up others on a harvester in the belief that they were on a generation ship. It was all Gregor's idea, and he was proud of it. "What is a human without hope?" he'd often say. The breeding lab contained pregnant livestock.

The three buildings at the end carried out food production. One was a slaughterhouse and butchery, while the middle one carried out meat-processing.

The final building packaged the food for consumption.

Nearly everybody ate the product delivered in silver trays. The croatoans, human livestock, harvester crews, and of course: the bastard hierarchy in the ships who would have those on the ground send up large containers of supplies on a daily basis.

The only people who didn't eat the cream-colored slop were Gregor and his team. He liked to keep some sort of personal standards.

This seemed to be the standard camp set-up wherever they went.

He held his door open at the entrance to the chocolate factory. "This way, please, Mr. Augustus."

Alex came around the side of the building and whispered, "He's waiting by the paddocks."

"Thanks. Come with me," Gregor said.

Augustus walked past a large table surrounded by the helmeted surveyors and acknowledged them with a raised hand. A couple nodded their helmets, clicking excitedly.

The small delegation arrived at the bank of monitors. Vlad swiveled in his chair.

After good results in Russia, Gregor was promoted to North America as the Operation switched during a seasonal change. He took key members of his former gang, or at least the most subservient. Marek, Alex, Igor, and Vlad had all joined him on the shuttle over the Atlantic.

"Vlad, take Mr. Augustus though events as you saw them."

The small, greasy-haired man pushed his glasses toward his face with his index finger. "During the removal of a resource, due to reaching the age of mental deterioration, the harvester took some external damage. The onboard team couldn't manage to switch to back-up or control the situation, so I ordered them to the rear for our guard to deal with. After this, we lost all contact. A report is due from the patrol at any moment."

Augustus leaned forward. "Is this the same as the other two times?"

Vlad glanced at Gregor.

"Look at me, not him. I'm the one asking the question," Augustus said.

"Very similar, apart from the resource switch, but—"

Augustus turned to Gregor. "It seems you haven't managed to get a grip of the local situation. Are you capable of handling it?"

"I was going to report to you today, Mr. Augustus," Gregor said. "We suspect one of our team with collusion. I'm going to personally deal with it."

"Is this true, Alex?" Augustus said.

"Ye… Ye…" Alex said.

"Stop stuttering, woman. Is this true?"

Alex nodded.

"I'm not sure I believe you. But execute him anyway.

Put his body to good use."

"We've got him waiting by the paddocks. Would you like to see it?" Gregor said.

"That's your business. I'm going to spend the day talking to the croatoans. I want to get a good feel about local progress. You better get focused on sorting things out. If another harvester goes offline, you go offline. Do you understand?"

"Of course, Mr. Augustus," Gregor said as he imagined strangling him.

"Meet me back here in three hours. We'll talk once we know more."

Gregor left the building with Alex. They cut between the two warehouses and headed toward the farm. Igor waved as they approached. He stood by the eight-foot electric fence that surrounded eight separate paddocks, each forty square acres.

Humans clustered together in the paddocks like flocks of sheep, dressed in dirty white sheets. Most under the makeshift shelters, some sitting around, eating from silver trays.

"You wanted to see me, Gregor?" Igor said.

Gregor approached and held his arms out. "Brother Igor, we've had another harvester sabotaged. Can you believe it?"

"It's the little wasp. I know it. That piece of shit," Igor said and spat on the ground.

"Augustus's pissed. He came down straight away," Alex said.

"I saw the shuttle. What did he say?"

"That we need to sort things out," Gregor said. "Have you been speaking to anyone about the harvesters?"

Igor shook his head. "They're not part of my job. Are you suggesting I've been giving their intended paths away? I'm not the one who got caught with my pants down. You need to speak with Marek."

"Are you telling me what to do?" Gregor said. Igor stood motionless, mouth hanging open. "Do I have to ask you twice?"

"No. You can trust me implicitly to do what's best for the team."

That was Gregor's main concern. What Igor thought was best for the team probably involved him being boss. The individual problems were mounting, but at least he had license to execute the Russian if needed.

Chapter Eleven

Ben squinted at the sudden flash of light.

The place smelled fresh and unfamiliar, a scent rooted in nature and in stark opposition to the sterile smell of the harvester. He breathed it in deeply, the damp atmosphere moistening his throat and lungs. The underground room accommodated the five of them plus Denver's dog. Shadows gathered in the corners, cast there by a small, battery-powered lamp of sorts hanging from an overhead wooden beam, rough-hewn from a trunk.

Ben remembered watching a video of humans of old cutting trees and planking the logs with simple machinery. Agricultural, Jimmy used to say, when denoting something wasn't hi-tech.

It seemed to Ben that this world, his home that he never had chance to know, was now a mix, but humanity weren't the ones with the tech anymore.

"Sit down and be quiet," Charlie growled, indicating a log that had been placed on the dirt floor. Maria and Ethan did as they were told and huddled together. They were used to receiving orders. Ben, however, refused and remained standing.

Denver pulled back at a tatty curtain to reveal a screen. A grainy image of armored figures like the one that had killed Erika played out a curious film. There were four of them in a diamond pattern. Each one carried a pistol like the one Denver had fired at one of the smaller creatures.

"What's happening?" Ben said, approaching Charlie.

"We're being hunted. They're trying to locate your GPS signal."

"Our what?"

"You really don't know anything, do you, kid?" Charlie shook his head as he looked at Ben and his colleagues. He turned his attentions to Denver at the screen, joining his son with an arm over his shoulder.

Denver whispered something to Charlie and looked back at Ben.

Infuriated at being left in the dark, Ben stepped forward only to walk into the barrel of the alien pistol. "Hey now, this isn't on—"

Denver turned round. "Get back, sit down, and shut up. We're trying to save your asses here." Denver's red beard hid the scowl, but Ben could see it in his eyes. Even though he was young, there was a severe degree of hardness there.

If what they had said was true and this was how they lived, Ben couldn't blame him. Being constantly on the move, hunted, stalked, that must take its toll.

"How?" Ben said. "If they can track us ..."

"Jammers," Charlie said, lowering Denver's arm. "It'll scramble the signal but won't hold up to a close inspection. GPS means Global Positioning System. You have a chip embedded near your collarbone that transmits a signal. These fuckers pick it up and use it to trace you."

Ben opened his mouth to ask a question, but Charlie's face told him that wasn't a good option. He turned and sat with Maria and Ethan as Charlie said, "Look, I know this is all a lot to take in right now. Once we're safe for a moment, I'll explain everything in finer detail, but right now, we need to be quiet and calm."

Even though Ben was eager for answers and determined to get to the bottom of this, even if it was just to pay tribute to Jimmy and Erika, he knew not to push it. He sat down with his colleagues and waited.

"Have you seen that?" Ethan said, pointing to the end of the room into a dark nook that had been dug out of the dirt.

"I don't like it here," Maria said, keeping her voice low so Denver and Charlie couldn't hear. "They're going to get us killed—or worse."

Ben narrowed his eyes to see what Ethan was pointing at. His vision eventually adjusted to the low light, and it came into focus. One of the small aliens, like the one Denver killed back at the harvester, was pinned up against a wooden board.

It was cut open from sternum to groin, the pale-grey skin pinned back to reveal its inner biology. A number of wires and what looked like probes or electrodes were stuck into its organs. Its wide-set eyes were rolled back to reveal black orbs.

On the either side of the room was another nook, this time holding a series of shelves, on which, collected together, were a number of foil-packed rations.

A number of square, gray boxes that he guessed were batteries were on the next shelf. Wires travelled up the dirt walls and across the boarded ceiling like the alien's exposed arteries.

"I don't trust them," Ethan whispered. "We need to find a way to get loose."

"I agree," Maria said. "I think we should give ourselves up, go back with the aliens. Perhaps they'll understand."

Ben scowled and shook his head. With a harsh whisper, he berated his colleagues, unable to understand their reasoning. "Are you forgetting what they," he pointed to the aliens still patrolling through the forest as shown on the screen, "did to Jimmy and Erika?"

Maria leaned in closer. "What if they attacked us because of Charlie and Denver?"

Denver's dog stood up from her bed: an old box with a blanket hanging over the edges. Pip growled and pointed her nose to the entrance hole.

"What is it girl?" Denver said, kneeling to the hound and running his hand across the dog's neck. The dog continued to growl.

Fragments of dirt fell from the ceiling and the boards that supported it shook.

"Fuck, they're here. Must be a second squad out of view," Denver said in a hushed voice.

"How are you even seeing all this?" Ben said, also keeping his voice low.

"We've got a number of cameras rigged up outside," Denver said. "Got to have eyes all over the place in order to stay alive in this world."

"Have you always lived like this?" Ethan asked.

"Shhh," Charlie said as he apparently moved the cameras to cover different angles.

Ben counted six of the aliens now. Four wore the gray-mesh armor like the harvester guard while two looked like the smaller ones, wearing thinner material and gold-tinted visors.

"Shit," Charlie said, "They're running radar."

Ben saw the two smaller ones put a pair of poles into the ground and then refer to a clear, tablet-like device. It resembled the control tablets they had used back in the harvester.

The idea that it wasn't actually a generation ship would take some getting used to, Ben thought. All his life, he'd thought of it as a ship in space—such an elaborate ruse just to use him as nothing more than a worker drone. And now here were Charlie and Denver. Although clearly human, he felt as alien to them as he did the croatoans.

"It's time," Charlie said to Denver. "They'll find us within minutes if we don't."

"It's a one-shot deal, Dad. Are you sure?"

Charlie looked to Ben and the others. "We don't have any choice."

Maria stood and stretched her arms. She looked scared, on edge. "Can you tell us what you're talking about? I'm scared and just want to return to the ship." Her eyes welled with tears.

Ethan got up from the tree trunk and hugged her. "There is no ship, Maria; that was all a lie. We have to stick together, okay?"

Charlie ignored them and moved through the shelter until he reached the shelf of batteries. He pulled out a metal box, its surface mottled and worn. Old green paint was chipped away to reveal a dull grey beneath. On top of the box was a red dome the size of his palm. It shined glossily in the low light, the crown of the dome polished through what Ben presumed was lots of use.

A wire trailed from the box to the battery and up into the dirt ceiling.

"Everyone sit down and place your hands over your ears," Charlie said.

Denver ushered Ben, Maria, and Ethan to the far end

of the room. "Seriously, do as he says for your own sake."

Placing his hands over his ears, Ben nodded to Maria and Ethan to follow. Denver crouched beside his dog, covering her ears and holding her close into his body. She licked his face before facing Charlie.

Everyone was looking at him now.

Charlie watched the monitor with the metal box in his hands.

Ben also watched.

The two smaller aliens were now just outside of the crumbled wall. Ben could see its edge, rounded with time, and covered in green foliage. Beyond, into the thicker greenery of the forest, the two aliens drove their metal poles into the ground.

Three heavier-armed croatoans stood in front and behind them, their weapons raised to their wide chests. Their heads hidden within helmets turned in wide sweeping angles. It was then that Ben managed to get a good look at them.

Their knees seemed to work the other way compared to humans, and their legs were twice as thick.

They didn't just look powerful: they looked agile too. Given the way the one back at the harvester had so easily dispatched Erika and stalked the others, Ben was relieved he didn't have to run away from one. He imagined being caught would be a trivial matter for the croatoans.

"Now," Denver said.

Charlie hit the dome with his palm. The metal on metal made a short, clapping sound. At first, Ben didn't think anything had happened. And then a sound like the harvester crashing erupted, sending dirt falling down from the ceiling.

The rumble vibrated through the walls and floor and up into his spine.

On the monitor, the two surveyors flew up into the air. The heavier aliens fell backwards as a cloud of dirt and debris blasted up, followed by a large flame.

Two further blasts came from further away.

Charlie wore a discreet but satisfied smile as he placed the metal box on the shelf and strode across the room to stand in front of the monitor. Everyone waited for a few minutes. Denver joined his father and nodded with satisfaction.

"I think it got them all," Denver said.

"Looks that way, but we're compromised nonetheless. Our cover is blown, literally."

"My God," Ethan said. "You killed them all? How?"

Charlie turned to face Ben and the others. He pulled a knife from his belt scabbard. "Explosives," Charlie said. "We don't have long. I'm sorry I don't have anything for the pain. We're going to have to do this the old-fashioned way." He walked forward until he was standing in front of Ben, Maria, and Ethan.

Denver joined him.

"You," Charlie pointed to Ben. "You're first. Open your shirt and bite down on this." Charlie handed him a piece of wood from his pocket.

"Why?" Ben said, unable to take his eye of the wicked-looking knife. Its blade was at least ten inches long, and the tip curved backwards. "What do you think you're doing? What the hell is this about?"

Charlie leaned in, grasping Ben by the shoulder, and with his knife he pointed to the blue bead around his own neck. "You've got one of these inside you. It's how they track you. I'm sorry, but there's no way out of it. It has to come out. I'll be as quick and painless as I can. I'm not new to this."

Ben swallowed his fear. Turned to the others. Maria and Ethan stared at him wide-eyed like scared rabbits. Not wanting to let his crew down and show weakness, he turned to face Charlie.

"Is this the only way?"

"No," Denver added. "There's one other option."

Maria looked up. Hopeful. "What the other option?"

Without emoting, Denver replied, "Death."

Maria's hope vanished as she slumped on the log.

"If you take these beads out," Ethan said, "what then? Where do we go? Are there others?"

"You survive," Denver added. "Fight back. Or you don't and you die. Those are your choices. I wish it were different, but that's how it is now."

"He's right," Charlie said. "And we're running out of time. We need to get this done now and get on the move. Get to a town. They'll send another scout group. We can't be here when that happens. Your choice, kid."

"Do it," Ben said, unbuttoning his grey overall top and exposing his collarbone. He took the piece of wood from Charlie, placing it in his mouth, wondering how many other people were in this same situation.

Denver took a box, metal and painted green with a white triangular icon on its front. It looked like an older version of the ship's first aid kit. At least they were going to see to his wound.

"This will hurt," Charlie said as he pressed his thumb into Ben's collarbone, locating the bead. "A lot."

Instinctively, he bit down into the wood as he nodded

and closed his eyes when he felt the cold tip of the knife touch his skin.

As Charlie increased the pressure and the knife's edge split through his skin, Ben gripped the loose material around his legs and let out a long, pain-filled scream, all the while driving his teeth into the soft wood.

Sweat poured from him, and his eyes filled with tears.

Charlie dug his fingers into his shoulder, holding him into place as he twisted the knife slowly, seeking that damned alien bead. Ben fought the urge to vomit and breathed heavily though his nose.

"I've got it," Charlie said.

Warm blood flowed down Ben's chest, pooling into the grey cloth of his uniform. Denver stepped to the side and placed a wadded cloth against his chest to soak up the rest.

"Hold on, kid, we're nearly done here," Charlie said, prizing the tip of the knife against the bead.

Ben could feel the resistance. Feel the hard, stubborn alien tech press into his bone. And then there was the sensation of something popping, coming lose, and the knife blade retreating.

Denver moved the wadding to the wound and pressed it down.

When Ben looked down, he saw that the material was coated in an orange substance. A tingling sensation occurred within his wound, deep into the tissue, and then it burned. He shut his eyes and held his breath. It felt like someone had lit a match and pressed it into his flesh, but as he thought he would never stop, the burning reversed, turning cold.

He fell forward and breathed in a deep breath.

When he sat back up, Denver removed the material,

and to Ben's astonishment, the blood had already clotted around the wound. The orange substance formed a sticky patch over the cut. The pain was still there, but it was manageable, no worse than a headache.

Removing the wood from his mouth, Ben looked up.

Charlie stood beneath the overhead lamp, holding the now-cleaned bead up to the light. It was light blue and shimmered. "Here, catch," Charlie said, dropping it into Ben's hands.

The bead zapped him with a bolt of electricity, making Ben instantly let go. "Crap, what's it doing?"

"Phoning home," Charlie said. "It's what they do when they're removed. They alert the croatoans. Okay, Maria, Ethan, which of you are next?"

Before anyone could speak, the tree trunk that sat above the entry hole to the shelter lifted up and was thrown away.

Light streaked through the hole for a brief second and then they were in shadow again as an armored croat-oan looked down inside, holding a rifle version of those strange, angular pistols.

Denver and Charlie both dived into the shadows.

The alien fired once, sending up a clod of dirt inches from Charlie's diving legs. It readjusted the aim and was about to fire one more when its head snapped back with a sharp blast. Ben looked to his left, fully expecting to see Denver with his rifle in hand, but what he saw was Maria, her arms shaking, barely able to hold on to the black alien pistol. Vapor lazily drifted from the end of its barrel. The smell of ozone filled the room.

Maria dropped the weapon, collapsing back to the trunk. Her shoulders shuddered as she sobbed, placing her face in her hands.

"Good shot," Denver said. "You might survive for longer than we expected after all."

Ethan stood and bore down on Denver. "Can't you see she's scared, damn it? God, we all are, and all you can do is make smart comments."

"Calm down," Denver said, standing over Ethan, his wiry but powerful frame intimidating Ethan. "We don't have much time. We need to get those beads out of you and get going."

Denver turned his attention to Maria, kneeling in front of her, placing his hand on her shoulder. "It's okay," he said, his tone softer now, which surprised Ben. So far, he'd only seen a cold side to the kid. The only affection shown was for his dog. "Listen, you did good, okay?"

"I killed someone," Maria said. "I can't believe I actually killed someone."

"And you might have to kill many someones if you're to have any kind of life out here."

"I want to go back," Maria said, turning to Ben, reaching out for him. "Please, can we go back? We can explain things, tell them it wasn't our fault. We can have our jobs back, the safety …" she trailed off and slumped back against the dirt wall.

Ben so wanted to do what she suggested. Although life wasn't brilliant in the ship, at least it was safe, predictable. They were in the right place there, the right time. Out here? It was too chaotic.

But regardless, Ben knew Charlie and Denver were right. This was their home now. They owed it to all the people who were killed by the croatoans as the aliens terraformed the planet for their own will. They owed them resistance.

"No," Ben said, standing. "We go on. We learn and adapt. We can't give in now." He turned to Charlie, who had stood up and joined the group. "Do it. Take their beads, and let's get out of here before any more come back."

Chapter Twelve

Gregor peered out of his office window at two passing croatoans. The light blue, triangular insignia flashes on their shoulders told him they were from the mother ship.

They carried a rigid stretcher with a large electronic device on it. The device was encased in a solid, sea-green, transparent material about the size of a coffin with circuitry and wires inside and five circular holes on the side.

He pushed the window open. "What have you got there?"

One at the front of the stretcher glanced at him and clicked a few times in what Gregor thought was a hostile tone.

They carried on toward the warehouses, ignoring him.

He thought the croatoans from the ship were always a lot more dismissive of humans, unlike the ones who had regular ground duties. The grounded ones probably had some mutual respect. Especially the ones from Europe, where he'd shown them what he could do. If they wanted to farm humans, fine, but they still needed to know how to treat them to get the best results.

Gregor played the role of sheepdog well; admittedly, it was better than being in the flock or an alien stomach.

A handheld radio crackled on the desk. "Gregor, are you there?"

He swiped it up and depressed the transmit button.

"Layla, what did you find?"

"Another attack. Looks like land mines placed in the path. There's extensive damage to the right hand side of the harvester. It's worse than before. Mr. Jackson seems to be learning."

Gregor screwed his face and clenched his fist.

Charlie fucking Jackson—the little wasp, again.

Gregor sat down and let out a long breath. "How bad? Will it be another three-week job?"

"It's croatoan tech, who knows? We need to send over an engineer for a proper evaluation."

"What about the crew?"

"Two dead—by croatoans hands—and three missing. We're trying to find them. I've lost contact with our patrol. They were tracking a weak signal."

"Have your squad sweep the area. They're new, confused. They can't be far away."

"Okay. I'll let them know. Out."

He grabbed a pair of binoculars from his desk, stormed outside, and headed to an ivy-covered brick garage attached to the exterior left wall. The rusty door's mechanism screamed as he wrenched it up. It shuddered open. Flecks of loose, dark red paint dropped around his boots.

Daylight filled the space inside. On the right stood a table supporting a bottle of water and a bowl of slop.

In the middle of the room, Marek squinted. He'd fallen over sideways along with the chair he was secured to with rope. He tried to speak but only managed to cough.

Gregor gripped Marek's shirt and the chair, hauling them both upright. "There you go. What have you been doing in here, old friend?"

Marek gulped hard. "Why are you doing this?"

The decision to put Marek in an improvised prison cell wasn't taken lightly. Gregor feared the croatoans might demand his friend be turned into dinner. He'd been captured by wild humans—no real surprises by whom, Gregor thought. Marek had shown weakness. Gregor was sure the aliens were watching how he handled the situation. He'd tell Marek when the time was right. For now, it had to remain as realistic as possible, not even a wink.

It was for their own protection, especially with Augustus sniffing around. That bastard seemed to know everything.

"You look terrible. Can I get you some food? Water?" Gregor asked.

"Why, Gregor?"

Gregor picked up a bottle of water and a tray of the croatoans' slop, still sealed up tight. "I need to know I can trust you again. You were missing for two days."

"I've told you—"

"I don't believe in coincidences. We've suffered another outage today. Now, open wide."

Marek spluttered as he tried to drink. Gregor emptied the bottle over Marek's mouth and face. "Are you hungry?" He peeled off the lid and dug a plastic spoon into the cream-colored contents. He pushed the spoon against Marek's mouth.

Marek twisted away, spitting away the food around his lips. "I'm not eating that shit. Gregor, please."

He threw the tray to one side. "I want to hear again about your supposed captors. Did they say anything about attacking harvesters?"

"We've been through this. They only asked me questions. One was blond-haired, late forties or so, the other much younger, perhaps mid-twenties, red head. Both had beards and looked like they've been living in the forests."

"They didn't mention the harvesters? Not once?"

"They wanted to know about the warehouses and the shuttles. What was coming down, what was going up, that kind of thing."

Gregor walked to the entrance and reached for the door. "I'll give you another day to think about it."

Marek tried to shout. The screeching hinges drowned out his words. Gregor slammed the door shut and wiped his hands on his jeans. A rumble of thunder rolled in the distance. He looked up at the gathering clouds, wondering if the weather was starting to match his situation.

***

Rain fell steadily over the camp. Gregor squelched through mud toward the chocolate factory.

Two croatoan hover-bikes shot over the trees from the distance, coming toward the main square. Layla was on the back of one, ducked behind the croatoan rider, shielding herself. The droning grew louder as they hovered for a moment before descending, joining the other parked bikes in a smart line.

The square was busy with aliens. They seemed to be fascinated with the rain. Whenever it started to fall, they'd leave the barracks and stand in it, looking up, taking off their gloves and waggling their spindly olive fingers.

It was times like this that Gregor thought they were almost child-like. A quick look at the pulse cannon on a shuttle or the meat-processing warehouses would quickly push the idea from his mind.

Layla dismounted and headed toward the chocolate factory, looking uncomfortable in her soaked black trousers and jacket.

Gregor met her by the entrance.

He glanced at the riders who joined the others, marveling at the grim weather.

"They never get bored of it," he said.

"I do. Let's get inside," Layla said with a scowl.

The chocolate factory was deserted apart from Gregor's man at the monitors, lit up by their glare. Charts, pens, and the croatoans' shoebox-shaped computer devices lay around the large table. The little surveyor bastards were probably out enjoying the rain too.

"What's that?" Layla said. She pointed to a number of objects in the corner. The odd plastic thing he saw earlier. It'd been hooked into the power source and glowed light green, highlighting an electronic system inside.

Three transparent boxes were stacked next to it.

"I saw them carrying it here. Probably came down with Augustus. His shuttle's still here."

"What does he want?"

He let out a grunt. "You're the anthropologist. You tell me."

She crouched in front of the glowing object and ran her hand along its exterior. "I've got no idea what this is, but I'll find out. They brought some large crates down the other day and stored them in the barracks. Something's going on. Seems like they're preparing for something. The sneaky fuckers are always up to something."

She flashed him a smile, her hazel eyes picking up the green glow from the device. She'd pulled her blonde hair back into a ponytail. Her face was smudged with grease and orange root. For a scientist, she didn't have any problems with getting stuck into the physical side of things.

Gregor had warmed to Layla over the last couple of months. When he had first arrived in North America, she was introduced as part of this operation.

They'd picked her up in England. She was a social scientist, whatever that entailed. Gregor never really knew. Her job at the facility was to look for efficiencies in the way they ran operations—improve the human resources and the harvesting root yield. He was sure she hated him, it was her aloof style, but he felt protective of her.

She'd introduced a number of improvements on the farm that increased their food and reproduction output. In Europe, he ran the paddocks like his parents ran their pig farm. She suggested changes in human livestock management like providing shelter to limit exposure. Another key improvement was feeding livestock produce from the food processing warehouses instead of swill. He was impressed with the pragmatic circular nature of the coldly delivered suggestion. Its effectiveness after deployment was tangible.

He wondered, though, how far her coldness truly extended.

Though from one perspective, what they were doing here, treating humans like cattle was barbaric, but it was the world now, and now people like Layla knew it. She had the smarts to exploit a situation, something Gregor had decided to keep a close eye on. He had no doubt she'd step on him if it furthered her agenda, whatever that might be.

"Did you figure out the details of what happened at the harvester?" Gregor said.

"They shot the guard on the platform and suffocated the driver. You need to get a grip on this. We might all go down."

"They seem okay at the moment," Gregor said, nodding his head toward the main square where the aliens were doing their weird rain dance nonsense. "It's Augustus I'm concerned about. He came down straight away, asking questions."

Layla smiled. "Let me work on him. I've got a few questions of my own—"

Alex burst through the metal swing door entrance. "We've got signals again."

She held a croatoan tablet out, a detachable one from a hover-bike they used to track humans with. Gregor remembered the rage he felt when his bead was inserted. The advantages became clearer when he was assigned human resource manager and tracked missing stock.

"Where? How many?" Gregor said.

"We've got a cluster of signals, maybe three. Not far away from the harvester. They could be underground. Keeps fading in and out."

Gregor grabbed the tablet and orientated the red dots to a map on the wall. "I've picked up something there before. Couldn't find anything."

"Fifteen minute rule?" Alex said.

Gregor nodded. The croatoans didn't place huge value on individual wild humans. When they took him or his team out hunting for new livestock, they'd only be allowed to pursue a target for fifteen minutes.

The logic behind their rule was the aliens didn't want to waste their time in a game of cat and mouse with one of the more slippery and resourceful humans. He thought they viewed it as the same as catching a rabbit in a garden. It was slightly annoying but wouldn't hurt them; they could crush it if they really wanted. Alternatively, the signal could be from a corpse buried in a shallow grave.

"Three croatoans are scrambling. I need to take the tablet back," Alex said.

"The crew might be with the little wasp," Layla said.

"That's what I'm hoping. Can you go with them?" Gregor said. "Try to convince them that this is the shit who's been attacking the harvesters?"

Layla puffed her cheeks. "They won't go on a wild goose chase. I don't see what use I'll be."

"At what point will they start caring about the bastard who's screwing our production statistics?" Gregor said. "I don't want him slipping through our fingers."

"I'll get right on it," Alex said.

The door flung open, and a group of surveyors entered, visors covered in droplets. They surrounded the large wooden table and started working on their computers, studying charts and busily clicking to each other.

Gregor leaned toward Layla. "You're the one they trust and I trust. Please, go with them. We need some human intelligence on the ground."

"Okay. I'll get them to bring him in alive if I can."

"Thanks. Alive or dead, I'm easy with either option."

They left the chocolate factory. Layla and Alex headed for the central area, where three croatoans sat on hover-bikes, watching their approach.

Gregor walked between two warehouses and scanned the paddocks. His men were distributing food. One drove a large tractor around the grassed areas while two stood on the trailer it towed, throwing out silver trays to outstretched hands.

Some humans sat and ate at the spot they received their

food. Others protectively took their trays to an individual spot, cautiously looking around while scooping the contents into their mouths with their hands.

One shot from a croatoan weapon was all it took to turn them into brainless cattle during capture. Yet, after a few months in captivity, some started to display more advanced kinds of behavior, a broken attempt at language, an attempt to climb the paddock fence, or an assault on a guard.

This made the meat-processing selection easier. The guards would splash paint across any human showing danger signs. They would be the first in the back of the truck for the weekly meat-processing run. The rest would be picked at random.

Three hover-bikes roared overhead, accelerating away.

Gregor instinctively ducked even though they were fifty feet overhead, their pink circles opaquely shimmering. Layla waved downwards from the rear bike.

Within a few minutes they were little black specks in the distance, their vapor trails quickly vanishing in the breeze.

Gregor turned to look at the camp. Augustus walked toward him, flanked by two croatoan guards from the shuttle, his usual escort. He raised his robe clear of the muddy ground, exposing his skinny white ankles as he crossed the more muddy thoroughfares.

He shook his head and cursed as he approached.

"Have you come to see the paddocks, Mr. Augustus?" Gregor said.

Augustus straightened his mask. "It's time you and I had a little chat."

Gregor held out his arms. "I trust you've found that everything is in order?"

"We're shifting the focus of the farm. I've got some new targets for you."

"New targets?"

Augustus flashed his yellow teeth through a gap in the mask, hiding some inner delight. Gregor imagined his skinny body fed into the meat-processing machines but instead smiled back and waited for the bad news.

Chapter Thirteen

Charlie halted Ben and Ethan, brought them behind a large tree. Its trunk was at least twenty feet in diameter. Up ahead, Denver and Maria, with Pip following close behind, had stopped and gestured to the others.

They were heading east out of the forest. Charlie knew it as Allegheny National Forest, Pennsylvania. During his exploration of the area in previous years, he and Denver had come across an old hunting lodge.

Within the derelict shack, he'd found some brochures extolling the beauty of the forest. Back then, he was sure it was a national beauty full of wildlife and a wide variety of flora, but now, with the root in the atmosphere and the croatoan terraforming after the frozen years, a new arrival had appeared: a croatoan tree that looked like a redwood but grew like a weed.

The brackens and hawthorns had a weird look to them too and excreted a waxy residue. He discovered it was a very useful waterproofing agent. Although the aliens were slowly terraforming the planet, there were some benefits to the things that they were growing.

The root had plenty of uses, healing being one of them. Charlie doubted he'd be as physically fit and strong as he was without learning how to distill the oil from the root. Still, those gifts paled into a pathetic joke compared to what was lost.

"How you kids doing?" Charlie asked as he waited for Denver to return to him.

"Good, I think," Ethan said, rubbing his collar. "It's healing fast."

"I can barely feel it now," Ben said.

"Yup. The root is handy like that."

"Is that why the aliens are harvesting it?" Ethan asked, seemingly over his frustration and getting into the spirit of learning how to survive.

"Among other reasons," Charlie said. "It's difficult to really know. I just don't have the information. But there's a …" how could he put it without freaking them out again? Human farming was not a subject that he had any easy way into, and he didn't want to get into it now with the sun setting and the croatoans probably not far behind them.

The beads felt heavy in his pocket. They seemed to gain mass when they were transmitting, but he knew it was just gravity. It still wasn't natural, he thought.

"You were saying?" Ben said.

"There's a facility to the east of here. A center of operations if you will. There's a number of the aliens there along with human … sympathizers who work on their behalf. They've been shipping the root harvest up to a mother ship via shuttles for the past few years. But this year is different."

"Different how?" Ben asked.

"I don't know exactly. The crop is different, more potent. They've upped their harvesting, and the air … It's not right."

Charlie ended it there as Denver and the others joined them. Pip nestled into Charlie's leg and licked at his hand as he stroked the dog's neck. Despite himself, he thought of *his* Pippa back before the uprising.

Ironically, she wasn't a dog person, preferring the company of cats.

His thoughts were probably due to Maria. She had a fragile strength to her like Pippa. Although she looked soft on the outside, he could tell she possessed a desire to survive. She wasn't afraid of her emotions like the others.

"There's one patrol," Denver said. "They're already on the other side of the river. We're good to go."

"Okay," Charlie said, gathering everyone in. "Listen carefully. What comes next is particularly dangerous. Don't speak even when prompted. Let me and Denver deal with them."

Ethan opened his mouth to ask a question, but Charlie carried on, wanting to get on with things. "I want you all to follow Denver as soon as we've broken cover. I'll take the beads."

"What are you going to do?" Ben asked.

"Let's say that our galactic friends will have a little surprise waiting for them. I'll rejoin you once I'm done. Den, you know what to do?"

Denver nodded. "I'll keep to the north side, don't worry."

"It's not you I'm worried about," Charlie said, looking at the others.

"What?" Maria said, stepping forward. "Have we not shown you trust? We've done everything you've asked."

"I'm not talking about you lot. Just stick with Denver, and keep those weapons at the ready. Okay, Den, these are all yours. I'll catch up with you in ten minutes tops."

With that, Charlie left the others behind and darted into the darkening forest.

A few minutes later, he reached what used to be the

edge, but the alien-influenced flora didn't stop on the threshold anymore. It carried right on into the town once known as Ridgway.

The trees and bushes plagued the town like a slow swarm of locusts. Branches and ferns and ivy covered almost all available surfaces. The old blacktop on Main Street had broken up. Mosses and other lichens had colonized the surface, making it slick underfoot.

Charlie oriented himself by the layout of the ruins.

To his right, he could just about see the tops of a series of warehouses.

The Clarion River flowed parallel to the street. The water was thick and brackish and like the air, under certain light, had taken on an orange cast.

To his left, the small, low buildings of dwellings were just visible through the trees and vines. Small pockets of lights, drum fires, and candles glittered behind grimy windows deep in the foliage.

He and Denver had seen a group of survivors in the town the last time they were here. It gave him a little sense of hope that they appeared to still be here, still surviving, which made him feel guilty about bringing the beads here.

The croatoans would come. Hopefully, the human survivors would have the sense to hide and put out their fires when they heard that dread-whine of the hover-bikes.

Further along Main Street, Charlie came into the center of town. The river had changed course and headed north, going under a bridge. Charlie crossed it until he came to an area where the vegetation wasn't as thick.

Rows of houses stood like rotten teeth. Their roofs had long collapsed, and the ice damage had crumbled most of the walls, but among the damage, there were one or two that remained—or at least had been rebuilt, patched up, and saved.

Finding an ideal spot, a large warehouse unit with an alley leading down to the side, Charlie removed the beads from his pocket and a cube of C4 from his backpack.

He had salvaged the explosives from his old Army base where he'd spent a few years in his childhood as a National Guardsman. Although he was running low, he could spare some for this.

He found an old, rusted dumpster, its insides now home to a range of flora. He placed the beads on top of the C4 and covered it with a series of fern leaves behind the dumpster. He inserted a blasting cap into the plastic explosive and wired up a trigger to a trip wire, which he ran across the narrow alley. In the gloom, no one would detect it.

The only worry he had was that some idiot survivor might wander in and set it off before the croatoans tracked the bead's signal.

On his way back out, Charlie heard a series of raised voices in argument and the barking of a dog—Pip.

Seemed Denver had found the survivors.

Charlie put his backpack on and took the knife from his belt and headed further into the town toward the voices. Whatever it was about, they needed to shut the hell up before the damned aliens turned up.

Further into the town, the foliage gave way a little to brick and concrete. Some of the old multistory brick buildings had survived, mostly on account of being solidly attached to each other, providing mutual shelter from the encroaching trees.

Denver and the others were surrounded by a ragtag

group of post-thaw survivors. Their torches flickered in the dark sky, illuminating the red and cream brick of a substantial building. An old iron cannon, its black paintwork now peeling with rust, kept guard out on the grass in front.

For a moment, the building distracted Charlie.

It looked almost completely intact.

Ornate, cream arches over tall windows contrasted with the deep red brick. As he looked up, he could just make out the spire and the clock tower in the gloom.

A tatty U.S. flag fluttered gently on a breeze from a flagpole that was bent over at the top, and yet it still hung on, still flew that flag with defiance to what had happened.

"Stop!" Charlie shouted, silencing the bickering, his word echoing off the building like a gunshot. The group turned to him as he approached.

When he got nearer, he lowered his voice. "You lot are gonna get us all killed. Keep your damned voices down. What's the problem?"

The group consisted of three women and two men. All of them had the gaunt look of desperation about them. One of them, a dark-haired, hard-faced woman wearing clothes that looked like she had made them herself out of a mix of plaid and chino material, stepped forward and sneered.

Turning to the rest of her group, she let out a laugh. "Look who it is, the man and the myth. Charlie Jackson, the survivor, the savior of humankind. You're not wanted round here, Charlie. You'll bring those damned aliens after you. We saw what you did with the harvester. Why do you have to keep poking them, eh? Why do you always have to antagonize them?"

"Yeah," one of the men said, stepping forward into the torchlight, the flames showing his ruddy face behind his unkempt beard. He stood considerably shorter than Charlie, barrel-chested, and wore a patch over one eye. "We've made a life for ourselves here. We had a peace. They didn't bother us, we didn't bother them. Now your meddling's gonna change all that. When are you ever gonna let it go, Charlie? It's over, man, they've won. It's done, finished, over."

Charlie leaned in and grabbed the man by the lapels of his filthy jacket. "It's not done while I've got breath in my lungs. You lot can skitter about like cockroaches in the night, but I won't stand by while those fuckers slowly kill us all off. I will not go extinct. Goddamnit, I was there! I lost everyone I loved, but I kept going for us, for humanity. And you just want to give up? To hide? No, I will not go down like that."

He pushed the man back, and he stumbled. The other man in the group stopped him from falling completely. They glared at Charlie, and he could see hatred in their eyes.

How had it come to this? Survivors he often met mocked him as a myth, a useless old man with nothing to offer while they hid in the shadows like scared ghosts.

"Now you lot have a decision to make," Charlie said, pointing the group.

Ben, Maria, and Ethan watched on in tense silence. Denver, as ever, cast a quiet determination, backing up Charlie with Pip at his side.

"What are you talking about?" the woman said. The rest of her group stepped forward. Enemy lines were drawn between the two groups now.

"You either do the right thing and let us shelter with you for the night or you choose to do the wrong thing and refuse. But if you choose the latter, let me tell you now, I will not consider you my allies. I will not consider your lives worth saving. Like I said, your choice. Live and die by it."

The woman backed off and turned to her group. They muttered for a moment before she turned back to Charlie and the others. He saw she held a pistol in her left hand. "Keep on going, Myth. You're not welcome here."

"So be it," Charlie said, gripping the knife in his right hand to try and channel his anger somewhere the others wouldn't see.

The woman stepped back, and her group parted, leaving a way through the old road. She pointed eastward out of town. "Go, before things get difficult."

"Wait," Ben said, "take us in with you. We can help you. We've only just met Charlie and Denver. We're not like them; we just want to stay out of the way."

The woman laughed and shook her head.

"On your way," she said again, waving the pistol.

Charlie and Denver, along with Pip, moved on. All the time, Charlie kept an eye on the woman's trigger finger. Denver had his rifle across his chest. Charlie knew his son would be quicker on the draw even with the larger weapon; it was like an extension of his body.

When he was twenty feet clear of the other group, he turned back and saw Ben, Maria, and Ethan pleading their case with the other group. It stung him that they'd be so quick to jump ship even after he and Denver had liberated them and saved their asses.

Without the beads, they wouldn't be tracked. They had

a chance of life now, and at the first opportunity, they'd betrayed his trust and loyalty.

As if reading his mind, Denver patted Charlie on the shoulder. "Don't worry, Dad, it's their damned choice. We can't make them follow us. Some people just have to see the world for what it is themselves first. Some people were born to die."

"Not us," Charlie said. "You and I, son, we'll keep going. We'll endure. I'll make sure of it."

"Where do you wanna go?" Denver asked. "Mohan Run?"

"Yeah, the shelter there should still have some supplies unless these scumbags have looted it." The Mohan Run shelter was in a thick part of the woods on the outskirts of the town. It was one of the first Charlie and Denver had set up when they travelled west from New York when Denver was just thirteen.

It was easier back then. Fewer harvesters, and the croat-oans were still building the infrastructure after the thaw. Like their previous shelter, it was just a hole in the ground, but it was better than nothing.

With his personal reputation not worth a damn these days, he didn't like the idea of staying in Ridgway with the other group running around. People like those had built up a myth around Charlie and had distorted who he was, casting him as some kind of villain.

But that was often the case with post-thaw survivors.

They didn't have the perspective of what the world was like before. They had no way of understanding that the earth wasn't a giant farm for the croatoans, that it was humanity's home. They looked at towns and cities and couldn't picture how people had lived and loved, how a society worked.

It was every man and woman for themselves now despite his attempts at uniting them against the invaders. Ben and the others' actions were no surprise to him. He had hoped that unlike the others, these would be different; they would show more willingness to fight back.

He'd set them free, but what they did with that freedom was their choice.

Charlie turned his attentions back to the east road, what used to be Highway 219. A twisting vine that looked like a serpent choked the white sign on the side of the road. The numbers were fading but remained.

Five minutes on their journey out of the town and he heard footsteps racing up behind him. Pip growled by Denver's side, but they didn't stop. Just kept on walking. Eventually, it was Maria who spoke first, as Charlie'd expected. Ben wasn't the type to admit his mistakes. He and Ethan were still trying to find where they fit into the world.

Maria already knew. "I'm sorry," she said. "About back there. It's all so confusing."

"Forget about it," Charlie said. "No need to say anything else." He spared her the humiliation of asking to rejoin them. They had nowhere else to go. This would be a good lesson for them. They'd now discovered an important lesson in trust.

Trust no one.

Chapter Fourteen

Layla gripped the silver handles on either side of the hover-bike, turning her head against the wind chill. The feeling of weightlessness contrasted the aching in her fingers as they shot through the air over the densely vegetated land. Each trip helped her get a better idea of how the machines operated.

The controls were quite simple. Moving the handlebars forwards raised the bike. A twist grip on the right handle increased speed. The alien rider would twist the left grip when they wanted to hover. All gentle movements. It was like being on a huge hair dryer and sounded a little like one too.

She looked over her shoulder at the disappearing camp and farmed area beyond. From this height, it looked like the world had been split in two. One side, a brown cloak with an orange tinge; the other a sea of green with occasional smashed ruins peeping above the canopy. The derelict remnants of her former world.

Layla wondered if Gregor and his gang were nearing their expiration date. Manual labor and resource management was good, but it was nothing the croatoans couldn't do themselves once they picked up on the implemented systems. She felt a little safer as long as the improvements and tweaks kept yielding results based on her scientific knowledge of the species.

She'd actually found it easier than she'd originally thought. It was pointless fighting a superior force, so improving conditions of the captured survivors provided a justification in her own mind.

Augustus appreciated Layla and told her she was the brains of the outfit, although he'd disparagingly called her Doctor Mengele when he was in one of his melancholic moods and cackled at her reaction from behind his weird mask.

Layla peered over the croatoan's shoulder at the tablet. The green 'v' that indicated the bike's position was nearing the group of red dots. The alien twisted the left grip to hover. The bike pulled around above a small clearing.

Surrounding branches and leaves rocked and rustled in the downdraft created by the three descending vehicles. A rabbit ran from the clearing followed by loose twigs blown away by the force of the hover-bike's thrust.

The croatoans dismounted after the bikes settled and drew their brain pistols. That was Gregor's nickname for them. He could always be relied upon for his subtlety.

They each keyed in something on their wrist devices. They weren't checking the time; croatoans had no concept of the human way of measuring it. The wrist devices controlled appearance. All three suits and helmets took on a disruptive camouflage pattern of brown, green, and cream.

An alien clicked free a tablet from the front of a bike and held it toward Layla. She took it, holding the screen away from the sunlight now poking through the clouds, giving the mossy clearing a slight luminous feel.

A blue arrow marked their position, and as she turned, it did the same like a spinning compass, pointing in the direction of the dim red spots.

"Right guys, follow me."

She led the way into the dark forest, picking her way through the damp undergrowth. After a hundred yards, the gap on the tablet closed to half. At least they hadn't landed right next to their intended targets, although the hover-bikes would've been spotted or heard by anyone above ground.

Layla glanced ahead for any clues, a fresh-broken twig, footprints on the wet, soft forest surface, a scrap of clothing on a thorn bush, anything to indicate a recent presence. The unfarmed landscape was increasingly turning into rainforest typically associated with the southern hemisphere. She wondered what conditions would be like in the Amazon.

A group of noisy birds fled from close proximity with a chorus of exotic squawks. Layla crouched and turned. The three croatoans ducked behind individual trees. Hover-bikes hummed overhead. She caught a glimpse of two between a gap in the trees powering through the air high above alongside each other.

She waved the croatoans alongside and pointed at the tablet then toward a lighter area in the distance. "Over there. Might be the remains of a small town, highway, or something like that."

One of the aliens nodded and gently pushed her forward.

Proceeding with caution, with croatoans on either side, Layla picked up a beaten track, worn into the ground, running toward the target area. It wasn't surprising that humans would be taking similar routes. Land, or at least cover, was becoming less and less available as the continent transformed into a vast area of alien agriculture.

The places left alone were the concrete jungles. The last she saw was Nashville, now transformed into a slimy green outcrop. Layla felt like Juan Crisóstomo Nieto discovering the lost city of Kuelap. The conducive climate of thick, moist air had made conditions perfect for a quick colonization of plants and trees. Whatever the harvesters didn't chew up and spit out, nature took advantage of, regaining its stronghold.

At the edge of the tree line, Layla paused. The forest floor gradually turned into slippery concrete. Ahead was a main street of a small town. Thick vines climbed the buildings. Ivy sprawled over the walls. Most shop front windows were smashed, probably during the mini ice age. Wooden doors had rotted from the top and bottom, a couple creaking in the breeze. PVC ones were covered in black and green-speckled mold, their windows dulled and dirty. Several vehicles dotted along the street, all at various stages of decay, rusting away to become dark red shells.

The road was still visible through the weeds and ferns that popped and spread through the fractured surface. It led a hundred yards back into a forested area.

Layla checked the tablet. The signals came from dead ahead. At the far end of the street by one of the larger buildings, a dumpster, which resembled a large plant-pot stuffed with weeds, marked the likely signal source.

"Okay. It's right along there. How do you want to play this?" she said.

One of the croatoans pointed to himself and another then slowly started advancing. Layla and the other alien waited.

They moved from rusted vehicle to doorway to plant.

Moving a few yards at a time, covering each other as they headed along the street. When they reached halfway, the alien next to Layla clicked a few times and followed the others.

As she wasn't armed, Layla followed behind, using the alien's body as cover. She let out a small yelp after falling to one knee, her foot sliding on a clump of loose moss. The croatoan span around, aimed at her, its helmet almost blinding as a ray of sun reflected toward her. After a short moment, it held out an arm, and Layla pulled herself up. They continued forwards.

It wasn't quite as bad as her college field trips. Layla was always treated like the ugly duckling. Teased for being a geek and marginalized by her peers because her theories went against the conventional wisdom of the lecturers. The more she studied human behavior and became a victim of their spite, the more she hated humanity and realized it was on the wrong path. Her parents were an exception, but the ice age took them quickly. At least the croatoans didn't judge, tease, or bully her.

The two aliens ahead stood behind a truck yards away from the dumpster. They sprang out from their position and behind the dumpster in their strange, bouncy style. Layla edged to one side for a better view. They headed for a side alley.

She heard a twanging noise. Something flicked into the street.

The two croatoans froze, looked at each other.

A huge eruption followed a blinding flash of light.

Layla flew backwards, skidding across the road surface. Small chunks of debris hit her body and face. The sound of masonry dropping, glass breaking, and a booming echo through the buildings deafened her.

The alien pulled her up. She found it difficult to balance, tried to focus and patted herself down. They were surrounded in a veil of light brown dust. Rays of sun tried to break through it.

Her ears rang with a high-pitched tone. The croatoan clicked in an urgent tone and pulled her toward the dumpster, pointing its weapon from side to side.

Layla squinted and blinked. The dust stung her eyes. She coughed and swallowed, trying to clear her dry throat.

They came across the bottom half of a croatoan leg, boot still attached. Close by, half a broken visor rested in the weeds. An arm protruded from a pile of rubble.

The street became clearer as the dust settled. One of the lead scouts was still intact, slumped against a brick wall in a mangled shape. Its suit had returned to its former gray color, ripped in various places around the armor plates. The helmet visor was splintered, punctured in two places.

She felt the grip release on her shoulder. The alien dropped to one knee, bowed its head, and clicked more slowly. It appeared to be grieving. Layla hadn't seen this kind of emotion before, although she'd never witnessed one being killed in front of another.

Her opinion of croatoans since being recruited by Augustus had gradually grown to a solid appreciation. They were pragmatic. Working in small teams to achieve their objectives, never being led astray to carry out petty injustices or wasting time debating their moves. The aliens had a clear focus on the big picture.

An old human saying was look after the little things and the big things will take care of themselves. The croatoans tackled *things* in the opposite direction. So far, it was working out.

Layla sighed and put her hand on the alien's shoulder. The rhythm of its sounds increased, going from something similar to the tick of a grandfather clock to a fast, dripping tap. It stood up, holstered its weapon, and grabbed Layla's ponytail, forcing her head down to the side of its hip.

"What the hell are you doing?" she said.

"Hu-man," it croaked.

"Get off me. I'm on your side."

It ignored Layla and started dragging her toward the forest. She stumbled over plants and debris, trying to maintain its pace while keeping balance.

They crashed through the undergrowth, back in the direction of the hover-bikes. Her legs caught on weeds. The croatoan curled an arm around her chest and ripped her free.

"Please. Why are you doing this?"

The top of her head ached from the constant yanking. She staggered alongside, and they reached the clearing. The croatoan wrestled her onto the back of his hover-bike and raised a finger.

She nodded. "I won't do a thing. I'll help you report it. None of this was your fault … our fault."

The engine started with a roar, and the alien thrust the bars forward. They shot up to an unusually high altitude faster than she'd ever seen the bikes move. They were usually graceful and steady. The croatoan twisted the right grip fully back, and they surged forward, increasing to a dizzying speed, the trees below merging into a green blur.

Layla clung on for her life. Wind blasted against her face. The seat vibrated below her, and she yelped as they occasionally bounced like a jet-ski.

The warehouses quickly came into view.

They dipped like a shooting arrow near the end of its arc, heading straight for the square. The buildings grew in size by every second. She felt herself pressing against the alien because of the angle of descent.

At the last moment, as Layla feared some kind of mad emergency landing, the croatoan twisted the left grip, and the bike shuddered to a hovering halt. It calmly pulled back the handlebars, and the bike smoothly descended to the end of the line in the square.

The croatoan ignored Layla, dismounted, and quickly walked to a barrack warehouse. She stood up and took a few deep breaths and rubbed her hands together to stop them shaking.

Alex raised her hand from the chocolate factory entrance. She walked across to the parked bikes. "Is everything okay? You look like you've seen a ghost."

Layla put her arm around her, leaned on her as they walked back toward Gregor's office. "They're changing, Alex. Is Gregor about?"

"He's chatting to Mr. Augustus, something about new targets."

Chapter Fifteen

Gregor grabbed a forty-year-old bottle of whiskey from his kitchen cupboard. He'd intended to open it when celebrating something. Appeasing Augustus would have to do, something to take the edge off him.

Single malt wasn't going out of date any time soon unlike most other pre-alien produce. It was a shame Augustus hadn't rotted away like an unwanted microwave meal in a derelict supermarket. He sat at Gregor's desk, caressing his stupid robe with an armed croatoan behind each shoulder.

Gregor placed the green bottle down with a reassuring thump and turned the tartan label in Augustus's direction. "Would you like a drink, Mr. Augustus?"

"Don't you offer all of your guests a drink?"

Gregor frowned. "I didn't think that—"

"No, I don't want a drink. We've got serious business to discuss."

The croatoans clicked in unison. Augustus sat forward, placed his elbows on the desk, and clasped his fingers together. His sunken eyes fixed on Gregor.

Gregor told himself to keep calm, not to betray a flicker of emotion. He wanted to gut Augustus like a fish just like his former boss during Gregor's successful putsch in 2009. Augustus and his old boss shared a lot of the same qualities. They made the men feel uneasy, behaved like kings, and ultimately acted for themselves instead of for the wider gang benefit.

"It's been raining a lot this month," Gregor said. Augustus dismissively waved his hand. "You said something about new targets, Mr. Augustus?"

"A global change of plan is required for all camps and farms. I'm here to tell you about the new directive and to set your targets for the next month."

Gregor shifted uneasily in his chair. "Change of plan?"

"You're required to double the land conversion statistics. We're not going fast enough. I need a major push in the next few days."

"That's impossible. The six harvesters are working twenty-four—"

"Five harvesters at the moment. You've let another one get sabotaged today."

"I'm going to take care of that. It's the same person," Gregor said. He tried to think of a way to articulate the implausibility of the new expectations. The ground team were already fully maximized meeting the current requirements. "Will you be providing me with more equipment and resources?"

Augustus drummed his fingers on the table and slowly nodded. "It's time to be frank with you, Gregor."

He turned sideways, slipped his bony fingers around his robe's hood, and pulled it back. The mask encased the front half of his head and was held on with an elastic strap. Blotches of pink scarring covered the back half surrounded by wispy, brown hair. Augustus reached behind his crusty, misshapen left ear and clicked the fastening loose. The mask sprang away and hung to one side. He turned back to Gregor.

Gregor clenched his teeth, trying to keep a neutral exterior. Augustus looked like he'd been attacked with a knife and had the wounds cauterized with a blowtorch. Scarring covered at least fifty percent of his face. His left cheek folded inwards as if sewn to his tongue. Small islands of dark stubble spread around his chin and jawline.

"What are you doing?" Gregor said.

"I'm showing you the price of failure. I'll be checking how you're getting on in a couple of days. My face should serve as a reminder of what will happen if we're not on schedule. I'm sure you can figure out the punishment for repeated failures?"

"How do you expect—"

"I don't expect. The croatoans expect. You're not a special case. It's the same the world over."

The door flung open, and a croatoan bounced in. The two guards initially turned their weapons before relaxing. It started communicating with Augustus using staccato alien noises. Gregor tried to discern Augustus's reaction, but his mangled face was impossible to read.

"I need a moment outside," Augustus said.

He left with the new arrival. The two guards remained inside, helmets angled down at Gregor. He reached for the whiskey bottle. The guard on the right flinched, nudging its weapon up.

"Steady, my friend. I'm just having a drink," Gregor said.

He filled a shot glass and swallowed the whiskey in a single gulp, refilling immediately and drinking again. Gregor clenched his fist to keep his hand steady.

Augustus was setting him up for failure. Without doubling the harvesters, they had no chance. Even if the croatoans provided the machines, the ground team didn't have enough trained humans to work in the Operations Compartments. The key to running the harvesters around the clock was the ability to carry out isolation procedures from the local control room to allow continuing functionality. The croatoans couldn't or wouldn't resource it, which was part of the reason he thought his team were still alive. They needed humans for work as well as food.

The door opened. Augustus returned, mask in hand. "I take it you've heard the latest news?"

Gregor raised his eyebrows. "Latest news?"

After sitting back at the desk, Augustus dabbed a white folded handkerchief against a dribble of saliva running from the corner of his mouth. "Ten croatoans dead. Ten. The harvester. You're bringing a lot of heat down on this operation."

"Ten dead?"

Augustus repeatedly jabbed his finger against the desk. "Two at the harvester. Two surveyors. Four searching for their killers. Two blown up, killed in a trap, following signals. Ten. T. E. N."

The left corner of Augustus's mouth twitched.

"It's Jackson and his bastard son," Gregor said. "We'll get them. They can't keep hiding forever."

Augustus sighed. "You said that last year after they crashed a bulldozer through the paddock fences. Are you sure it's them?"

"I'm positive. The harvester attacks have all followed the same pattern. Whenever we've interrogated survivors, they always blame him. Trust me, most of them want to keep out of our way and hate him as much as me."

Augustus stood and cupped the mask around his face, clipping it back in place behind his ear. "You're incapable of sorting this out. So I will."

"What's that supposed to mean?" Gregor said.

"I'll see to Mister Charles Jackson. We've got a limited resource available for such situations."

"A limited resource? I can do this, just give me time."

"Your time will be occupied with the quotas. We had a similar situation in North Africa. A pain in the ass that wouldn't go away. I'm sending down a croatoan hunter."

Gregor remembered a larger, more aggressive alien during the battle of Eastern Europe. He hadn't seen one for twenty years. No nonsense and formidable. If it crushed the little wasp, he'd shake its hand.

"Thank you, Mr. Augustus. With him out of the way, we'll have a better chance of meeting your targets."

Augustus held the door open, and the two guards left. He turned to Gregor. "They're not my targets, I've already told you. Oh, one more thing …"

"Yes, Mr. Augustus?"

"Wash your clothes. You smell like horse manure."

***

Gregor followed Augustus and his two guards back toward the shuttle. Augustus had an annoying strut, like a peacock. He hadn't spoken a word since his aroma barb. It was all right for Augustus; he probably had croatoans scrubbing his velvet robe and running him luxurious bubble baths on the mother ship.

The cobalt shuttle's primed engines blasted hot air in Gregor's face. He stopped by the edge of the clearing as the entourage headed for the graphite ramp.

Augustus glanced back; Gregor raised his hand. The

robed cretin didn't acknowledge him and shuffled into the craft followed by the two guards. The ramp slid into the main body, and the door hissed across and shut.

The ground rumbled as the engine noise increased, blowing dust in all directions.

The shuttle raised a few feet, paused, and zipped away in a smooth, diagonal line above the trees. Gregor shielded his eyes from the lowering sun and watched the craft bank to its left before shooting through the clouds toward the distant, vague outline of the mother ship in the spring green sky, the shuttle's pink rings quickly disappearing into orbit.

Dust settled, and surrounding trees gently rocked to a halt, leaves brightly glistening with a greasy sheen.

A hand rested on Gregor's shoulder. He flinched and turned, feeling for his gun.

Alex and Layla stood behind him.

"Don't sneak up on me like that," he said.

"We need to talk, Gregor. Things are happening, strange things," Layla said. "One of the croatoans grabbed me by the hair after the booby trap. I haven't seen them behave like that before."

Gregor shrugged. "You should have told me about that. I had to learn about it from Augustus."

"You were already in with him when she got back," Alex said. "We were waiting till he left."

"If you want to know about strange things, you should have been in my office when Augustus took off his mask."

"What did he look like?" Layla said.

Gregor ran his fingers down his cheeks. "Like he'd been bobbing for apples in acid."

He started walking back to his office. Layla tugged at

his sweater. "I meant what I said. Something's going down; we need to talk."

"Talk in my office. I've also had some news." Gregor glanced through the trees toward the chocolate factory as he led the two women away. Three croatoans were testing a large anti-gravity trailer at the back of the warehouse. It hovered three feet in the air. One alien balanced on top of it. The other two stood at either end, moving it around in a circle.

Gregor led the way through his front door, closing it behind Alex and Layla, twisting the key and securing the bolt. He peered through the window blinds before pulling them shut.

"Augustus wants us to double our land conversion stats. We've got a few days to do it," he said.

"How are we supposed to that?" Alex said.

Gregor sat in his chair and poured a whiskey. "I don't see a way. We bent over backward to meet the current targets. The new goal came attached with a threat."

"Jesus. What?"

"You don't want to know. Layla, any bright ideas?"

Layla looked down, rubbing her chin. She moved across to a chart on the office wall and placed her finger on an area north east of their current location. "This is all former farmland. We concentrate here for the next few weeks. Progress will be quicker as the woodland is less dense. I'm not saying it'll double the conversion, but if we focus on these type of areas …"

"It'll catch up with us," Alex said. "At some stage, we'll be left with thick forest and cities. Then what?"

"I'm just providing a short-term solution. Last week, I mapped the individual harvester statistics to the old charts. If we want to meet Augustus's short-term targets, this is how we do it. When we get the damaged one from today repaired, we send it to start on the forest. Okay?"

Short-term, long term, it didn't matter to Gregor. As long as he could keep the plates spinning. He downed his whisky and slammed the glass on the table. "Makes sense. Can you work on this together and send the new coordinates to the harvester drivers?"

"Leave it with us," Alex said. "I'll have the instructions sent out tonight."

The thought of Alex and Layla working together pleased Gregor. Both seemed to have a mutual dislike for each other since meeting ten years ago. The time hadn't managed to bring about a thaw, unlike the croatoans' weather control.

Alex was long-serving and loyal. Friends from the pre-alien days were at a premium. Layla had provided him with yet another solution to keep the wolf from the door. Without her, he could have been hanging on a butcher's hook.

His thoughts turned to Marek. With Augustus out of the way and the new directive in place, it was all hands on deck. A safe and justifiable time to release his old friend.

"Alex. You're in charge of the ground team again. Marek's back as my number two," Gregor said. He brushed the blonde to one side and unlocked the door. "I'll leave you two to it. Let me know if you have any problems. I don't like looking clueless in front of that masked bastard."

"Gregor, wait, they're up to something," Layla said.

"Who? The croatoans? They're always up to something."

"Not just the quotas. Have you noticed there's more of them in the warehouses? Numbers have doubled in the chocolate factory. The equipment they're bringing down too. I'm telling you, this is more than usual operations."

"They come and go. So what if they have a new floating platform or funny device?"

Alex stepped toward him and said with a genuine look of sincerity, "She's got a point. It's not just because of today; it's been going on the past two weeks. They're not communicating with us either."

Gregor paused for a moment. He couldn't deny that things were changing, but for the sake of survival, they had to concentrate on what would work for them. Worrying over alien experiments or motives wouldn't help. Meeting the targets and keeping the livestock healthy and fit for consumption would.

"Do some digging. See what you can find out," he said.

As he left the office, Gregor gazed at sky. It started to turn a gentle orange during the hours of dusk and dawn over a year ago, perhaps two. It became more accentuated as they covered larger swathes of the continent with the initial planting of croatoan crops.

Gregor heaved up the metal garage door, wincing as it screeched on its rusty mechanism like giant nails running along a chalkboard.

Marek peered through the dim light, twisting his shoulders against the bound rope around his upper torso. "Gregor, you've come to see me."

"It's over, my friend. You're back as my number two."

"Why did you do it? You know you can trust me."

Gregor picked up a knife from the table on the right-hand side of the garage and jabbed it toward Marek. "It was an act to keep you alive. Do you think Augustus liked the fact that you'd been captured and interrogated by the little wasp?"

"You could have told me," Marek said.

"And let Augustus's aliens beat that information out of you? We'd both be dead. I'm sorry, you have to understand."

"We need to put a stop to Jackson once and for all. He's going to get us killed."

"They're sending down a resource called a hunter to end him."

"A hunter?"

"Probably one of those croatoans they used in battle."

Gregor slipped the blade underneath the rope and used the serrated edge to saw through it, making quick work of the frayed braid. He passed Marek the knife to release his ankles from the legs of the chair.

"I heard Igor talking to Augustus outside the garage a few hours ago. Couldn't quite tell what they were saying," Marek said.

"Igor's slyer than a fox," Gregor said. He resisted the urge to kick the table and pulled Marek to his feet. "If he's colluding with Augustus, I need to know what they're discussing. We'll do it first thing tomorrow morning. Tonight, you get a whiskey and a comfortable bed."

Marek unsteadily shuffled toward the door. He flung his arm around Gregor to stop himself falling. Gregor wrapped his arm around Marek's back and started leading him to his office.

A faint roar echoed overhead. Gregor glanced up into the darkening sky. A bright light shot across it like a shooting star although the trajectory was more deliberate. It was arcing down from the mother ship toward Earth. He tried to recall the last time he saw a croatoan fighter.

Chapter Sixteen

The screeching sound of a bird startled Ben.

A cold sweat had soaked his clothes, making him shiver in the dark. Sleep had evaded him, coming in shallow, brief moments, lulling his subconscious into a semi-awake state. Daydreams lingered like memories lost to time, their residue remaining, pointing to something substantial but ultimately out of reach.

Ben turned over and reached out his hand to switch off the phantom alarm clock. His arm moved on instinct, a behavior burrowed into his muscles from years on the ship. And there, the phantasm of truth glared bright in his mind.

He wasn't on the ship.

The place was dark and cold, and the sounds of others snoring reminded him that he lay ten feet under the ground in a tomb dug out by Charlie and Denver. The dampness of the blanket beneath him transferred the coolness of the soil.

Worms, insects, beetles, and things far worse than his imagination could conjure no doubt crawled beneath him, waiting to devour him, bring his energy to the soil.

Sitting up with a startled breath, he clawed his way forward in the dark, desperate to escape. The cold, pressing confines of the shelter making him gasp for air. Fresh air.

Ethan and Maria were pressed tightly together to his right, their bodies warm to his touch as their chests moved rhythmically with their quiet breath.

Charlie lay to his left. He snored loud and long, the slumber of someone who had grown up with this, someone who had chosen this over acquiescence with the croatoans. The sleep of the confident.

Ben wondered if he would ever have that inner peace again in a world where it was he that felt alien.

Dirt compacted beneath his fingers. He continued to crawl forward until eventually, with out-stretching hands, he found the wooden ladder.

Above him would be his escape, his freedom.

It was only as he climbed the ladder leading to steps cut in the earth and pushed the cover of leaves away that he realized Denver was missing from the shelter. Pip too.

Cool air wicked away the sweat on his brow, and his lungs felt the chill of pre-dawn air. The scene before him was a de-saturated landscape; the monochromatic touch of the moon delineated the outline of the leaves and trunks.

An excited yip from beyond the tree line of the copse caught his attention. Through the foliage, he could see the slick, oily surface of a river, the silver light creating specular reflections as the breeze manipulated the water.

But the breeze was not the only instigator.

Moving closer, treading carefully across the loamy, damp ground, Ben pushed through between two wide trees until he stood on the threshold. A dark shape sat at the river's edge.

Ben watched as the figure lifted what looked like a medieval crossbow, pointed it into the darkness beyond the river, and fired a near-silent bolt. Only the twang of the wire and the thunk of the bolt hitting its target made any noise.

A rustling came then. Pip's tail wagged within the tall grass, the white tip catching the half-light. The dog disappeared for a moment and returned with a small creature in its mouth. She crossed a tree trunk that had fallen across the river and dropped the prize at the shape's feet.

Ben stepped forward.

"Can't sleep?" the voice from the dark shape said, confirming to Ben that it was Denver. The young man didn't turn around as he pulled a small hunting knife from his jacket and made a series of straight cuts across his catch. "Don't just hang around there behind me. You make a man suspicious."

"Sorry." Wrapping his arms around his body to retain the heat, Ben stepped forward until he saw what Denver was working on: field dressing a rabbit. In front of him, a rack made from twigs held half a dozen fish and three skinned and gutted rabbits.

"Breakfast," Denver said, his voice like a cold growl. "I don't sleep much either. Sit down; you're making me nervous, hanging over me like that."

"Sorry."

"And stop apologizing. You don't have anything to apologize for. I get it," Denver said as he placed the skinned rabbit on the rack. "This is quite the change of lifestyle for you and the others. I'd be freaked out too."

"I don't want to be here," Ben said. "I just want to go back, work on the ship. I was safe there."

Denver turned to face him. His pale skin seemed entirely without color beneath the pre-dawn starlight. "Really? What do you think happened to those that came before you? You think they're enjoying retirement? That's what you were told, wasn't it? All those tuition videos you had to watch, telling you how you were heading for a new planet, how you'd do your job and you'd get to retire in a life of comfort."

Unable to stand his glare any longer, Ben turned his head, trying not to think of Jimmy and Erika. Deep down, he knew that's what retirement meant.

"They recycle you. Did you know that?"

"What do you mean?"

"They use us as food source, a labor force, lab rats. They see us as nothing more than animals designed to further their cause. We are rabbits."

"Food source?" Ben said, "What do you mean exactly?"

"They farm us. We're just protein and nutrients after all. Stick us in a meat-processor, and we're no different than beef or chicken. On the harvesters, when your shift is done and they retire you, you go to the unit. Those silver trays of food they give to you ..."

"No," Ben said, standing up, shaking his head. "They wouldn't do that ... That's ... I can't believe it."

"That's your problem," Denver said. "Believe or don't believe, it doesn't change the situation, does it? They're still here. They're still changing the planet, it's just a matter of time now."

"Changing how?" Ben asked.

"You've seen the air, the water, the land. That orange root compound is getting into everything. It's what's in the aliens' backpack and respiratory system: a gas made from the compound. They can't breathe our air unaided. Well, for now anyway. The atmosphere will soon be right for them."

"And then what?"

Denver didn't say anything as he stood up and stretched his arms.

"Denver, what's going to happen?"

"What do you care, Ben? You're not really with us, are you? I can tell you don't want to be out here, surviving. You want to go back, don't you?"

A flush of shame and truth warmed Ben's cheeks even as he turned away. "I don't know what I want. It's all just so much to take in."

Denver put a hand on Ben's shoulder. "I know it's difficult. What if I could give you a third option? You can't go back to the harvesters, and you're clearly not cut out to stay here. I won't lie; it's a tough life in the wild. I've seen dozens of people just give up, give in, unable to adapt. But there's one other course for someone like you."

"What do you have in mind?" A mix of fear and hope swirled in Ben's guts, but there was something in Denver's eyes that told him it wasn't going to be an easy option, but then he believed nothing was going to be easy again.

"Work for us. On the inside. Help us get these fuckers off our planet for good."

"It sounds dangerous," Ben said, slumping his shoulders as the hope died before it even had time to blossom. "What do you mean work for you?"

"Sit down. Have a drink. I'll explain everything."

Denver indicated a log. He had a tin can of water that was steaming from an earlier boiling. The glowing remnants of a fire sparkled within a mound of leaves and twigs.

Ben sat down and received the warm cup from Denver. "Thanks." He took a sip and screwed up his face at the bitter taste, but he still drank, quenching the thirst of spending the night in the underground shelter. "What is it?"

"Root compound. We learned how to extract the active ingredient. It'll make you feel better," Denver said.

"Is this why your father is still in such good shape? How old is he anyway?"

Pip came over to Ben and lay down on the warm ground in front of the log, resting her head on Ben's foot. Denver patted the dog and looked up at Ben.

"Dad's fifty-eight this year and is probably fitter than I am. He had to be. He's one of the very few to have survived the ice age and the thaw. He saw it all. Even fought in the people's militia during the initial struggles when the croatoans came up from the earth. Later, they came from space, overwhelmed the population, and Dad had to go in hiding with the other survivors."

"How long was the ice age for? What brought it on?"

"Twenty years. We believe it was the first part of the croatoans' terraforming process. They had this huge mother ship that altered the atmosphere, changed the world's temperature. Dad reckons it was preparing the lands to grow the root they so desperately need. When the thaw came, the trees and vegetation grew rapidly as did the root, which is why they're now harvesting it."

"So about this other option," Ben said. "What is it you want me to do?"

Denver pointed to the west back toward the forest. "There's a farm back there, a few miles from your harvester. You can go there. They'll take you in."

"Is it run by the aliens?"

Denver shook his head. "No, someone far worse. A betrayer of humankind. A jumped-up gangster from pre-ice age days. He got in with the croatoans early, selling out his own kind. Gregor runs the farm on their behalf and manages the harvesters."

"That's why you attacked it? Revenge?"

"Vengeance? No, that doesn't even scratch the surface. Gregor and Dad go way back. They've been fighting since the start. The more pressure we can put on Gregor with his harvesting quotas, the more pressure the croatoans will put on him to meet his targets. If he can't, then … Well, he'll become livestock for all those poor bastards in the farm."

Ben was starting to get the picture. The thought of a human farming others of his kind as livestock turned his stomach. How could he work for something like that? How was that any better than being out in the wild?

Ben's hope was well and truly gone now.

"I don't see how this is a good option," Ben said. "How do you even know they'll just take me in and not throw me in with the livestock?"

"That's a good question," Denver said as he took a piece of root from his camo jacket's pocket and chewed on the end. "At least you're thinking now. You'll have one thing that Gregor wants almost as badly as his career trajectory."

"What's that?"

"You'll go to him with information on my dad. That'll buy you almost anything you want. You can have a comfortable life there. There's others with Gregor. You'll likely make friends, find a purpose, and do some good along the way."

"Farming our species is not my idea of good."

"But you see," Denver said, leaning in, his face shining in the moonlight, smiling conspiratorially beneath his straggly beard. "Once you're in, you can feed information both ways. You could bargain for things in return for what you've learned about us: where our shelters are, how many people we have on our side, what our plans are. And in return, you'll gain their trust and feed us information. If we can take out Gregor and free the people he's using as livestock, we can start to take down other farms, freeing those people, until we … You get the picture."

"So you want me to be a double agent of sorts?" Ben said, remembering a James Bond film he'd watched.

"Something like that."

Ben looked down at Pip. The dog was snoozing now, her breath making a quiet rumbling on his foot. It was the first time he'd ever really understood man's fascination with animals.

During his orientation training, they were shown a number of films produced to show them what they would be doing when they got to Kepler B, their so-called colony planet. They were told that along with humans in stasis, there was a Noah's ark of animals too. Dogs were among the most prized for their loyalty and their uses in colonization.

"Man's best friend," Ben said, reciting one of the lines from the film's narrator.

"Pardon?"

"Oh, nothing, just something I heard once about dogs."

"Pip's the best friend I'll ever have aside from my old man," Denver said.

"I can see why."

Ben sighed and leaned forward onto his knees, clutching his head in his palms. He felt stuck, unable to truly make a decision between a life on the run, living in the dirt, or going back to some kind of civilization although brutal and unfamiliar.

There was a risk too that this Gregor might not even accept him into the fold. What if his information wasn't good enough? Ben turned to Denver, who just stared out across the river, a stern expression on his face. It wasn't right that a man so young should be so jaded. Ethan would likely be the same too.

Of course, that was another consideration. Could he really leave Maria and Ethan behind? Would they go with him? If they did, he'd be responsible for them like he was supposed to be responsible for them on the harvester. And that didn't end well for anyone.

If only I didn't go to the stasis, he thought. If only we'd just stayed where we were and waited it out. We'd have been fine. They would have fixed the harvester, and they would have never been exposed to the truth.

"If I did go," Ben said, "what information exactly can you give me that will guarantee my life? It seems to me I'm the one taking all the risk here."

"We'll give you a map to one of our main shelters. We've got dozens between here and New York, but one in particular not ten miles from here will be of interest to Gregor. We've got weapons and supplies stashed there. If he were to find that and take it, he'd think he would be impacting our ability to survive a great deal. And there's one other thing that'll seal it completely."

"What's that?"

A hand grabbed Ben's shoulder, making him yelp with surprise. Pip woofed as she moved away from his sudden movement to lie at Denver's feet.

"This," Charlie said, looking down at Ben from behind

him.

Ben held out his hand as Charlie dropped his blue-bead necklace into his palm.

"Consider it a trophy. Gregor knows what it is, what it means, what it represents. Behind Den, it's my most precious thing."

It was warm in Ben's palm where it had been around Charlie's neck just moments ago. The bead was just like the one that Charlie had cut out of Ben's collar. Only this was wrapped in a cocoon of semi-transparent material.

"It's what started all this in motion," Charlie said. "The very first find, and the item that was the catalyst for the invasion. It was also the item that I kept to remind me of my beloved Pippa."

"I can't," Ben said. "It means so much to you."

"Which is why it's perfect. Gregor knows this. If you turn up with it, he'll know you stole it as he'd never believe I'd give it away. It's your way in and your ticket to safety. I'll be honest with you, Ben. You seem like a good kid, but you're not cut out for this life out here. What you've experienced so far is easy street. It only gets harder from here on out. You won't survive. I know that; you know that."

Ben closed his hand around the bead and looked up at Charlie and Denver. They were right. He wasn't cut out for their life. He needed security, a job, someone to guide him. And if going to the farm meant he could help these people, then at least he'd be doing something good.

"Okay, you're right. I'll go. But how will I get information out to you?"

"By radio of sorts. Here." Charlie handed him a metallic object resembling a coin. The surface was dark grey and rough to the touch. "I took this from a croatoan helmet.

It's what they use to communicate. They've been paired, so they share a frequency. Don't worry, they're secure. Den and I have been using them for a while. As long as we keep things short, you'll be okay. To work them, you just activate the transceiver by pressing those two notches on the side there."

Ben did as he instructed and spoke into the transceiver. He heard his voice come out via the other one. "Okay, I got it."

"Keep it to a minimum though, and make sure you don't let it out of your sight," Denver said. "If it's found, just plead ignorance. It's unlikely they'd suspect you of being able to take it from a croatoan."

"One week from now," Charlie said, "you'll contact us, tell us what you've learned about the shipments to and from the mother ship. We want to know if there's a schedule, how it's handled, who oversees the packing."

"So what exactly is your plan?"

"Better you don't know, son," Charlie said. "If you don't know, they can't extract that from you. But it won't come to that. Just do as you're told, be a good worker, and you'll have no problem. When the time comes, we'll get you out of there as there'll be no more croatoans left."

Chapter Seventeen

The howl of a croatoan fighter craft flying a low circuit over the camp kept Layla awake for most of the night. She punched her pillow and checked her watch after being awoken from the latest pass, probably an hour's sleep if that, not much chance of any more.

At first, the sound evoked memories of the battle of Britain. Flashbacks to shortly after the vessels appeared from the sinkholes stuffed with ground troops who spread from the freezing smoke like locusts. The fighters appeared almost immediately in support, taking everything out of the sky in short order, firing powerful weapons at targets on the ground. They left almost as quickly as they appeared after annihilating the global population. That's when she first met Augustus, after the overhead howling stopped, before the mini ice age took hold.

Layla thought about his threat to Gregor and wondered if he'd seen the same side of Augustus that she had.

A group of croatoan foot soldiers rounded up survivors, including Layla, who had been taking refuge in a supermarket. He appeared in his mask and robe and announced that everyone was to be interviewed in the warehouse.

Layla was fifth in line out of the twenty-five-strong group.

When she entered the warehouse, Augustus was sitting

behind a desk, holding a pen. A pile of four bodies lay to her right-hand side. He told her he was carrying out a skills assessment for future operations, and it was her chance to shape a new world. She was the only survivor to leave the building alive, and witnessed Augustus sliding his pen across his neck after each person that confronted him revealed their skills and was apparently found unsuitable. They were executed on the spot by a croatoan soldier.

Light was already starting to seep through the drapes, illuminating the tatty trailer's brown and cream interior. She commandeered it after the team arrived in Pennsylvania. The usual process was to grab the closest available accommodation to Gregor's choice of office.

She peeled a large carrot in the kitchen sink and took a bite. A sour, metallic taste burst around her mouth as she crunched. Layla gagged, spat it out, and took a drink from a plastic water bottle, swilling the fluid, attempting to wash away the taste. For years, she'd always tried to keep a vegetable patch on the edge of camp. The yield was gradually becoming worse; this year's crop was almost entirely inedible.

The alien root was having a larger combined effect on the ground and atmosphere. Layla decided that now would be a good time to check out the chocolate factory. Dawn was breaking, and the croatoans didn't usually start work for another hour. She could slip inside the warehouse and have a good look around their equipment, check their latest charts, and maybe even try and make sense of their computers. It wasn't worth risking before, but things were moving, and she wanted to know the direction.

She slipped on a black sweater and carefully opened the door, trying not to make a sound.

Thunder rumbled in the distance as she neared the chocolate factory. The last thing she needed. It was like an alarm for the aliens to go outside and revere the adverse weather. Layla tried to appear as casual as possible as she walked around the side of the building toward the front entrance.

Thin light shone out of the barrack buildings into the quiet main square, reflecting off the hover-bikes parked in the middle. Some aliens were busy. Layla could hear faint sounds of clanking and humming, nothing really unusual.

She reached for the chocolate factory door. It flew open, striking her hand as she attempted to pull it away.

A croatoan surveyor stood in the entrance and looked up. It carried a shoebox-sized device under its right arm, not one of croatoan computers; this had a luminous green display and several circular blue buttons. A transparent pipe curled around the box like a vacuum cleaner hose.

The croatoan clicked a few times and held its free arm to one side in a gesturing motion.

"Good morning. You're starting early today," Layla said.

The alien shuffled past her, followed by four of its colleagues, each carrying the same thing.

Layla stood on her tiptoes and peered into the gloom behind the outgoing procession. The place was a hive of activity. Nothing like she'd ever seen before.

Two more aliens filed past, carrying the large object on a stretcher. It was the first time she'd observed the back of the glowing sea-green piece of equipment. Five circular holes ran along the side, funneling into the internal machinery.

She stepped inside and walked past the croatoan worktable. A group of eight surveyors stood around it, busily communicating with each other, holding up their tablets, pointing. They stopped and turned as she passed. Layla pointed toward the back of the room where Vlad sat gazing at the screens, dutifully monitoring the harvesters.

Vlad remained transfixed on the screens as Layla approached. She said, "People are going to start to think you're a chocolate factory ornament."

Vlad twisted in his chair. "I'm not the only one who works here."

"You are for at least sixteen hours a day."

He grunted and spun back to face the screens. Layla remembered him close to breakdown when he worked with the livestock, turning up increasingly drunk for work, losing his temper before sobbing in open view. Vlad was the one member of the gang that didn't seem to be able to simply brush things under the carpet for the sake of survival; he had little choice but to go along so he carved out a niche in the most bearable work. Layla got it; Gregor didn't. He called Vlad *the wet lettuce.*

"How's the conversion rate since the change last night?" Layla said.

Vlad twisted his chair around. "Seems to be doing the trick. I'll have a better idea in a few hours, but the early signs are good."

Layla glanced back to the croatoans. "How long have they been here?"

"About three hours. Came in the middle of the night. I've never seen so many of the little freaks buzzing around. One of them brought over a tray of food," Vlad said, twisting his face into a grimace.

"You'll let me know if you see anything strange?"

"Look around you," he replied, and started writing

something on a notepad.

***

Layla decided to follow the croatoans as they left the chocolate factory in a busy gaggle. She shadowed them left, into the eight-foot gap between the factory and training building toward the paddocks.

A loud, short electric buzz echoed ahead. The warning sound before the paddock gates were opened. She reached the other side and saw red lights spinning on either side of the entrance.

Two surveyors pulled the tall mesh gates open.

Humans remained at the opposite end of the paddock huddled under the shelter, staring over with blank faces at the croatoan activity.

To Layla's right, the gravity trailer drifted past across open ground.

Four croatoans kept it on course at each corner. A large transparent structure, about the size of a single decker bus and split into five sections, balanced on top. Each section had a small, circular hole at one side and a door on the other. It must have been assembled in one of the warehouses. To her knowledge, nothing that size had come off a shuttle. That's the way croatoans did things, assembling their equipment like hi-tech, flat-packed furniture.

The croatoans pushed the trailer through the gate and brought it down in a clear grassed area. They slid the structure off the trailer and moved it to one side. Other aliens joined them, carrying over their pieces of electronic equipment.

Layla crouched by the electric fence and observed

their movements. Another roll of thunder boomed in the distance; the aliens collectively looked up for a moment before carrying on.

Each of the five devices was twisted in place around the holes of the large structure, one for every compartment. Two croatoans attached the hoses from the devices to the larger one that was carried over on a stretcher. It took on the appearance of a control panel once the whole thing was interconnected. Most croatoans gathered around the glowing, coffin-sized device, fifteen of them.

The remaining five made their way toward the far end of the paddock. Each pulled a single human out of the flock and led them at gunpoint back toward the main group and lined them up outside each individual compartment, all dressed in dirty sheets tied around their bodies.

A croatoan approached the back of the first compartment and knelt by the attached device. A series of lights started winking on it. A whirring noise drifted over to Layla.

As the alien moved along each compartment, the noise became gradually louder. It sounded like being next to a bank of servers with multiple running fans. All five shoeboxes collectively winked and hummed.

The left hand compartment started to fill with dark orange smoke. Its neighbor took on a lighter tone. The middle compartment was slightly more transparent. The one after that was only tinged with orange. The left-hand compartment remained clear.

Croatoans moved all around the structure, investigating it, checking the shoeboxes probably for readings, and pressing their gloved hands against the plastic-looking shell.

It looked to Layla like they were creating different types of atmosphere pressurized in individual compartments.

The aliens stood in a circle for a few moments before one broke from the group and opened the individual doors to each compartment. Puffs of orange smoke drifted into the cloudy sky after the last three doors were released.

Layla edged behind a tree stump and peered over. She was starting to feel that this was an experiment she needed to see and didn't want to be chaperoned away by a paranoid alien.

A croatoan guarding the man outside the left-hand compartment opened its door by raising a lever, then cajoled the confused-looking man inside at gunpoint. It slammed the door behind him and secured the lever downwards.

The same thing happened in turn to all four humans outside the other compartments until all five sections were occupied. It looked like a strange zoo as the croatoans stood around the structure, checking the smaller devices and crowding around the larger console. The humans looked around, pressed against the interior. One sat cross-legged on the floor. A croatoan approached and ushered him up with a gun.

Through a gap between the aliens, Layla could see they were peering down to a light blue square on the larger device. Probably giving them data or readings from individual sections.

Dense, orange smoke billowed into the left-hand compartment, quickly filling it from top to bottom. Its black-haired inhabitant clutched at her throat, sinking to her knees. Layla momentarily lost sight of the human in the smoke until the top of her head pressed against the bottom edge.

After observing for a few minutes, looking between the console and the compartment, a croatoan released the door and pulled the lifeless body out by the hair.

Smoke pumped into the next compartment, having the same effect on the human. Because it was less thick, Layla could see a visible outline thrashing around inside. The man dropped to his backside and tried to kick at the door with his feet, eventually stopping and rolling to one side. He was dragged out shortly afterwards.

Fists thumped against the transparent middle section. The woman inside had seen what was coming. She tried shouting toward the croatoans. The structure must have been soundproof. One walked up and stood directly in front of the struggling woman as if mocking her, matching her actions as she slowly perished. Aliens clicked loudly from the console.

She was unceremoniously dumped on the increasing pile of bodies after five minutes.

The humans in the final two compartments were facing each other, hands placed on the internal separating wall against each other.

Layla cupped her hand over her mouth and breathed, "Oh my God."

A light orange tinge surrounded the man in the second to last section. He looked around, squinting, and wiped his eyes. He remained standing for two minutes before doubling over and dry retching several times. He leaned against the side with his eyes tightly shut, nursing his stomach. The woman in the final compartment watched on. Her head gently rocked as she clasped her hands on her cheeks.

After a few more minutes, two croatoans opened the final compartment doors. The man staggered out and fell, gasping for clean air. A croatoan pulled him up by his filthy white toga and pushed him back toward the flock. The woman was also encouraged at gunpoint toward the shelter. She didn't need a second invitation and sprinted, tripping and tumbling, before glancing back and hurrying away.

All doors on the five compartments were left open. Croatoans crowded the console and seemed to be communicating the results of whatever they were testing. Some were more animated than others, raising their arms and pointing at individual sections of the structure.

A croatoan with a red-rimmed visor stood on top of the console and raised its arms. The group fell silent. A minute later, five aliens walked to the front of the structure and stood in the individual sections; one secured each door behind them.

The whirring started and each compartment filled with various shades of smoke like before, going from thick to thin from one end to another. The aliens inside pressed their gloves against the walls, moving them round in a circular motion. More visible from right to left.

Layla edged back and observed from the trees. The croatoan with the red-rimmed visor checked the small devices attached to each individual compartment, signaled back to the aliens at the console, and then thumped its glove against the middle section.

The croatoan inside removed its helmet, revealing its ugly, tortoise-like head. Aliens surrounded the section, clicking loudly; others from the left and right of the structure were released and joined the mob. All excitedly went back and crowded around the console.

Their objectives started to make a little sense although Layla didn't know the true motivation behind it. Were they testing an atmosphere where they could survive and a human would die, or was it a test to just try and find an atmosphere that they could survive in on Earth with enough of the root extract mixed into the atmosphere? Regardless of which one it was, Layla knew either way was bad news for humans.

Increasing the land conversion statistics now started to make a little more sense. The urgency of the request baffled her at first, but after seeing this, it seemed a full colonization and extinction event was planned.

Chapter Eighteen

Charlie stoked the fire with a stick, inhaling the succulent scent of roasting rabbit.

"The boy done good, eh?" Charlie said as he used his hunting knife to cut a piece from the spit, waiting for it to cool before he took a bite and delighted in the tenderness of the meat. He nodded. "Yup, you caught a good one there, son."

Charlie wiped his knife on a rag tucked into his belt and slapped his son on the shoulder. Ben and Ethan picked at the rabbit with a set of old forks as though it were some alien creature ready to reanimate at any moment. Maria tentatively took a bite, analyzed it, realized the taste suited her, and returned for a second serving.

"You two are too used to eating processed grey slop, right?" Denver said, pointing his knife to the two men. "The stuff they fed you from the trays?" Grease dripped from his lips and soaked into his beard. He dabbed at it with the back of his hand.

"It wasn't so bad there," Ben said.

"You won't have to put up with this much longer," Denver added before he cast his eyes back to Maria as she chewed on a rabbit leg.

For a very brief moment, Charlie had a flashback to sitting with Pippa by a fire in their ice cave, cooking up a fox they'd caught. Maria's mannerisms and easy nature were so similar. Either that or the distance of time had compressed Pippa into a half-remembered mimic whose real personality was but a ghost.

Charlie had noticed that since Maria and Ethan had joined them by the riverside, sitting on logs surrounding a fire, Denver had barely taken his eyes off Maria. And he didn't blame him.

Aside from her physical attraction, Charlie could see what Denver saw in her: a good, healthy balance of emotions that she wasn't afraid to show or act upon. Some people, like his old National Guard officer, thought that those who were best equipped for survival were the ones who throttled their emotions.

In the years since the old officer had died during the ice age, Charlie had learned that he was wrong. Those that could survive weren't repressed. They were in tune with their emotions and in a good position to act upon them.

He'd seen too many good people die because they repressed their fear.

As far as Charlie was concerned, there were no such things as negative emotions. Each one served an important role, and the individual who had those in harmony were the ones that outlasted those who were devoid.

Maria was one of those people who had that harmony.

Even now, after all the stress and fear of the day before, she was delighting in the simple pleasures of spit-roasted rabbit and fish, caught naturally.

Ethan sat back, crossing his arms, parallel lines etched

into his forehead. "I know something's going on," he said, looking up at Denver.

At first, Charlie thought he meant Denver's not too subtle glances at Maria. But then the boy continued and looked to Charlie as he spoke, uncrossing his arms and pointing his finger.

"You're in on it too. In fact, I think I must be the only one you haven't told. You're planning something. I know it."

"What are you talking about?" Maria said, shaking her head with annoyance.

"The atmosphere's changed. Hasn't it, Ben?" Ethan said.

After having sat there silently for the best part of an hour, his right fist shut around the bead, Ben looked up at Ethan and then Maria. His face tightened as though he was in pain.

Internally, he probably is, Charlie thought. Ben had clearly made up his mind to leave for the farm, but the thought of leaving his friends behind weighed on him heavily. Even his shoulders were hunched as though his concern was real and solid.

"I'm not staying," Ben finally said.

"What?" Ethan replied, his eyebrows twitching upward.

"Staying here? None of us are, Ben. We're moving on later today," Maria said, not really getting what Ben was saying.

He stood up, brushed the dirt from his now-tatty-looking uniform and took a breath. "I'm leaving you. I mean here with Charlie and Denver. I can't do this; I'm just not cut out for it."

"I don't understand," Ethan said. "What is it you're saying?"

"Explain, Ben. You're not making much sense," Maria added.

"Like I said, I'm not cut out for this. I can't survive out here. Not like you two. I don't belong here. I'm going to do a job for Charlie. I'm returning to the croatoans on a farm run by a human called Gregor. Charlie and Denver have explained everything, and it's the right choice for everyone concerned. I'm doing this for me but also for you two. You'll stand a better chance if I do this. We all will."

For the next ten minutes, Charlie and Denver briefly explained the plan to Ethan and Maria, leaving out certain important pieces that could get them into trouble if they were to be captured, such as the bead and the location of the decoy shelter.

"And there's no changing your mind?" Maria said.

"None."

"Well, that's that then," Maria said. "I understand and respect your decision. But I hope we'll get to see you again soon. I'll miss you."

"And I'll miss you too," Ben said, moving to her, leaning down, and hugging her. He broke away and hugged Ethan. "And you too, Ethan. But you're young enough that you'll soon adapt out here and thrive. I'm not so adaptable."

"This might be what a funeral felt like," Ethan said. "Like the ones on the video recording. I never knew it'd feel so bad. It's worse than losing Jimmy."

A hush descended on the camp as people processed that thought in their own way.

For Charlie, it was the picture of hundreds of graves he had personally dug in order that those who had perished would at least get some kind of sendoff.

Even if almost all of them were strangers, given the state

of the world, having to bury anyone, even someone with no personal connection, still felt like a loss. Every human counted for so much more when there were so few.

"Denver, be a sport and get Ben's pack ready."

"Sure thing." Denver stood up and moved to the shelter, Pip following right behind him like she was his shadow.

"Before I go," Ben said, "Can you tell us what it was like before all this? How did it happen? The knowledge might help me on the farm."

Charlie looked at the three of them staring back at him with the rapt attention of children at story time. With the fire burning to embers and the morning's chill burning off, he thought it as good a time as any. Once Ben was gone, it'd be one less thing to go through for the others, and Ben was right. The more he knew, the stronger position he would be in.

"Okay, let's start at the beginning." He leaned back and crossed his legs and began his tale. He filled them in about how society was back then, how he'd worked for a production company, and that fateful day when he went down into the sinkhole.

"How did you survive that?" Maria said, her mouth gaping with surprise.

"Pippa was on the surface looking down. She saw the alien craft before I did. She got the firemen and the police to haul me and the boy up, but he perished as the great metal orb climbed out of the hole and crushed him into the sides. I managed to land on the front of it and use its momentum to ride up and out.

"When I got to the surface, everyone ran. Once I was clear of the ropes and harnesses, Pippa and I managed to get into my truck before the croatoan orb dispensed the gas.

"That's what killed most people on their first surfacing. We don't know what it was exactly, but later, talking with some guys from the Army who had tried to fight back initially, it seemed it was some kind of neurotoxin."

"What did it do?" Ethan said, not understanding the term.

"It paralyzed people. But it didn't stop them from feeling pain. Most of the afflicted died through starvation and thirst while others died from heart attacks and other blood-pressure-based illnesses."

"That's terrible," Maria said. "I can't imagine how scary that must have been to be paralyzed and know you're going to die but not being able to do anything about it."

Charlie shook his head at the memories. "If only you knew the half of it. It was a terrible time. Numbing. No one could truly comprehend what was happening. The croatoans' orbs came up at the same time and continued to surface for a week all over the world. There must have been hundreds of thousands of them.

"Pippa and I estimated they were in the ground for thousands of years. Before even humans fully evolved. We should have known it sooner. The signs were there. Over the ages, many societies and cultures had experienced them in some way or another.

"We discovered cave paintings that in hindsight were obviously early croatoans. When you go back through human history and look at some of the strange reported events, it's clear the aliens were involved. I can show you in more detail when we reach our destination. Pippa and I researched a lot of this once that initial phase was over."

"Initial phase?" Ethan asked. "What else happened?"

Lighting a root cigar, Charlie took a long drag and exhaled the orange smoke. The root made his brain tingle, and a warm sensation crawled over his body, clearing away the tiredness, making him feel alert and a little high—an energetic high, one that he had come to rely on to keep him vital and healthy.

"When the military initially resisted, they busted open one of the orbs. It had one of those smaller aliens inside. Shriveled up and aged but still alive. We carbon dated one. They're essentially immortal as long as they maintain their chemical composition. Within the pod were a number of tanks filled with this root compound.

"Additionally, there were other tanks filled with the toxin. That initial attack crippled humanity. They destroyed our satellites and jammed our radio signals. Our computers stopped working as each orb acted like an electro-magnetic pulse station. Together, they networked, increasing their capability and reducing us to using flags to communicate.

"The second phase was when the mother ship arrived. It altered our atmosphere and brought on the ice age. Along with the gas the orbs emitted, they did something to drastically shift the temperature of the planet.

"Those that weren't killed by the gas were killed by the extreme weather. It took six months for the ice to take hold. During that time, the mother ship sent down thousands of raiders—ships that bundled humans together and took them up there for whatever reason. Testing, experiments, food. It didn't matter. All that mattered was hiding, staying alive."

"That's when you met Gregor?" Ben asked.

"A few years later, yeah. I stayed in North America,

joining up with some military friends.We retreated to their Army base with Pippa and formed a group of survivors.

"We were forced south where we found a cave system that we used as our new base of operations. We would go out and search for survivors, bringing them back and helping those that we could. One day, Gregor and half a dozen of his Armenian brethren turned up. Somehow, they'd travelled all the way from Europe.

"They brought tales of the thawing and the harvesters. Within a few years, the thaw came to America, but Gregor was long gone before then. He and I didn't mix well. He had certain ideas I didn't agree with. He wanted to join with the croatoans, co-exist with them."

Maria shook her head with a look of disbelief. At least one of them was finally getting it. Ben, however, had remained impassive, listening, taking in as much as he could.

"I refused to be a part of that. Some of our group went with him while a few others stayed with me."

"What happened to them?" Ethan said.

"Most of them died," Charlie replied. "A few survived but left the group to seek shelter elsewhere. Many people headed for their hometowns, wanting to be someplace familiar. There's pockets of people all over the place, but over the years, most have come to distrust each other. You saw an example of that back in Ridgway."

"So they're doing all this just for the root?" Ethan said.

"No, not just the root. They also benefit from human resources. We're cattle to them, remember? We're beasts of burden, a food source, even amusement. I don't know what's special about our planet, but they've always known, for thousands of years, that it would come to this. I suppose this is more their home than it is ours."

"But we can't just give it up to them," Maria said.

Charlie smiled, liking this woman more and more. "Exactly. We won't. Not without a fight. Co-existing is not an option. They know it; we know it. They just think they've already won."

Pip gave a little bark as she dashed over and sat by Maria. The woman stroked the dog as it panted excitedly. Denver followed behind with an Army backpack. He placed it at Ben's feet.

"Okay, Ben," Denver said, "I've packed everything you need for a few days' journey, though it'll only take you a day to get to the farm, but I packed extra just in case there's any problems and it takes a little longer. There's also one of the alien pistols in case you need to defend yourself."

Ben's face lost its ruddy complexion and became pale as the reality seemed to set in. But he nodded his thanks. Standing up, he hauled the pack on this back.

"You sure you want to do this?" Ethan said.

"I'm sure," Ben said. "Charlie's tale is even more convincing. That they think they've already won means this is an opportunity I must take if I'm to play a role in our fight. I can't stay out there, but from within, I can hopefully do my duty."

"We'll take you south around Ridgway," Charlie said, "to avoid any confrontation there. From the edge of the forest, it's about half a day's walk. Den, did you pack him the map and compass?"

"Yeah, it's in the pack side pocket. Do you know how to use a compass?" Denver asked Ben. The other nodded.

"We were trained in basic navigation, and we had them installed on the harvester. We thought we were … Well, it doesn't matter now. I should go now before I run out of time."

Ethan and Maria took their turns in saying their good-byes. Charlie was expecting a more emotional affair, but both of them were quite stoic and practical and weren't as upset as he imagined them to be. Adapting already. He liked that. Gave him hope that they would become good allies and assets. Ben still gave him doubts, but the information he gave him about the shelter was a good test.

If Gregor's people or the croatoans went there instead of coming back here, he would know Ben had stuck to the plan. Regardless, Charlie was prepared for either eventuality.

It took an hour to cut south around Ridgway. They came to the edge of the forest, through which they could make out the rising smoke of a distant burner. The farm.

"This is it, Ben. Be confident; stick with the plan, and you'll be fine," Denver said.

Ben stepped into the forest before looking back. "I'll miss all of you. Hopefully, it won't be long before we'll meet again. And thanks, Charlie, Denver, for everything. I may not have shown my gratitude, but I can see now that setting us free from that lie was the right thing to do."

He waved as he turned and disappeared into the forest.

"I can't believe he's actually gone," Ethan said.

Maria stared ahead, quiet.

Charlie gave them a few minutes of respect and reflection before putting his hands on their shoulders. "We should go; we've got a plan to enact."

"Where exactly are we going?" Maria said. "I get that you didn't want to say in front of Ben, but if we're to come with you, I'd like to know where it is we are going and why."

"We're going to Manhattan," Charlie said. "As for why … This is the start of the fight back. Today marks the day we bring a war to the croatoans."

Chapter Nineteen

A low-level mist hung around the damp forest floor outside camp. Gregor flinched after dew dripped from the canopy above and splashed against the back of his neck. He peered down, searching the shrouded ground for one of his first rabbit traps placed along a prominent run two weeks ago. Nothing.

He hoped for a sunny day and a rabbit in a noose. Anything but to eat a silver tray of slop. Supplies were running out. A few cans of out-of-date Spam, some cake mix, and Layla's revolting vegetables. It was time for a trip to an urban area, a town, or a city where survivors could be robbed.

Footsteps thudded across the wet ground in close proximity. Gregor darted behind a tree, crouched on one knee, and peered around the trunk toward camp. Layla stumbled through a clearing with her hands on her head, and went around the back of his house to her trailer, slamming the door shut after entering. She'd have some explaining to do later.

Too many people seemed to be acting unilaterally nowadays. Igor would be the first to answer questions today.

As he approached his office, a croatoan fighter shot through the distant sky, blazing a light pink vapor trail. From this distance, it looked like the outline of a cruising swallow. The hunter was searching the immediate area for a sighting of Jackson, his bastard, and the traitors from the harvester.

Marek groaned, turning on the couch as Gregor entered his office.

"What time is it?" Marek said.

"Early in the morning. Get washed; we've got work to do."

Marek stood in his filthy white vest and jeans, pulled his fingers along his mousy beard, and stretched his back. "What's the plan?"

"We're going to hitch a ride with the croatoans. Two were killed in a booby trap yesterday in a former town nearby. Let's see if we can find any evidence or survivors, information to crush the little wasp."

"I thought they were sending a hunter to deal with Jackson?"

Gregor snorted. "We'll get him first. This time, I'm serious."

"You've said that a hundred—" Marked paused after Gregor raised his hand. "And Igor?"

"He's coming with us," Gregor said. He smiled, picked up one of Layla's cucumbers off his desk, and snapped it in two. "After we rob any survivors, he's going to talk."

He threw both pieces at Marek, who took a bite, chewed, and spat vegetable sludge onto the floor. "Is this her latest crop? It's worse than the last."

"Which is why we're going out. Just like the good old days, brother."

Marek nodded, yawned, and headed for the bathroom.

Gregor thought back to them both as young men in Armenia, terrorizing local villages. The villagers, young and old, had no reason to pay protection money, but they wanted to stay on the right side of the gang. Fresh food and the best wine was the price for being left alone. Gregor prided himself on providing the best for his team as a reward for their work. It was becoming harder during the last few years. The croatoans were the main gang. He had to live off the dwindling scraps of humanity.

Marek called from the bathroom, “Who’s going to feed the livestock this morning?”

“Take Igor after we get back. If he comes back.”

The *big* operation Gregor took control of was starting to feel smaller. Too many other things were starting to happen locally, things he didn’t know about. It was time to get a grip of the situation. He was doing the right thing. Jackson was the troublemaker and the one putting the remnants of the species at risk.

Marek returned to the office. “Okay, I’m ready.”

“I’m going to wake up Igor. You grab three of the croatoan attachments and make sure they prepare their hoverbikes.” Gregor handed Marek a small, folded map and pointed toward Ridgway. “We’re going here, but not so close that the sound of the bikes puts any inhabitants on alert.”

“Okay, I’ll have them ready in five minutes.”

“They might be a little pissed. Ten of them were killed yesterday.”

***

Igor had taken a large wooden shed as his place of residence. The whole thing looked on the verge of collapse. Its moldy pine timbers rotted, and the roof wrap was torn and curled away from the structure on both sides.

Gregor carefully trod across the wet grass to its filthy, cobwebbed window and glanced around the edge of it. Igor lay on a mattress, half under a duvet, snoring. Gregor pulled out his gun and moved to the front entrance.

It creaked as he slowly opened it. Igor flinched in bed, rolled to one side, and carried on snoring. Gregor dropped to his knees and placed the barrel of his gun into the two-faced Russian's mouth.

Igor's upper teeth clanked against it. He opened his eyes, blinked, jerked backwards, stared up at Gregor, and held his hands to one side.

"What are you doing?" he said.

Gregor smiled. "Come on. We're going scavenging."

He placed the pistol back in his hip holster and looked around the shed. Faded pictures of topless women had been pinned around the walls. A bottle of vodka sat on a workbench next to Igor's revolver. His clothes were folded in a scruffy ball by the end of the mattress. Nothing in view smelt of Augustus.

"Why do you need me? I'm on feeding duty in an hour," Igor said.

"You'll be back in time; don't worry. We're going to a town where two croatoans were killed yesterday. It's too dangerous for just Marek and me to go. We need someone else."

Igor grabbed his sweater and shook it before placing it over his head. "Marek's free? Why not take Alex?"

"Questions, questions. We need some short-term supplies until we get near a big city again. Are you coming or not?"

"Do I have an option?" Igor said while pulling on his

jeans. He slipped on his boots and glanced up at Gregor with his sneaky eyes.

"I'll throw this one back. Do I have to ask you or tell you?"

He let Igor take the lead past the chocolate factory. The small-time Muscovite was handy with a gun; Gregor had witnessed it early in the ice age when they came together. It took Igor five seconds to kill four armed survivors in a barn during the early battle for the remaining territory and resources around Vladikavkaz. Gregor's gang were forced north and regrouped in the southern Russian city. Igor was pushed south; that's where they'd met.

Gregor guessed he was a petty jewel thief or a lone wolf for hire in his previous life. The more the years went by, the more his claims of running a Moscow operation became exaggerated. Fat lot of good his bullshit did him in their situation. It's not like the croatoans would give a flying fuck.

To his left, he noticed an anti-gravity platform being pushed from the paddocks with three humans slumped on top of it. Their orange skin looked like they were coated in fake tan like the ladies who used to hang around his hide-out in Yerevan.

Igor turned. "What the hell is going on over there?"

"No idea. I've got Layla on the case. Speaking to her when we get back."

Gregor liked to delegate and deal with things in bite-sized chunks. Supplies and Igor were his immediate focus. Delegation brought a sense of responsibility and loyalty; people felt involved. That was something else the Russian could have learned instead of obsessively grooming his ridiculous moustache.

Marek waved across from the hover-bikes and walked across to meet Gregor. The square was a hive of activity. Three croatoan riders were in position. The engines were already quietly humming. Clusters of aliens milled around the entrances of every building. The whole place crackled with croatoan speak.

"They seem in high spirits this morning," Marek said. "Is it National Croatoan Day or something?"

"What's up with them?" Igor said.

"Who cares? If they're happy, I'm happy," Gregor said. "Do they know where we're going?"

"Yep, all set," Marek said.

Gregor swung his leg over the closest hover-bike, gripped the side handle with one hand, and tapped the rider on the shoulder.

The bike rose above the height of the buildings and thrust forward.

It tore over the paddocks at a low level. Gregor looked behind to see the other two bikes following in line. Below, a strange, transparent object sat by the gates, a couple of surveyors around it.

As they reached the far end of the paddock, humans scattered away in all directions from the flight path, running for the shelter or bushes that had sprung up since the area had been cleared. It was one of those moments where the feeling of power was magnified.

In the distance, an orange haze covered the vast farmland. A feeling of pride swelled up in Gregor. He hadn't been up on a bike in months to get a high level view; there'd been too much to sort out on the ground level. The scale of the project came back to him.

He gripped the other supporting handle as speed

increased. They roared over the forest for five minutes before the bike gradually reduced to a slow cruise as the alien's tracking tablet reached the coordinates that Marek had supplied. The engine softly purred as they slowly approached a rocky area below. The rider brought the bike around above it and hovered, waiting for the other two bikes to arrive.

Igor waved as he arrived. Gregor nodded.

All three bikes lowered simultaneously. Gregor's came to rest at a slight angle. He hopped off. "I'll be back in thirty minutes."

The alien didn't acknowledge him. It sat silently, looking straight forward.

Marek pulled a map from inside his jacket. "It's a five-minute walk from here. Follow me."

Gregor checked his gun and held it up. He followed Marek and Igor into the forest, occasionally pointing his gun at the back of Igor's head and pulling away. The wet night chill had already left the woodland, and humidity was building. Gregor wiped a thin layer of sweat from his forehead with his sleeve.

Sporadic rays of sun seeped through gaps in the trees, highlighting thousands of midges, busily hovering in clusters. Gregor felt an itch and slapped his neck. Igor spun around and faced him.

"Paranoid about something?" Gregor said.

Igor frowned. "Anything could happen out here. I'm staying alert."

Leading the way, Marek crunched along the forest floor. He crouched by a fallen, rotting tree and checked his laminated map.

"Are we here?" Gregor said.

Marek pointed his gun over the dark brown, lice-infested trunk. "It's just over there; we're two-hundred yards away."

Two people moved in the distant clearing. Gregor gripped Igor's shoulder. "Get down."

They observed the area for five minutes, creeping closer from tree to tree until the three were fifty yards away. Two people stood on a former street, heating a large metal pot on a fire.

Rubble was spread around the road, probably from yesterday's explosion. Not that it mattered. The place was slowly dying. The fifth harvester, once repaired, would put it out of its misery. Gregor remembered watching in awe when he first saw one plow through a small town. Chewing up buildings, gouging out foundations, and spitting them behind in minute pieces mixed with surrounding soils.

"We'll take them head on. Don't do anything unless I say," Gregor said.

Igor spun the wheel of his revolver and clicked it back in place. Marek held his gun in both hands.

Gregor moved from behind the tree and quickly broke from the forest. A man and woman turned, wide-eyed. She dropped a ladle. He attempted to say something, then turned to run.

"Stop right there," Gregor shouted. "We mean you no harm."

Both put their hands up. The man shuffled round to face him, his bottom lip quivering on his dirt-smeared face. They were in filthy clothes stained with years of grime. If Augustus had a problem with Gregor's sweater, he couldn't have met many of the population. These two were throwbacks from a bygone era, peasant-looking types he'd only seen on period dramas before the shit hit the fan.

Marek moved around the right-hand side, covering the flank. "Are there any others we need to know about?"

"It's only us. Please, we've got nothing," the woman said.

Igor moved ahead of Gregor, looked into the pot, and pointed down. "Nothing, you say? What's bubbling away here?"

Gregor clenched his teeth and felt his left eye twitch. He bit his lip to keep the appearance of a team.

"It's just a simple stew. You can have some," the woman said.

"Mallard and root. We call it *duck a l'orange*," the man said. He nervously laughed, abruptly stopping when it was clear that Gregor didn't find it remotely amusing.

"Give us your supplies, and we'll go," Gregor said. "You have time to loot some more. I don't."

Igor wrapped his sweater around his hand and grabbed a handle on the side of the pot. "We'll start by taking this."

"No," the woman said. She reached for the other handle. The pot flipped over, and the contents splashed over Igor's ankles and feet. He jumped back and yelped.

Gregor tried to stifle his laugh. The woman edged backwards.

Igor thrust out his revolver and fired twice into her chest. She collapsed backwards, her right hand flopping onto her chest over the wounds.

The man held out his arms and momentarily froze before kneeling by her side. He clutched her left hand and shook it. "Ellie … Ellie …"

The shots echoed in the distance. Igor picked up a piece of boiled duck by his feet and tossed it into his mouth. Gregor glanced at Marek and nodded.

The man looked up with tears in his eyes. "What have you done? What have you done? This is all we have. You've … you've killed her."

Igor stepped forward and fired again. The blood sprayed from the back of the man's head as the round exited. Igor turned to Gregor. "Whiney pieces of—"

Gregor aimed his weapon at Igor's face. "Drop it, now."

Marek quickly moved to Igor's side and took aim. "He said drop it."

The revolver twitched in Igor's hand. He ducked slightly before holding his left palm toward Gregor, crouching, and placing his revolver on the ground. "Steady, old friend. They meant nothing to us."

Gregor wanted to shoot him. But the years they'd spent together since the invasion had a freezing effect on his trigger finger. "I said don't do anything unless I said so."

"She was just a hag," Igor shrugged. He spat out a piece of duck. "The food tasted like shit anyway."

"We'll never know if they had supplies," Marek said. "We can't search this whole town. You've made this a wasted trip."

"And you've fucked our chances of getting info on Jackson. You're an idiot," Gregor said.

Igor smoothed his moustache with his thumb and forefinger. He stared at Gregor with his piercing, light blue eyes. "What's this really about? She was just a hag, an old witch with a cauldron."

"What's going on between you and Augustus?" Gregor said.

"Me and Augustus?" Igor said. He shrugged and pursed his lips.

"I heard you talking to him while I was in the garage,"

Marek said.

Igor's eyes half closed as he shot a glance at Marek. "He's the one you shouldn't trust. I wasn't captured by the little wasp."

"Forget about Marek. I'm the one asking the questions. What were you and Augustus talking about? Don't even bother denying it," Gregor said.

"He asked me how things were going. I told him we're in good shape. What am I supposed to do? Ignore the skinny old bastard?"

"Is that all he said?"

He held his hands toward Gregor as if they were in invisible cuffs. "Would I lie to you, old friend? The things we've been through to get here. Seriously?"

Gregor grunted. "If I didn't need you, Igor … Lead the way back to the bikes. I'll take your revolver."

"Have it your way," he said and started walking away.

Marek picked up his revolver and handed it to Gregor. He whispered, "Are you just going to let him go? He's up to something. I know it."

"We need him for the moment with the new targets. I can't afford to be a man down on the farm."

"You're the boss. But don't say I didn't warn you," Marek said.

Gregor smiled and patted his shoulder. "Trust me; he won't live to see next winter. Until then, he can work with the livestock and meat-processing."

Igor turned and waited by forest edge. Gregor longed for the good old days when things were less complicated.

Chapter Twenty

Ben cursed the others and then the aliens and then the whole damned world. A twig snapped against his face as he passed through the dense forest. He pressed his fingers against his cheek and felt the dampness of a stinging cut.

Every sound had him on edge. He held the alien pistol in front of him, aiming at any movement or hint of shadow. The compass kept him on track, and occasionally, he'd come to old trails, buildings, and even some automobiles.

There were a number of them, rusted hulks, their windows and doors sans glass and consumed by weeds and vines and other creeping, green foliage. One thing that struck him was just how quiet it was walking out here on his own. Very few birds or other animals. Certainly, nothing that screeched like the animal that had kept him awake all night.

Tiredness mired his progress and weighed down his legs. The pistol felt heavy in his arms, and the backpack filled with supplies was like an anchor, its hard edge wearing a sore groove into his lower back.

Fuck this, he thought, slumping down on a log. Hefting the pack off, he rubbed his back and looked out ahead of him. There was a clearing maybe only thirty feet away. A few streams of golden light cut through the green gloom, highlighting the dust particles and small, buzzing insects as they looked for their next meal.

Splitting the light every few minutes, the solid shadows of the shuttles descended from the mother ship, whose shadow bled through the dark clouds above. He realized he wasn't very far off at that point. The weird, pink lights of the shuttles bathed the tops of the trees and then disappeared beyond the cover.

The sound of a voice came to him then. Different accent to the others. Harsher. Foreign for this land. Not wanting to be caught flat-footed and in the open, Ben slipped behind the trunk, pulling the pack with him.

The voices died off, but he could still hear the snapping of twigs getting louder, closer. Perhaps a single person given the regularity of the noise. The trunk made a good rest for the pistol. Ben braced his shoulder against the tree as he looked down the grooved channel that made up the sights.

Dull black, heavy, but accurate and deadly, Ben remembered how lethal the pistol was in Denver's hands. There's no way Ben's aim would be that good, but he knew if this threat came close enough, he'd have more than a good chance of hitting it.

His pulse quickened; his breath became shallow.

Twigs continued to snap, getting closer to the edge of the clearing that Ben focused on through a pair of tree trunks. He could see right across the clearing to where the tree line started again.

A figure stepped out.

Ben, although expecting it, still found it startling in his heightened state and pulled the trigger too quickly, sending his shot firing high above the figure's head. The person ducked and rolled. At the end of the roll, the person rose to a knee and held out a gun, sighting across the tree line, tracing where the shot had come from.

What is he doing? Ben thought as the figure seemed to sniff the air and then smile before rising to his feet.

"It's just me, Igor. That you out there, our little croatoan friends? Firing on your allies now? I'm not sure Augustus would be so happy with that."

The man spun around, his weapon by his side. "Come on then, show yourself. I'll get you back to the farm."

The farm! Igor … Ben pulled his pistol away and took his finger off the trigger. He remembered Denver and Charlie talking about an Igor, along with a Marek, Alex, and of course Gregor. All the people who worked on the farm.

Grabbing his pack, Ben vaulted the trunk and ran out to the tree line, making sure he kept the pistol in hand but pointing down to the ground. He didn't want to accidentally threaten Igor and get shot himself for the effort.

Excitement and relief built within him as he rushed forward into the clearing, holding his free hand up. "Igor? Please, can you help me?" He didn't really know how else to start.

Igor, with his shaved head, droopy moustache, and deep scowl, aimed his pistol with both arms out in front of him. "Stop where you are and drop that damned weapon," he said. "Who the fuck are you? And more importantly, what the hell are you doing shooting at me?"

Making a wet thudding noise, the alien pistol struck the loamy soil as Ben did as he was told. He held both arms up, having seen people do it in Western films. "I'm Ben. I'm from the ship … vI mean harvester. I escaped from Charlie. I was trying to find my way back."

"Oh really?" Igor said, cocking his head to one side. He

looked over Ben, watching the edge of the forest, probably suspecting some kind of trap. "And is he chasing you?"

Ben shook his head. "No, I slipped away in the night. No one knows I'm here. He killed the rest of my crew shortly after he damaged the harvester. Please, you've got to help me. I can't stay out here."

"Why'd you fire on me?" Igor asked, stalking closer, his pistol solid and unwavering, the barrel pointing right at Ben's head.

"I was just scared. I thought Charlie and his psycho son were stalking me. I panicked. I'm not used to it out here. I've only ever known my ship, my cabin, but all that's gone now, and my crew ..." Ben dropped his head to really sell the ruse. Although not exactly experienced in body language, he gathered this Igor wasn't the prize wrench in the toolbox.

"Stand up," Igor said, "and turn around."

For a moment, Ben hesitated, thinking he was going to be executed. But Igor's bark made him jump and follow the orders. Then the man's hands were on his arms, pulling them behind his back. Something plastic locked his wrists in place. Igor's breath was on his neck as he threatened him.

"You're coming back to the farm with me, Ben, but if you so much as move or breathe out of place, I'll put you down like a pig and feed you to the cattle. You understand?"

Ben nodded furiously, wondering what the hell he had got himself into, and if Denver and Charlie had set him up and all the nonsense about the plan was just a way of getting rid of him, to get him killed by these other people.

Not that he could do anything about it now. He thought

of showing Igor the bead that he kept in his shirt pocket beneath his zipped jacket but didn't want to waste his best gambit. He decided to wait until he met this Gregor character.

Still, while Igor placed the alien pistol into the pack and hauled the latter onto his back, Ben said, "I've got information about Charlie and Denver. I know things; I can trade."

Igor kicked him in the lower back, forcing him toward the edge of the clearing. They were moving back from where Igor had come. "I don't doubt that, son, but you're mistaking me for someone more generous if you think I'm going to trade anything with you. I'll get that information in my own special way; don't you worry about that. Now get moving, and don't make as much as a squeak unless I tell you; otherwise, I'll put a bullet in your head. Is that clear enough for you?"

Ben was about to speak but chose not to. Instead, he nodded.

"Good, little pig. Good."

***

Ben stifled a scream as the gaffer tape, as Igor called it, was ripped suddenly away from his mouth, the adhesive tearing away small patches of skin on his lips and cheeks. His eyes filled with tears. Igor placed his clammy hand over Ben's face. Leaning in, he whispered, "Make a noise, little pig, and you'll join those."

The former gangster pointed to a rack of meat hooks upon which hung half a dozen men and women, their hands and feet pointing downwards, their chins resting on their chests, the hook embedded deep into their backs.

Below them, flowing in a channel to somewhere further off in the slaughterhouse, was a tiny river of blood. It dripped from a series of cuts among the people's bodies, now stained dark brown with dried blood, forming external arteries like dried rivers.

The smell made Ben gag: a heady mix of coppery blood and lung-scorching bleach. Every breath brought with it a stinging sensation, making his guts turn. He fought to keep the bile down as it rose into his throat.

Igor backed away. Beneath the bright white glare of the overhead strip-light, a piece of dark leather material wrapped around Igor's waist, presumably for protection, shone glossily. Red stains covered the white, ankle-length jacket he wore beneath.

Trying to move, Ben realized his wrists and ankles were shackled to the legs of a steel chair bolted to the floor. A steel desk stood in front of him. Pieces of meat that were once limbs filled a series of containers.

A yellow glow surrounded the edge of a door beyond the hanging bodies.

"No-no," Igor said, standing in front of him, blocking his view. "There's no way out unless I say there is. Now, let's get this party started, shall we? I'm on a schedule."

Before Ben could say anything, Igor placed his left hand over Ben's mouth, and with his right brought out a small blade from a front pocket. The blade glinted beneath the strip-light as Igor brought it close to Ben's face. His eyes hurt as they tried to focus close up, but the image just blurred as he screamed and thrashed against the chair.

Aggravating the wound on his face caused by a twig, Igor's blade dug deeper into the flesh, widening the wound. The blade scraped across his cheekbone, making him yell out, but Igor's hand was too tightly clasped over his mouth for it to escape the slaughterhouse and raise an alarm.

Ben sobbed with the agony as Igor cut him three times more on the cheek and once across his forehead. The blood dripped down into his eyes, making him blink as the world became dark and blurred.

"Now we've got the introduction out of the way," Igor said, "I trust you'll do as I suggest. Nod if you understand me."

Of course Ben nodded, unable to do anything else as his face felt alive with pain, burning and unyielding.

Through his darkened vision, he saw Igor's face come closer. He wore a sick smile. Ben realized then that he'd done this kind of work many times before. Just what the hell had Denver and Charlie got him into?

"First of all, tell me everything. If you lie, I will know, and I will continue to cut you. No one knows you're here. I have the only key to this facility. We could be here for days if need be. I'm sure you understand that the truth is the only way out of this for you now?"

"Anything," Ben said, spitting the blood from his lips. "I'll tell you anything."

"That's good, Ben, you're learning. I like that. Okay, let's start from the beginning. If you leave anything out, or if you lie, I will start with your eyes and work my way down to your testicles. Trust me, there's no easy to way to do this. It will hurt. A great deal. And what really gets people is that they sometimes think I'm bluffing. They don't think that for very long."

With the threat of the blade just inches from his face, Ben answered every question Igor gave him. On it went for what seemed like hours until finally, his voice hoarse and his will truly shattered, Igor left for a smoke.

He returned two minutes later with a small, silver tray containing a needle and thread and a clear bottle of orange liquid.

"You did well, Ben," Igor said, setting the tray on the table. "Let's get you fixed up, and then we'll introduce you to Gregor. You will remember what to say when he questions you, won't you? I won't have to visit you in the night and continue where I left off, will I?"

"No," Ben said firmly. The pain had started to dissipate. The first injection of root compound acted quickly. Any desire to sob and beg had long gone. His will had been broken; his fear had run out. All he felt now was a savage desire to end Igor's life and that of anyone else who would use him.

Throughout the hours of pain and threats, Ben came to realize the futility of it all. Life to these people meant nothing. It was bad enough what the croatoans were doing to the people, but so far, he'd learned that humans were far worse to their own kind.

He eyeballed Igor as the torturer wiped Ben's face clean and stitched the wounds. Just a few hours ago, those skilled fingers had brought pain, but now, they sutured his wounds with delicate skill.

That Igor wanted Ben to lie to Gregor told him more than he had told Igor. Despite the pain, he hadn't given up his friends. For all Igor would ever know, Maria and Ethan were dead, and Charlie and Denver had disappeared into the forest, leaving him behind. Ben would continue with the plan, give Gregor the bead and the location of the decoy shelter, and make sure he dealt with Igor before the bastard had a chance to act on his threat.

There was a clear division on the farm between Igor and Gregor. Ben thought about it as Igor continued treating his wounds. It seemed that Igor wasn't happy with his status and planned some kind of coup against Gregor.

This gave Ben something to work with. An angle he could exploit. Although Igor was highly skilled in pain, he wasn't very smart when it came to language and intent. His motivations became obvious during the interrogation. He hadn't even realized he had shown his hand early.

Even on the ship, Ben was the best poker player, figuring out the other crew members' plays before they did themselves.

"There," Igor said, "that's the last of them. You'll tell Gregor that Charlie did these. You will tell him about a decoy shelter to get him out of the way and play along, and tomorrow, I'll go visit the real one. Have Gregor take you at dawn. And if the weapons you promised aren't there … Well," Igor turned and indicated with a sweeping gesture his future fate among the meat hooks.

"Don't worry," Ben said. "I understand clearly. You will get everything you deserve. Now, shall we go see Gregor? I'm eager to get this over with."

"Good little pig," Igor said, smiling, showing his yellow, decaying teeth.

Yes, Ben thought, you will get everything you deserve.

Chapter Twenty-One

Charlie pulled back the camouflaged tarp, revealing a rusted Ford F-150. The once-red paintwork had given way to a colonization of orange rust. Among the conquering march of time and decay, small islands of defiant paint remained.

Leaves and twigs covered the hood, clinging to the surface.

Charlie swept them off and cleared the debris from the cracked windshield.

The noon sun streaked through the surrounding trees and gleamed off the glass, the cracks refracting a rainbow of light in thin slivers.

A solid metal lockbox took up a quarter of the rear bed. It contained a few days' supplies, water, ammo, a pair of shotguns, and an old Army tent.

Pip jumped up into the extended cab as soon as Denver opened the passenger door, curling up on an old grey blanket between the two front seats.

Ethan stood by the river's edge with his mouth open as he stared on. They'd hidden the truck in a tight copse of trees and shrubs the week before as they scouted the harvester's route.

Charlie waved him and Maria forward from their temporary camp.

"Does it run?" Ethan said, running his hand along

the fender as though it were an ancient relic. To Ethan, it probably is, Charlie thought. He'd have only seen them on whatever brainwashing videos the aliens had given to them to watch.

"Yeah," Charlie said. "Of course it runs."

"How did you keep it working all through the invasion and the ice age?" Maria asked as she joined them.

"My old Army friend was a mechanical genius," Charlie said. "Between him and a colleague of mine, we sourced spare parts and kept it running. With so many people dead and so many vehicles abandoned, it's not difficult to source fuel and parts. Back in New York, there's a number of Ford dealers and warehouses that we got replacement parts from."

"So where are we going?" Maria said as Denver loaded up more supplies and the weapons taken from the croat-oans.

"Going to take a trip to the East Coast. The Big Apple. Come on, get in; we need to set off if we're to get there in good time. It's going to be a long journey. The roads aren't exactly easy these days," Charlie said. He held the rear passenger door open and waited for Ethan and Maria to settle in.

Denver jumped into the front passenger seat.

Once inside, Charlie turned the key, and after a few splutters, the old diesel power plant roared to life, belching out a little black smoke before purring like a wild cat. He put it into drive and slowly pulled away from the hiding place, keeping the wheels on the harder parts of the forest floor.

From their shelter in Mohan Run, a small clearing within the forest, Charlie drove the truck out through the trees, only once scraping against a branch, and joined the hard surface of Interstate 219. The plan was to head south to I-80, which would take them all the way into New York.

Fragments of blacktop had long peeled off the road. Multiple croatoan-engineered environmental changes, especially the ice, had conspired to ruin the surface. But as long as he stayed vigilant, they could make good time.

"I would have expected more cars and trucks," Ethan said, leaning forward from the rear.

"That's the kind of thing you see in the films," Denver said.

"He's right," Charlie added, steering around a ten-foot-wide pothole and accelerating onto a clear patch. "When the invasion happened, it took many by surprise, but the war waged for a number of years. Plenty of time for people to get off the roads and go somewhere safe. You'll see most of the cars still parked near people's homes or service stations and car lots. The roads were deserted during the war to allow military traffic to get into position without worrying about the public."

"Where are all the bodies?" Ethan asked. "I'd have expected to see more."

Charlie looked at the young man through the rearview mirror. He didn't really know what he was asking. The idea that billions of people were butchered had to be entirely alien to him. There just wasn't a way for someone like him, so detached from his own species, to fully comprehend what had happened.

But he'd soon get the idea.

"Most were buried," Charlie eventually said as he found a clear patch of road. Even without the blacktop in place, the hard concrete provided a brief section of smooth ride.

"Despite the situation, many families, neighborhoods, and government organizations did their best to give everyone a proper burial, but sometimes, that wasn't always possible."

"So what happened then?"

Charlie wanted to tell Ethan to drop it, to focus on survival rather than the dead, but as painful as it was to bring back those memories, it could just be what he and Maria needed to bring some perspective.

"I'll show you," Charlie said. "For now, try and get some rest. We'll be travelling for at least nine, maybe ten hours. If we're lucky."

He thought about the croatoans. They wouldn't be happy with the previous day's losses. That was as many of the aliens as Charlie and Denver had killed since the war. Up until now, he and Denver were probably just a minor thorn in their sides, but now ... If he were on the other side, he wouldn't take those losses without some form of vengeance.

Charlie stared out of the windshield and thought that it didn't look too bad. The trees, bushes, and vines that had built up beside the road and some that had sent roots through the concrete and gravel broke it up into large fragments. It looked quite beautiful.

But the cost of attaining this natural beauty wasn't worth the blood in the soil.

At one point, the branches that stretched across the road were so thick, they had to get out and chop their way through with machetes and blades Charlie had fashioned from the alien metal. An hour later and they were back on the road, finding clearer spots, making good ground.

When they approached towns or cities, Charlie always took the outer route, preferring to avoid going into the center where there were likely to be pockets of survivors. At one point, a distant sniper fired upon them, a warning shot, hissing over the hood.

"I don't understand why they would fire on us," Ethan said. "Surely with so few of us left, they'd leave us be."

"They're just frightened," Denver said. "Not many with working vehicles. Probably think we're scouting for the farms."

Charlie noted the change in Ethan's thinking by the use of *us*. Good, he thought. The kid is starting to think the right way. If his plans to take down the croatoans were to work, he'd need people like Ethan and Maria to see that humanity was not at war with each other for resources or survival. They had to be united in their struggles.

***

A further four hours passed without incident; they'd crossed into New Jersey and were only a few hours from their destination of Newark. Charlie drove the truck up a hill; the road had crumbled away to dirt and gravel, but the F-150's 4-wheel drive dug in deep and pulled them up to the summit. Putting it into park and engaging the emergency brake, Charlie got out, leaving the engine running.

He opened the door and gestured for Ethan and Maria to get out. They looked at him suspiciously. "I just want to show you two something," Charlie said, turning his back and approaching the edge of the hill.

Ethan and Maria joined him, and both took a sharp intake of breath.

Down in the green valley beyond, a two-hundred-foot-wide sinkhole scarred the earth like a huge wound. Around its crumbling edge, houses and other buildings were left in ruin. Half of their walls had collapsed long ago, their open sides providing shelter for shade-loving plants or trees.

But it wasn't the ruined homes that caused the surprise; neither was it the huge CAT diggers rusting away on the perimeter. It was what was in the sinkhole that caused the reaction.

The very thing Ethan had expected to see.

Bodies.

Or more accurately—skeletons.

"When things got really bad, after the gas and the initial attack, it became impossible for the authorities, what were left, to handle so many bodies," Charlie said. "Hospitals were overrun. Funeral homes and cemeteries were full to bursting. Families, those that survived the initial stage, buried their dead in their gardens or in makeshift graves in the woods or other common areas.

"But when the numbers got too huge, the remaining militia, in an effort to prevent the spread of disease, used the same sinkholes the croatoans created to come to the surface to bury the dead.

"All over the country, you'll find huge ones like this with thousands and thousands of bodies in them."

Charlie stared away into the distance. The evening sun silhouetted a dozen birds as they glided above the sinkhole. But there was no meat on the bones anymore. They were picked clean by scavengers and the elements years ago.

"That's terrible," Maria said, her voice barely a whisper. Ethan remained silent, taking in the scene, realizing what he was looking at.

Charlie didn't want to have to show them this, but he needed them to understand what was at stake, what had happened to humanity. They had no sense of the numbers or what life was like before. But this would help bring the necessary perspective.

They all got back into the truck, silent, haunted by what they had seen. Charlie didn't say anything, just let it sink in, let the enormity of what happened finally get through to them.

He turned around on the summit and headed back down the hill, rejoining I-80 and moving toward Newark Bridge. He gunned the engine, taking advantage of a rare section of clear road. He wanted to get to the bridge before sun up. They'd have to complete the rest of the journey throughout the night, swapping driving duties.

Over the sound of the engine, he heard a throaty roar streak by them overhead. An icy chill crept up his spine. The last time he'd heard a sound like that was when the croatoan fighter craft first descended upon the earth.

Chapter Twenty-Two

Layla huddled under her duvet with a flashlight, poring through personal notes from the last few years. She needed irrefutable evidence before going to Gregor with her findings. Something to join up the dots.

She cursed under her breath as she read her last two diaries. Self-indulgent, whiny, and lacking solid information. With the benefit of hindsight and clear focus, it felt like she was reading extracts from her college days. The Layla that thought the world was against her, living like a hermit in her student apartment, studying the very thing she purposely avoided.

Her notebooks weren't much better. A lot of hurried scrawls about the livestock condition, available food, and observed human-human and human-croatoan interactions. Clouds surrounded the notes filled with written ideas about how to improve things. Nothing about the noticeable rise in humidity, increasingly amber skies, or the greasy film that was starting to coat the region's foliage. She kicked herself for not paying attention to the bigger picture.

Layla checked her watch. Three in the morning. The only thing for it was a clandestine trip to the chocolate factory. She slid open a window next to her bed and listened.

Distant clanking came from the meat-processing warehouses. Nothing unusual; the automated machines ran around the clock. Layla had only been inside those buildings on a single occasion. That was enough. She'd narrowly avoided throwing up.

An owl hooted.

She gently rattled open the flimsy trailer door and crept past Gregor's office. Light streamed through gaps in the blinds. She heard raised voices coming from inside. Probably talk of *the good old days* with Marek after a few drinks.

Layla glanced into the clear, navy, starred sky. The mother ship was more revealing during the hours of darkness. It must've been hundreds of miles away but still appeared large, vivid. A bright strip ran across its center.

Pouring in and out of the strip, minute specks of light headed to and from earth, shuttles on their supply runs. Hundreds of them like worker bees, probably landing at different farms around the world in other time zones.

The moon looked like a scarred apricot as it had for a while. She'd seen it that color before when on vacation in Sydney. A bushfire took hold in the Blue Mountains, smoke scattering the rays of light from Earth's natural satellite.

Layla knew the croatoans were terraforming but avoided the inconvenient truth. The requests to update land conversion and the experiment on the paddock brought it into sharper focus. Survival instincts that motivated her to work on the farm were now pushing her in the opposite direction.

Monitors faintly glowed through the frosted glass of the chocolate factory door. Vlad was probably watching them at the far end of the building. Nothing in the immediate vicinity suggested the presence of surveyors.

The square was quiet. No signs of any outdoor alien activity.

She slowly twisted the handle, slipped through the gap, and closed the door behind her. Vlad slumped over the desk in front of the bank of monitors, probably getting a snatch of sleep. It wasn't a huge issue to doze on shift. The harvester alerts sounded like the grating buzz of an old, electronic alarm clock.

Ambient light was sufficient enough for Layla not to use her flashlight. She crept around the empty surveyors' table to a walled-off area on the left-hand side.

Croatoans usually carried their equipment and charts there before leaving. The space was used by the alien with the red-rimmed helmet visor. It usually sat surrounded by three of their little computers. Layla watched the alien enter the chocolate factory two weeks ago. The devices sprang to life when the croatoan touched them. She hoped it would be that simple. Just like their tablet devices.

All three trapezium-shaped computers were folded open. Layla took a deep breath and touched a central pad with a silver outline on the first.

The screen filled with bright electric-blue background. A black square in the middle streamed unrecognizable, light green digits. Layla swished her finger across the pad. Nothing happened.

She touched the middle computer. The screen burst into life and split into four sections, each showing a different graphic. The top right was a bizarre picture of planet Earth; the bottom three-quarters of the globe were orange-tinted. It spun around, showing hundreds of black dots across the continents, probably farms. In the top left was a graph, some kind of measurement, impossible to read.

The bottom two pictures showed North America. One she recognized as the land they'd farmed colored in red. It wasn't a surprise that the croatoans were also tracking progress; she expected that. The final picture had a shaded-in area of previously untouched land to the north of their location. She guessed it covered a hundred square miles.

Layla focused on the last image and wondered if she was looking at the tipping point for the required atmospheric change. It looked too small.

She touched the last computer. It flashed awake.

The display looked like a timeline. Thirty tasks in alien language. Twenty-eight struck through. Whatever they were doing, it looked close to completion.

None of the information was as compelling as the experiment. Collectively, it all led to the same logical conclusion.

Something gripped Layla's shoulder.

She flinched. Turned.

Igor smiled, his face bathed in a blue glow from the computers. "Fancy seeing you here."

Layla put her hand to her chest and felt her rapidly drumming heart. She let out a deep breath. "Jesus. I thought you were …"

His right arm was behind his back. He never failed to look shifty and dangerous.

"Thought I was an alien?" Igor said. "What are you doing here?"

"I could ask you the same thing." She glanced to his side. "What have you got there?"

Igor stepped toward her. "Things are going to change around here. You need to make sure your colors are nailed to the right mast."

***

Gregor poured a whiskey into a shot glass, slammed it onto the table, and pushed it across to Ben. The dog from the harvester had earned it.

"Drink. It'll put hairs on your chest," Gregor said.

Ben frowned and twisted the glass. "What is it?"

"The water of life. Now drink. Do not insult me."

Ben the dog held the contents of the glass in his cheeks and swallowed with a single, exaggerated gulp. He screwed up his face, squeezed his neck, and coughed.

Marek, who stood beside Ben, roared with laughter. "Looks like he enjoyed it."

"You do realize what's going to happen if I find out you're lying?" Gregor said. He swiped a finger across his own throat.

"Why would I lie? It's been a nightmare since he attacked our harvester."

Gregor held up the necklace and gazed at the bead. "Jackson pretended to be my friend when I first arrived. It was all an act. He was gathering information for his assaults. He risks all our lives."

Marek pointed at the dog. "What are we going to do with him?"

"I'm with you guys. You can trust me," Ben said.

Gregor stared at the dog, mulling over three options. Ben quickly broke eye contact and looked down at his empty glass.

They couldn't return him to the Operations Compartment of the repaired harvester. This dog had seen the outside world. He could easily open his mouth during a moment of weakness and compromise the whole crew. The second option was to turn him into silver trays of slop. It seemed like a waste.

"I'm going to reward you," Gregor said. "Because of the information you provided, you can have a job on the farm. Be under no illusion; what I give I can take away with a bullet. Do you understand?"

It wasn't much different from the speech Gregor used to give to new recruits in Yerevan. Before anyone became fully integrated, they had to prove themselves. Ben the dog had already done this to some extent, but Gregor was wary. Jackson had shown to be a sly operator in the past. Leopards didn't change their spots.

Gregor smiled as the frightened dog nodded.

"Yes. Thank you, sir," Ben said.

Gregor winced. "Don't call me—"

Two knocks boomed against the door.

"Who the hell is that at this time?" Marek said.

Before anyone could respond, Layla flung the door open. She looked immediately at the dog.

"Strange time for a visit," Gregor said.

"I've been carrying out a little bit of the investigation work you asked me to do. Who's he?"

"Let me introduce you to Ben," Gregor said. He held up the necklace. "He's given me the location of a hideout used by the little wasp. Jackson tried to use him as his new bitch. Recognize this?"

"Is that?" Layla said.

"Jackson's necklace. Yes. I'm going in a few hours." He turned to Ben. "He'll show me the way. And you're coming with us."

"Me?"

"If you're bullshitting, I'll leave you in the forest."

Layla sat on the couch. "We've got bigger things to worry about."

"Bigger things than Charlie Jackson?" Marek said. "We've wanted that bastard for years. What could be bigger?"

"Yesterday, I watched the croatoans carrying out a test. Did you see a large transparent structure in the paddocks?"

Gregor nodded. "We passed over it. Why?"

"It was some sort of atmosphere box. They tested five different levels on humans and aliens. Let's just say we wouldn't survive in an environment where they can take their helmets off."

"It doesn't take a genius to work that out. They wouldn't wear them in the first place if they didn't need them," Marek said.

"You're missing the point," Layla said. "Look around you. The sky during dusk and dawn. Go out and look at the moon. The increase in land conversion. It's all building."

"They want more root. So what?" Gregor said.

"They're terraforming the planet. The root is how they're doing it."

"Even a fool can see they're changing the place. What are we supposed to do about it?" Gregor said.

"Why would we run away to live in a ruined city?" Marek said. "Somebody else would just step in. The croatoans needs us. We've proven that."

"I've just come back from the chocolate factory. There was information on the computers that collectively pointed to something happening very soon."

"Very soon? Collectively?" Gregor said.

"Graphics and a timeline," Layla said. "They looked close to concluding whatever they are trying to achieve. I think the experiment backs it up."

"I think you're being a little dramatic," Gregor said. "We provide them with food. Manage the farms around the world. Why would they choke us to death?"

Layla rolled her eyes. "I don't know. To live on our planet in conducive conditions?"

"No need to get sarcastic. I can't risk everyone's lives based on your theory. You might be completely wrong."

"And if I'm not?"

Ben cleared his throat.

"Do you have something to say?" Marek said.

"Charlie thinks the same," Ben said. "That's why he's been trying to stop it."

"Who gives a fuck what he thinks?" Gregor said. Ben looked back at his boots. "I can see things changing. We can all see things are changing. It's a question of to what level, the timing, and our personal survival. Layla, I'm not going through this in the middle of the night."

"We might not have time to wait," Layla said. "I told you the other day they're acting differently. It's happening soon. I know it."

Gregor twirled the necklace around on his finger. He sat back in his chair, stroking his chin. "First I deal with the hideout. Layla, try to find out more. We'll get together this evening and decide our next steps. If we act, we have to be one hundred percent sure. I'm not risking everything on a hunch."

She nodded.

"It's crazy," Marek said. "We've been doing this for ten

years. Why now?"

"We'll discuss it tonight. I need a couple of hours sleep before heading out," Gregor said.

"There's something else," Layla said. "Igor came into the chocolate factory. I think he knows what's going on. He threatened me and said things were changing."

"Don't worry about that Russian scumbag. I've got him just where I want him," Gregor said.

"Have you?" Layla said. "Or does Augustus?"

"Screw that freak," Gregor said, resisting the urge to insult Layla. He jumped from his chair and grabbed the back of Ben's neck. "I've got my eye on a different prize at the moment."

Chapter Twenty-Three

Morning broke with a rich purple stain across the sky. An hour later, the color burned away to be replaced by a thick tobacco-orange.

Denver parked the truck at the edge of the broken road, what used to be the New Jersey Turnpike, where it met the Newark Bay Bridge. The structure lay half in the bay. The thick, sludge-like water rolled slowly back and forth across the debris.

From their position, they could see across to Manhattan. The broken shards of hundreds of towers pierced the orange sky like shattered, grey teeth. They spoke of the initial devastation during the first invasion.

Charlie got out of the truck and helped the others. Ethan and Maria had slept for the entire overnight journey. Charlie got a couple of hours when Denver took over driving, but his body could have done with a few more. He needed another intake of root to really feel awake again, but now they were in the city. Root wasn't so easy to come by.

His current supply would have to last. If things went well, they'd be heading back out by noon anyway. Just a few hours here to get the device and they'd be done.

"Wow," Maria said, stretching her arms above her head as she stared out toward the city. "That's incredible. This is the old world?"

"Yeah. Used to be one of the greatest cities on Earth," Charlie replied.

"This is the place where you worked?" Ethan asked, impressing Charlie that he remembered. "Must be hard to deal with the memories of your colleagues when you come back."

Charlie shrugged. He'd lost so many over the years it was difficult to still grieve for individuals. Occasionally, he would think back to the young lad he'd tried to save in the sinkhole, Luke, and his supervisor, Steph. That fateful day would always remain with him. How he and Pippa and a single fireman were the only survivors from that day.

"Right. It's where we're headed," Charlie said to break himself from his memories and cut any more inquiry into his grief.

"How are we going to get across?" Maria asked. "It's not like we were taught to swim."

"Follow me," Charlie said.

Leading them across the deserted bridge until they came to the point in the middle of the bay where the concrete road split apart, Charlie leaned over the side and ran his hand along it until his arm was submerged up to his elbow.

It took a moment, but he found it. A rope. He pulled on it, and from within the murk of the water, he pulled up a plastic container with weights on the side. "I need some help over here," Charlie said.

Ethan and Denver grabbed the rope, and the three of them hauled up the eight-foot by four-foot plastic container and dumped it onto the concrete road.

"What is it?" Maria said.

"Transport," Charlie said. They unclipped the plastic

ties of the container, leaving the lid on the broken road. Inside was a rubber dinghy with a small outboard motor. A compressed-air tank would self-inflate it. They lifted it out and depressed a button on the canister and watched as it took form over the course of a few short minutes.

"Come on," Charlie said, "Let's get this in the water."

The dinghy hit the surface with a wet slap. Charlie sat in the back, manning the outboard. The others sat on the hull with Denver at the front, facing the mainland, his sniper rifle shouldered, scope to his eye. He scanned in slow, sweeping arcs, keeping them protected.

Progress was slow across the bay as the prop struggled to propel the boat through the thick water. They had to stop a number of times to get around dense weeds that had grown up from the bay's bed. They looked like vines, alien and entirely out of place for the water. But then that's what those bastards wanted: to turn Earth into their world.

They eventually reached the mainland and pulled the boat up into a wooded area. The weather was getting cooler. Charlie zipped his camouflaged combat jacket. He'd have to get Ethan and Maria some better clothes; their uniforms from the harvester were getting badly torn and damaged, and being blue and orange were standing out too easily for his liking.

"Where now?" Maria said as Pip pointed her nose toward the foliage-strangled city. Her head tipped up as she picked up a scent. Charlie could smell it too. Roasting meat.

Charlie held up his hand. "Okay, listen to me. The city will have pockets of survivors. Some will be friendly, others won't; don't do anything stupid. Just follow Denver's lead and mine. By the smell of it, there's a group not far from here, and the wind direction is telling me they're just beyond this copse of trees."

"So why don't we just go round and avoid them?" Ethan asked.

"Too far," Denver replied. "Most of the city was totally leveled during the war. Entire buildings and towers were toppled, roads destroyed. It won't be easy, and the longer we're out in the open, the longer we're a target for anyone who doesn't want us around or wants our supplies." Denver pointed to the three backpacks of gear, food, and water they had brought with them.

Charlie hefted one onto his back, Maria and Ethan took the other two, leaving Denver free to carry and aim his rifle. As the best shot in the group and with vision that would rival an eagle, it was better to have him free to move.

"Let's go. Lead the way, Den," Charlie said.

His son nodded once and turned his back. With two long strides, he moved into the forest, Pip dutifully staying by his side.

It was cooler inside the forest with the thick tree cover blocking out the morning sun. The smell remained though, carried on a breeze. It didn't take long for them to hear the sound of voices, thankfully human.

Although the problem with that was that it wasn't always clear what their motivations were. Just because they were human didn't mean they had the same outlook as Charlie.

All this time under the new alien paradigm had really shifted people's perception of what it meant to be human and what society should and shouldn't be. Sure, he had to be selfish at times to ensure his survival, but wherever possible, he sought ways to be inclusive.

It's why he sent Ben to the farm. There was certainly

no love lost between them and Gregor, but Charlie knew that Ben would find a way into their support and would be taken care of. There was no way he'd be able to cope on his own in this kind of environment. He needed a more clear-cut structure and someone strong to lead him.

Despite what Charlie thought of Gregor and his methods, he was certainly a strong leader and would take care of Ben at least long enough that they could get the inside info from him and free those poor bastards trapped on the farm.

Pip stopped and wagged her tail. Denver took a knee and held his hand up. The rest of the group stopped as Charlie walked slowly to kneel beside his son. "What's up, Den?"

"A group of three, about forty feet away around a fire. One's armed with a pistol. They're just eating, chatting. They seem to have set up camp. There's no obvious way around."

Denver pointed to the artificial valley caused by two collapsed buildings to either side of the camp. The large, concrete mounds with sheer sides where the towers had fallen directly down meant they had no easy way around.

Going too far around would lead into the busy area of west Manhattan, putting them far out of their way and exposing them too much. Charlie took his monocular from the webbing on his backpack and took a closer look.

He hoped to recognize some of them. Since his time going back and forward to his old office, he had come to know some of the survivors. Most of them were with him in the caverns where many had lived out the ice age, but not this group. Two of them were young, post-ice age. Charlie didn't recognize the older man.

Weighing up the odds, Charlie thought about going in with firearms and dealing with it quickly, but the two young ones, two girls, looked like they were suffering from malnutrition. The roasting meat smell came from a tiny, charred squirrel over a poorly made spit. These people weren't surviving particularly well. That catch wouldn't feed one person let alone three.

"What's going on?" Ethan said as he clumsily sat by Charlie, knocking a pan from the side of his backpack. The metal vessel struck a rock, ringing out. The three survivors moved with unexpected swiftness to the source of the sound.

The older man raised his pistol and fired twice into the trees, directly at Charlie and the others. They ducked, but the bullets were already going high and wide, striking the thick trunks of the alien redwoods.

"You damned fool," Charlie said, pushing Ethan away. Charlie shrugged the pack off his shoulders and grabbed his own firearm from the holster around his belt. "Stay down."

Another two shots whipped through the trees, striking branches and leaves. He was getting closer. Denver raised the rifle and chambered a round. The three survivors were now just a few feet away from the tree line. They'd be instantly killed from that range.

"Wait," Charlie said, this time speaking loudly so that he could address everyone, including these other three. "We're human, friends; don't shoot." He touched Denver on the shoulder and whispered, "Hold your fire, son."

"Show yourself," the older man said, still aiming his pistol into the trees.

Charlie placed his pistol back into the holster, covering it with his jacket. He could still draw it quickly if he needed, having modified the holster so nothing obstructed the gun.

Maria gave him a concerned look. Ethan looked scared but in control. This was progress. They were getting used to life out of the harvester. "Wait here," Charlie said, "and watch. Keep me covered if the shit hits the fan."

With that, Charlie tapped Denver twice on the shoulder and stepped out with his arms up. The three survivors stepped back to give him room. The older man, his face craggy and white hair tied back in a ponytail, kept the weapon trained on him. He squinted his eyes, scrutinizing Charlie. "Who are you? What do you want?" he said, a noticeable shake making his weapon judder within his grip.

"We mean you no harm," Charlie said. "We're just passing through. If you let us, we'll be gone right away. We don't want to cause you any trouble."

"Who are you?" He asked again.

"My name's Charlie Jackson; I'm like you, a survivor."

"They all say they're like us, but then they always say something." The old man looked to the young girls. Up close, Charlie could see the resemblance now; they were clearly his daughters, and he could just imagine what some of the other people would want with them. They both looked to the ground, unable to hold Charlie's eye.

"How many of you are there?" The man asked.

"Three others beside me," Charlie said. "I suggest you put that weapon down. There's no reason for anyone to get hurt, is there? Listen, you don't look well. Why don't you let us go about our business, and I'll leave you something to help."

One of the young girls looked up then, her dirty face hiding a pretty personality. Her blonde hair was matted and covered with twigs and debris. They looked as though they'd been living in the ground, which made no real sense given the number of dwellings and buildings they could choose, but then he'd known people like this before, people who would refuse to go back into the cities and preferred to stay outside with nature. There was something comforting about being around trees, animals, and bugs.

It reminded people they were still on Earth. Day by day, things were getting more and more removed from the Earth they used to know, but it was slow enough that most people didn't really notice, like a slow-growing cancer tumor.

"What's your name?" Charlie asked the man, making sure he didn't look at the girls for too long. He didn't want to give the old guy any reason to shoot.

"Jan," he said. "I used to work here before …well, before everything. They've left us to die out. They don't care."

"Who?"

"The croatoans. For a while, we thought they'd help us, take us to their colonies."

"They're not colonies," Charlie said. "They're farms. You don't want to go there unless you have something you can offer them."

Jan looked to his girls and back to Charlie. "I know. It's why we stay out here. You said you could help?"

"We can if you put the weapon down."

Jan hesitated for a moment before eventually lowering his gun. Charlie thought it was more likely through exhaustion than anything else. The old guy slumped to an old wooden crate he was using as a seat.

Charlie turned to the trees and beckoned the others out. Denver kept his rifle pointing to the ground so as not to spook them. Ethan and Maria came through carrying Charlie's pack between them. From that pack, Charlie took three days' worth of dried ration packs—foil-wrapped, just-add-water soups that he had recovered from the Army base. They'd last a century apparently.

In addition to the rations, he took out his supply of root contained within an old tin and cut off a third.

"Here, for your daughters." Charlie handed him the root and the ration packs. "It's not a lot, but they look like they need it. It'll give them something to get them by for a while until you can find something more substantial."

Tears welled up in Jan's eyes as he took them. He bowed. "Thank you so much. I don't know what to say … I …"

"Don't say anything," Charlie said. "Just have yourselves a meal and share the root. It'll give you enough energy to move. Go north, upstate, away from the trouble."

"What trouble?" Jan asked.

"The trouble I'm going to be giving to the alien scum. Trust me, go north."

With that, Charlie motioned goodbye to them. The two girls smiled and thanked him with quiet, whispering voices.

They headed through the camp and came out onto a road that hadn't quite succumbed to the encroaching forest.

Here, humanity, in the form of concrete and steel and glass, remained defiantly. Charlie navigated his way through the ghost town of Manhattan until he came to the Quaternary headquarters. Though the building was charred on the outside and pitted from various munitions, it remained standing.

But it wasn't the upper floors he wanted.

He led his group through a pile of debris, a maze of corrugated metal doors and wooden obstructions, until a dark hole greeted him. At the end of the tunnel was a metal door with a heavy lock. He took a key from his pocket and opened it.

Bright white light flooded out.

"Go on, inside," Charlie said, pushing the others inside while he watched behind him to make sure no one else was watching him. Once Ethan had gone through, Charlie followed inside, closing and locking the door behind him.

A basement room greeted him. Lights strung across the ceiling with looping wires illuminated the room. All around the wide-open space were desks, parts littering every surface. Wires and batteries, mechanical parts, anything and everything that could be salvaged.

Ethan and Maria turned around, taking it all in, their eyes wide with wonder.

A shadow came from behind a screen, then a bright red and blue sweater around a thickset man with a beard that reached to his chest.

"Charlie, Denver, strange new people! You made it. So great to see you." The man opened his arms wide as he approached Charlie, embracing him with a bear hug. Releasing him but gripping his arms, the man smiled.

"Mike," Charlie said.

"Charlie."

"How's the weapon coming along?"

"Huh! All business as usual. That can wait. Come the fuck in and grab some coffee first, eh? You're not a damned savage, and you have shiny new people to introduce to me."

Charlie smiled, enjoying his old colleague's unflappable personality. But behind the joviality was a keen mind, the very mind that Charlie needed to bring down the croatoans. But before they got to that, he would do as he suggested. A cup of coffee was always welcomed before the destruction of an invading force.

Chapter Twenty-Four

Ten years of cat and mouse would finally be ended in the next few hours. The thought of it made Gregor smile. He checked the working parts of his gun. There would be no mistake with Charlie Jackson if he were close to the shelter.

Ben had told him that Charlie planned to move to another location. He might still be there. So could his supplies.

Marek loaded six grenades into a small backpack and slung it over his shoulder. "Ready to do this?"

"Get three hover-bikes ready," Gregor said. "I'm going to pay Igor a visit."

Marek left the office. Ben shuffled after him.

Gregor slid a magazine into his pistol grip, put a round in the chamber, and followed. He left the other two heading for the square, turning by the side of his office and striding over to the moldy shed.

The moody morning sky would no doubt soon give the croatoans a treat. A shuttle approached. Its noise grew louder.

He looked through the cobwebbed window. Empty.

The shed gently shook as warm air blasted downwards.

Layla's trailer door rattled open. Her head appeared around it. "What are you—?"

The descending shuttle, arriving for a morning supply collection, quickly drowned her out. It smoothly dropped toward the landing area, obscured by trees. Gregor pointed toward his ear, shrugged, and headed off to the square.

Marek and Ben were already waiting on two bikes. Igor stood next to them. He licked the edge of a cigarette paper and rolled it in his fingers.

"Still smoking that shit?" Gregor said.

"Morning, Gregor. How are you?"

Gregor grunted. "Shouldn't you be helping Alex feed the livestock?"

Igor rubbed his hands together. "Just come to wave goodbye. I hear you're hunting a wasp."

Wave goodbye. Like Igor ever did that. His time was coming. Not here though. Too many croatoans around. He was priority number two today.

Gregor swung his leg over the hover-bike and tapped the alien on the shoulder. He turned to Igor. "Have a good day, my friend."

"You too, my friend."

Igor smiled and raised his hand as Gregor's vehicle ascended. A horrible false smile. The type he'd seen Igor use when interrogating people with his knife. Igor's modus operandi was strapping somebody to a chair and playing tic-tac-toe on their face. He'd gone lightly on Ben but left his unmistakable fingerprint.

As the bike lifted above the warehouses, hugging the farmed land, Gregor gazed at the distant, orange haze. Thoughts of Layla's revelations spun through his mind.

He had too many moving parts to consider. Jackson, Igor, Augustus, the croatoans. Removing two of them would bring more clarity.

They zipped away from the farm. Alex stood by a tractor in the paddock, throwing food to the livestock. She looked up and they passed. Gregor saluted.

The plan was to land half a mile away from the shelter and move quickly along the riverbank. Zero tolerance against anything that shifted. The same policy applied to Ben if he was found to be lying.

Gregor glanced across to the two bikes flying next to his in formation. Marek looked across and returned a nod. Ben's eyes were shut tight. He hunched behind the croatoan rider, turning his face against the rush of wind.

Ahead, the river came into view like a large brown snake winding through the overgrown land into the distance.

Rain started to fall, tinkling against the bike's metal as it powered through the sky. A minute later, they reached the river, momentarily hovering above it before lowering onto a thick grass bank. A couple of birds took flight from the undergrowth.

Ben jumped off the back of his bike and unsteadily walked to a tree. He leaned against it and doubled over. A long trail of saliva hung from his mouth as he dry retched a couple of times.

A dead spotted redshank caught Gregor's eye after he dismounted. He walked closer to inspect it. Its feathers were coated by a stringy paste. The river slowly flowed past like a large, foamy beer. He rubbed a greasy fern between his fingers. The change was becoming more rapid. Gregor just hadn't been noticing the little things. Now they had his full attention.

The croatoans stood in a circle, tick-tocking away.

Marek patted him on the shoulder. "Come on. We've got work to do."

***

Igor watched until all three specks disappeared into the distance. This was his chance to cement a place as number one in Augustus's eyes. To raid Jackson's den and bring back information, or better still, kill him. He'd do what *the boss* had failed to manage.

Gregor was past it. Ten years was long enough being in the tin-pot Armenian's *gang*. It was time for Igor to run the show. Augustus had already verbally promised him the job; there'd been too many mistakes. Harvester damage, livestock escapes, and dead croatoans: It all added up, and it was time to pay.

Augustus had informed him yesterday that Gregor would be taken on a one-way trip to the forest. Left for animals to nibble on his stinking corpse. These things were best done in private.

Layla, Vlad, and Alex were still required and would all have to fall in line. The croatoans wouldn't give a shit.

Igor waved toward the barracks. His croatoan rider exited the door and took its position on the hover-bike. He held a map forwards and pointed to a location. The alien punched in coordinates on its tablet before clicking it into place above the handlebars.

The bike drifted over the warehouses for a couple of minutes. They had to wait for the shuttle to take off. The brilliant blue craft shot into the sky. Its six pink rings glowed against the gray clouds before slipping through them, out of sight.

Below, the little surveyors left their barracks and headed to the chocolate factory. That would be the first thing Igor renamed. Gregor and his stupid nicknames. He should have had more respect for his masters.

They cruised over Gregor's office. Much better than a shed. Soon, the whole place would be Igor's. He hadn't decided on whether to take Alex or Layla first.

He tapped the croatoan's shoulder.

The alien jabbed its head to one side. He rolled his finger around, trying to signal an increase in pace. "Faster, faster."

No response.

Sedately traveling over trees gave Igor a better view of their immediate surroundings. If he was going to be boss, it was a good chance to see potential looting spots. Overgrown buildings with trails leading from them or signs of smoke drifting out of the forest. Both signs of habitation.

After spotting two thin streams of smoke curling out of the trees, he looked back to the farm to orientate their positions. Only a few miles away. He'd treat survivors like the hag near the ambush site. They had no value unless young enough to process.

The bike lowered in a clearing not quite at the specified location but close enough. Igor recognized the vague, broken lines of a tennis court. Shrubs and weeds filled the cracks brought on from age and ice. Remains of a rotting net stretched across the middle, raised by bush. A rusty chain link fence surrounded the court, half-smothered in ivy. The bottom of it had mostly broken away and curled upwards. Only two sections remained in place.

Igor slipped a compass out of his pocket and checked his map against the tablet location. Just under a mile north.

"I'll be back in half an hour," Igor said.

The croatoan ignored him.

"Whatever," he whispered to himself as he checked his watch.

He pulled up a section of the fence and ducked underneath. The forest was dark ahead. It suited his approach. Stealthily moving from tree to tree, keeping a close eye on his bearing, Igor made quick progress.

After ten minutes, he sensed he was getting close and slowed to a deliberate creep, placing his feet away from any twigs or branches. Revolver to the front.

Igor crouched behind a large rock and searched the woodland. Ben had directed him to this spot. If this was a wild goose chase, he vowed to beat the little shit's brains out.

Through the gloom, Igor saw it. A dark slit slightly raised off the forest floor. A man-made entrance. Charlie Jackson wasn't as clever as he thought. A couple of obvious trails led to the opening.

He waited five minutes. Observing, searching for signs of movement. The place appeared to be deserted. If Jackson or his bastard weren't around, some of his supplies or any available clues to his whereabouts would have to do.

Igor moved around the side of the shelter and edged forward, aiming at the entrance.

From a distance, it looked like a small hump, blending in with the surrounding forest floor. Up close, steep dirt steps were cut into the ground, leading into what was probably a bunker. Igor thought about shouting a threat but decided against it. If anyone was here, he'd take them by surprise.

He crouched, listened by the entrance. Not a sound from the inside. Trees rustled above in the gentle breeze.

Igor leaned around the corner, peered down. Holding his revolver through the entrance, he started to climb down.

A loud bang filled his ears. He felt searing pain in his

right knee. Igor instantly buckled to the ground, dropping his revolver and sliding down the steps.

He desperately fumbled in the dark. A boot stamped on his wrist.

A shotgun barrel pushed against his cheek.

Through the gloom, Gregor's face appeared. "Say goodnight, you Russian fuck-rat."

Igor groaned. "Wait. I wasn't here to kill you. I followed and came to warn you."

Gregor forced the barrel harder against his check. "Stop lying. It's over. Your only mistake was thinking you were smarter than me."

Igor had seen Gregor in this kind of mood a hundred times. There would be no stay of execution. "Get it over with. You're a dead man anyway. A ship's coming to complete the process. Augustus told me—"

***

Gregor's ears rang with a high-pitched tone after his two deafening shots reverberated around the bunker. The effort of dragging Igor's body up the steps helped his anger subside. Ben was right; Igor was playing a dangerous game. The two-faced bastard was trying to get one over on him. He searched the Russian's pockets, then tossed the revolver to Ben.

Ben caught it and wiped mud from a groove in the cylinder. "Is this mine?"

"Look after me, and I'll look after you. It's that simple," Gregor said.

"You've done well," Marek said. "He was a bad apple."

"Tell me about it," Ben said, pointing to his face.

Gregor lifted Igor's legs and nodded toward the bank. "Grab an arm each. We'll throw him in the river. Don't want to leave a calling card for Jackson."

The other two gripped the corpse under each shoulder, and they staggered and crashed through thick ferns thirty yards across to the bank.

"What was Igor saying about another ship?" Marek said.

"Something about completing the process. I'll pass it on to Layla. He was probably bullshitting to try and save his own pathetic life."

They dropped Igor by the edge, and Marek rolled him into the water. The body rolled onto its front and slowly floated away.

All three stood amongst the foliage, catching their breath.

"Remind me to thank Jackson for the use of his shotgun. When I kill him," Gregor said.

Marek smiled. He'd found an AR-15 wrapped in plastic complete with three full magazines. He tapped the stock. "Not if I get to him first."

Ben frowned. "He's not that bad. A bit of a dick, but …"

"A bit of a dick?" Gregor shook his head. "Do you think you're the first crew that met him?"

"I don't know," Ben shrugged.

"I'll tell you a little story about the *hero*, Charlie Jackson. Our farm was based near Jefferson City a few years ago. He blew up a harvester and kidnapped two of the crew. One was sent back to place a bomb in the chocolate factory. It detonated, killing several croatoans and my cousin. At the same time, he and his bastard son flattened a paddock fence with a log strapped to the roof of a small truck."

"They used it like a battering ram," Marek said. "Livestock fled through the gap."

"Wasn't he just trying to help other humans?" Ben said.

Gregor scoffed. "A few croatoan soldiers were still around back then. They hunted down every human they could find. Livestock, survivors, whoever. They purged the area clean."

"How did Charlie and Denver get away?"

"It's the same every time," Marek said. "They just vanish like ghosts. Probably into a network of hideouts like the one over there."

Gregor looked over the ferns. Something caught his eye: a flash. He whispered, "Get down."

Marek shouldered his rifled, aiming it toward the shelter. "What is it?"

"I don't know. Someone's out there, close."

A twig snapped. Gregor peered through the ferns.

Three figures moved through the trees forty yards to their left. Unmistakable croatoan movement. Bouncing along as if taking individual one-legged jumps, short pauses between each one. An alien passed through rays of sunlight that streamed through the trees in two thick beams. Its visor glinted in the sunlight.

"Looks like our riders," Gregor said.

"What the fuck are they doing here?" Marek said.

Gregor put his finger to his lips. The aliens stopped short of the shelter and stood behind three individual trees. After several seconds, they sprang out and rapidly moved to the entrance. All had weapons drawn.

"Holy shit. They're attacking," Gregor said.

"Attacking who?" Ben said.

"Exactly."

One pulled a tennis-ball-shaped silver object from its belt and threw it into the shelter. An alien grenade. The croatoans stood to one side.

Gregor had seen them plenty of times before but usually carried by the croatoan soldiers, not the smaller patrollers that looked after farm security and local transport. They wouldn't carry out an action like this unless under orders.

Smoke drifted from the entrance following a dull blast.

"Get your grenades ready," Gregor said.

"What?" Marek said.

"We're taking them out. Give me the rifle; get a couple of grenades ready to go. Now."

"What do you want me to do?" Ben said.

"Two croatoans disappeared down the stairs. I'll shoot the one above. We sprint straight to the entrance. You drop the grenades, and I'll provide covering fire. Got it?"

"I hope you know what you're doing," Marek said.

Easy from this range, Gregor thought. His shot smashed through the side of the alien's helmet.

Marek immediately jumped up and ran with a grenade in each hand. Gregor followed, aiming at the alien who sank to its knees and keeled over backwards. Ben appeared by his side, holding his revolver forward. Not what Gregor had anticipated but a welcomed bonus. He'd thought Ben would be a useless coward.

Diving to the ground next to the entrance, Marek reached around it and threw down both grenades in quick succession. A shot fired out of the opening. The metallic snaps of a croatoan gun.

Gregor knelt by the side with rifle shouldered. Ready to take out anything that appeared. Ben trained his weapon from the opposite side, aiming at an angle.

Both grenades erupted in quick succession like a thunderous double-tap.

Mud and smoke spewed out of the shelter.

Smoke cleared. An alien hand shakily reached out of the entrance before flopping to the ground.

Marek sprinted to the downed alien outside and grabbed the weapon by its side. Gregor edged around the entrance, aiming into the hazy gap. One alien lay against the dirt wall. Its uniform was ripped around its body armor, and its helmet was smashed. The other slumped at the top of the stairs, the bottom half of its right leg missing.

Gregor gritted his teeth and stamped on the croatoan's visor, smashing it like an eggshell. The alien let out a light wheeze as its skin crackled.

"What the fuck?" Marek said.

"We need to warn the others," Gregor said. "The croatoans are turning. Layla was right. It's happening now."

He glanced at the three dead aliens and scowled.

Augustus. It had to be him.

Chapter Twenty-Five

Layla sat in the chocolate factory peering at monitors. Results increased by fifty-five percent since they designated harvesters to the land she'd helped pinpoint. It wasn't what she wanted anymore. It wouldn't be what any human wanted.

She'd arrived at the monitors as Igor was taking off in the square, the same time as the surveyors. They buzzed around in the usual fashion, business as usual stuff. Mixing soil samples in glass tubes, poring over charts, and generally appearing fussy. To avoid looking too suspicious, Layla moved to the back of the building.

Vlad slumped against the desk, oblivious to it all. He yawned and twiddled a pen. "Do you want a coffee? I've still got some of that freeze-dried crap left. A bit gravelly but …"

"No thanks. Have you seen anything different around here in the last couple of weeks?" Layla said.

"What do you mean? Like croatoan stuff? It's all alien to me."

Vlad seemed to have thrown up the mental shutters long ago. He didn't care about anything, at least not when she tried to strike up a conversation. Layla couldn't decide whether to feel jealous or sorry for him.

Her planned task for today was to check the occupants of the breeding lab. Events of the last two days had a horrible effect of pushing reality to the surface. Survival was no longer an excuse. The thin self-justification for her actions had vanished, and she knew it.

She got up and sighed. "I'll leave you to it. Speak later."

The job still had to be done. It wasn't all about her personal feelings. Twenty women, humans, needed their welfare checking.

Croatoans streamed out of the door ahead of Layla. Outside, it was raining.

They circled around, taking off their gloves and jiggling their fingers. She hugged the side of the building to keep dry and headed for the breeding lab.

Livestock still had sex. One of the remaining human instincts or urges that hadn't been stripped away by the croatoan regime. It was a daily occurrence in the paddock, embarrassing at first, but she'd gotten used to it.

At least the croatoans had stopped finding human intercourse a source of interest. They'd often gather around the paddock and watch, pointing at the male's penis and clicking loudly.

The novelty wore off after a few months. Layla thought it was childish, like her former student colleagues who'd giggle at clips of animals having sex.

A tractor rumbled across the square. Alex, wearing her bright yellow waterproof, drove it from the meat factory toward the paddocks. She stopped when she saw Layla and called, "I took one in yesterday. Give me a shout if they need any more food."

"Will do, thanks," Layla said, holding her thumb up.

The tractor rumbled away, cutting a dirty track across the damp ground.

Any female exhibiting a bump would be identified,

usually by Alex, during feeding time, and they'd be sent to the breeding lab. They were fed slop, kept inside, and monitored until they gave birth. Alex played midwife. Layla would assist if she were around. She hadn't been required lately although a couple of women were only a matter of days away.

Layla took a deep breath and opened the door.

Inside, the roof echoed with the sound of a single woman's quiet sobbing.

Symptoms of stress were common. Women would bite their nails, refuse to eat, and often shake. The paddock was their natural environment, unlike the enclosed walls, a single bed, and waste bucket. Layla had given up trying to offer comfort. It had a scarring effect. And when one started crying, others in adjoining rooms would often join them.

She walked along, glancing through small square windows on individual doors.

The layout inside was quite simple. A long corridor ran along the middle of the warehouse with brightly lit, sparse cells on either side. Forty in all. At the moment, they had a fifty percent occupancy rate.

The inhabitants were identified by room numbers, which Layla had painted on the doors.

One woman sat hugging her knees, rocking backwards and forwards. Another pressed her hand against the plastic pane as Layla passed. The majority of the twenty lay placidly on their black plastic mattresses.

In the second to last room near the end of the corridor on the floor, a woman was lying, spread out on her front. Layla took a sharp intake of breath. She knocked on the window and received no response.

She twisted the circular locking mechanism. It opened with a clank. Layla pushed the door, forcing it the last couple of inches with her shoulder to move rigid legs out of the way. Creating enough space to enter through a narrow gap.

When she reached down and grabbed an arm, it was pale and stiff. Too late. Rigor mortis had set in.

Next to the woman's outstretched hand was a small, humanlike figure crafted from twisted, dry grass. A charm or keepsake. The first she'd seen created by livestock.

"Oh my God," she breathed.

Layla hadn't witnessed a death in the building before. She'd only heard about it occurring. The procedure was to hit the green call button by the entrance. Layla hurried along the corridor with her head in her hands.

She depressed the saucer-sized button. It flashed and let out two soft, electronic beeps.

A minute later, two croatoans walked across the main square carrying a gray metal slab, heading straight for the breeding lab. They didn't move with any great urgency and stopped to talk to a group of aliens by the hover-bikes before finally reaching the building.

The first one bumped through the swing doors and looked at Layla. She led them along the corridor and pointed into the cell. The croatoans briefly paused. One clicked, and they both jerked forward.

They placed the slab on the floor, grabbed the body by its hair and robe, and rolled it on. The front area of the woman's clothing was stained dark purple. Layla closed her eyes tightly and put her hand against the corridor wall for support.

The patter of alien feet passed her. She opened her eyes

and watched them bounce along the corridor.

Faces started to appear through the little windows. One woman wailed. Then another. As the croatoans carried the body to the entrance, the whole place echoed with crying and moaning.

Layla followed the aliens, watched them bump back through the doors. They crossed the main square, around the hover-bikes, and straight into the meat-processing warehouse.

She leaned with her back against the wall. The wailing continued, penetrating deep inside her. She wanted to run but didn't know where. She clasped her hands around the back of her head, bringing her elbows together in front of her face. Her back slid down the wall until she ended up in a crouching position.

A woman peered through the closest window, sobbing. Layla shuffled sideways toward the door, out of view, gulped, and took a deep breath.

She couldn't hold it in any longer and joined the cacophony of weeping.

***

Layla composed herself in an empty cell, took a few deep breaths, and wiped tears from her face with her sweater sleeve. Something had to change. It was impossible to carry on at the farm now.

Perhaps it was time to find Charlie Jackson.

The breeding lab's door banged open. Footsteps ran along the corridor. Vlad flashed past the open cell door. She heard him skid to a stop. He hurried into the cell.

"Layla, you're wanted at the monitors. You need to come

with me." He fidgeted with a pencil, scraping his thumbnail against the sharpened end. "Layla. You have to—"

She sniffed and looked up. "Wanted by who?"

"Hey, are you okay?"

"I'll be fine. What's happening?"

Vlad held his hand toward her. "Augustus. He wants to speak to you. Says it's a matter of great urgency."

Augustus never spoke to Layla on an individual basis. She'd talked to him at meetings with Gregor, and he'd made the odd passing comment to her around camp. This was the first time he'd directly requested her presence.

"Why me? Did he say anything else? Was he angry?"

She grabbed Vlad's hand and hauled herself off the bed.

"He specifically asked for you. As for angry, who knows?" Vlad shrugged. "He wears a mask, and I struggle to understand his accent."

Augustus's accent was a mystery. He spoke with the fluency of a native English speaker but didn't sound like any Layla had previously heard or met. Gregor had asked him where he was from a few years ago. Augustus replied, *Earth*.

The rain had abated outside, and surveyors crowded around the chocolate factory table. They ignored Vlad and Layla's entrance, more interested in a tablet that was being passed around like a hot potato.

She could see the outline of Augustus's head on the main monitor, surrounded by color, waiting for her.

"Do you know where he's transmitting from?" Layla said.

Vlad pointed upwards.

When she reached the desk, Augustus leaned forward. He stroked his mask. The wall behind him was decorated with a series of bright rings. The largest outer circle was light pink, the inner ones different shades of blue.

This was her first glimpse inside the mother ship. It looked like Augustus was in a psychedelic brothel.

"Please take a seat, Layla," Augustus said. She slid a stool from under the desk. Vlad flopped in his customary position. "I didn't tell you to sit down, Vlad. Leave the building. Return in five minutes."

"I'll grab a bite to eat," Vlad said and moved out of view of the monitors. He raised his eyebrows and repeatedly circled his ear with his finger before walking away.

"You wanted to see me, Mr. Augustus?" Layla said.

"Where were you at three o'clock this morning?"

Layla felt her stomach knot. "Excuse me?"

"It's a straightforward question."

"I was sleeping. Why do you ask?"

She clenched her hands tightly underneath the desk.

"We had a security breach. Somebody, a human, came in here last night and looked through secure croatoan data."

"It wasn't me. Have you checked with the others?"

The only person who saw Layla last night was Igor. If he was in Augustus's pocket, he'd probably spill the beans. Another reason for her to run. Her only option left.

"We're carrying out some print analysis on one of the devices. You'll all be required here tonight. The guilty party will receive swift justice."

Layla would be gone by then. She wasn't hanging around for Augustus to pass his sentence. "What's so important about the data?"

Augustus tutted. "It's the principle. We still need farm workers, especially for the breeding lab. If somebody doesn't want to play the game, I'll be the one to blow the final whistle."

"No problem, Mr. Augustus. See you back here tonight."

He waved his bony finger. "I haven't finished yet. There's some news you need to be aware of. Gregor's gone."

She leaned back on the stool. "Gone?"

"As we speak, he's having his employment terminated. I need you to step up. Are you with me?"

"He's being terminated?"

"Why do you insist on repeating me? The details are a trivial technicality, none of your concern. I'll assume that you are still part of our team. Which reminds me, is Igor around? I need to speak with him."

Layla's mouth felt dry. She gulped. "He left this morning. Haven't seen him since."

"Send him here as soon as you do. I can't get in touch."

"Is that it, Mr. Augustus?"

"For now."

The screen flashed back to monitoring the two most northern harvesters. Little red trails across the map, expanding the root coverage. All critical measurements showing green.

They'd murdered Gregor.

Augustus had all but confirmed Igor was in cahoots with him. Igor knew about her clandestine trip to the chocolate factory. It was only a matter of time. Layla focused on short-term survival. There was nothing for it but to grab some personal items from her trailer and get as far away as possible.

Chapter Twenty-Six

Mike was still smiling at Charlie when he handed him a chipped mug of steaming tea. Charlie took a deep swig and enjoyed the burning sensation. They sat around a dirty desk only slightly less cramped with stuff than Mike's former desk above them in the Quaternary building.

"Since the invasion," Charlie said to the others as they sat around the table, "Mike's been in his element. Look at this place. It's a tinker's paradise. Every imaginable device is here, though most are in various stages of actual usefulness."

Ethan had taken to Mike right away as Charlie's old colleague gave the kid the tour. When they came back, it was obvious where Ethan's future would lie. Right here with Mike building weapons and devices.

There was one problem however. Mai—Mike's kinda-wife and fellow engineer. They'd set up a cozy existence together. Mai, a Chinese-American nuclear physicist, was one of the survivors within their cavern during the ice age. She and Mike had hit it off right away.

"So," Charlie said, placing the mug on the table. "Now we've got the pleasantries out of the way, what's the status on the device?"

Mai entered the screened-off area carrying a silver Samsonite case. She cleared a space on the table and laid it flat, opening the lid and displaying for all to see the device that they'd been working on for the last five years.

It was all Mike's idea. And it'd taken Charlie those five years to source the parts needed.

Maria looked over Charlie's shoulder and Ethan over Mike's. Denver was paying no attention, preferring to make a fuss of Pip, making sure she didn't go sniffing into something dangerous. There was no telling what Mike and Mai had stashed around.

"What is it?" Maria said.

The device was the size of a laptop and was in fact built on the chassis of an old Lenovo Thinkpad. They were built with longevity in mind, and they'd certainly achieved that. In the early days of the design, Mike ironically wanted to use an Alienware machine.

"It's a bomb," Mai said, her accent now completely neutral. In the early days, she still had a lilt of Chinese to her, but with all the time spent with Mike, she'd come to sound just like him.

"Well, not exactly a traditional bomb," Mike added with a smile. He pulled his long gray hair back, revealing a thinning pate. Not surprising considering his age. He was in his late seventies, but like Charlie, regular imbibing of the root kept him young and able.

At least that was one thing to thank the alien bastards for.

"So, what does it do if it's not really a bomb?" Ethan said, leaning in further for a closer look.

Where the laptop screen used to be was now a rounded, metal shell. The track pad had been swapped out for a small OLED screen from a smartphone. The thing looked like a designer '70s toaster with some modern tech cobbled onto it, but beneath that shell was one of the most potent weapons ever devised, assuming it'd work.

"Well," Mike said, putting his arm around Ethan's shoulder. "What do you know of EMP devices?"

"Erm, nothing? Yet."

Mike smiled, seeming to like the kid. "It stands for Electro-Magnetic Pulse."

"Or Extreme Magnetic Pain," Mai said with a wicked grin. Her leathery face and its many folds hid her intelligent eyes. She was younger than Mike by twenty years, but they could well have been twins on personality. Both wore wacky sweaters, and both had a brain that Charlie could only wish he had.

"So what does it do?" Maria said. "And how will this save us all as Charlie said?"

"It'll tear the aliens a new asshole and send them packing back to the ass-end of the galaxy," Mike said. "Once detonated, those turtle-looking fuckers won't know what hit 'em. Inside this unassuming shell is a nuclear bomb that makes Hiroshima look like a bee-sting. When it goes, it won't just blow anything up, it'll destroy anything electrical for hundreds and thousands of miles around."

Maria seemed to understand as she turned to Charlie. "So for this to be effective, it'll need to be set off within the croatoan ship? That means someone has to—"

Charlie stopped her with a hand, "We'll come to that later. Mike, what's the situation; it's not ready to go, is it? And I can tell something's up."

"No," Mike said. "We need one more part."

Mai leaned against the table, regarding Charlie with her wise eyes. "Someone will need to make a trip to the Ford warehouse north of here. There's a special kind of magnet they used in their last models. It'll help regulate and deliver the pulse. We found an old one, but it wasn't efficient enough. We need a new, unused one from the parts warehouse—if there's any there of course."

"Fuck it," Charlie said, turning his back. "Sorry, I don't mean to be an ass, I just thought ..." He took a deep breath as Denver entered the room and stood in front of him.

"It's not a problem, Dad. We'll go get it. It's only an hour's walk. We'll get the part and be out of here. The plan can still go ahead."

"You're right, son. I just wanted ... I'm just getting impatient in my old age."

"Here," Mike said, handing Charlie a small black disc the size of an old dollar coin. "That's the burnt-out one we found. We need something like that; two, if you can find them, would be even better. Always good to have a backup."

"You got it. We'll go now. Quicker we get it, the quicker we can carry out the rest of the plan," Charlie said. "How long will it take you to fit?"

"A few minutes," Mai said.

"Come on, son, let's go for a midday stroll into town."

"We're coming with you," Maria said. "If it's this important, we can be of help. Be spotters or something, some extra backup."

"No," Charlie said. "It's too dangerous. Anything and anyone can be out there. They're not all gonna be like the last lot. The city dwellers are more hardcore. We need to move quickly and without fuss. It's better if it's just Den and me."

"Fuck that," Ethan said, surprising everyone. He slapped his hand on the table. "We've been through all kinds of crap to get here. I appreciate you looking out for us, but

Ben's been sent off to who knows what fate, and now you want us to just sit back. What if you get into trouble and we're just sitting around waiting for you? No, we're going."

Mike grinned at Charlie as he patted the kid on the shoulder. "Looks like they've made their own minds up, Chuck. Let 'em go with you. You can't protect everyone. At some point, everyone has to call their own shots and stand on their own two feet."

"Exactly," Maria said. "It's our choice, not yours."

Shrugging his shoulders, Charlie turned his back and headed for the exit tunnel. "Grab your guns and follow me. On your own heads be it."

***

The midday sun was just passing noon, creating thin, stubby shadows on the broken sidewalks and roads where the blacktop had long splintered off to expose the concrete beneath.

Few trees had managed to settle within the city, but there were still overgrown areas of bushes and shrubs, contrasting their natural hues with the monochromatic palette of human endeavor. Charlie and Denver stuck to the main streets where possible. If there were any survivors in the area, they'd likely be in the houses; many had set up homes there or in the low-rise apartment buildings, almost as if nothing had happened.

There were some who still thought it meant something to live in Manhattan. But the place was a ghost town now with little to offer anyone apart from the most basic of shelters. Unlike Mike and Mai's basement that had power from the building's rebuilt diesel generators, almost none of the makeshift domiciles had any power. Years before, Charlie had been part of a fuel group whose task was to extract fuel from other generators, cars, and trucks.

The yield was low, but given the sheer number of sources, they'd managed to gather enough to keep the Quaternary basement running with power for decades to come. Most of that was due to Mai's genius in mixing the diesel generators with solar and wind power.

They'd made their way about halfway to the warehouse, weaving in and out of streets, making sure they were covered at all times by shadows or dilapidated buildings. Denver, as ever, took point, using his scope to observe their intended route.

Maria and Ethan took up the rear and watched the flanks.

Charlie kept his attention on the sky. He didn't want to worry the others, but ever since they'd arrived, he'd seen the shadow out of the corner of his eye and the glint of something in the clouds. It was flying in stealth mode now, but after hearing the roar earlier, he knew it was here.

Which of course was one of the reasons he didn't want the others to come with him, but like Mike said, they had to make the choice; he couldn't protect them at all times.

They crossed a street, rounding a pair of rusted limousines. Most of the road signs had lost all their lettering to the elements. Given the destruction, he couldn't tell exactly where they were but knew they'd walked for thirty minutes, always heading north. The Ford warehouse wouldn't be much further.

As they turned left out of a tight avenue, they came to a wide road that led straight forward. Before Charlie could warn the others, having just seen the shadow the instant he walked out onto the road, an alien fighter craft—triangular, flat, and deadly black—landed at the end of the street no more than a hundred feet away.

"Get into cover," Charlie shouted as he dived behind a pile of rubble on the left side of the street. Denver joined him. Maria split to the right, and Ethan remained in the middle of the street looking confused, his attention on the alien craft.

It looked nothing like the regular croatoan shuttles and was more advanced than the first fighters that had come down after the invasion. This was something new.

A door opened. Blue light surrounded an alien creature with an almost neon glow. This was no ordinary alien. It was twice as tall as any croatoan soldier and featured a form-fitting, matte-black suit. Its head was flat and pointed, resembling the triangular hull of its craft.

Before anyone had time to do anything, a blast of blue energy shot out down the road. Charlie screamed for Ethan to move, but the kid was too slow, too scared. The bolt of energy coalesced into what looked like ball lightning.

It struck Ethan with a crackling explosion.

The boy's body seemed to be ripped apart at the cellular level as he screamed. A few seconds later, all that remained was a charred, black stain on the street's surface. He'd been completely vaporized.

Another bolt, smaller this time, fired down the street, crashing into the debris. Charlie and Denver jumped back just in time. The shot destroyed half of the concrete before it ran out of energy. The air crackled with electricity. Maria screamed from the other side.

"Get down! Stay down," Charlie screamed over to her. He pulled the pistol from his hip and aimed at the alien.

It was on the move now, walking purposefully down the street, reaching behind its back.

"Mother fucker," Denver said as he raised his rifle, using a part of the partially melted rubble to steady his aim. He adjusted the scope and took a deep breath.

Charlie fired off three controlled shots, aiming for the giant alien's legs and torso. His aim was off. Something about the way the alien moved made it hard to focus. "Shoot the fucker," Charlie said, urging his son.

Denver obliged. The crack of the rifle echoed around the buildings. The shot was true, but the alien seemed to shift physically in a blur. Charlie fired off two more shots. They went right through the weird-phasing movement of the alien, striking the craft with a spark behind him.

Maria, screaming, shot out from her position, lifting her shotgun.

"No!" Charlie screamed. "Get back. Now."

It was too late.

Maria stood in the street directly opposite the alien. Charlie could tell now with Maria as reference that the damned thing must be at least seven and a half feet tall. Its limbs were twice as thick and muscular as any soldier croatoan.

When the phasing stopped, it came into full focus. The black, form-fitting armor seemed to harden. Maria fired off two shots. The buckshot bounced off its armor.

It lifted the rifle-like weapon, its barrel square and at least a meter and a half long, and aimed it at Maria. Its long, talon-like fingers curled around a trigger.

Chapter Twenty-Seven

Crashing through the ferns, Gregor led Marek and Ben along the riverbank. Speed was of the essence. They had to get to the bikes before any more patrols arrived. The aliens had clearly been ordered to kill them and leave them out in the forest.

Ten years of loyal service down the drain.

Gregor wanted Augustus's mangled face under his boot.

Igor had approached the shelter from the opposite direction. His croatoan rider wouldn't be too far away but would wait until it received further orders.

Gregor reached the bikes and rested on the closest one to the river. Marek and Ben stood in front of him, both with hands on their knees.

"You're serious about using these?" Marek said.

"I'm not leaving Layla, Alex, and Vlad to the mercy of those bastards," Gregor said. "Three of us, three of them. We take the bikes."

Ben mopped sweat from his brow and looked over the controls. "They look familiar to what I used in the harvester. Have you ridden one before?"

"It's easy. We used to have a bike for our team," Marek said. "Until Igor crashed it. After that, we had to request a ride. They've been pretty good about it up until now."

Gregor grunted. "Sit. I'll show you."

Ben jumped on the bike and pointed down. "I know

that button switches on the engine."

"That's right," Gregor said. He patted each part, explaining, "You push the handlebars forward to rise, back to lower. Twist the right handle to speed up, let go to slow down. The left to hover. Don't turn them at the same time. Nice and easy."

"You do know left from right?" Marek said.

Ben frowned. "Of course I do. What about landing?"

"Twist the left and pull the handlebars back. Not too fast."

Croatoans loved tracking everything. The blue beads in humans, harvester locations, land conversion. Gregor rubbed his chin and looked at the bikes. He leaned over Ben's controls and ripped the tablet from its fastening and passed it to Marek.

"Good idea," Marek said and unclipped the other two from the bikes. He spread the tablets around a bush a few yards apart.

Ben's engine hummed into life. "Where are we going first?"

"Follow me," Gregor said. "We'll set down at the landing strip; it's got partial cover. We'll round up the others, deal with the threat, and get the hell out of here."

"To where?" Marek said.

Gregor mounted his bike and slung the AR-15 over his shoulder. "I'll think about it on the way. Maybe to a city. They tend to avoid those places."

"It's dangerous. They'll see us turn up without the riders. For all we know, the others are already dead."

"The next shuttle run isn't for a few hours. Without the pulse cannon, we're dealing with the surveyors, which a child could kill, and a few jumped-up security guards. If we faced a squad of croatoan soldiers, I'd agree with you."

"I've known you for too long, Gregor. You're going kill the aliens."

Gregor smiled and started his engine. "Every fucking last one of them. Augustus is going to regret the day he ordered our execution."

Ben looked back. "What if the shit hits the fan as soon as we arrive?"

"We split and come up with something else."

Marek mounted the final bike and started the engine. He shouted above the humming engines, "If we take out the farm, they'll come after us."

"There's thousands of these farms around the world. They won't care about one."

***

The bike maintained a steady pace, smoothly powering toward the distant farm buildings. Gregor stood at the handlebars once he was comfortable with the balance of the bike. Wind rushed through his greasy brown hair.

He guessed they were traveling at half the bike's maximum speed. A sensible pace considering Ben nearly fell off his after a shaky take-off, and both he and Marek were out of practice, although the controls came back easily, like riding a bicycle.

Gregor didn't feel an urge to punch someone or something. Instead, he felt butterflies of excitement in his stomach and as if a weight had been taken off his shoulders. Back to gangster Gregor, answering to no man, liberated.

A mile from the farm, he slowed down and descended to a few feet above the canopy. Marek and Ben joined him on either side. The bikes slapped occasional branches, but it took a lot more than that to down one.

The lack of a patrol in the air was a good sign.

Perhaps the alarm hadn't been raised just yet.

Gregor hovered momentarily over the landing strip, ensuring the vehicle was steady before lowering down, bumping against the ground with a little less grace than a croatoan rider. Marek and Ben quickly followed.

Nothing moved in the immediate area apart from trees rustling in the breeze.

Gregor raised the AR-15 and nodded toward his office. He had a few weapons stashed in his bedroom. Nothing as good as the rifle, but ammo was limited. Anything they could get their hands on would do.

He dashed across the strip in a crouching run. Straight for the tree line. Marek and Ben had their guns drawn, covering each flank.

Pausing behind a thick old oak, Gregor dropped to one knee and observed his office through the last line of trees.

Marek ducked by his side. "What are you waiting for?"

"We don't want to run straight into a trap. They're not the toughest croatoans, but they're not stupid."

Something moved in Gregor's peripheral vision.

He swung his rifle left.

Layla stepped out of her trailer with a small pack on her left shoulder.

Gregor whistled, trying to sound like a bird, hoping to attract her attention. She crept toward the forest in the opposite direction.

To sound more distinctive, but not to croatoans, he decided to whistle a tune. For some reason, "Happy Birthday" was the first thing that came into his head.

Layla paused. Turned. She squinted in their direction. Marek waved his arms above his head. Layla took a few steps closer.

"Layla. Layla, it's us," Marek said.

His words seemed to give her focus. She leapt into the trees and ran for their location, her panic-stricken face quickly appearing through the gloom.

She knelt between Marek and Gregor. "Jesus. I thought you guys were dead."

"Why would you think that?" Gregor said.

"Augustus summoned me for a chat. He said you were being terminated."

"He was here?"

"No. It was on-screen. He wanted to know who was in the chocolate factory this morning. Said they're going to receive his justice. Igor saw me. He's with Augustus. I need to—"

Gregor put his hand on her shoulder. "Calm down. You don't need to worry about Igor. He's the one that's been *terminated*."

"You killed him?"

"He used Ben to try and double-cross us. I did what I had to do."

Ben began to speak. Gregor held up his hand.

"And then our riders tried to kill us," Marek said. He pointed back through the woods. "We came back on their hover-bikes. Set them down on the shuttle landing strip."

Layla rubbed her hand though her hair and puffed her cheeks.

Gregor saw clothing stuffed into her backpack. He nodded toward it. "You were making a run for it?"

She sighed. "What did you expect? We're not surviving

on the farm. We're creating our own deaths. Mine was just around the corner as soon as Augustus worked out it was me who messed with their computers. I thought you were already dead."

"So we're all officially unemployed," Marek said. "Did you get any info on your theory?"

"It's not a theory. It's happening. I just can't work out how they'll achieve it in the short-term."

"So we've got time?" Gregor said.

"I wouldn't count on it."

"Igor mentioned something about another ship coming to complete the process," Marek said.

Layla's eyes widened. "Oh my God. That has to be it. Did he say anything else?"

Gregor looked away, sweeping the immediate area through the rifle sights. Still quiet. Igor's driver hadn't returned. They would've seen the bike. "Let's get to more immediate business and talk about this later. We're getting Vlad and Alex out and leaving. We'll find a quiet area to regroup, somewhere inconspicuous."

"What's the plan?" Ben said.

He tapped the AR-15. "This is the plan."

"Seriously?"

Gregor cleared leaves and weeds away from the ground with his boot. He picked up a small stick and drew a rough layout of the farm. "Gather round and listen up. This is how we're going to do this."

"Seriously, Gregor. Igor's info, it's …" Layla said.

Gregor pointed the stick down. "Marek will go through the back window of my office, retrieve guns and ammo from my drawers. I'll provide cover and keep watch. While you're in there, Marek, check through the front blind to see if the coast is clear to the chocolate factory."

Marek nodded. "No problem."

"We'll head to the main square. Shoot the barracks windows through; choke the bastards who haven't got a helmet on. Any alien that comes out is a dead alien."

"What about us?" Ben said.

"You and Layla move around the other side of the chocolate factory in a right-flanking maneuver to provide covering fire. The surveyors, mechanics, and meat-processing ones are armed. Shoot any that leave their buildings."

"This sounds like a kamikaze mission. There must be an easier way," Layla said.

Gregor shook his head. "I thought about it on the way over. If we give them a chance to get armed and organized, we're done. We take them while they're not expecting it. There's not that many croatoans here."

"Three from today. Igor's rider and the ones Jackson killed yesterday must leave around six of the bigger croatoans. Unless the shuttle brought replacements this morning?" Marek said.

"Not that I saw," Layla said.

"The little croatoans are cowards," Gregor said. "They'll hide until more of their big boys show up. We do it now or leave Alex and Vlad. Show of hands for who wants to leave them."

Gregor looked around the group. Nobody moved or said a word.

Three metallic snaps pierced the air in quick succession. Dirt burst from the ground just in front of Gregor.

Gregor dived for cover. Placed his back against a tree. Glanced around it.

Six croatoans were advancing around his office. Three on each side.

Layla's trailer exploded into flames.

Three croatoans on the right of the office fired again. An alien projectile whistled past Gregor and slammed into a tree behind him.

The odds were stacked against them. The croatoans must have worked out what happened at the shelter. Without the extra weapons and element of surprise, they only had one option. He didn't like it, but they might just live to fight another day.

"Run for the bikes," Gregor shouted.

***

Gregor let off four rounds in the aliens' direction. They scattered for cover.

Layla dropped her backpack and sprinted away.

"Get moving. Now," Gregor said.

Ben seemed to freeze. He crouched behind a tree, breathing heavily, holding the revolver up in both hands. Marek grabbed him by the collar and yanked him away.

They stumbled to the clearing, weaving between trees. Gregor followed, occasionally turning and firing in the direction of the office.

Branches snapped, and dirt and leaves flew from the ground as the croatoans fired through the woodland.

On open ground, the group would have been cut to pieces. Gregor doubted the aliens intended to stun them and use them for livestock.

He stopped at the edge of the clearing next to the others, turned, and shouldered his rifle. "Get the bikes started.

We're going north. I'll cover."

Shots ricocheted around the trees, but there was no sign of an alien advance. Gregor returned fire until he emptied the magazine. He replaced it with one that Marek had given him earlier.

Behind him, three hover-bike engines started to collectively hum.

Gregor turned to see two already rising. Marek and Ben. Layla looked back at him, frantically gesturing him over.

He fired twice more, spun around, and sprinted.

Layla clutched the handlebars. "Come on. Get on."

"I'll fly it—"

"Just get the fuck on, Gregor. We haven't got time to debate it."

Without thinking further, he grabbed the rear handle and swung himself onto the back seat, keeping his rifle in his right hand. "Go, go, go."

They thrust vertically into the sky, faster than he'd ever experienced. Gregor clung on tightly with his left hand and squeezed his legs against the seat as if riding a wild horse. He jerked into Layla as she twisted the right handle grip.

The bike quickly progressed to a rapid speed, moaning loudly, bouncing slightly, like taking a powerboat over a lake. Something Gregor used to do in the good old days when entertaining overseas clients, organizing drug deals.

He was impressed with how Layla controlled the beast. They passed the other two bikes in a matter of seconds and cut north through the headwind.

Looking back toward camp, four small dots rose above the main square. Gregor leaned forward. "They're coming after us."

Layla reinforced her hands against the bars. There was no detectable speed increase.

Marek and Ben had upped their pace after Layla passed. Gregor signaled to both, pointing to the camp and raising four fingers.

Shuffling around on the seat like a clumsy pommel horse gymnast, he faced backwards. The croatoans closed in, flying in an extended line formation at least a mile behind.

Gregor bent back until his head brushed Layla. "Can't this thing go any faster?"

She turned momentarily. "What? I can't hear you."

"They're catching up. Can you get more out it?"

"Hang on," she said.

Gregor slung the rifle and grabbed both handles. The bike banked left and swooped down to a few feet above the trees.

The tactic was safe at a cruise. At this speed, it was dangerous. The reaction time to avoid less obvious things like old overhead power lines or stray lampposts was minimal. He understood her thinking. At least two aliens had crashed at low levels when they were based in Florida.

Ben and Marek followed, plunging down behind them.

Gregor didn't hear the sound of the alien weapons first. Tiny projectiles hissed past the bike.

One clanked against the rear housing.

He reached over Layla's shoulder and pointed down. The aliens were faster, and their only protection was his rifle. They were sitting ducks in the sky for the advancing pursuers.

Two more projectiles whizzed past, between the bikes.

Gregor returned fire, trying to take aimed shots. The

bump of the bike made it impossible. Something flashed to his immediate left, followed by a metallic rattling sound. He glanced across.

Marek's bike must have taken a hit in a key area. A jet of red gas sprayed from the side. It began to arc downward. Gregor's life-long friend slumped against the handlebars, right arm limply hanging by his side.

He looked up at Gregor with a forlorn expression and opened his mouth.

A second later, the bike smashed into the trees at high speed. Marek had no chance.

"Take us down. Now," Gregor shouted.

Layla swung the bike left and right. She must've been searching for a clearing. Anything to get them out of the sky.

The croatoan riders hovered over Marek's crash site, giving them a moment's respite.

A reservoir appeared below. Layla dropped altitude. Ben followed suit. Flying yards above water, they blasted two white trails along its glistening, dark brown surface.

Ben looked across, his face full of panic. He pointed to the side of his own bike. Through the roaring wind, Gregor detected an inconsistent tone. Ben headed for the edge, toward a building at the head of the dam.

Gregor carefully watched behind, searching for the arrival of the croatoans over the trees. He grabbed Layla's shoulder. "They're not here yet. Do it now."

Layla decreased their speed to a cruise and reached a grassy area to the right of the building. The bike reared slightly as she twisted the left grip, bringing it to a hover. She pulled back the handlebars. The bike dropped five yards and thumped against the ground.

Ben gently approached, his engine spluttering. Before he reached dry land, the bike nose dipped and entered the reservoir, spraying a thick sheet of water. He was thrown over the handlebars and splashed in, head first.

Ben quickly surfaced and flapped his arms around. "I can't swim. Help."

He was ten yards away.

"Hold this a minute," Gregor said. He passed Layla the rifle, pulled off his jumper, and waded in, pushing off to a swim after a few yards. He grabbed Ben under one arm and started dragging him to the side.

"They're here," Layla said. "Hurry up."

Gregor looked into the distance. Three bikes roared over the trees, advancing along the reservoir, heading directly for them. He staggered out of the water, dragging Ben by his side. "Head for the building."

Layla ran for a faded red wooden door of an industrial-looking building, Ben and Gregor followed. She jumped over a partially collapsed metal fence and walked through a patch of waist-high weeds. She reached out and rattled the handle. "It's locked."

"Out of the way," Gregor said.

He carried on his forward momentum, roared, and slammed the bottom of his boot against the door's midsection. It crashed open, revealing dark space inside.

A croatoan hummed into view, stopping at a hover fifty feet away, thirty feet in the air.

Gregor aimed and fired. His round sparked against the side of the bike.

A return shot thumped against the building yards away. Dust puffed from the stone wall.

"In. Now," Gregor said. He quickly backed away, keeping the bike in his sights, slamming the door closed.

"All three of you. Stay exactly where you are," an unrecognizable voice said through the shadows.

Layla held up her hands. "We're being attacked. Haven't you seen what's just happened?"

A tall, thin man wearing a hunting jacket stepped out of the shadows holding a crossbow. He aimed at Gregor's face. "I saw you three arrive on alien machines. You've brought them to us."

Chapter Twenty-Eight

Denver fired his rifle, hitting the alien's hand, knocking its own weapon to the ground. The alien leaned down to reach for the gun, but Denver chambered another round and fired. This time, the bullet struck its torso, but like before, it seemed to activate some kind of temporal shifting ability.

While the alien phased in and out of vision, seemingly making it invulnerable to Denver's rifle, Charlie dashed out into the road and grabbed Maria, who stood there shell-shocked, her eyes already haunted by seeing Ethan vaporized.

"You go," Denver said. "I'll keep this fucker locked down while you get Maria somewhere safe. I'll meet you back at Quaternary."

"Don't do anything stupid," Charlie said from across the street. "We don't know what the hell this thing is or can do. You understand me, boy? Get your ass to safety ASAP."

"I got it, now go."

The alien's form flickered, phasing through the visual spectrum. While it was doing this, it moved back to the craft. Denver reloaded his rifle and fired again. As he'd thought, the bullet went right through the alien and struck the metal surface of the craft.

Blue light continued to spill out of the doorway that acted as a ramp from the central triangular section of the craft. Denver looked over to see his dad and Maria head for the shadows of a half-collapsed hotel. They'd just hit the side when the alien spun to face them. It brought out a long tube, placing it on its shoulder. A rocket with more of that blue energy firing behind it shot out, striking the side of the decrepit hotel.

With a blast that made Denver's ears pop, the remaining rubble of the structure collapsed in a huge cloud of smoke and debris. The single shot leveled the entire building. Denver's heart seemed to stop as he waited for movement.

Come on, where are you?

He considered going over there, but the alien had dropped the tube and regained its square-barreled rifle. It walked down the street, firing at Denver's position, each round booming like a cannon as the sound reverberated around the remaining buildings.

From the corner of his eye, he saw Maria wave at him. His dad dragged her away. "Go," his dad shouted. "Get out of there, Den. Don't fight it, just run; go back through the forest's edge."

Denver nodded and waved his hand to urge them to get out of there before the alien saw them. Another round flew just over his head, the heat scorching his crown. That got his heart pumping again and the adrenaline flowing.

He fired back at the alien, making the beast stop in the street and kneel behind a burned-out taxi, its chassis mostly rust. Through the windows, Denver saw the alien attend to its gun, probably reloading. It was no more than twenty feet away now. Looking to his left, Denver spotted a narrow alley with a low wall at the end.

Taking the opportunity, he dashed out of cover and

dived into the alley. The expected explosion of the alien's gun didn't come. This didn't make him feel any better. It made him feel like prey to an advanced and highly capable hunter.

He sprinted down the alley, holding the rifle close to his chest. He clambered over the wall, slipping where the smooth vines had broken through. Hitting the ground hard on his side, he gritted his teeth until the initial pain in his side dissipated. He stood and continued to sprint, taking just a quick glance behind him. As he reached the end of the alley and made to turn right out into a street that looked like the carbon copy of the one he'd just come from, he caught sight of the alien's long, agile legs.

Holding the rifle with one hand now and using it like a relay baton, he sprinted down the length of the street, dodging in and out of cars, piles of rubble, and fallen buildings. Each time he passed an alley, he looked down it to assess his position. When he came to the fourth one, he ducked inside and made his way to the end, heading back to the first street, doubling back on himself.

If the alien was tracking him, at least he'd be getting some distance and putting obstacles between them. When he came to the end of the alley, he saw the alien craft a few feet back down the street.

Waiting for a moment with his back against what used to be a bank with its expensive marble wall covering, half of which was now charred with signs of war, Denver poked his head around the corner to look back down the alley. When he saw no signs of movement, he stepped out behind the alien's ship, kneeling in its shadow. He looked out beneath its cone-shaped nose that was a few feet off the ground.

The alien had returned to the shadow of the car. It appeared to be communicating with someone. Its sharp, turtle-like snout moved up and down in erratic movements. It was definitely croatoan but looked like some kind of genetically-enhanced version. Way bigger, stronger, faster. And certainly better equipped.

While the alien's attention was elsewhere, Denver crept around the front of the craft and walked up the ramp, stepping inside. The atmosphere made him choke as though it was filled with a noxious dry ice. He pulled his shirt over his mouth to help filter the air.

The walls inside were white. To the left was the cockpit section with a single seat in front of a curved glass touch-surface. There was a discernible hum coming from the center of the craft. The whole thing was no more than about thirty feet long and ten wide.

What caught Denver's attention though was the cabin to the right. On two surfaces of the walls were racks holding what clearly looked like munitions. He reached out and touched a set of three disc-shaped items. They looked like mines. He lifted them off the rack and placed them in his backpack. Not wanting to spend any longer than necessary, he turned to leave, but something on the lower rack caught his attention: A rifle like the one the alien wielded.

He looked at his own rifle, then the alien one. It was a tough choice. He'd owned his for years, but it was starting to show signs of wear and tear, and he was running out of ammo. He'd have to make some more, but right now, he needed something to fight this hunter.

The alien rifle was longer by far, but the tubular barrel was vented and made of some extremely lightweight material. He placed his rifle on the rack and lifted the alien weapon. It felt good in his hands and weighed less than half of the old Remington.

"Fuck yes," Denver whispered. "You're coming with me."

He took the alien rifle and the three black boxes next to it, which he assumed to be ammo. They too were extremely light and fit snugly into the webbing around his pack.

Design-wise, the gun wasn't a million miles away from human weaponry, but then he guessed that firing a projectile through a barrel only had so many designs. The stock was large, designed for the hunter's torso, but it still fit snugly in the crook of Denver's shoulder. The sights were electronic. A slider on the side adjusted the magnification.

The gun had a button above the trigger. When Denver pressed it, the gun hummed, and a blue light flashed on the two-inch-square sight window, which seemed to be the weapon's general feedback mechanism.

Something within the rifle whirred, and the trigger moved forward a hair. A metallic click coming from the main body of the gun told him that it was loaded. The blue light faded away, and a green dot appeared in the middle of the screen.

He ducked his head outside for a moment, confirmed the alien still had its back to the craft. Heading back inside, he had an idea.

He followed the vibrations of the humming through the ship, going past the weapon's rack into what he guessed was the engine compartment. A four-foot high cylinder stood within a vat of blue gel-like substance. A pink tinge came from the perimeter, reminding him of the pink circles on the underside of the shuttles.

It must be the engine; there was nothing else in the ship.

Not wanting this fuck-bag to have the luxury of transport, Denver took one of the mine-like devices from his pack and inspected it.

Like all croatoan tech he'd come into contact with over the years, it was the pinnacle of simple, efficient design. If they were to design computers, they would have invented Apple machines, he thought, having seen them back at Mike's basement.

The mine had just a single mechanism. The same small screen as the rifle's sights, upon which was a single icon. Denver placed the disc on the top of the cylinder. One had to experiment with these kinds of things if they were to understand what the damned aliens were capable of.

His lungs were starting to protest about the poor air quality, and from outside, he heard the alien shooting his rifle again. When the rounds didn't hit near the craft, he realized it must have spotted Maria and his dad.

"Fuck it," Denver said, pressing the icon on the mine. It flashed blue, then pink, then started to pulse. He turned and dashed down through the corridor of the ship, carrying the alien rifle with him.

He stumbled out and rolled down the ramp before scrambling to his feet and sprinting for the alley. As he did, he shouted at the alien, who was leaning against the hood of the old car, his rifle supported out in front of him.

"Hey, fucker, over here!"

The alien turned his head and they locked eyes. Denver stopped just inside the alley and held out the alien's own weapon. "Look what I found. You want it? Come get it?"

As soon as Denver ducked back inside the dark coolness of the alley, the air took on a strange feel as though it suddenly filled with static. Then the explosion came, cutting short as the craft's hull muffled the sound, but blue and black smoke billowed out of the open door.

The alien roared, grabbed its weapon, and sprinted down the street toward Denver. But then it stopped halfway as Denver's dad stepped out from behind a building and fired two shots at the back of the alien hunter. Both missed narrowly, striking the ground at its feet. It spun round and seemed to be undecided on what to do. Apparently it decided Charlie was more of a threat, and instead of firing its rifle, raced after him.

"Dad, go!" Denver screamed.

"Get to the warehouse," his dad shouted back. "You have to get the part, you understand? Forget about us, the part is all that's important."

And then he was off, darting into the shadows, his root-infused muscles not making it easy for the alien hunter. Denver was left there on his own, the alien craft destroyed, or at least temporarily broken, and the hunter on his dad's trail. And of course there was Maria. Could he leave them? What if the hunter caught them? Despite his feelings, he knew his dad was right.

The part would mean the bomb could be completed. It meant they could take out the croatoan mother ship for good. He closed his eyes and rested his head against the cool concrete of the old bank.

Sacrificing yourself for the greater good was one thing, but having to sacrifice those you loved weighed much more heavily. But what could he do? Deciding that his dad had always proven himself to be right, and knowing the hunter wouldn't have it all his own way, Denver decided to go for the warehouse. He just hoped his dad and Maria had a plan.

He aimed the alien rifle into the sky and pulled the trigger. The gun barely kicked back as it fired with a loud but short crack, making his ears whistle. The motors inside whirred again. At least he knew how it worked. He'd come back for the hunter after he got the part. He just hoped he'd be back in time.

Chapter Twenty-Nine

Two more figures stepped out of the gloom: a man with a shotgun and a woman with a large, rusty knife. As Layla's eyes became accustomed to the light, she could see they'd been using this place as a home.

A camping stove sat in the corner of the filthy, dank room. Next to it, a jumble of metal pans and plates. Supplies were moderately stacked against the wall. Some old cans, probably out of date; pitiful-looking vegetables, even more so than hers; and several large bottles of cloudy water. Clothing hung on a line near the ceiling. A drip of water fell from a frayed pair of cargo pants.

Croatoan bikes distantly hummed outside.

"They're landing," a voice called from above.

"Who are you? Why did you come here?" the man in the hunting jacket said.

Layla touched Gregor's arm. She said, "We're running from the creatures outside. These two were attacked this morning in the forest and killed three aliens."

"Seems a bit strange," the woman said. "They don't usually go after survivors. You're from that farm, aren't you?"

"Fuck this," Gregor said. "Do you want to stand around here chatting while they come in and blow our brains out? If your man upstairs can see them, let me join him. Give me a clear shot."

He held his rifle forward.

"Listen to his accent. He's from the farm," the woman said.

The man with the crossbow edged back, lowering it. "He's right though. We'll deal with this first. Then we talk. Are you armed?"

Before Layla could answer, Gregor said, "Yes. They're coming upstairs with me."

"This is the only way in," the man with the shotgun said. "It's a side building. Only one entrance to protect."

Gregor grunted. He grabbed Ben and pushed him forward.

As much as she'd thought he was a cold bastard throughout the years, Layla couldn't help admiring Gregor's leadership qualities when the shit hit the fan. He was decisive and made decisions based on what was best for the team rather than himself.

For the first time since she could remember, she felt part of something. Gregor risked himself to come back and save her. And now he didn't want to leave her downstairs with strangers.

Layla felt integrated like never before, following Gregor as he thumped up the dusty, concrete staircase in his heavy boots.

Upstairs, a man crouched on the right hand side of the room, holding a pistol. He peered through a sliding hatch the size of a small pizza box created halfway up a boarded window. He squinted against the sunlight streaming through the gap, lighting up his face.

"I saw you arrive," he said. "Where did you learn to ride those things?"

"I used to work in a harvest—" Ben said.

"Shut up, Ben," Gregor said. He joined the man by the hatch. "Can you see the aliens?"

"They've landed and taken to the trees. Must be planning something."

"Let me look," Gregor said and stooped down.

The room above was the same size as the one below, about thirty square feet. Its three windows were covered by wooden boards, painted black. Light streamed in through cracks around the edges. Four single mattresses were spaced around, blankets scruffily drawn over each one.

The floor was spattered with various-colored dry blobs of candle wax. It reminded Layla of a Jackson Pollock painting she'd seen at the Guggenheim Museum in New York. A can of Spam held more value in today's world.

"Use the other window," the man said, nodding to his left.

Layla gripped the edge of the other hatch and eased it open along its squeaking rails. A ray of sunlight burst through the gap.

Across the grassy area seventy yards away, three hoverbikes sat by the edge of the forest. She briefly saw the edge of a croatoan behind a tree before it quickly vanished.

Gregor nudged her out of the way. He dropped to one knee and aimed his rifle. "Get behind me. If I'm hit, take the rifle and carry on the fight."

Layla stood to one side. Ben peered over the man's shoulder, revolver in his right hand.

"What are the aliens packing?" the man said.

"Similar to our conventional weapons. Guns, grenades, that sort of the stuff," Gregor said.

"No cannons or those guns that flatten small houses?"

"Those soldiers aren't around here," Layla said.

"Are you sure?" the man said. "I saw one of their fighters yesterday. First time in years. If the aliens get in touch with that thing ..."

"If it was coming for us, we'd know about it," Gregor said.

Layla wasn't so sure. If the hunter was under Augustus's command, he could give it a new mission. There was nothing stopping the croatoans outside from identifying their location.

Gregor's grip tensed around his rifle. Layla looked over his shoulder.

An alien scuttled from behind a tree toward the hoverbike she'd previously parked. It stopped a few yards short, took a silver ball from its belt, and threw it.

Gregor fired.

The croatoan clutched its torso and slouched to one side. Its grenade exploded with a hollow pop, creating a cloud of white smoke.

Gregor aimed at the shroud as it slowly cleared, drifting away on the gentle breeze. The blast shunted the bike onto its side. The alien lay flat on its back, helmet blown clear by the force of the explosion.

"Nice shot. One down," Layla said.

She'd never expected to hear herself utter those words.

"Two to go. And I can't see them," Gregor said. "Anyone else?"

A loud thud shook the building. Layla instinctively ducked. Flecks of paint dropped from the ceiling.

"What the hell was that?" Ben said.

"Sounds like they're next door," the man said.

"Joe. Get down here," a voice called up the stairs.

"Sorry guys. They want me downstairs," the man said.

He shrugged and hurried away.

"We could make a run for the bikes," Ben said.

"It'd be a turkey shoot," Gregor said. "We stay. Our hosts have offered to be the first line of defense."

The building shuddered again after another internal boom. Layla pressed herself against the wall. "What if the croatoans kill them? Use grenades in here?

Gregor rubbed his chin and looked around the room. "Stack the mattresses in the corner. Do it."

Layla grabbed the edge of the closest and dragged it to the end of the room. Its filthy gray blanket slithered off. She kicked it away.

Ben had already placed one in the corner at an angle. Layla stacked hers against it. He slid a third mattress across the floor and said, "This won't protect us. You saw what—"

"Do you have any better suggestions?" Gregor said.

After Layla completed the barricade, she returned to the gap in the left window. Ben paced around the room, mumbling to himself.

The three hover-bikes still sat in position by the trees. Another cut through the sky, it must've been the fourth one, circling their position.

Something moved outside, close to the building. Flicking in and out of Layla's line of vision.

She sprang on her toes, tried to get a better angle. The position of the hatch wouldn't allow it. "I think they're outside the door."

A shotgun blast and two pistol cracks came from directly below.

Croatoan weapons started snapping.

"Fuck this," Gregor said. He slammed his shoulder against the boarded-up window. It crunched into the plywood, splitting it horizontally across the middle. Gregor kicked the bottom section away and leaned his rifle out.

Ben jumped behind the barricade, holding his revolver over the top of the mattresses.

An alien grenade exploded. Gregor flew back, skidding on his backside, clutching one side of his face. Smoke coiled through the window.

Screams of pain came up the stairs, punctuated by the firing of croatoan weapons until both abruptly stopped.

Layla ran over to the makeshift barricade and slid behind it, next to Ben.

Gregor moved to the side of the stairway entrance and crouched with his rifle shouldered.

He put his finger to his lips. The slap of boots on concrete started to echo up the stairs. Gregor nodded with every slow, deliberate step as if mentally counting. Blood trickled down the side of his face.

Ben's hands shook as he held the pistol forward.

A croatoan boot appeared through the entrance.

Gregor dropped to his back and fired five times. He rolled away and covered his ears. Layla ducked behind the mattress. She grabbed Ben's shoulder and pulled him down.

The building vibrated after a thumping boom. Smoke gushed into the room, leaving a sour taste at the back of Layla's throat.

Silence followed.

She climbed over the barricade and approached Gregor. He sat up and dusted himself down. Layla went to touch his wound. He jerked his head away.

"Are you okay?" Layla said.

"Fine. Let's get the hell out of here."

"What happened?" Ben said. "Did you get them?"

"Shot them both. The front one had a grenade ready to go."

Layla squinted. The smoke stung her eyes. She pulled her sweater over her nose and mouth and followed Gregor downstairs.

Near the bottom, she stepped over the twisted figures of two dead croatoans into a room bathed in light. The entrance door had been blown off its hinges. A body lay underneath.

Gregor grasped Layla by the shoulder. "Don't look to your left. You don't need to see this."

She focused outside. Gregor pointed his rifle upwards and dashed out, turning amongst the weeds, looking up through his sights. Ben joined him and searched the sky.

Layla tentatively joined them. There was no sign of the previously circling croatoan. She approached the alien by the overturned bike. Its weapon lay a few feet away in the knee-length grass.

She picked it up, pointed it toward the forest, and pulled the trigger. It easily depressed like she was squeezing a tube of toothpaste. The alien rifle kicked against her chest as a projectile whistled out and thumped against a tree.

Gregor ducked. "Be careful with that."

"I'm not going through another situation unarmed," Layla said.

He appreciatively grunted and started heading for the forest.

"Where are we going?" Ben said.

"Away from here. Who knows what might turn up next? I'm not waiting to find out," Gregor said.

"We could take the hover-bikes," Ben said, gesturing to

the three parked by the forest's edge.

Gregor spun and grabbed Ben by the scruff of his neck. "Do you want to end up like Marek? Do you?"

He pushed Ben away. Ben stumbled after him. "I'm sorry. I didn't mean … I just …"

For the next hour, they picked their way through dense, slimy undergrowth. Gregor probably chose the route to provide cover. Layla breathed hard, swiping away branches and kicking away weeds that knotted around her feet.

They eventually hit a former road. Gregor leaned against a rusting SUV and wiped sweat from his brow. He gazed into the distant sky at the thin outline of the mother ship. This was probably the first time he had to stop and think about Marek. Layla decided to leave him to his own thoughts.

She shuddered at the thought of a new alien hulk in the sky. An instrument of death that would shortly bring about their demise. They had to do something.

Ben stretched out on a rock twenty yards away. Layla went over to him. "Are you okay?"

"A few scratches, nothing major."

"Do you have any idea where Jackson went? Think. We need to put our differences aside. Fight this thing together."

He shrugged. "Charlie and Gregor? You're joking, right?"

"I'm being serious. Unless we come up with something soon, well, you know what'll happen." Ben flashed a glance at Gregor, who still stared into the clear blue sky. He sheepishly looked back at Layla. She lowered her voice, "If you know something, now is the time to say."

"Charlie's got a plan. I don't know what exactly, but he's been working on it for some time. I know where he'll be,"

Ben trailed off.

She resisted the strong urge to punch him in the face. "I swear, if you don't start talking—"

Ben failed to spot Gregor moving around behind him. He wrapped his arm under Ben's chin and squeezed tightly.

"I'm giving you a minute before I snap your neck," Gregor said.

Ben's face reddened. He gasped. "I'll tell you. Please. Let go."

Gregor loosened his grip and grabbed the back of Ben's hair. Layla leaned toward him. "This is no time for games. Where will he be?"

"Ridgway. The clock tower. Noon tomorrow. I'm supposed to meet him. Give him information about the shuttle runs."

"Did he say why?" Layla said.

"That's all I know. I wasn't going to meet him. I'm with you guys. Honestly."

Gregor released his hold and slapped the palm of his hand against the side of Ben's head. "You treacherous little shit."

"What are you going to do?" Layla asked Gregor.

He threw Ben to one side. "What do you think I'm going to do? Tomorrow, I'll be in Ridgway, waiting for Jackson to show his face."

Chapter Thirty

Charlie wiped the debris from his face. His ears were still ringing from the grenade explosion. Using the cloud of smoke and concrete to hide their position, they'd managed to outmaneuver the hunter, using Charlie's knowledge of the alleys and side streets to get some distance and return to Quaternary HQ.

"What about Denver?" Maria asked as they cleared the sheet metal out of the way and headed into the basement.

"He'll be okay." Charlie locked the door behind him and took a breath. Even though the root kept him fit and strong, his age meant that he still felt the fatigue once the adrenaline and the root's effect wore off. "Come on, we need to go up a few levels."

Before they entered the basement area, Charlie stopped at a small room previously used by janitors. Mike had converted it to a gun rack. Charlie took a Barrett .50 caliber rifle. If anything would stop that damned croatoan bastard, it'd be that.

Taking the stairs two at a time and wincing with the effort, Charlie led Maria into the third floor, where his old office used to be. His, Mike's, and of course Pippa's. It was like a mausoleum.

Desks and computers were still in the same place since the day he'd left it. Papers and books littered the floor, disturbed by the vibrations of war. He made to reach up to the bead necklace and remembered he'd given it to Ben.

It didn't matter. Pippa's face was still clear in his mind. She smiled at him with that quirky look of hers. He pictured her bouncing into the office, dirt smudged on her face as she excitedly talked about their next project or some surprising find.

"Are you okay?" Maria said, touching his arm.

"What? Yes, sorry, I just … It doesn't matter. Okay, stand back from the window, but from somewhere you can use this to spot for me." He handed her the monocular sight.

"What is it you want me to do exactly?" Maria asked.

Charlie opened the boarded-up window and balanced the Barrett's barrel across the sill. He rested the rest of the gun on the edge of a desk that he pulled closer.

"That bastard alien is going to have to approach from that street down there. Everywhere else is too dilapidated. It'll know we had to come this way too. I want you to be a second of pair of eyes to help me focus on it."

"Okay," Maria said, pulling a wheeled office chair closer so that she could rest and still get a good view out of the window.

Charlie got himself comfortable, brought the scope to his eye, and checked his distances. All seemed good. He just had to wait. Even if the hunter came at them from the shadows, there was still a ten-foot section of open space it'd have to cross. Hopefully, they'd spot it before it got to that section and gave him time to aim.

They sat in silence for five minutes. Sweat beaded on Charlie's forehead. He knew Denver would have the part by now and be on his way back. As though he had conjured him with his very mind, Maria excitedly said, "Den's there, look."

With an alien weapon in his hands, he came out of a side street, looking to either side, always on alert. "You keep watching him," Charlie said, not loving this at all.

His fears were born of good instinct. As Denver stepped further out into the open, forty feet behind him the shadows shifted, and the hunter slid out of his position. The bastard was probably there the whole time. Charlie couldn't quite get a good aim on him. A fallen wall obscured his vision, but he could see the shadows moving now that the noon sun had dipped lower to the west, lengthening the shadows across the sidewalk.

"Oh God, he's going to see him," Maria said, tracking Denver's movements.

"Just wait," Charlie said.

"We have to warn him." She placed the monocular down on the desk and approached the window. Charlie pushed her out of the way and took the Barrett to the next window across to get a better angle. That did the trick. He could see the hunter edge out from behind a half-yard-thick fallen wall.

Maria moaned as she got to her feet. "What the hell do you think you're—"

"Shut up," Charlie said, glaring at her. She took a step back but kept her eyes on Denver as he came further down the street.

On its knees, the alien raised the rifle and brought its scope to its eye. The glow of the screen illuminated its transparent visor, revealing the tough, leathery skin of its face and a glowing amber eye. This was definitely not a run-of-the-mill croatoan. But even with its fancy tech, Charlie doubted it could withstand a .50 cal round.

"Denver, run!" Maria said from the window, shouting

at the top of her voice. Den looked up then behind him and dashed to the side. Charlie was about to yell at her, but when he looked back, the alien had come further out of the shadows. It had heard Maria. It pointed the rifle up at Charlie. They locked eyes, and Charlie pulled the trigger before launching himself to the side.

Both rifles exploded. The alien's shot rocked the walls of the Quaternary building. A chunk of masonry flew away from the window frame, narrowly missing Charlie's face.

"You've hit him," Maria said, now standing further back but still watching through the monocular sight.

Charlie took a risk and lifted his rifle to peer through the scope. He saw the hunter crawl away, clutching its right leg. He was surprised that the leg wasn't severed, but the alien armor was damaged, and its suit took on a lighter color. Yellow blood stained the ground.

"It's wounded," Charlie said. "But I don't know how long we'll have. We need to leave. Now."

He grabbed the rifle and Maria's arm and headed back down the stairs.

Mike and Mai pulled Denver into the basement and locked the door behind him. They all rushed into the workshop area. Breathless, with sweat pouring from him, Denver shrugged off his backpack. They all looked at him expectantly.

"Well?" Charlie said, "Did you get it?"

"What do you think, old man?" Den said between panted breaths. Pip joined him by his side. He knelt down and made a fuss of the dog. "I ain't just a pretty face, am I, girl?"

"No," Maria said, before realizing he was talking to the dog. She turned away to hide her embarrassment.

"Oh," Mai said, lifting out a disc-shaped object from Den's pack. "What's this? Looks alien, of course."

"Bomb," Denver said. "I used it to take out the anti-grav engine of that bastard's ship. You just press …" Denver reached out and grabbed Mai's wrist to stop her from touching the small screen. "Jesus, Mai. That's what activates it."

Mike lifted the second one. "I'll have to make some safeties for you. Wouldn't want it going off by mistake. But as nice as these are, what about the magnet?"

Denver fished out a box with a Ford label stamped on it and handed it over. "These?"

"Holy crap, Den, there's half a dozen here."

"I think there might be more there," Den said. "I saw boxes everywhere and grabbed the first one I saw. I wanted to get back before … Well, before we all got killed by that thing out there."

"What is it?" Mai asked. "A soldier?"

"Worse," Charlie said. "I don't know what it is. One of the croatoans' experiments perhaps, some other alien imported from God knows where. But it took a .50 cal to the leg and was still alive, still moving. We've got to clear out right now before the bastard tracks the way in."

"On it," Mike said, heading to one of his over-filled desks. Mai joined him. Together, they opened the case of the bomb and started to install the part.

Maria sat down on a plastic chair and wiped tears from her eyes. "I can't believe what happened to Ethan. One minute he was right there by me, the next …"

Denver knelt down by her, held her hands within his. "I know it's hard," he said. "It's a shock. It's difficult and brutal, and it hurts. But right now, we have to remember him and everyone else that died at the aliens' hands. We have to remember them and go on because what we intend to do will honor them. We can't lose focus on that. We can grieve later. Take the pain, but don't let it consume you, okay? You're with us; you're one of us. We'll stick together."

Maria looked down at Denver, her face blemished with dirt, the tears tracking the stains down her cheeks. "You were so brave," she said, "to go off like that. How can I be that brave? I'm so scared. It feels like danger waits in every shadow. I'm not sure I can go on."

"It's understandable," Denver said. "This is all new to you, but believe me, as dangerous as this seems, it's like a vacation to how it was. We have to put all this into perspective and carry on. If not, then what else is there?"

"Waiting to die," Maria said.

"And I'm not one for waiting," Denver said, flashing her a smile. "So what say you come with us and let be what will be? Let's do this, bring down that mother ship, strike back at these bastards, and show them that they've underestimated us."

Maria wiped her eyes and took a deep breath. "I guess we have no real option. Count me in."

She stood and hugged Denver.

Charlie smiled and turned away to prepare their exit. On the other side of the basement was a fire exit that led across the street. Mike and a few others who had sadly passed on had dug a tunnel further through until they came out into the subway system. Although flooded, the water level wasn't so high that they couldn't get an inflatable raft in there.

In emergencies, they'd used it a few times before. If they followed the right route, they could get through enough of the train system to get clear of Manhattan. They kept a smaller raft stored in the basement. The other dinghy was too large.

Now their load was lighter, they could squeeze onto the raft and get out. It'd be tight, but it was better than risking going over ground. All the shooting would have stirred up other survivors lurking in the city.

"Hey, Chuck, it's ready," Mike said, calling out from the other end of the tunnel.

Charlie walked back to find them standing around the device. Mai had a satisfied look on her face. "Your boy done good," she said, winking at Denver. "It works perfectly. But here's the thing. You'll have one shot at this. Once activated by using the touchscreen here, there's no going back. If it malfunctions for whatever reason, the regulating magnet will be fried, and no offense, you won't have the expertise to wire in another in time and figure out what's wrong."

"Understood," Charlie said.

Denver's forehead wrinkled. "It doesn't sound very … solid. I mean, it's a huge risk going up there. If it doesn't go off, it'll be for nothing."

"That's my worry, son. We've talked about this already. It's my time. I'm going up there. I trust that it'll work. You'll just have to trust me."

"Wait," Maria said. "So what you're saying is this is a complete suicide mission? There's absolutely no way you're coming back if it works or not?"

"We all have to make a sacrifice," Charlie said, "and this is mine. Okay, that's enough of the philosophy. Let's have less chat and more action. Mike, prep the bomb and make it safe for travel. We've got to go. I suggest you get Mai out of here too."

“Will do, Chuck,” Mike said. “And don’t worry about us. We’ve got transport waiting for us.”

Mike placed the bomb inside a plastic flight case and made sure it was clipped tightly shut. He handed it to Charlie with his left hand and extended his right. Charlie took it and shook it firmly. “I’ll miss you, you crazy old bastard,” Charlie said, trying to swallow the lump in his throat.

“And you too, you reckless fool. One of these days, you’ll get yourself killed.”

“One of these days. But not today.”

Chapter Thirty-One

Augustus pulled the cannula from his body after the last of the root compound had flowed into his bloodstream. With a sigh of satisfaction, he sat back on his human-leather recliner.

The cool, white-blue lights of the mother ship made his skin look pale and diseased, but he knew he was never in better health. Every nerve tingled and every hair stood on end as the root compound did its magic in repairing any aging cells.

He took this shot a few days early, having caught a bug from one of the cattle-scum down on the surface. Probably from Gregor, he thought. That reckless fool mixed with people without any concern for his health. Gregor was a walking, talking disease factory. Like they all were.

After all this time, human beings were still barely better than pigs and cows. Even the livestock had the same herding instinct as cows. Still, they made for a good, nutritious food supply while the root took hold. And for now, the second crop appeared to be perfect. More perfect than many of the planets the croatoans had terraformed.

Though he had been in and out of stasis since his last day as Roman Emperor Valens, he wasn't one to dwell much on the past. Especially given it was so long ago. But stasis within a croatoan pod had the effect of compressing time. That fateful day during the Battle of Adrianople, the ninth of August, 378 AD, was still clear. The Goths, led by the maggot, Fritigern, defeated his Roman army and set about the destruction of the Roman Empire as it was known. He, Emperor Valens, removed his habit and disappeared into a village, escaping as nothing more than a battle-wounded peasant.

For five long days, he'd wandered through the woods of Thracia until he'd managed to seek voyage across to Greece.

Augustus closed his eyes, the fatigue of post-root injection making him tired. Though it was nothing like the fatigue of his escape; this was more of a spaced-out bliss. His body rejuvenated, growing young and vital again.

His senses sharpened during this state. The soft, cyclical vibrations of the mother ship's engines synchronized with his heartbeats so that he was one with the ship, a part of the larger system, a part of the Croatoan Empire.

An empire that made his Roman Empire look like a backwater village.

That revelation came to him within days of settling in Greece. The croatoans never did explain how they knew who he was, but one night, while he was working alone on a fishing jangada, hauling in the evening's nets, he was approached on the beach. At first, he thought he was sick, hallucinating.

The first impression he got of the croatoan was that of a large, helmeted turtle, standing on two reverse-joined legs in a strange suit. The eyes were large and held intelligence within them, but the overriding feeling he got was that it was ancient.

For two weeks, the croatoan would visit him during the night, talking to him in broken Greek, but enough for

Augustus, or Valens as he was then, to understand. The promises seemed unreal to begin with: eternity, a life without pain, which appealed greatly due to the wounds he'd suffered at the hands of the Goths.

Even back then, he required the wearing of a leather mask or a deep-brimmed hat to hide the disfigurement. When he saw the creature's pod, he knew the promises were real, that they had substance. He thought the Romans were advanced in their use of materials and technology, but the stasis pod, half-buried within a deep cave, told him that humanity hadn't even started yet.

And then came the first taste of the root. Within the pod, a system of root compound within a slow-feed drip ensured that the aliens could live indefinitely once in a stasis mode. It was like a voluntary coma but one that with some thought could be come out of at will or at specified times.

For the first time in decades, he felt young and powerful again. The compound stitched his wounds, made him stronger. Even his thoughts sped up. It brought him out of the self-imposed prison where he'd placed himself, and now he could see the world of opportunity in front of him. He had a chance to build a new empire, to rule again, but this time without the limits of humanity and politics.

Hagellen, the croatoan that approached Augustus, explained many historical incidents of how the aliens had intervened or taken candidates to work with them when the Earth's conditions were right.

When Hagellen said that he'd be in stasis for more than fifteen hundred years, the period of time needed to make the Earth's ecological balance suitable for growing the root, Augustus laughed, but Hagellen had shown him relics from the Egyptians and further back still.

It'd be like waking from a dream, Hagellen said. Within the stasis pod, the compound would keep him alive, compress time, so that when he woke and the croatoans rose from deep within the Earth, it would feel like no time at all.

And he was right.

Augustus sat up as the tingling sensation began to wear off. The compound was almost finished with him for this month. He shook his head. The memories of being Valens dissipated. It was always strange how this procedure would send him back to his former life. But despite the time-compression, it was a long a time ago. He wasn't that cowardly emperor any longer.

He was Lord Augustus. Earth's first post-alien leader. Or at least he soon would be.

"On screen," he said, leaning his elbows against the glass desk in his office. They'd decorated it to look like a Roman court. This part of the ship, one of the lowest levels, was designed to support him as a human, but soon, he wouldn't need a special atmosphere to suit him. Soon, he'd have the procedure that would make him more croatoan than human, and he would take his rightful place at the top of Earth's new hierarchy.

The wide screen, embedded into the curved white walls of his office, switched on and glowed the familiar blue briefly before it patched into the communications network. Thousands of smaller squares in a grid showed him all the channels to the farms down on the surface.

"Message to all farms," he said, and waited for each square to gain a white border to indicate the communication connection established. The screen beeped after a few moments, confirming the connection.

Within each square, he saw the faces of the farm workers looking at him expectantly, the requisite level of fear in their eyes. It made him smile beneath his mask. As Valens and now Augustus, he could always draw that level of fear from his fellow humans, though he wasn't so conceited to believe it was at him directly.

No, it was due to his position. He'd always known that. It was why he'd ducked out of the battle of Adrianople. It was clear the Goths would win. He'd seen the winds of change and knew the Romans' time was up. He would no longer have the position to instill that fear, so he left to cast fear upon the fish in Greece.

Some men would feel they took a step down, but not Augustus. Even back then, he knew the order of things. Dominion over fish was no different than dominion over man.

"Farmhands, this is Lord Augustus; we're coming to a new stage of our development, and you are placed at the forefront of this transformation. Your actions next will determine not only your individual fate but also the fate of humankind. Fear not; your action is a simple one. I want you all to activate the pressurization protocols on all breeding facilities. The time has come to seal those precious breeding units from the harm of the atmosphere."

As though perfectly orchestrated, he saw three thousand pairs of eyes widen in fear and realization. By pressurizing the breeding facilities, it was clear that all those outside of the buildings would perish when the atmosphere changed. But they knew better than to question him.

"Atmospheric metrics are being downloaded to your systems now," Augustus added. "Once complete, activate the protocols. As for yourselves, I want to thank you personally for your work and tireless dedication. Without you, humanity would not be able to continue. Your sacrifice has ensured the continuing survival of our noble race.

"Each and every one of you will be remembered in the records. I will see to it personally. In its current state, Earth has but a few more days left. Say your goodbyes and perform any last rituals you need. The end has come. Thank you, and good luck in the journey of your afterlife."

One by one, the individual video links to the farms glowed yellow as the data packs downloaded. The ones that turned green indicated they had activated the pressurization process, sealing off the breeding facilities and, so doing, sealing their own fates.

Augustus took a great deal of joy from watching his orders being executed as the large screen became a sea of green squares. Hundreds activated at once, and within a few seconds, the entire farm network had activated the protocol although … He leaned forward and noticed that there was one that was still yellow.

Of course. It had to be that one. He'd expected as much.

"Engage Farm 1038."

The sickly image of Vlad, one of Gregor's old gang members, came up on screen. The revolting man's face was grey and puffy. His eyes were rimmed with red sores, and his brown hair lay lank and greasy against his scalp. He reminded Augustus of the street peasants back in Rome. Even then, they never looked after themselves. Some things never change. Some humans are just not as worthy as others.

"Mr. Augustus, sir, I …" Vlad began to say. A girl appeared behind him, the one he remembered as Alex.

She was barely more capable than Vlad.

"Why haven't you activated the pressurization protocol?"

Vlad looked to Alex. Her face tightened. It was clear they were hiding something. The tension of their bodies said it all.

"What's going on there?" Augustus asked. "Do I need to send a squad down there to take over?"

"No, sir, it's erm, fine, really, just a few minor issues with the livestock. We've got it in hand."

"Then activate the procedure."

Augustus kept the channel open and waited. Vlad fussed at the console and looked up through his lank hair. But he wasn't fooling anyone.

"There's a problem with our mainframe, sir. I'll get it fixed right away."

Augustus brought up a second console window on his desktop screen, patched into Farm 1038's system, and ran a diagnostic. In hindsight, the croatoan hierarchy should have made everything automated from the mother ship. It was too risky to have left any procedure in the hands of the humans, but the aliens were hot on trust. They said many times over the centuries since being on the Earth that trust was always the first way to cooperation. Force should only come if that trust was proven to be less than optimal, and force could fix anything that trust broke.

Looking down at the diagnostic report, he felt the bounds of trust retreat from the breaking point. It appeared that Vlad was indeed telling the truth. The mainframe was reporting an error in one of its processor cores.

"I'll give you an hour to fix it before I send help," Augustus said, emphasizing that last word.

"Thank you, sir, we'll send a report right away when it's done. Sorry to delay things."

"I'll expect a report within the hour." With that, Augustus closed the connection and shut down both screens. Immediately, a new session started. This time, the screen filled with the image of his old friend.

Hagellen smiled on screen, stretching his wide, turtle-like mouth, his ancient face shown in super-high definition. Augustus didn't know how old he was but, from his stories, calculated he must be at least five hundred thousand in Earth years. The compound had made his leathery skin look almost like bark.

The alien was one of the hierarchy members. Although Augustus would never fully understand their cultural organization, the mother ship had a clear organization structure. There was Hagellen and three others that made up a command module; they decided what happened here on Earth and set the schedules.

Beneath them was a council of five others who oversaw various aspects of planetary colonization. Augustus was an honorary member of that council with his role earmarked as taking over the planet once the terraforming was complete.

The idea was that once things were running well, they would move a population of croatoan citizens to live on Earth while the mother ship and its hierarchy would head off to their next project, which could be thousands of years in the making, with Hagellen and the others going back into their stasis pods until whatever planet they had found would be ready for the same procedure.

"Hagellen, old friend, to what I do owe this pleasure?"

"Valens, my friend," the alien said in his clicking

language. Augustus had picked it up over the years. Although he would never fully understand the nuance, he knew enough to be able to translate on the fly. “The terra-forming ship is one of your days away. We’ll soon dock and initiate the final procedure. Is all well with your systems?”

“All working as expected. There’s a small delay on one of the farms but nothing that will prevent the plan from going ahead.”

“I noticed that you ordered Baliska to the surface. That seems a drastic action at this time. Is there something I and the council should be aware of?”

Baliska was the hunter Augustus had ordered down to deal with that meddling little bastard, Charlie Jackson. Seeing as Gregor couldn’t cope with him, he needed to do something. Though in the grand scheme of things, Jackson wasn’t a huge problem. “There’s a tiny resistance on the surface. Baliska hasn’t been hunting in three decades. After he arrived here from his sojourn on your jungle planet, he wanted a new challenge, so I decided to take advantage of his desire to find and eliminate this resistant human before he had the opportunity to become a bigger issue later.”

“That’s understandable,” Hagellen said, shaking his head side-to-side slowly, which was the croatoan way of agreeing. The aliens had a complicated set of body language that Augustus had never quite got the hang of. It seemed to change on so many different nuances, and with him not understanding the language at a fundamental level, he was never exposed to those nuances. With a race as ancient as the croatoans, he didn’t expect to learn all that in just a few decades of waking time.

“Was there anything else, old friend?” Augustus said.

“Not for now. Inform me when the final farm has initiated the pressurization. I'll inform you when the terraforming ship has successfully docked with us."

"Will it take long, the atmospheric change?"

"Everything is but a blink of our eyes, Valens. You know this." Hagellen squinted his large, black eyes slightly, which meant that it was a lighthearted phrase. The croatoans never laughed as such, rather, via their eyelid movements they indicated acceptance or rejection of the attempt at humor.

Augustus never bothered to figure out what made them 'laugh.' There was too much risk of insulting them. He'd lasted this long by usually only speaking when spoken to and keeping his interactions with them strictly about business. To get personal with a croatoan council member was to go into a battle with a multi-headed hydra with the ability to kill you faster than you could blink.

"We'll talk tomorrow," Hagellen said before the channel on the screen closed.

Augustus leaned back in his chair and closed his eyes. He let the hum of the ship enter his body. He pictured Earth, a bright blue marble in the dense black of space. "Soon, you'll be mine."

Chapter Thirty-Two

Gregor watched the front of the clock tower from inside the remains of a crumbling brick building. The cover from here was perfect. He was obscured by thick ivy that almost completely wrapped the building. Poking his rifle through the plant gave him a perfect shot.

Ben lay snoozing next to him. They'd spent all night walking by the side of roads and fighting their way through woodland, trying to find the former town in time to set up an ambush.

Charlie Jackson would not catch him loitering by the clock tower. This meeting was going to be on Gregor's terms.

His stomach growled, but food could wait. All he'd eaten in the last twelve hours were two unripe apples from a nearby tree. Gregor kicked himself for not grabbing some supplies from the building by the reservoir. By the time he realized his error, they were heading to Ridgway. At least it wasn't raining. The sun beat down on them through a large hole in the collapsed roof.

Layla knelt beside him and swiped some leaves to one side. "Still no sign of them?"

"Nothing," Gregor said. He looked at Ben. "Do you think he was telling the truth?"

She checked her watch. "If he was, Jackson's nearly an hour late."

"Or he's got his own vantage point. I'm not moving first." Gregor shook Ben's leg. He twitched awake and looked back, bleary-eyed. "Are you sure he said noon?"

"Positive. I've told you several times already. Why would I lie?"

Ben's question was exactly what had started preying on Gregor's mind. He could lie to lead them into an ambush. Jackson might've been in the process of surrounding the area.

The instruction was given in the belief that Gregor was still running the camp. Maybe it was to draw him away so Charlie could attack.

He wondered if Alex and Vlad were still alive. The croatoans didn't seem to recognize feelings or attachments between humans. With a bit of luck, they'd still be feeding the livestock and monitoring inside the chocolate factory. Gregor had to get them free before Augustus got his claws into them.

"I'll be back in a few minutes," Layla said.

"Where you going?" Gregor said.

"Do you really want to know?" she said, rolling her eyes.

"Oh. Fine. I want to have a little chat with Ben anyway," Gregor said.

Layla hopped over a partially collapsed internal wall, its chipped plaster surface covered with dark green mold spores, and disappeared to another part of the building.

Gregor grabbed Ben's shoulder and squeezed with enough force to make it unfriendly. Ben returned his stare with a nervous smile. "Gregor?"

Back in Yerevan, they'd used Marek's basement for extracting information from unreliable people. A thumb-screw was usually the best way to make people talk, usually after the first crunch of bone. Sometimes even the mere fitting of the medieval-looking torture instrument was enough to prize out information. It depended on the backbone of the person and what they had to lose. It was certainly a cleaner approach than Igor's amateurish knife-related strategy.

A verbal thumbscrew would be enough for Ben.

"Treachery will always come home to the traitor," Gregor said.

Ben tried to edge away and winced as Gregor tightened his grip. "What's that supposed to mean?"

Gregor drew his rifle from between the ivy and jabbed the muzzle under Ben's chin. "It's an old proverb meaning if you betray me, bad things will happen to you."

"I'm not. I swear. How many times do I have to say it?"

"Do you want to know my own proverb? I've made it up especially for you." Ben didn't reply. "If you've betrayed me, I'll rip off your arm and beat you to death with the soggy end. Have I made myself clear?"

Ben rapidly nodded. "Crystal."

A foot crunched over broken glass in an adjacent room. Layla coming back. Gregor let go of Ben and aimed his rifle back between the ivy.

"Well, well, well. I didn't expect to find you here," a voice said.

A voice that Gregor hadn't heard for years. That he'd dreamed of hearing scream with agony while strapped to his garage chair as Gregor slowly pulled out his individual fingernails with snipe-nose pliers. Reminding him about his cousin.

He tensed. Didn't want to turn. Didn't want to give Jackson a moment's satisfaction before the bastard pulled the trigger.

Ten years of his shit. Ten years of survival. He'd been led into a trap. It was all so simple. It made his life seem trivial. Too much effort for such a stupid end.

"Get it over with, Jackson," Gregor said.

Ben scrambled to his feet.

"Stay right where you are," another voice called out.

Footsteps approached. Gregor glanced to his side.

A red-haired, rangy-looking man strode through the rubble, peering down his sights. Denver Jackson. Last time he'd seen him, he was Charlie's feral pet, learning tricks from his master. A dog scampered behind his legs and barked.

Gregor snorted. "Look at you, all grown up."

"Shut the fuck up. I don't remember giving you permission to speak," Denver said. "Hold out your weapon. Nice and slow."

He held out the AR-15 by its grip and placed it on the ground.

"Did you get the information I asked for?" Charlie said.

Ben thrust up his hands and took a couple of steps away from Gregor. "I didn't have time. Gregor knows. We're not with the croatoans."

Charlie chuckled in his distinctive, sarcastic way. Gregor hated it. To Jackson, everything was black or white. He should have guessed that Ben wouldn't have been allowed to just stroll back into the farm. Jackson's necklace and the opportunity to get him had a blinding effect.

Gregor looked up at Ben and scowled. The turncoat backed away another couple of steps.

"We've tried to get information from them before. They won't help—" Charlie said.

"Drop your weapon," Layla shouted.

Keeping his hands spread above his shoulders, Gregor rolled onto his back. Layla must've heard the Jacksons. She'd rounded the building and stood behind Charlie, pointing the croatoan rifle at the back of his head.

Charlie's hands were raised. He didn't look much different from ten years ago. Gregor had caught glimpses of him through the last decade but never close up like now. Bearded, piercing blue eyes, miserable.

A woman stood next to Charlie wearing a harvester uniform. Another lie from Ben about the fate of their crew. Gregor reached across for his rifle.

"Pick that up and I put a bullet through your forehead," Denver said.

Gregor withdrew his hand. "If you shoot me, your plastic father gets it in the head."

Denver hadn't even glanced back to Charlie. He focused down on Gregor with an intense expression and twitched his head to his left. "Then I kill your helper."

A distant overhead noise like an ongoing extended roll of thunder echoed from the clear blue sky.

"Leave us with Gregor," Charlie said. "You go back to the farm. We won't hurt you."

"We want the same thing as you. To bring down the croatoans," Layla said.

Charlie shook his head and groaned. "You've sure got a funny way of showing it."

The rumble grew into a roar. Everyone looked up. A large, white cloud formed in sky. Eight huge bright rings appeared through it. A blast of lukewarm air rushed down, spreading dust around the building. Pieces of plaster dropped from the decaying internal wall as the ground shook. Denver's dog repeatedly barked.

A massive object in the shape of a key moved in front of the sun, casting a shadow over the area. The mother ship had lowered, but something larger was attached. A rectangular vessel with four large funnels protruding from its side. The circular mother ship appeared to be connected to the bottom of it.

"What the hell?" Ben said.

"This is it," Layla said. "The data, behavior, experiments, and Igor. It was leading to this. They needed more than the root to terraform."

"What are you saying?" Charlie said.

"I'm saying we haven't got time for disagreements," Layla said. "You and Gregor sort out your differences later. We've all got bigger things to worry about."

***

Charlie looked at Gregor and slowly shook his head. Gregor glared back. The woman in front of Layla turned and said, "What do you know?"

She seemed non-aggressive, unlike Charlie and Denver. Layla had only ever known Charlie as a vague acquaintance during her first year in North America. She'd found him a little abrupt. It all changed after they moved to the farm. Gregor and Charlie became equally as obsessed over one another. Sabotaging anything around each of their respective operations, employed in a dangerous game of one-upmanship.

Layla jabbed the alien rifle into the back of Charlie's head. He shuffled forward a few inches. She said earnestly, "You need to listen to me. I've observed what they're planning to do. Croatoans testing with an atmosphere box. A timeline near completion. Igor mentioning a ship to complete the process. You only need to look around you to see the place is primed for it. The ship up there is the final part. We need to figure out a way to stop this. Together."

Charlie shrugged. "I've already got a plan. Been working on it for years while you've been sucking up to the croatoans and butchering the population."

"And you can hatch it in a day?" Layla said. "Because I reckon that's all we've have. Maximum."

"What's your plan, Jackson?" Gregor said.

"Wouldn't you like to know?"

"He wants to put a bomb on the mother ship," the woman said. "Blow it out of the sky. Ben was supposed to get information about the shuttle runs."

"Shut up, Maria," Charlie said.

Layla moved around to Charlie's side in order to get eye contact. "Trust me. It's do or die for all of us."

"Charlie," Gregor said. "Call off your two pet dogs, and I'll give you the information you need. We'll do this together. After that, you and I will sort our differences the traditional way. Do we have a deal?"

Gregor stood up and dusted himself down. Charlie nodded toward Denver. He lowered his rifle.

Layla lowered hers. "Good. Now we can talk like civilized people. Do we have a deal?"

"There's nothing civilized about you," Charlie said. "But you have a deal. The overall requirements for the planet are bigger than Gregor's ego. Then again, they always have been."

"Replace my name with yours and the statement still makes perfect sense," Gregor said.

"For God's sake. Will you two knock it off?" Layla said.

She looked skywards again at the joined vessels. They'd maintained a position high above a few puffy, light orange clouds that drifted lazily past.

"How can you get me on a shuttle to the mother ship?" Charlie said.

"Easiest way is to put you in a food container," Gregor said. "If we still have people left at the farm, it'll work."

"You mean processed humans?" Denver said.

"Does it matter now?" Layla said.

The last thing they needed was to keep raking up their individual choices for survival. Layla noticed Gregor's eyes kept flicking toward Ben. He nervously edged further away until he flinched as his back hit the semi-collapsed interior wall.

"We arrange oxygen to be left behind the stacked trays," Gregor said. "You get in before the container's loaded onto a shuttle. Alex or Vlad can divert the croatoans elsewhere. We launch a diversionary attack on the farm. The shuttle will make an emergency take off."

"And we get shot with the cannon on the roof of the shuttle?" Denver said.

"The croatoans are pragmatists. They don't fire cannons toward their own buildings."

"You sure that'll work?" Charlie said.

"I can't think of another way. You sure the bomb will work?" Gregor said.

Charlie walked over and stood a couple of yards in front of Gregor. "It'll work. But don't bet on me not coming back, *my friend*."

Gregor's eyes narrowed. "Don't test me, Charlie. I could—"

Masonry exploded inwards.

Layla jumped back, covering her face.

A light blue beam shot through the room, passing between Ben and Charlie. It punctured a basketball-sized hole in the opposite wall.

Bricks clacked to the ground. Dust filled the air.

Gregor picked up the rifle, spun, and pointed it through the ivy. "There's a big, ugly alien outside."

"Is everyone all right?" Charlie said.

Gregor fired two shots; both went clean through with no damage. "What the fuck? It turned into a blur."

Charlie crouched over Gregor and pulled leaves to one side. "We met that thing in New York."

"Augustus sent a hunter after you."

Layla ran across the room and knelt next to the gap that had been blasted out of the wall. She leaned around and saw a large croatoan prowling outside. It threw its weapon to one side and drew a sword from its thigh-sheath. The blade shone as though as it were made from chrome. Circular holes ran down the middle.

She squeezed the trigger. The rifle bucked against her shoulder. The croatoan shifted to its left at an unbelievable speed. Denver joined her by the hole and fired his rifle. The alien dodged again in a blur.

"It's impossible to hit the thing if it's facing you," Denver said. "We need to split up."

The alien raised its sword and moved toward the building.

"Take the bomb to the edge of camp," Charlie said. "Get everything prepared. Gregor says this thing's after me. I'm going to create a diversion."

Denver nodded and ran to the back of the building.

Ben stayed against the wall, shuddering. Layla decided not to argue and followed.

"Get moving now," Charlie said.

She stopped and looked back. "Take the croatoan rifle."

Layla threw it to Charlie. He caught it in his left hand.

Ben scrambled past her. Charlie jumped through the ivy and stood in front of the building. The alien pointed at him with its graphite gauntlet and swung its sword in a circular motion above its head. Charlie rushed to his right, back toward the forest in the opposite direction to the farm. The alien hopped after him.

Chapter Thirty-Three

Denver wiped the sweat and dirt from his eyes. The journey back from Manhattan had been long and tedious. He'd only caught a few hours of sleep as they drove back overnight. The weight of the bomb, the mines, and the other supplies in his backpack seemed heavier than his usual load. Luckily, his alien rifle helped balance things out.

Pip trotted by his side, staying close. Even she didn't like Gregor that much, and Denver had come to learn his dog's intuition was often worth paying attention to.

He'd noticed Gregor glancing at him and the weapon with an expression of jealousy, but then he had an automatic weapon, so he had nothing to concern himself in terms of who had the biggest penis replacement.

They walked in a tense silence through the forest, heading for the farm. Gregor and Layla led the way. Maria hung back with Denver, and Ben floated between them. Denver pitied him really. A man needed a family or at least a close circle. Ben didn't seem to fit particularly well anywhere, but at least he'd followed the plan and hadn't sold Charlie and him out.

And having Gregor and the others armed now seemed like great foresight considering the croatoans' change of behavior. Denver wondered if Charlie had already foreseen that. It wouldn't be too surprising.

One didn't survive for as long as Charlie Jackson without noticing small changes and having the smarts to plan ahead. Though the plan hadn't gone down as expected, the result was the same: using the farm as a way into the ship.

He thought about Charlie going up there with the bomb and not coming back. Up until now, it had felt like something that would happen in a future that wouldn't have real consequences. A part of him perhaps thought it wouldn't work out like this, that he'd come up with another plan. Of course, he had that bastard hunter on his tail, but Denver had full belief in his dad. Charlie knew these woods better than anyone.

By following them here overnight, the hunter had made a big mistake. He'd given himself a massive disadvantage. This was Charlie's playground. Advanced alien species or not, he was fighting Charlie Jackson in his backyard. And this backyard was loaded with surprises.

"He'll be okay, won't he?" Maria said as Denver held back a thick branch to let her step through the trees into a clearing with a path worn into the compacted grass.

"Yeah," Denver said. "He's like a ghost in this place. Don't worry about him. Just keep your eyes open for anything waiting for us. We don't know if the bastards up there have sent reinforcements yet or if they even know what's going on."

"They won't," Gregor said, looking back over his shoulders. "I dealt with the guards. There's none left to get word back. They'll know when they don't report in for the evening's update, but we'll be in position by then. Besides, Augustus thinks I'm dead."

"How can we be so sure?" Ben said, speaking for the first time since they left the clock tower. "Wouldn't their bike's movements send an alarm?"

Gregor stopped and glared at Ben, clearly not liking someone questioning him. Ben flinched away when the gangster stepped closer. Denver put his hand on Ben's shoulder and, towering over them, glared back at Gregor. "Drop this macho bullshit. We need to work together now. Just answer the question. Is there any way the ones that chased you or the ones at the farm compound could have raised an alarm?"

Looking up at Denver, a smile of derision stretched across Gregor's face. "A chip off the old block, eh? Just like your own old man, though he ain't really your old man, is he? You were just something he stole from another family like a magpie."

Pip growled low in her throat, but she became quiet when Denver reached down and scratched behind her ears. "It's okay, girl."

The bait attempt was obvious. Denver let the jibe wash over him. He didn't care for word games. It was the sign of the inferior man. Denver didn't need words to back up what he was capable of. "Time's getting on," he said. "We can stand around all day behaving like kids, or you can just cooperate and work as a team. What is it? You want to take out your frustrations with my dad on me? Fancy your chances, do you, Gregor?"

The older man seemed to size Denver up but hesitated. He smiled and shook his head. "Yeah, just like your old man. And for the last time, no, there is no alarm raised. And how do I know?" He pointed to the sky. "There's no fucking craft or shuttles coming down from the mother ship. If the croatoans from the farm raised an alarm, we wouldn't be standing here right now. For all they know, the ones that chased us had dealt with us. The orders were to kill me. Without any other update, there's no reason to suspect anything else has happened. So let's just shut the hell up and get to the farm while we still have the element of surprise."

Layla shrugged her shoulders in a silent apology to Denver and the others. How Gregor could have retained the loyalty of a woman like her, smart, capable, and beautiful, Denver would never know.

But strange times called for strange alliances—even with someone as low as Gregor, the killer of Charlie's true love, Pippa.

"I wanted to thank you," Ben said to Denver as they headed across the clearing.

"Why's that?"

"For making things clear for me before I came here. I know it's not how it was supposed to go down, but it was the right decision. With poor Ethan gone, I know I would have been useless in that kind of situation. I'm not cut out for this kind of thing."

"We just have to keep going," Maria said. "Make sure Charlie gets the bomb up there, and we can have our revenge for Jimmy, Erika, and Ethan. Just focus, Ben. It'll be over soon."

A hush descended as they made their way through the next section of forest. Fifteen minutes later, Gregor stopped everyone. "Just beyond here is my office and the rest of the compound. We need to get to Vlad and Alex."

"And secure the breeding rooms," Layla said.

"So how are we playing this? We can't go in all guns blazing," Denver said. "We need that shuttle to complete its routine pickup and wait for Charlie to get back."

"What if he doesn't?" Maria said. She instantly held up

her palms. “I know, I know, I’m just thinking of contingencies. In the unlikely event he doesn’t meet up with us.”

“I’ll go,” Denver said. “I had Mike show me how the bomb works. If my dad’s not back in time for the shuttle, I’ll take his place.”

Maria squeezed his arm, and a pained expression distorted her lips where unspoken words formed. He knew she cared, but he knew his duty. This was always his plan. And if he had the choice, he’d go instead of his dad anyway, regardless. He even considered somehow getting onto the shuttle before his dad so he didn’t have the option, but he knew it would hurt him too much. So he accepted that this was Charlie Jackson’s call, and as his son, he’d do as he was told.

“We wait here,” Gregor said. “Give your old man a chance to show up. The shuttle isn’t due for another two hours.”

“And in the meantime,” Layla said, “I’ll go and prep Vlad and Alex.”

“Are you crazy?” Gregor said.

“Not at all. Think about it. There’s no more of the larger croatoans left, only a handful of engineers and surveyors. They won’t have orders to kill me; that was for you. As far as they’re concerned, I’m no problem.”

Gregor paused for a moment, probably assessing options, figuring out the various issues. Finally, he nodded. “If there’s any sign of problem, shout, scream, do whatever, but get our attention, and we’ll come in to help.”

“I’m hoping it won’t come to that,” Layla said. “We’ll only get one chance at getting that bomb on the shuttle. When it goes back, they’ll know what’s happened.”

“While you’re in there,” Gregor said, his face lighting up

with an idea, "sabotage their communication rig. That way, if things get fucked up down here, those up there won't have a clue."

Layla took a breath and checked herself over, smartening herself up. "I'll tell them I just went out for a scout and got attacked by a survivor," she said. "If there are any questions."

"The way Vlad is, I doubt he'll even notice," Gregor added. "Go now, and Layla? Take care, won't you?"

She gave him a wink and disappeared beyond the trees. Denver just hoped there wasn't a welcome party waiting for her. But she seemed strong and intelligent. He had confidence she'd figure something out.

And he hoped his dad would get here soon. He'd been listening for sounds of gunfire and landmines, but the forest had taken on a heavy silence. He didn't like that one bit. It always seemed to be a precursor to something unnatural, something dangerous, like the insects and birds and the few remaining mammals knew before any human. Even the trees seemed too still.

But there was nothing left to do now other than wait.

***

Charlie vaulted a log and sidestepped the rusted remnants of a water tower stanchion. Serpentine branches had woven through the crisscross metal supports, creating a solid green barrier. Skidding like a kid playing baseball, he dug his foot into the dirt and swung around behind the natural cover.

Sweat clung to his camo shirt, sticking it to his back. His lungs ached with the exertion. Having taken the last of the root compound before the drive back, he was feeling the effects of his old muscles.

Despite that, he'd still managed to outfox the alien hunter. He looked through a gap in the branches and saw birds flutter high above the tree line, indicating something moving below.

The snap of a twig ahead of him confirmed it. He raised the alien rifle and sighted down its aiming groove. He didn't understand fully how the damn thing's armor worked, but having shot it in the leg before, it seemed that it could be caught off guard.

A rustle of leaves twenty feet away and a darting squirrel made him tense, ready and waiting. But then nothing.

The forest became still, almost as if the hunter had placed a blanket over the place.

It was a trap.

The hair on the back of Charlie's neck stood on end, and his pulse spiked.

He spun round to see the dark shadow dart out from behind a huge redwood. The hunter focused on Charlie, raising its sword.

Even with the injured leg, it sprinted across the ground, eating up the distance.

Charlie tried to spin out of the way, but his elbow got caught against a branch, unbalancing him and making him stumble over a root.

The rifle slipped from his hand. He hit the ground on his ribs, winding himself. But with the adrenaline making his reactions faster and the remnants of the compound still active, he managed to twist in time to avoid the slash of the sword as it struck the ground inches from his head.

The alien's thick legs, knotted with muscles beneath the

form-fitting armor, planted on either side of him, pinning him in place.

Looking closely, he noticed the armor was actually a mesh. He could see a jagged hole just above its reversed knee. The fabric had torn away to reveal a thick coating of orange gel: the root as a healing agent.

The alien lifted its sword from the ground.

Its face, visible through a clear visor, seemed to smile at him. Its solid black eyes grew small.

It struck out, but Charlie had anticipated the head strike and leaned forward. The sword swung freely over his head, the creature's arm crashing into Charlie's right shoulder.

He took the hit with a grunt and reached over with his left hand to pin the alien's arm. Charlie kicked forward into its left knee, collapsing it to the ground.

Charlie knew he'd never be able to out-power it, but he could outsmart it.

Grabbing a fistful of dirt with his free hand, he smeared it across the visor, and, letting go of its trapped arm, rolled away, coming up on his knees.

From his flanking position, he noticed two pipes that connected its breathing apparatus to a slim tank on its bank.

Before the alien had the chance to re-orient itself, Charlie launched himself onto its back, grabbing the pipes and pulling on them.

They resisted at first, and the hunter tried to fling him from his back, but Charlie clung on and screamed with a deep roar as he put everything he had left into breaking those pipes.

He felt the right one give, so he let go of the left and with both hands yanked on the right pipe. The alien dropped his sword and reached up and over with his hands, grabbing Charlie by the head.

The damn thing's strength was incredible.

Charlie thought it'd crush his skull, but as it continued to thrash and buck, it pulled Charlie over its head and flung him away. The pipe came away with a loud hiss as Charlie collided with the ground; his head banged against a rock, making his vision swim.

Through the dizziness, he watched as the hunter frantically tried to rejoin the connection to his breathing tank, but Charlie had the broken part in his hand. He dropped it and reached out for the alien rifle in front of him.

Squinting to help combat his fuzzy vision, he pulled the trigger.

The blast hit the alien square in the chest, throwing it back against the ground with a thud. Its arms collapsed by its side. Charlie heaved himself up and approached, holding the rifle in front of him.

The alien was still. Yellow blood dripped from its chest, the wound raw and ugly, exposing its weird biology. Even its face, previously black behind the visor, had turned a sickly yellow color, its mouth held open in a silent snarl of final anguish.

"You ugly fucker," Charlie said, kicking at it to make it sure it was dead.

No movement.

"You're the best they've got, eh? Welcome to my world, motherfucker."

Charlie spat blood from his mouth and turned, leaving the dead alien behind in the dirt for the animals and bugs to feed on. If it wanted Earth so much, it could have it.

Chapter Thirty-Four

Gregor scanned through the trees past his office toward the chocolate factory. Layla had been gone for just over an hour. A hover-bike breezed overhead and lowered into the square. Nothing out of the ordinary. The massive shape in the sky was, and it started to move again, rumbling along, creating a sound like a continuous blast from a distant foghorn. The croatoans on the ground, he observed, seemed oblivious to the new arrival.

In the near vicinity, Layla's trailer was reduced to a black, charred skeleton. Gregor wondered if the croatoans would kill her on sight, although it was him they were after and only acted on direct orders or procedures. Alex and Vlad's trailers were still in place without any noticeable damage, as was Igor's rotting shed.

Maria shuffled alongside him on her elbows. "They told me you were responsible for the set-up inside the harvester."

Gregor shrugged. "I didn't build them. Just passed the idea along to Augustus. He's the real boss. Besides, you were safe in there. Had hope."

"Until my *retirement*." She slapped him across the face and shuffled out of arm's reach. "Now I can work with you."

"You can have that one for free," Gregor said. "But only that one."

"Can't say you didn't deserve that," Denver said.

The slap momentarily stung, but it was worth taking if it meant having Maria fully onboard. He needed trust when leading the diversionary assault on the farm. Not a former harvester worker with a grudge, taking him down before they achieved their goal.

Gregor turned to Denver. "There's a lot of things you and your fake dad deserve too. All good things come to he who waits."

"Do you know what he once said about you?"

"Fuck this," Gregor said. "I'm going to sweep the forest. Make sure they're not sneaking up. You should know all about that."

Ben was propped against a tree. He'd sat and agreed with everyone for the last hour. Gregor resisted the temptation to kick him in the face as he passed.

"How long you gonna be?" Denver said.

"Not long. Layla should be back soon."

Gregor needed time to think away from the group. Every few minutes, Denver chipped away at his nerves. Maria was like a parrot on his shoulder.

He wanted to think of a disaster recovery plan. If Charlie couldn't get on the shuttle, they needed another play. Something effective. His mind blanked. It seemed like they had a one shot deal.

Cutting through the trees, scrambling over obstacles and surveying the damp ground for fresh croatoan boot marks helped release some of the tension he felt building inside.

Above, he heard the increasing hum of the shuttle descending toward the farm. The others would see it shortly. They'd positioned themselves in woodland between the landing area and warehouses. A trail was cut through the woodland to allow the containers to be transported for loading. As soon as the croatoans appeared on the trail, the plan was to attack the warehouses. Starting with the barracks.

Something moved in the trees ahead.

Gregor ducked behind a moss-covered rock and peered over it.

A figured darted between two redwoods, heading toward him.

Human.

Charlie Jackson.

Gregor looked down the sights of the AR-15. Aimed at Charlie. Followed his movements as he closed in. Fifty yards. Forty. Thirty.

His finger itched on the trigger. Gregor had waited years for this opportunity. Denver would take the bomb if his father didn't show.

He couldn't fire. Yesterday, Jackson would've been worm food. But not today.

Charlie hadn't spotted him. He was twenty yards away. Gregor kept the rifle shouldered and stood. "Managed to deal with the alien?"

Charlie abruptly stopped. His hand twitched against the alien rifle. He darted behind a tree. "Waiting to ambush me, Gregor?"

Gregor knelt back behind the rock. "I wasn't going to shoot. I could've easily killed you if I wanted."

He peered over the moss. Charlie's head shot back behind the tree.

"We need to finish this, Gregor. Lower your rifle."

"Both of us come out after I count to three. Leave our rifles on the ground."

"Why should I trust you? You don't have to pretend to care. Nobody else can see you out here."

"You need to get that bomb onto the ship. It's in all of our interests. I'm arranging a place for you on the shuttle and leading the attack on the farm. Why would I jeopardize the plan?"

"Because you're a dick who has no respect for life."

Gregor scowled and bit his fist. "The shuttle's arrived. There won't be another run until tomorrow morning. *If* there is another run. You heard what Layla said."

A sickly-looking rabbit with greasy fur shuffled between the rock and tree. Time was against all native species. The shuttle would be gone in less than an hour.

Gregor stood, placed his rifle on the rock, and held his arms out.

Charlie looked around the tree. He placed his rifle on the ground and stepped out.

They stood twenty yards apart. Charlie walked to his side. Gregor moved to keep an equal distance until they were ten yards away from their weapons.

Charlie rolled up the sleeves of his camouflage shirt. Gregor took off his watch. They started circling a large rock, staring at each other.

"Why did you kill Pippa?" Charlie said.

"It wasn't me. I swear on my mother's grave."

"Your mother was a whore. Stop lying. Why did you do it?"

Gregor winced. He'd slit throats for lesser comments. "I killed the man who did it yesterday morning. You, on the other hand, killed my cousin."

"He was collateral damage. I blew up a croatoan building. If you lot didn't have your tongues stuck up the croatoans' shit pipes, unlike us survivors—"

"Stop right there. You won't get a rise out of me. I did what I needed to keep my team alive. Those humans, livestock, they're bred for food. They didn't have a previous life like you or me. I only went after people who attacked my operation."

Charlie shook his head, maintaining his cold stare. "You think it's acceptable? Do you? I mean, deep down in your commie soul?"

"I'm not a commie, and the ice age froze my soul. We're never going to agree, so let's get this plan out of the way and meet back here."

"You know I'm not coming back, Gregor. Whenever I think about Pippa, I can't help seeing your ugly face. Do you think that's the last thing I want to see up there?" Charlie pointed to the sky.

Gregor stopped and reached for his pocket. Charlie stopped opposite and narrowed his eyes.

They walked toward each other. Gregor produced the blue bead necklace and held it toward Charlie. "Here. I think you'll want this for your journey."

Charlie paused. Looked down. He snatched the necklace from Gregor's hand and briefly closed his eyes. "If you lay a finger on Denver after I've gone …"

"We'll go our separate ways. You have my word on it. From now on, my enemy's enemy is my friend."

Charlie started walking back toward his rifle. "Let's do this."

***

Making their way back to the group, Gregor kept a healthy

distance between himself and Charlie. A suspension in hostilities was all they needed. They were never going to be friends. There was too much water under the bridge.

Four people squatted against trees when he approached. Layla frantically gestured him over when she saw Gregor coming. He quickened his pace and crouched next to her. Charlie stooped on her other side. They briefly glanced at each other, then Layla.

"How'd it go?" Gregor said.

"They're starting work right away. Alex is going to stall the croatoans," Layla said. She looked at Charlie. "Vlad will help you in the warehouse. He's going to put some equipment in a container for you. An alien rifle and some oxygen equipment."

"What about the farm? Any step-up in security since yesterday?" Gregor said.

"Some reinforcements came down on a shuttle last night. Just the usual ones, nothing like that thing we saw in Ridgway. Besides Augustus asking them to pressurize the breeding lab, it's been business as usual."

"Breeding lab. You fucking people," Charlie said. "Can we rely on them?"

"Augustus's message put a rocket up their asses. It doesn't take a genius to work out why he wants to do it."

Gregor raised his eyebrows. "Because they're changing Earth into the middle box?"

"What's he babbling about?" Charlie said. He looked at Gregor and slowly said, "They're doing it because that ship is gonna complete the terraforming process."

"I know that," Gregor said. "I was referring to a scientific experiment. Something that's probably way above your head."

"Look above my head," Charlie said. "There's two ships that want to kill us."

Layla grabbed Gregor's sweatered arm and twisted. She did the same with Charlie's shirt. "Knock it off. The pair of you. Charlie, there isn't much time; move to the back of the meat-processing building."

"We're both committed; don't worry about that," Charlie said. "How will I know the difference between Alex and Vlad?"

"Alex is a woman," Gregor said. "You might've met Vlad before. I'm not sure."

Denver moved over and joined the huddle. "Well? Are we ready to go?"

"We?" Charlie said. "There is no *we*. I'm doing this on my own. You've always known it."

"I'm coming to make sure you get into that container. Once Gregor attacks, I'll come in from the other side. Add to the confusion." Denver glanced at Gregor. "Are you okay with that?"

Gregor raised his left shoulder and pursed his lips. "Fine with me. I'll bring the other three in." He looked at Ben and Maria. Both held their respective weapons and peered through the trees. Hardly Special Forces, but it'd do.

Charlie walked over to Maria and said something in her ear. She watched him walk away with a genuine look of sorrow, holding out an arm toward him before letting it drop.

As Charlie passed him, Gregor held out his hand. "Good luck."

Charlie stopped, looked into Gregor's eyes, firmly shook his hand, and slowly nodded.

Chapter Thirty-Five

Charlie and Denver sprinted around the farm facility's perimeter, keeping to the shadows. Through the trees, they saw the one called Alex stalling a couple of croatoans by the shuttle. They were expecting the next load of meat and root and weren't happy about the delay.

"It's coming," Alex said, raising her voice and talking slowly as though that would get through to the increasingly agitated croatoan. It raised its hand to the shuttle and nodded its head, indicating that it needed loading.

Charlie clutched the bomb case to his chest and duck walked to the edge of what Gregor had told him was the meat-processing building. For a moment, Charlie doubted himself, wondered if this wasn't some sick, elaborate plan on Gregor's part, but even if it was, it still represented an opportunity to get on that shuttle. Even if he had to kill every last alien and fly the damned thing up there himself.

Denver took a quick glance around the edge of the building. "We're clear," he said, his body pressed against the building, the alien rifle in his hands across his chest. "They've gone back to the shuttle. Alex is making her way to the other side of the unit. Are you really sure this is the only way?" Denver asked, looking directly into Charlie's eyes.

"You know it is." It really wasn't the time to get into another discussion. He understood his son's hesitation, but this was personal. He wanted to do this. Needed to do this. So much had happened since the day the aliens rose out of the ground. So many people close to him were cruelly killed as nothing more than inconvenient insects.

A shadow passed overhead, sucking the light away from the farm compound, bringing with it a chill and a stirring of wind. The new alien craft made the mother ship look like a speck in comparison.

He shook his head and mumbled, "What if it's not enough?"

"What do you mean?"

"The bomb. I trust Mike and Mai implicitly. They're great at what they do, but look at the size of that thing. With the mother ship conjoined to its underside like that, even with the bomb and the EMP, will it even scratch the surface of this new thing?"

"Maybe it doesn't even have to. Maybe by taking out the mother ship and its anti-grav engines, gravity will do the rest and pull that damned thing down."

Charlie pressed himself closer to the wall of the meat-processing unit as the massive terraforming ship stopped. It had turned so that the long, straight section pointed west. Following the line of the ship brought Charlie's vision to the shuttle.

There wasn't really any longer to delay things. Through the open, mud-covered square, Charlie saw Gregor and the others spread around like small, dark lumps on the perimeter of the farm. The 'livestock' no longer wandered the fields, having been brought in by Alex earlier.

The thought of those poor souls steeled Charlie's resolve. How could he let the enslavement of his race like that go unpunished? Though it did occur to him that his actions would be like a bull assaulting humanity for farming cows.

He didn't think the aliens were evil—certainly no more evil than humans—they just thought humanity were nothing more than tools, cheap labor, and a source of food.

Charlie waited for a count of twenty.

When no croatoans appeared in the square from any of the units or the shuttle, he took one last look up at the terraform ship as though it were watching his every moment. Then he slid past his son and around the side of the building. He could see Vlad and Alex standing outside by the ramp.

Inside would be the empty container—if Gregor and Layla had stuck to what was agreed. That they were waiting in hiding, preparing for the distraction, gave him some confidence, but the icy energy of anxiety still prickled at his nerves.

Denver followed behind, his steps deliberate and quiet. The rear of the shuttle was open and pointed thirty or so degrees away from the ramp that led into the unit. As agreed, when Charlie was within a few feet of Alex and Vlad, he whistled quietly and then ducked onto his haunches, close to the front wall.

For a moment, neither of Gregor's colleagues moved. But then Vlad mumbled something, nodded, and headed inside. Alex took off and moved toward the shuttle. The distraction he needed to go inside. When she was completely obscured from sight, he heard her voice rise as she set about arguing with the aliens.

A quick sprint later, and Charlie, with Denver right behind him, found himself inside. The smell made him want to gag. Even in the darkness, he could see the terrible machines that made food from people. Large, metallic boxes where the people were ground up, their bones crushed and liquidized.

He was instantly reminded of the movie Soylent Green, and his stomach turned.

Wide conveyor belts, now still, told him of their levels of production. People ground down to their constituent parts, nothing more than fat, protein, and carbs all mixed together into a paste.

"You should be ashamed of yourself," Denver whispered to Vlad. "You fucking traitor. How could you work here of all places, treating your fellow man and woman like nothing more than meat."

"I'm beyond your outrage," Vlad said, pulling them further into the building. "So you might as well just shut up and stick to the plan. There's a breathing mask and oxygen tank inside. Along with the supplies of meat and root. I had to guess your weight, including the bomb, to load this properly." Vlad looked Charlie up and down. "You're smaller than the myth that precedes you. We might be a few kilos off."

"I don't care as long as that shuttle gets into the mother ship."

Vlad shrugged, appearing as disinterested in this as though it were just another day at the human-meat factory. Charlie didn't hide his disdain as he looked into the container. There was a small space provided between the silver, foil-wrapped containers.

The mask lay to one side, a pipe connecting to a tank hidden beneath the packages. Vlad looked up. "Get in now; they're coming. You hide," he said, pointing to Denver.

Glancing back, Charlie saw Alex remonstrating with the aliens as she walked back toward the building. Charlie dove into the container, hurriedly placing the mask on his face and placing the bomb across his stomach.

Denver leaned over and extended his right hand. Charlie grabbed it and squeezed. He noticed his son blink away a tear. "You go," Charlie said. "Remember I love you, always. Never give in. Remember what I taught you, and save as many as you can. Now go!"

He wouldn't let go, just stared down at Charlie, shaking his head. Vlad displayed a surprising strength as he wrapped his scrawny arms around Denver's shoulders, pulling him away into the shadows.

"I love you," Denver said as he hunched down in the shadows beyond the unit's opening. Charlie nodded and smiled, doing all he could to stop himself from jumping out of the container, but the world was bigger than him. The stakes were greater than his own personal losses.

The time was now.

He slumped into the hole, fixing the oxygen mask over his face. As soon as they were in the shuttle, it'd pressurize to the croatoan atmosphere. It would take about fifteen minutes to get to the mother ship. He hoped that the oxygen tank Vlad had arranged contained enough air.

With a solid, metallic clang, Vlad slammed the lid down on the container and locked the latches down on either side. It felt like the underground shelters he'd first used after the initial invasion. Too tight, too dark, but he was used to it. He just had to relax, control his breathing to avoid using up all the air, and wait until the shuttle was in place within the ship.

Simple really. A quick journey, a press of a button, and it would all be over.

Vibrations rumbled through the metal box, knocking

him against the packages inside, packages containing his fellow humans.

Through the lid, he heard the croatoans clicking their displeasure at the delay.

The container stopped.

Charlie's chest tightened and his pulse raced. He tried to keep his breathing short and shallow. The latch on the right side pinged open, the lid buckling. A spray of light bled in. He'd surely be spotted. He thought about Gregor again, thought that this was a setup, and rued the lack of foresight to bring in a hand-weapon with him.

The croatoans were getting angry, their clicks turning into barks. The container rocked violently to one side, the lid opening further, exposing him to anyone or anything that decided to look inside.

Gregor! Come on, he thought. *Where the hell are—*

Crack, crack, crack.

The sound of gunfire erupted, making the croatoans panic, their barks now high-pitched sounds of alarm. The lid was slammed shut and the latch closed. Feet shuffled away. Something pneumatically hissed and thumped, and then the whir and whine of anti-grav engines.

The ruse worked.

Gregor came through.

This was it.

He clutched the bomb close to his body like a precious newborn. In a way, he thought, if all went well, it would give humanity a rebirth.

If it went well.

Chapter Thirty-Six

Fifteen minutes had passed since the Jacksons' departure. A distant buzz grew louder. The strange croatoan version of a forklift truck swept between trees up the trail.

The vehicle buzzed along, a few feet off the ground, containers stacked at the front, balanced on two large, metallic prongs. A little croatoan controlled it like the aliens who navigated the harvesters. It sat in a transparent box and shifted levers around.

Layla hoped Charlie was in one of the containers, clutching his bomb. Their survival depended on it. Everyone's did.

Four aliens stood next to the shuttle's open hatch at the rear, roughly the size of a garage door.

The forklift reached the shuttle and slowly dropped to the ground. Its prongs started to extend, moving the containers into the back of the craft. They slowly disappeared from view. The forklift pulled back the empty prongs and reversed before turning. It started to head back to the warehouse.

"Is that it?" Maria said, "Or do they have multiple loads?"

"Just one," Gregor said. "On my signal. We turn and attack the farm."

Ben raised his head from a patch of long grass he was lying in. "I thought it was a diversion? You shoot and the shuttle takes off."

Gregor grimaced. "The fight back has begun. Charlie isn't sacrificing himself for us to act like chickens. We kill every leather-faced bastard we find."

"So he's your hero now?" Maria said.

"Be careful, little lamb. I'm not the enemy. You don't want me as one."

Layla listened but watched the croatoans. One appeared from the side of the shuttle carrying a scanner. The tennis-racket-shaped object gave off X-ray-like images on the clear, circular part. If Charlie was in a container, they'd identify him. The weight must've been slightly off, triggering suspicion amongst the aliens.

Another croatoan joined the one carrying the scanner, and they disappeared into the back of the shuttle.

"We need to do it now, Gregor," Layla said.

"Just seen it," Gregor said. "We watch them take off, move straight through the trees to the main square. Make your shots count. Barracks first. Get their weapons. Okay?"

Layla nodded. "Now or never."

"Ready," Maria said, holding up her pistol.

"I'll be right behind you," Ben said.

Gregor aimed through the trees toward the forklift that was still moving slowly along the trial.

He fired three times.

The forklift picked up speed and disappeared from view.

Croatoans at the back of the shuttle started to move with urgency. The two outside hopped straight into the side entrance. The two inside the back compartment sprang out and followed. The rear door smoothly closed with a pneumatic hiss. The graphite ramp slid into the body of the vehicle, and the side door slammed shut.

Engines roared into life. Dirt blew across the landing strip.

On the shuttle roof, the pulse cannon's turret started to turn toward the forest.

"Run," Gregor said.

Layla followed Gregor as he crashed through undergrowth like a wild boar. She glanced back. The shuttle was above the trees. Its cannon built toward a high-pitched crescendo.

Gregor dived down and covered his ears. Layla did the same, landing with a squelch in a brown, stagnant puddle.

The cannon boomed. A flash of brilliant light flooded the forest.

Debris flew over her head. Branches landed on top of her.

The shuttle's engines whirred. Their noise started to drift away.

Layla glanced up. The six pink rings were getting smaller, like a colorful domino in the sky, heading toward the mother ship, carrying its deadly payload.

"Is everyone okay?" Gregor said.

He stood and helped Layla up by her arm. A section of forest to their left, the size of a basketball court, had been obliterated by the cannon blast. Trees were smashed to the ground, their jagged black stumps smoking from the heat of the shot.

Ben rustled through the leaves of a thick branch that had blown off a tree. Maria crouched next to Layla. "Do they have those things on the farm?"

"No. Stick with Gregor. Do what he says. You'll be fine."

Gregor moved off at pace again. He broke the tree line

and raced past his office. Layla kept focused on the ground ahead, trying to keep up, searching for any croatoans who would have heard the shuttle fire.

Single rifle shots came from the far end of the camp. Denver, carrying out his assault.

Croatoan rifles started to snap closer to them, coming from the square.

They moved along the side of the chocolate factory. Gregor paused at the end. Layla looked over his shoulder. Three aliens were mounting hover-bikes. Three fired toward the warehouse. Layla thought her heart was about to burst out of her chest as she struggled to control her breathing. This wasn't her environment, and she wondered if Gregor really was the one to get them out of this. But with Denver back toward the square, she had no other choice but to trust and follow.

Adopting a prone position, Gregor fired at three alien engineers standing in the square. One dropped forward, clutching its helmet. Denver must've hit another as it fell back between Gregor's shots. The third croatoan started hopping away. Gregor cut it down before it could reach its barracks.

"Maria, Ben, you take the chocolate factory. They're unarmed. Layla, come with me," Gregor said.

They rushed across the square. Three hover-bikes thrust into the air and turned to face Layla. She ducked behind a parked hover-bike, tumbling down in a heap next to Gregor. She breathed deeply, steadied her hands, aimed, and fired.

Shots echoed from behind, coming from inside the chocolate factory. Denver came running into the square before he knelt and started firing into the sky.

An alien fell sideways off the closest hovering bike. It remained in its position, slowly spinning around. The two remaining bikes zipped away over the buildings in a southerly direction.

"Where are they going?" Layla said.

"Who knows?" Gregor replied. "Maybe to another farm. It's two less we don't have to worry about. Let's get those alien rifles. I'm nearly out of ammo."

Denver met them at the bodies as they each picked up a weapon.

"Did your dad make it?" Layla said.

"Yeah. He's in a container," Denver said. "Where to from here? I've dealt with the lizards in the meat-processing place."

"Shoot out the windows of the barracks." Gregor pointed to the buildings. "Drop anything that comes out of the doors."

They turned and collectively fired at the barracks windows. Thin, orange gas seeped from the bullet holes after the alien projectiles punctured through. A small croatoan, one of the surveyors, came running out without his protective visor and breathing equipment, his eyes wide with panic and terror. It was instantly felled by multiple shots.

Nothing else came out of the buildings for the next minute as all three stood in the middle of the square, aiming at different points, covering a 360-degree arc.

"If it's this easy, why didn't you do it before?" Denver asked.

"There used to be soldiers. We'd be dead if they were still here," Gregor said. "When they figure out what's happened, and if your old man doesn't manage to let off that bomb of his, you better be ready for their retaliation."

"This place has been ramping down for a while," Layla said. She peered up at the two hulks crawling across the sky. "I bet it's the same for all the farms. I thought they were moving to a management mode. It's probably due to the atmosphere ship."

"Gregor. Denver. Help," Maria called out. She staggered across from the chocolate factory.

"What's wrong?" Gregor said.

"Ben's dead. I'm out of bullets. The little ones ran to the end of the room and hid in a huddle. We fired from the door. Thought we'd got them all. Ben went to confirm, and two attacked him with small swords. Hacked him to death."

Gregor grunted and shook his head. "It was obvious he wouldn't survive."

"Come on, Gregor," Layla said. "He's played his part."

"Is this how you think of your team?" Denver said.

Gregor twisted around to face him. "Did you see where Alex and Vlad went?"

Denver looked into the distance. "Dead. Aliens must have got them early."

"If I find their bodies with wounds inflicted by your rifle, I'll rip off your arm, ram it through your head, and ride you around like a croatoan hover-bike. Do you understand?"

The thought of Denver enacting swift revenge on Gregor's team as soon as he had the opportunity sent a shiver down Layla's spine. Although not completely implausible, his story for Alex and Vlad's end didn't seem to fit with how the aliens on the farm operated. They would've assumed that both were still part of the team.

"Cut the empty threats," Denver said. "We still need to clear these buildings"

"I'll take the chocolate factory with Maria. You take the breeding lab with Layla."

"Can't I go with Denver?" Maria said.

"No. This isn't a family game," Gregor said, asserting his control. "You don't get to pick your favorite player. You're coming with me. Now."

Layla understood Gregor's logic. She'd grown more appreciative since seeing him more up close, how he reacted in dangerous situations. If they were going to be part of a team, start to forge bonds, this was a way to achieve it. The main issue was it left her with Denver.

"Which one's the breeding lab?" Denver said.

"Over there," Layla pointed. "You lead the way. Aliens don't go in there that often."

She didn't want to lead the way herself in case Denver took her out as soon as she got through the door. If he raised his weapon in her direction, Layla was going to fire first.

He moved quickly to the entrance in a crouching run while Layla remained a few yards behind with her finger on the trigger. Just in case.

Green lights blinked on a panel outside the door. The first time she'd seen them activated. The building had been pressurized to a conducive environment to keep human livestock post-change.

Denver kicked open the door. A flood of cool air rushed out. He glanced back as the control panel started to beep, lights turning red after five seconds. "You know the layout. I'll cover you."

Rifle fire crackled from inside the chocolate factory.

Layla was confident that Gregor would sweep the place clean. They were on the brink of securing the farm, and she knew he wouldn't hesitate to finish the remaining aliens. He was like a pit bull once he got something into his head.

While Denver was looking ahead, his attention away from her, she raised the rifle to the back of his head. "Did you kill Alex and Vlad?"

Denver looked around slowly, staring at the barrel of the rifle. He frowned and shook his head. "You really think that? How little you think of people outside of this place. From where I come from, we don't kill other humans. You ought to look closer to home for that behavior. Besides, this is our chance. My dad isn't sacrificing himself so we can squabble like petty criminals. So no, I didn't fucking kill Vlad or Alex. You got it?"

Layla felt the sincerity in his voice, the conviction, but Gregor would take some convincing. She could tell from Gregor's earlier reaction that he didn't believe Denver in the slightest and would carry out his own style of crime scene investigation to establish events. That was one situation she'd really like to avoid.

"It's one long corridor," she said, pointing into the lab. "You take the doors on the right, I'll take the left. We'll do it together," Layla said.

Denver nodded and spun through the door, pointing his rifle at the first window. He took a couple of steps back and breathed, "Holy shit." He glanced back at her, his eyes wide with surprise. "How are we going to get all of those women out safely?"

Layla checked the first room on the left. "We'll free them once the farm's secured. I've got it worked out. Don't worry, they'll be safe."

While moving from door to door, Layla kept Denver in her peripheral vision. They glanced into each cell before moving along.

She flinched as a croatoan rifle snapped. The glass on a cell door shattered next to her head, spraying fragments into the corridor.

She crouched and felt a sting on her cheek and a warm dribble down her neck.

Denver ducked next to her, holding his rifle to his chest. "It's only a nick. Do any of these rooms have external windows?"

Layla took a deep breath. Tried to compose herself. "No. One must've been hiding."

Another alien projectile whistled above them, slamming into the opposite door.

The weapons shook in her hands. She glanced at Denver.

He firmly nodded, stood, and fired twice.

Two quiet clicks came from the cell.

"Clear," Denver said. "Let's finish this and get out of here."

They proceeded to check the rest of the cells with more caution, creeping along the corridor, peering in with weapons pointed until reaching the end of the building. Layla immediately turned and headed for the entrance.

Denver walked alongside her. "You must have a sick or strong mind to have put up with this."

"I did what I needed to survive. I don't expect you to understand my choice."

A hollow pop sounded outside. An alien grenade.

Layla sprinted to the door and pushed it open. She knelt in the gap and scanned across the square with her rifle. Denver ran past her and took up a firing position a couple of yards away.

Gregor had a small pile of alien grenades next to him. He tossed one into a shattered window of a barrack building and ducked. Smoke belched out after an explosion. Maria huddled behind a hover-bike, her hands over her head. She looked pale, scared—the opposite of Gregor, who seemed to be enjoying this far too much.

"He's a fast mover," Denver said.

"You should consider that if we want to take the fight further. Destroy more farms. Start wiping out their crops. We need effective people."

"You think I want to team up with that piece of shit?"

Gregor tossed another grenade into a barrack building as Denver jogged across to Maria. Layla looked around the square, taking in the devastation and the pile of dead croatoans. It'd been quite easy. A coordinated effort around the world could wipe out the farms. The problem was communications. The aliens had effectively cut all long-range comms when they screwed the ionosphere. Humans were sparse. Spread far and wide as individuals and small groups, avoiding rather than confronting the croatoans after their initial show of strength.

If Charlie managed to take out the mother ship, they might just have a window of opportunity to destroy the remaining colonists, but they needed to pull in the same direction. A level of organization was required.

Denver swung his rifle in Gregor's direction. A barrack building door slowly opened, and an alien crawled out. Gregor kicked the croatoan in the chest. It collapsed to the ground. He stamped on its helmet visor, crushing it with the sole of his boot. Layla looked up. The shuttle had disappeared from view.

Chapter Thirty-Seven

Charlie took in a deep breath as the shuttle finished its docking procedure with the mother ship. The whole thing rattled violently, crushing him against the liquidized human food and root compound packages.

Sweat poured from his face and his leg muscles were starting to cramp. The container smelled of blood, but he knew it was just the foil coming loose on the silver trays.

Even that knowledge wouldn't get the terrible images of the meat-processing unit out of his mind. How terrified those people must have felt, standing in line, and one-by-one going into the machine to come out the other end a convenient meal.

Despite his temporary reconciliation with Gregor, he hoped Denver would make the bastard pay for overseeing that kind of treatment.

A low hum vibrated through the container's sides, making his teeth rattle.

It must be close now.

The sounds of whirring motors from somewhere behind him indicated that the mother ship had closed its docking hatch.

On clear days and nights, Charlie had watched the underside of the ship through his scopes. When the hatch opened, he'd often get a brief glimpse of the inside. It featured the usual croatoan pragmatic style: off-white smooth surfaces with light blue and pink accents much like their anti-grav projectors.

He wondered why they hadn't invaded during the '80s. They'd have got a kick out of the neon colors. That aside, he knew that shuttles were held in corridors just wide enough to accommodate the shuttle and someone to get into the cockpit on either side.

The sound of metal on metal came to him, and the shuttle rocked. He could feel movement. The aliens were coming into the storage area from the cockpit. His heart remained steady as he thought about this mission.

Once the container was taken out and delivered to the main distribution area, he'd have to find a way back toward the edge of the ship. He needed the bomb to rip a hole in the structure of the ship and preferably take out the anti-grav projectors.

The ship had eight of them in pairs at each corner.

Mike was sure that if they were to take out one corner, the ship would be destabilized enough to succumb to gravity. But with it now docked and a part of the terraform ship, that plan needed some modification.

The container rattled and moved, gaining speed down the ramp until it leveled out with a bump. The voices of the croatoans seemed more relaxed, their clicking and grunts less high-pitched. They continued to push the container further into the ship. After a couple of minutes, they came to a stop. Charlie felt the sensation of rising in an elevator. Up and up they went, and that's when he had the idea.

Throughout, he had only heard two distinct voices. And with this perpetual rising, they were probably in a confined space. He reached behind him and grabbed the small bottle of oxygen, making sure he didn't make any noise. Not yet anyway.

Once he had that tucked into his belt, he pulled his hunting knife free of its belt holster, keeping it low and hidden by his side. He'd pushed the bomb free of himself and hidden it under a number of foil-packed trays.

That's when he kicked out and banged his elbows against the container. He carried on until they stopped rising.

The latches sprung open, the lid twanging with the freed tension.

Two black barrels of croatoan pistols pushed into the gap before the lid was removed fully. The aliens looked down at him. Their faces didn't change, show surprise, or show any emotion. They simply observed before then breaking their attention and looking at each other, no doubt trying to figure out if there was a protocol for this.

The one on the left turned away, revealing that they were indeed in a kind of elevator. Circular with white walls, it must have been about twenty feet in diameter.

Ideal.

When the one on the right leaned further in, Charlie kicked up with his legs, scattering trays and foil packs over the edge, knocking the pistol away. He thrust up his arm, driving the knife underneath the alien's visor and the blade into its tough skin, but the knife was made from their own metal and honed over the years.

It broke through the hide with a pop and sliced easily into the alien's brain.

Its arms and hands twitched. Reaching up, Charlie grabbed the pistol and let the alien fall to the ground.

The other one spun round from behind the container, clicking and grunting in urgent tones. It mustn't have seen Charlie grab the pistol, for when the croatoan leaned over to point his own weapon, Charlie was already aiming and pulling the trigger.

With a loud reverberation, both pistols fired. White-hot blasts of pain burned into Charlie's chest. His oxygen tank hissed. Air started to escape from the valve before it popped completely, draining the precious air.

Yellow blood dripped onto his shoulder.

The croatoan slumped over the edge, its visor in pieces with a hole burned through it and through the creature's skull.

Charlie placed his hand over the valve to try and stop the flow of air as he stood up and got out of the container, stepping over the body of the still-twitching alien.

He checked his chest; the fabric of his camo shirt was frayed at the edges where the alien round had grazed by. The skin had risen into a bright red welt across his pectoral muscle. Kneeling, Charlie opened one of the root packs, grabbed a handful of milled root powder, and rubbed it in until the skin started to tingle, healing the cells.

While that continued to do its magic, he controlled his breathing, reducing his heart rate, and assessed the situation. He couldn't tell how sound proof the elevator car was, but the fact it stopped meant that someone would likely have noticed. Perhaps they were waiting for the delivery of the container.

Looking at the alien control panel, there was no way to guess of its destination or how it might work. A clear glass square, maybe eight by eleven, featured a series of symbols that he wasn't familiar with.

In all the time he had fought with the croatoans, they'd been careful not to leave any of their tech or communications behind.

Even the ones he had killed rarely had anything with their writing on it.

The valve continued to release the pressurized oxygen, and he began to feel lightheaded, not just from the shallow breaths, but the alien atmosphere within the ship.

Ripping off a foil cover and spitting into the remnants of the root powder, he made a paste and used the rippled foil to press and hold the paste around the broken valve. It wouldn't be perfect, but it'd buy him time.

A flash of light came from the glass control panel on the circular wall. A light blue ring spun around, reminding him of the waiting icon on PCs back in the day. And then the car jolted and started to lift.

It appeared that someone had realized there was a problem. Charlie knew he didn't have long now. Even with the oxygen mask, the atmosphere burned against his skin. With the alien pistol in his left hand, he reached over with his right to grab the bomb from the container, throwing it over his shoulder and putting his arm through the strap so he could wear it like a backpack.

He kneeled behind the container so he would be obscured when the doors opened. He knew it was unlikely he would get another chance at this.

One way or another, he'd set the bomb off.

For sixty long seconds, the elevator continued to climb until finally it stopped and the doors opened. Charlie saw the darkness reflect against the back wall. He gripped the pistol tight and strained his hearing, all the while trying to suppress the urge to cough.

The oxygen ran out. Each inhalation brought nothing. He cast the mask and the small tank to the side. He felt drunk, his vision spinning. Pain pinched at his nerves and muscles as they knotted with cramp.

Still he gripped the pistol and waited.

A voice called out to him. It sounded from somewhere far away and dulled as though his ears were full of water. Louder now, closer, the words became distinguishable.

"Oh Mr. Jackson, what have you done? The scourge of my employers fancied a tour of the ship, did he?" A shadow loomed over Charlie, and he knew this to be the one named Augustus. "Come out, little wasp, unless you wish to choke to a slow, painful death. I'm not concerned either way. Come see what you want to see. It's too late for everyone else now. Maybe you'll prove worth keeping around? Your choice."

The shadow retreated.

Charlie moved his aching body to the side and peered round the container into the dark corridor. He thought he was hallucinating. Outside the elevator, beyond the short corridor, was a room styled like a Roman court.

A colonnade of columns stretched into the distance like disciplined soldiers. The fluting was a perfect replica or Roman composite design. They'd even got the ornate, floral capital correct.

Marble surfaces adorned the floors, supporting lush, terracotta-colored rugs. A mist of pale air billowed out of the elevator, the alien atmosphere leaking into an artificial human one.

Even with the mask, Charlie knew he was human on the inside.

Augustus was wearing a red toga with a large, golden broach. He reached the end of the colonnade and turned. He waved at Charlie, beckoned him in. His mask glinted in the candlelight as he turned and disappeared into the gloom. Hallucination or not, Charlie couldn't wait any longer. He crawled out of the elevator and pulled his legs free in time for the door to shut behind and the car to descend.

Fresh, sustaining air flooded his lungs when he inhaled. His eyes watered, clearing the stinging alien atmosphere. Everything told him to just lie where he was and breathe, give into the pain and wait it out. But no, he couldn't afford to do that; this was bigger than him.

The bomb weighed heavily on his back despite its small and potent stature.

He got to his feet and walked after Augustus, small grenades of pain exploding in his muscles, but with every movement, he felt looser, stronger. The root compound continued to tingle on his chest, the soreness of which had reduced to barely a mild irritant.

With knife in one hand and pistol in the other, Charlie continued down between the columns until he came to the end. To his right, he saw more firelight flickering in the darkness.

He squinted, trying to make out more details, but the darkness and shadows were too encompassing. He had no choice but to go further into the space. His boots echoed on the marble surface. He stayed to the left-hand wall, using the torches in the sconces to navigate his way forward.

Unable to stand the quiet, he called out, "So what now, Augustus? You change Earth for good. Where does that leave you? Trapped up here in your little ode to a dead empire? You must know what happened to the Romans when the Visigoths came to town."

A flash of brilliant white light made him stumble to a stop and bring his arm up to his eyes. He heard the shuffle of feet too late. Something metallic struck out of the whiteness against his forearm, making him drop the pistol.

Charlie dashed back and hunched into a defensive stance, holding his knife out in front of him, ready to strike back. Through squinted eyes, he saw a sandaled foot kick the pistol away further into the wide white expanse.

"You're no Goth," Augustus said, the voice coming from behind Charlie. "At least they put up a real fight."

He spun round and slashed out with his knife, but no one was there. He realized his mistake too late.

A foot crunched into his back, sending him flying forward. He hit the marble floor; the side of his head cracked against the unforgiving surface, making his vision bleed with blotches of color.

Weight pressed down him, pushing the hard case of the bomb into his lower back. A blade cut the straps, and the bomb was taken away. Charlie spun onto his back, bringing his fists up, ready to protect himself, but Augustus casually tossed the bomb away, clearly thinking it was nothing more than a backpack of supplies.

Returning to Charlie, Augustus held a broadsword by his side. The man's silhouette blocked some of the glaring light. Charlie could now make out that they were in a large, open, office-like space. A desk sat centrally, and a large screen wall separated the space to its right. But more importantly, to the far right, thirty or so feet away, Charlie saw a porthole through which he saw the underside of the terraform ship just a few feet above.

He was near the top and, crucially, near the edge.

Charlie smiled and began to laugh.

"What's so funny?" Augustus said, bringing the point of the sword forward until it touched Charlie's throat.

"Just funny how things turn out. You spend so much energy worrying about something, worrying about how to achieve something, and yet if you just let go, life will often put you in the right place."

"Huh. Who thought you would be so philosophically minded? That you survived the confrontation with Baliska made me think you were just a savage. You see, I've seen lots like you in my time."

Augustus arranged the mask on his face where it had slipped slightly, exposing the knotted scar tissue beneath.

"Time's another funny thing, isn't it?" Charlie said, inching back away from the sword's point. He got a good look at it now and the hilt and recognized it as Roman design. "Funny how you're here in this advanced space craft, and yet you've had your quarters decorated in such an old style. Have a thing for the Roman Empire, do you? Fancy yourself as an emperor?"

Augustus laughed now, throaty and genuine. He lowered to his haunches, staring at Charlie with his one good eye. It was then that Charlie noticed how old he looked. Though his visible skin appeared in good condition, that eye was something else. It contained the years of someone who had seen so much more than they should have.

"Fancy myself? You fool, Jackson. I am one. Was one. Will be one again. But you're right about time. There was a time when I thought my time was over. Time, however, isn't linear like we think. Oh no, Mr. Jackson, it's pliable if you're willing to wait."

"And what exactly have you been waiting for?" Charlie said, wondering whether he was pushing things too quickly, the tip of the blade still within striking distance of his throat. The bomb lay just ten feet away. All he needed to do was open the flap on the bag and press his finger to the touchscreen.

Ten seconds later, and it'd all be over.

A tiny flicker in time is all it would take.

"I've waited for this moment, Mr. Jackson. This point in time when I slay the rebellion and make amends for the collapse of one empire and start another."

Augustus turned his face to regard something on the display wall, exposing his side profile. Charlie's mind itched with recognition. There was something familiar about him. Someone he had seen or read about. "Just who are you?" Charlie asked as Augustus looked back at him with a smile.

"If I told you, you would think me a madman."

"I already do."

Augustus inclined his head and brought the sword back to his side, unable to keep the weighty weapon in place. "I am Flavius Julius Valens Augustus, eastern Roman Emperor, Last True Roman."

Charlie let it sink in for a moment as he scrambled away, putting his back against the wall and bringing his knees up to his chest. Augustus, or Valens, stepped forward, blocking off his routes. Looking around the exacting detail of the place, the sword, and that recognizable face, Charlie wondered if the croatoans had perhaps cloned him or brainwashed him into thinking this, but for what reason? What purpose would that serve?

But beneath all that was the history. Charlie had studied the Roman Empire and knew full well who Emperor Valens was: the brother of his co-emperor Valentinian—the pair who signaled the collapse of the Empire. His body was never recovered at the battle of Adrianople. Many scholars assumed he had died in battle after removing his imperial robe and running headlong into combat, while others suggested he was burned by the barbarians at the behest of their leader Fritigern.

Charlie had his own theory.

"I don't understand," Charlie said. "How is that even possible?"

"They were always here, watching us, waiting," Augustus said. "I'm sure you read about what happened in Adrianople."

"It was a crushing loss for the Romans," Charlie said. "Humiliating, in fact. Valens was rumored to have left the field of battle, unable to face the catastrophic consequences of losing to the Goths. Others said Valens was a traitor, a coward."

The smile on Augustus's face twitched at the edges and his hand gripped the hilt of the sword tighter. He leaned down until his face was inches from Charlie's. "I survived, Mr. Jackson. Something you know a great deal about. Doesn't matter how you do it, you survive, breathe another day."

"So tell me then, how did you stand the test of time? Was it cryogenics? Cloning?"

"Neither. You remember the pods that rose up from within the Earth? I'm sure you realize now how ancient they were. Put two and two together, Mr. Jackson. It can't be that difficult to understand. Now, before I run you through, tell me, why come here now? Look out there; you see it, don't you? The ship that will change the world, remove the human disease from its surface. It's too late for you now. Your time has come to an end."

Augustus brought the sword back to Charlie's throat,

pushing the tip in until it broke the skin, pressing against his windpipe, cutting off his air. "I came for one reason only," Charlie said with a whisper as he squeezed the words out.

He reached up and grabbed the sword, but instead of pushing it away like Augustus was expecting, Charlie pulled it in, driving the sword further into his neck, but at the same moment unbalancing the old emperor.

Charlie capitalized on the move by grabbing his toga and yanking him toward him while simultaneously striking out with his legs, catching Augustus in the calves. The emperor toppled forward as Charlie slid to the side.

Augustus hit the wall with a heavy thud. His mask fell off and clattered to the floor. Charlie held his breath as he pulled the sword free, dropping it to the floor. On hands and knees, he crawled frantically like a cockroach to the backpack.

He reached out and grabbed one of the cut handles, pulling it close to him. Undoing the flap, he reached inside and pulled out the bomb. He spun it over, exposing the touchscreen. He brought his hand down and pressed his finger to the glass screen.

It beeped once for confirmation.

Charlie rolled onto his back as Augustus rose to his feet.

"What have you done?" Augustus said, looking down at Charlie, not understanding what he was smiling about. The emperor's face was gnarled and twisted, and Charlie realized the truth to him being burned.

A part of Charlie took great pleasure in knowing that he'd destroyed an emperor.

"They all crumble," Charlie wheezed, coughing out blood between each word.

"Crumble? What?"

"Empires. They all eventually run out of time."

Charlie coughed once and passed out. The last image he had was of Augustus reaching for his neck with his hands. But like before, he was too late.

The time was now.

Chapter Thirty-Eight

Sitting on the steps to Gregor's office, Denver held Maria's hand. Together, they watched the skies. A tense quiet had descended since the last of the croatoans were put down. The only noise came from the groaning and shuffling of the now-free humans, led by the now-conscious Alex, into one of their shelters. She'd only taken a glancing blow from a croatoan rifle. Vlad wasn't so lucky.

Denver blinked, waited, and watched the mother ship's pink circles, like alien eyes staring down at the Earth. They remained bright, still working. He pictured Charlie stuffed inside the container, the bomb tightly held as he waited for his time.

"What if he was caught before he had the chance?" he said.

Maria squeezed his hand and leaned in. "He'll make it, I'm sure. I might have been only outside of the harvester for a few days, but one thing I've learned is that if your dad wants to do something, there's no one who could stop him."

Denver glanced in Gregor's direction.

The old gangster, Charlie's nemesis, stood with Layla by the alien hover-bikes. They seemed eager to leave, but Denver didn't know where they expected to go. Nothing was settled yet. The people on the farm still needed to be cared for.

“Thinking of skipping out on us?” Denver said, raising his voice so they could hear him. He kept the alien rifle close by his side, one hand on the stock, ready to lift it into place within a fraction of a second.

Gregor tutted and looked away, not even trying to hide the disdain on his face.

Layla, however, stepped away and approached him. Her eyes were glossy and red. Dirt stained her otherwise unblemished face. Wiping a rogue hair from her forehead, she stood over him, casting a shadow.

Unlike Gregor, she wore no expression of disdain but rather sympathy, pity even. “I’m sorry for everything,” she said, regarding them both. “I’m sorry about your dad, Charlie. And you, Maria, I’m sorry that you’re the only one left from the harvester crew. I don’t know how much they taught you about grief and death during your education, but I just wanted you to know that I understand what it feels like. I lost everything and everyone I knew during the invasion.”

Maria brought her hands to her face as she sobbed, the pent-up emotion over the last few days finally coming out. “I can’t believe they’re gone,” she said between ragged breaths. “We’ve only just got free, and now Ethan and Ben are gone, leaving me behind. Why me?”

“It has to be someone,” Denver said. “We need the strong to survive, and as far as I could tell in all this, you were the strongest of that group. I’m sorry your friends and colleagues didn’t make it, but we’ve all had to make sacrifices. It’s how the world is now.”

“Holy shi—” Gregor turned to face the ship in the distant sky. Denver and the two women looked up.

The mother ship’s underlights faltered, flickered, and

became dull. A fraction of a second later, they heard the boom rip through the sky. The sound pressure hit Denver in his chest, rattling his organs inside.

Debris and hull wreckage blew out of the right-hand side of the round ship near the top where it had docked with the gargantuan new addition. The explosion continued to roar as the cloud of metal and smoke and flame continued to billow out.

All the lights on the various buildings of the farm went out. Maria squeezed Denver's hand as they both stood to watch the devastation above them.

"Motherfucker's done it … Goddamn," Gregor shouted over the noise. Almost half of the ship had blown away, leaving a ragged wound stretching front to the back, bisecting the craft and exposing its innards through the flames.

The whole thing tilted now that its anti-grav projectors were useless. The weight of the terraform ship docked to its top pitched almost ninety degrees up.

"It's coming down. Oh my God, it's really coming down," Layla said.

Throughout all this, Denver had remained quiet, his breath caught in his throat. A single tear fell down his cheek in both joy and an unending sadness at the loss of his courageous father. The one person whom he truly loved had done it: traded his life for a chance of freedom for all.

"He's done it," Maria said, hugging Denver around his neck. "He's really done it."

The sky turned black with the smoke. Thick, rolling clouds of alien technology melted by the nuke. Tinges of orange compound tainted the atmosphere as it burned up in the fire that had taken hold of both ships. The blast had torn away a huge section across the underside of the terraform ship.

It seemed to take an eternity, but eventually, a second explosion roared out as both ships crashed into the earth. Although they fell beyond the horizon, they could still see the cloud rise into the sky from the impact. Denver felt it too in the ground, the ripples feeling much like an earthquake. It reminded him of the stories Charlie had told him about what it felt like when one of their infernal machines created a sinkhole.

"Payback, you bastards," Denver whispered as he picked up his rifle and slung it over his shoulder. He walked off, leaving the other three behind.

"Hey, wait," Maria said. "Where you going?"

Without turning back, Denver said, "To the next farm. Freedom starts here."

***

The smell of fire was thick in the air even hours after the initial impact. Denver approached his truck and slid into the driver's seat. Pip appeared out of nowhere, having scarpered to safety hours earlier. She curled up in the middle space between the front seats and placed her head on his leg. She whined mournfully.

"I know, girl. I know."

Denver patted her on the head, smoothing her fur, all the while trying not to let his emotions get the better of him. He couldn't break down now. His dad would want him to go on, finish what he started, and that was just what he was going to do. Even if he had to do it on his own.

The engine fired, and he reversed the truck out from its hidden position within a tight group of bushes, backing it onto a dirt track that would lead out of the forest. He slammed on the brakes as he saw a silhouette appear in his rearview mirror.

Reaching for the pistol he kept in the door tray, Denver wound down the window and looked out. The shape moved toward him in the evening gloom. He opened the door with his free hand while keeping the pistol low, ready to fire.

The person crunched twigs and leaves as they approached the driver's side. Denver raised the gun and was about to shoot when a voice called out to him.

"Denver, it's me, Maria. Don't shoot!"

He lowered the gun immediately as she stepped close enough for him to see that it was her. "You followed me? I thought you'd stay with the others at the farm."

"There was a change of plan," Maria said, smiling.

More movement came from behind him as two more people stepped out of the shadows. "Layla, Gregor?"

Gregor grinned when he stepped forward, placing his arm over Maria's shoulders. "Your lady here seems to think we ought to stick together. Now don't get me wrong. I still don't like you, but you don't seem too much like your old man, and I like the way you shoot. What say we pool our resources?"

"What about all the people on the farm? The pregnant women?"

"Taken care of," Layla said. "Alex was okay, just got knocked out. She's staying behind to look after them. No point moving them if they're comfortable there. The plan is to join up with Eastern Farm Twenty a hundred kilometers from here. They've got reinforcements. We just need to get word and start the fight back."

Denver saw an excited look in Layla's eyes, not at the death of yet more aliens, but at the thought of freeing more people. Gregor's expression just seemed bloodthirsty, as usual, but every resistance needed its psychopaths to do the jobs ordinary people with morals wouldn't be comfortable doing.

He thought about it for a moment. The three of them stared at him expectantly, waiting for his decision.

That's when it dawned on him.

It was *his* resistance now. *He* was the one to lead this.

Instead of that prospect frightening him, it gave him a new shot of energy. After all, it was what his dad, Charlie Jackson, the Last True American, had spent all his time teaching Denver: how to be him. How to be the survivor. How to never give up and never stop until humankind was once again free from tyranny.

"Get in," Denver said. "We leave now."

Maria walked around and got into the front passenger seat. Gregor and Layla jumped into the rear after stashing a bunch of weapons in the truck bed.

Denver looked at Maria and smiled. "I'm glad you followed me," he said.

"Me too."

He held her gaze for a few seconds before turning to the others in the back. Talking to everyone now, he said with a grim tone, "Did everyone see what I saw before the initial explosion?"

They stared back at him in silence. Eventually, Maria asked, "What? What did you see?"

"At first I thought they were bits of debris, perhaps from the initial explosion, but their trajectory was all wrong. I only realized after, once the shock wore off. There were six of them. Pods, crafts, whatever you want to call them. Either way, some of the bastards up there escaped and came to Earth. Probably digging into the ground as we speak to recuperate. Well, we're not going to let them this time."

Denver turned back to face the front and engaged first gear. "This time, we're going to hunt them down and murder the bastards in the dirt before they think about rising again."

With that, he floored the accelerator and headed out into the night, promising to himself he'd do his dad proud. One way or another, the aliens would regret ever coming to Earth.

Other Titles by Darren Wearmouth

First Activation

Second Activation

Sixth Cycle

Fast Forward

Made in the USA
Monee, IL
02 May 2021

67506680R00215